ABSOLUTE CERTAINTY

MIDNIGHTS AT PEMBERLEY
BOOK 2

GISSANE SOPHIA

Copyright © 2025 by Gissane Sophia

All rights reserved.

No part of this book may be reproduced in any form or by any electronic or mechanical means, including information storage and retrieval systems, without written permission from the author, except for the use of brief quotations in a book review.

This is a work of fiction. Names, characters, places, business, events, and incidents are the products of the author's imagination or used fictitiously. Any resemblance to actual persons, living or dead, or actual events is purely coincidental.

No part of this book may be used to train generative artificial intelligence (AI) technologies or used in prompts to create content of any kind.

Edited by: Kate McGinn

Edited by: Sarah Tompkins

Cover Design and Illustration by Jenna Guidi

This one's for me and every writer who reached the type of breaking point they thought they'd never come back from, and for the people who held us up as the waves tried to pull us under.

And for the fictional characters who've been with us during some of the worst points of our lives, reminding us that we aren't alone.

"Elizabeth, still more affected, was earnest and solemn in her reply; and at length, by repeated assurances that Mr. Darcy was really the object of her choice, by explaining the gradual change which her estimation of him had undergone, relating her *absolute certainty* that his affection was not the work of a day, but had stood the test of many months' suspense, and enumerating with energy all his good qualities..."

— JANE AUSTEN

AUTHOR'S NOTE

Dear Reader,

Thank you from the bottom of my heart for picking up *ABSOLUTE CERTAINTY* and taking a chance on this story. This one's so special to me that I don't even know where to begin, but as I mentioned in my newsletter announcement, this story and I go way back.

Buried somewhere deep in my old emails, tucked away in some hard drive, is an even messier first draft of a book that's meant to live with the stray things in my memories. It was a story I wrote and carried with me for years, with characters who kept me company after my dad died, and after I'd convinced myself I would never write again. Jay was one of those characters, only he had a different job and a different character arc, but his gentle heart was a light at the end of the tunnel. A constant. A glimmer of hope. In that same draft is also the first line I ever wrote, a line that stayed with me, and a line I knew I couldn't give up on—[I think you'll know it when you read it.] I knew while mapping out the Midnights at Pemberley series that Sahar's story would come next, and it'd be with the screenwriter working at the coffee shop, but what I didn't know until I started writing *A CERTAIN STEP* was that he'd be Jay.

I go back and forth on names so much that it's actually one of the most exhausting parts of my process. But the second I started writing the first scene where we meet Jay, I wrote his name without even thinking, and nothing felt more right. *ABSOLUTE CERTAINTY* was the world he belonged in, and I suddenly knew exactly how to tell his story because he'd been with me for so long. He was fully in the driver's seat. And Sahar? My God, has she made me braver and better. There aren't enough words for her. Truly, none. Her big heart has been indescribable to write about, and I hope I've honored her love story.

This duology will always be so close to my heart for many reasons, so I can't thank you enough.

CONTENT NOTES: mentions of an abusive parent and spouse [off-page], crude language from an ex-boyfriend.

If any of these topics are too sensitive for you, please take care of yourselves.

All of the characters featured in this story are obviously fictional, as is their success. The shows or movies they are in and the experiences they have are all fictional. Some of them are big names in *this* world, and others are just getting started. Some mentions of shows or TV they watch and music they appreciate are drawn from real-life examples, but everything *they're* a part of naturally isn't.

1

——————

SAHAR

For the first time in a long time, Sahar Peck felt content. Heartbroken, but content.

Perhaps it was the dreamy weather, accompanied by her own fondness for the early days of summer, when everything always felt a little nostalgic. Delicate. Ineffable.

She loved the wistfulness, the vibrancy. The world rightfully loved New York City during the holidays, but in the early days of summer, it became its own unique spectacle of chaos and magic intermingling in every corner.

Anything was possible.

And today, her little world felt a lot more hopeful. After finally taking the plunge and dying her hair dark, crimson red like she'd been wanting to do since she was in her twenties, Sahar felt a sprinkle of life return to her. A form of control, after she had spent months molding herself into the perfect partner for her ex-boyfriend.

She was on her way to the Hyacinth Theatre for a two-show Wednesday in *Midnights at Pemberley: The Musical*, but not before stopping in at her favorite nearby spot, Amanda's Coffee.

Someone came barrelling through the street in a Statue of

Liberty speedo, and a pigeon plunged down for the discarded fries on the sidewalk. Sahar maneuvered through crowds, quickening her already fast pace.

When she stepped closer to the shop, located at the corner of the theatre's block, she noticed the manager, Jay Callahan. He'd been hunched over, sitting alone at one of the wrought iron chairs, his hand burrowed in his hair.

If he were taking a break, she'd see it as a good sign. The man hardly ever did when she saw him.

Only he didn't look like he was taking a break.

He didn't even look like he was okay.

She inched closer, careful not to disrupt him. Catching her approach, Jay's gaze rapidly darted up.

"Hey," she whispered.

"Sahar, hey," he said, plucking his eyeglasses from where they lay on the table. He put them back on and blinked, once, twice.

"Is everything okay?" she asked.

He dipped his chin in a quick move. "Yeah."

Questioning him, Sahar narrowed her eyes.

He stayed quiet, but the heavy exhale he released told her plenty.

Her face fell, her good mood muddied. She wasn't even sure why it bothered her that Jay wasn't okay. Though they'd built a pleasing rapport in the few months they'd seen each other from her regular visits, she didn't know him *that* well. Small talk about Man City here and there, commentary on the latest video game they were playing, and occasionally, Sahar would even berate him for not taking time off.

Huh, well. When she thought about it that way, she did know him. Outside of her coworkers, or her former boyfriend and *his* friends, Jay was basically the person *she'd* interacted with most.

"You alright?" she asked.

He nodded. "I'll be fine. Dahlia's inside. She'll get you."

"I'm not concerned about my coffee at the moment," she contested. Pointing to the chair in front of him, she wordlessly asked if she could join him.

Jay took a breath, then gestured for her to sit by extending his hand.

Leveled with his gaze after taking a seat, Sahar examined his features up close. Hidden beneath thick, long lashes, she noticed the shade of brown in his eyes with flecks of gold in his irises, made brighter by the sunlight cascading down upon them.

There was sadness there, too—something dark and weighty.

"Do you always seem this upset when taking a break?" she asked, finally.

"Sahar, I'm fine."

"I also hunch over in defeat when I'm fine."

He scoffed, signaling his irritation. Perhaps she'd pushed too far. All too quickly, fury eclipsed the sadness before he spoke. "Do you want to hear about how the feature film we shot and got through post-production was just scrapped by the studio for a fucking tax write-off? Or would you like to hear about how the network just said nah, never mind about the limited series we were about to sell?"

Fuck. There was a defeat in his tone she hadn't heard before, a different type of rage hanging at the edges of his words. Jay's voice was naturally deep, but the heaviness of frustration and agony clinging to his pitch made it sound so painful.

"Jay, I—" she started.

"Save it. Please. I don't want your pity."

"It's not pity," Sahar countered. "This industry is fucking shit. I was going to say it sucks. It really does. And you don't deserve to go through this."

"How do you know what I deserve? Maybe I do. Maybe I wronged a ton of people, and this is my penance," he argued.

"I have good instincts," she replied plainly.

He took a deep breath through his nose and looked at her again, eyes searching. "Your instincts are wrong."

Sahar swallowed, tilting her head. "You want to try that again?" she disputed.

The words tugged a small, barely there smile from him. And she'd seen his smile—it was massive and bright and so endearing that she was determined to get it out of him again. Jay's anger wasn't aimed toward her, she knew as much. The battle he was fighting was against external forces and, more harrowingly perhaps, with himself.

"Thanks," he managed, his voice still clipped.

She smiled, bobbing her head. And then she remembered the first audition she bombed—for *Romeo and Juliet* of all productions. She'd gone home crying, and to help her see that she wasn't the problem as much as jitters and external forces, her father had stopped working and convinced her to audition for him—no one else.

"Because I know you're capable, and I want you to believe it, too," he had said. And he was right. Sahar nailed down the monologue expertly, then persuaded the casting director to give her one more chance.

Now, sure, that was a university production and not as cutthroat as the West End or Hollywood, but she had the inexplicable urge to help Jay find his belief again. She wanted him to see that someone without any ties to him was interested in the story he had to tell.

"Can I read it?" she asked.

"Read what?"

"The screenplay for the limited series. Whatever you've got. I'd really like to read it," Sahar specified.

He grimaced, eyebrows pinched together like he couldn't grasp her sincerity. "You serious?"

"Why would I joke about that?"

"Why would you care to read a rescinded screenplay?"

"Because I'd like to see what you wrote. I knew you directed, but I didn't know you wrote as well."

She also knew that words could be personal—writers could be sensitive and their doubts were often like treacherous, unyielding currents. Once trapped in one, still, calm waters seemed impossible to reach again. For writers, artists, creatives —rejections fucking hurt. A lot.

He gazed at her, still undoubtedly questioning why she was interested in his work.

"Really?"

"You're quite distrusting, aren't you?"

"Can you blame me?" he countered.

She saw the rapids in his eyes—some tumultuous pain that had battered him must have forced him to build dams. Was it the industry? Something else? *Someone specific?* Lowering her voice, Sahar chose her next words carefully. "No. But I'm serious, Jay. I *want* to know what's in that brain of yours." In another life, Sahar would have been a psychologist, someone who had the chance to hear what people were thinking. She wanted to understand them—dive deep into the places where all their secrets lived.

He tipped his head, a bit of light dawning back into his eyes. He reached for his phone on the table, unlocked it, and handed it to her. "Here, add your email to my contacts."

Sahar took it from him, added her information, and gave it back. "I put my number in there, too," she said.

Pushing his glasses up the bridge of his nose, he glanced at the contact card. "I've always wanted to ask. Any relation to Gregory Peck?"

A guffaw struck out of her. "Ha! No, and thank heavens for that. I'd hate to withhold my attraction to him because we were somehow related."

That got a real, honest smile out of Jay. Judging by the following expression on his face, it seemed like he wanted to say something else but stopped himself.

He stood up and straightened his stance. "C'mon, let's get you your drink."

Opening the door for her, Sahar walked in ahead of him. He strode behind the counter, turning to face her again. "Where's Willa?" he asked, referring to her best friend, flatmate, and fellow cast member who was almost always with her when she got coffee.

"With Ethan," she told him.

He gave her a look, examining if that meant anything more than the usual. *Now it did.*

Willa and their *Midnights at Pemberley* principal star, Ethan Everett, were best friends for two years before they finally professed their feelings to one another and got together a couple of months ago.

"Did you not know they're together?" she asked.

"I wondered with the number of times they get each other's orders, but I didn't make a definite assumption."

"You're not on social media?" Sahar questioned.

"No," he replied.

"Lucky you," she remarked. "But yeah, the gorgeous fools finally admitted they're in love with each other."

He released a closed-mouth chuckle. "Well, good for them," Jay stated, his tone earnest and less prickly now.

He started on her drink right away. She walked to the register.

"It's on me," he called out, stopping her mid-walk.

"Because?" she contested.

"For talking me out of a breakdown," he replied simply. Oh, fuck, so it was bad. A part of her hoped she was seeing things and dramatizing the situation.

"You don't have to do that," Sahar said.

"I want to," Jay disputed.

She tried to smile, but the word *breakdown* was playing on a loop in her mind now. "Thank you."

"Of course."

Jay handed her the lavender latte she always ordered, as his eyes held hers for a beat too long.

Sahar blinked, breaking their contact. "I'll be waiting for those pages," she reminded him.

"I'll send them to you tonight."

SAHAR WALKED INTO THE THEATRE, signed in, and sauntered over to her dressing room. Contractually, she was obligated to *Midnights at Pemberley* until next March, so she hadn't thought of what would come next. She'd been in such a happy bubble with this job that, for the first time in a long time, she'd almost forgotten that there was rarely ever a constant in this industry.

She ached for Jay. She selfishly feared for her own career after this role. Sure, most jobs had their downfalls, but the unpredictable nature of the entertainment industry was never-ending. One minute, everything was steady, and the next, you were running from audition to audition, trying to prove your worth again.

The fact that she even had a principal role shocked Sahar almost every day because she genuinely never thought she'd get the part of Jane Bennet when she first auditioned. She also never thought she'd be nominated for a Tony Award.

And though she was sure she wouldn't win, it still felt like a dream she'd have to one day wake up from.

She took a sip of her lavender latte, and it was somehow even more excellent today than it had been before. She and Willa had basically sworn that they'd go to Amanda's even if they were no longer working at the Hyacinth Theatre. It was *that* good.

When they were no longer working at the Hyacinth Theatre. These thoughts shouldn't have been plaguing her like a dark cloud. It was only early June. They still had nine months. But the conversation with Jay was revolving around a wheel in her mind.

Things end.

Nothing is forever.

No promises.

She wanted to laugh. Why was she even shocked when her relationship ended just last month, because she was dating the world's biggest prick, pretending to be the most doting man in the public eye? Sahar's ex-boyfriend, Martin, was a rising, albeit mediocre star who people seemed to fawn over solely because of how attractive he was. He had a decent voice, sure, but it was nothing compared to their principal star, Ethan's. Or even her scene partner, Sam Butler, who played Bingley.

Oh, to be a nepo baby. Martin's parents were both actors. His dad was a piece of shit and a terror to work with, according to some colleagues. His mom was somewhat more enjoyable to be around.

Sighing, she turned over in her chair to face the mirror.

Thoughts of how Martin made her feel torpedoed through her previous ponderings.

Worthless. Too much. Less than. Selfish. Exhausting.

Sahar had been a hopeless romantic since she could remember. She'd believed that anything and everything could be lovely. She didn't have a big family—a few cousins here and there. But the love she had for her immediate family was what had made her the person she was.

Her father, Andrew, adored his wife and his two children above all else. The arguments she witnessed weren't crude or unkind. They wouldn't end with doors slamming or name-calling. There were compromises in her home, easy laughter, and quality time spent together as a family.

There had been a lot of tears when she sat her parents down to tell them she wanted to move to New York. It had been and still was the hardest thing she'd ever done, but their strength had carried her through. Their belief in her talent and their unyielding pride kept her grounded.

She loved love. She always looked for the kind of love her parents shared. She believed in its existence as if it were something tangible you could touch and see.

Yet, time and again, when it was in her grasp, it'd wither and die. Sahar always chose the wrong people, and they'd never choose her back. Not fully, anyway. Her first real boyfriend in secondary school cheated on her. And then another dated her only to make his ex-girlfriend jealous. When she was twenty-two, she fell hard and fast for a fellow actor, and the greatest heartbreak came when he told her she was only palatable in small doses.

That nearly ruined Sahar, shattering her in a way that she couldn't fathom overcoming. Then, a year later, she met a lovely chap named Dave, who'd been impossibly sweet, but he moved to California, and they never quite carried on the relationship after. He was married now, with two kids and another on the way, from what she could see on social media. She met Paul after Dave, and at twenty-five, she thought she'd been more mature—a better version of herself.

She was someone who *thought* she could read people. She was great at picking lifelong friends, after all.

But when it came to love...

Sahar had learned the hard way that no one could ever truly read a narcissist until it was too late. And Paul was a textbook narcissist, making her promise to herself that she'd see the signs better next time.

Unfortunately, she did *not* see the signs.

Sahar met Ryan when she first moved to New York six years ago, and while everything was great in the beginning, he turned out to be worse than Paul. Sometimes, when it was too quiet in her mind, she could still hear the last words he spoke to her: "You're the most exhausting fucking person I've ever met." He'd said that simply because she wanted to talk things through—because she wasn't willing to let an argument go without a resolution. Or, maybe, that was how she imagined it.

Maybe she was wrong in all this. Maybe they were right, and she was the problem.

By the time she met Martin, she was delusional to think that maybe, just maybe, he was actually the one because despite how shitty he was, he did seem to be genuinely into her. All that changed when she realized that he wouldn't celebrate her wins alongside his. He wanted her to hype him up while he slowly sucked the life out of her.

Ugh, she'd been so stupid.

She reached forward and grabbed the specific foundation designated for covering up tattoos from her vanity, starting with the hydrangea on the back of her shoulder first. She didn't have to cover all of her tattoos for the show, but some of the bigger ones needed to temporarily go. The hydrangea was one, and the crow on her forearm was another.

What if I never find love? What if I'm just the kind of person who's meant to be the friend?

Sahar doubted many things when times got tough, but she

never doubted the way her friends loved her—the way she adored them and the lengths she'd go to *for* them. *Yeah, but maybe sometimes you exhaust them, too,* her brain belted out. Fuck, did she?

She hadn't gone to therapy in years, but maybe it was time to revisit that. It'd been such a success for Willa in the past year that maybe Sahar should go back—find a release from the same old ghosts that continued to haunt her.

Speaking of the gorgeous unicorn. Willa had just walked into their shared dressing room.

"I'm never getting over your hair like this. It matches you so much!" she complimented.

Sahar flashed her a toothy grin. "You're too good to me."

Willa came up and hugged her from behind. "I got really sentimental last night and cried to Ethan about how much I love you."

"Aww, babe. Are you on your period?"

"He asked me that, too, and no. The picture you posted made me really emotional."

Ah, the picture. Last night, Sahar had been feeling reflective, so she'd edited one of her favorite photos from her birthday last year. Conveniently, even though Martin was there, he hadn't been in any of the photographs. Because why would he be when he was being a pissy dick all night.

The one Sahar had posted was one of her, Willa, Ethan, Sam, Priya, Declan, Carmen, Miles, Naomi, Jeanie, and Christian. She had a thing about editing the photos she took with various filters, adding a Polaroid frame, and posting them with a white background on her feed.

See, romanticism. She'd even done it with photographs.

Sahar squeezed Willa's arms. "I love you the most."

"And I love *you*," Willa returned before plopping herself down on her chair. "Oh, and Sam's been going on about how we need to get pizza today and eat together during break because our team building is lacking. Whatever that means."

"As in the whole cast?"

"Yeah," Willa confirmed.

Sahar let out a laugh. "We thought our separation anxiety was bad. Sam starts malfunctioning when we go a week without bonding."

"And this is why when the show ends, we have to come as a package deal."

When the show ends.

Willa couldn't have known that Sahar was mulling over that very same idea. Her heart threatened to crack in half at the thought of an uncertain future.

Not now.

There was time, still.

She had the summer and the fall and the winter, too.

But she was determined more than anything to ensure that, unlike last summer, she wouldn't spend this one chained inside the storyboard of a worthless man's happiness.

2

JAY

It was barely noon, and he'd already kicked out one person for harassing Dahlia and another for walking into the shop buck naked. Jay was almost always irritable at work, but especially on the days when he spent the night prior tossing and turning and then getting shitty news during his break.

With a pounding headache, he stared at the digital clock located at the corner of the screen as he made a quick adjustment for tomorrow's schedule.

Less than two hours to go.

The spreadsheet blurred in front of him as his mind trailed back to the conversation he'd just had with Sahar. Leaning back against the cheap fabric-swivel chair in the coffee shop's breakroom, Jay took off his glasses and pinched the bridge of his nose.

He appreciated the fact that Sahar wanted to read his work, but what would she think of him after? There was something extremely daunting about sharing your screenplay—*anything*—with people you admired, so his brain was now doing an excellent job of convincing him that his ability to write was mediocre at best, and she'd run the moment she read anything from him.

At this point, he was also sure that at the age of eight, his daughter Eloise was more talented.

Jay was no stranger to the metaphorical snares of insecurity, but because he wanted to impress Sahar, it was twice as agonizing now.

The two of them had only ever talked about other people's crafts, never their own, and it felt wrong to even think about or want her good opinion. She had a boyfriend. He knew as much because even though Jay wasn't on social media, she'd once mentioned that her boyfriend wasn't a gamer.

An exasperated sigh tumbled out of him. He put his glasses back on and stood up. He needed to get back to the front of the shop and stop thinking about her. But *fuck*, every time he saw her and every time they spoke, it grew harder for Jay to deny that he was enraptured by her. And there was still much to learn about her outside of what he already knew, like she was a Man City football fan, a gamer, a Broadway actress, and always, without fail, a ray of light.

He also couldn't deny that he loved the way his name sounded falling from her lips. He couldn't ignore the fact that she awakened something in him every time she walked into the shop and said *hi*. Jay hated his name, tarnished and foul, because he knew his deadbeat father chose it. But when Sahar said it... It was different somehow.

It was soft and honeyed in her husky voice.

Maybe that was what Jay liked most about Sahar. When she spoke to him, she had a way of making him feel like he was the only person in the room. And the only other person who made him feel like he mattered in this world was his daughter. His kid, whom he missed too much when she was in Philadelphia with her mother. His kid, who was the one reason he kept going.

But hell, he gathered that Sahar was like that with everyone, and her boyfriend was the luckiest bastard on the planet. Jay wondered if he was also an actor. Was he in *Midnights at Pemberley?* Sam Butler, he knew, was married to Priya Sharma. And Declan McNair, if he remembered correctly, was also married. Could she have been with Christian, maybe? He seemed close to both Sahar and Willa, but Jay also presumed that if he were Sahar's boyfriend, she would've referred to him by name. Maybe he wasn't even an actor.

You're not entitled to know who her boyfriend is, man. True. He had no business knowing any of this. The point was that Sahar had a boyfriend.

She was off-limits.

Plus, she was too lively and warm to be tangled with someone like him.

Dahlia broke him out of his thoughts as he finally stepped out of the breakroom. "Jay, have you already sent out the supply orders?"

"Yesterday. Did you forget something?"

"We only have one bottle of the Irish Cream syrup left," she answered.

He nodded. "Yeah, I noticed and added it."

"Oh, great. Never mind then."

He blew out a low breath. Supply orders. Rowdy customers. This damn street. He loved New York City and hated Times Square, yet he couldn't afford to dive fully into film, because every seemingly big break was either cut short or not nearly enough to live off. He initially started working here because his sister, Alex, needed him nearby, but he stayed because the promotion to management came with a surprisingly hefty raise.

Sometimes, he wished he could chase a different dream. If he only had the brains for medicine. Who knows, maybe he could've been an accountant, an attorney, an architect, a real estate agent. At least he'd have the income to live more comfortably. Though, scratch out the real estate part. He'd rather die a gruesome death than go into the same business as his piece of shit sperm donor.

He'd happily stay at this damn shop for the rest of his life so he wouldn't witness John Fucking Callahan gloat with the satisfaction of getting what he'd always wanted.

Now, *that* would destroy Jay quicker than anything else.

IT'D BEEN A LONG, *long* day. A slow, frustrating shift at the coffee shop, an unexpected delay at Penn Station, and an overly long train ride with his mind refusing to let up for two seconds. He couldn't even nap to pass the time quicker.

The only shining part of the awful day was the few minutes he got to spend with Sahar. It kept him going. Raking his fingers through his wet hair, he thought of how he'd recognized her voice seeping into his mind before he looked up to find her standing beside him. She owed him nothing, and yet... The look in her eyes when she'd said, *I want to know what's inside that brain of yours.* The dawning realization that her kindness ran deeper than the occasional conversations they would have every time she'd come into Amanda's while he was there.

Except everything was too fucking bleak right now to believe in anything.

Sitting at the edge of his bed, he glanced at the clock on his phone's lock screen atop the photo of Eloise's big, goofy grin at her recent birthday party.

It was almost nine-thirty now, and Maya, his co-parent, still hadn't called as part of their daily routine. He usually waited for her to do it while tucking Eloise in, but considering it was past her school day bedtime, he called instead.

Maya picked up after three rings. "Hey, I was just about to call you. We had a *day.*"

"Is everything okay? How's Ellie?"

Blowing out a sigh, Maya said, "She's fine, but she yelled at her art teacher today, and now she refuses to go back. It's been a whole thing."

Eloise was a spunky little thing, but she was mostly well-behaved. What possessed her to yell at a teacher? "That doesn't sound like her."

Maya laughed. "She's your kid in that regard, Jay. Apparently, one student was picking on another, and Ellie stood up for them. But when the teacher stopped her, she asked why *he* wasn't the one doing anything about it. She basically told him how to do his job. She's been super cranky during the last few lessons, so this was the icing on the cake."

A low huff slipped out of him. She was his kid, alright. "Let me talk to her."

"Do *not* enable this, please."

"I won't. But I'm proud as hell that she stood up for someone, aren't you?"

"Of course I am. But I don't want her yelling at teachers. There's a time and place." He could hear Maya opening a door. "Your dad's on the phone."

"Hi, Dad," came her clipped, small voice.

"Hey, kid. Your mom just filled me in. I'm glad you stood up for your classmate, but you know that yelling at your teachers isn't the way to go about things, right?"

Eloise sniffled. "I know. But, Dad, Mr. Johnson is really mean. I don't want to be in his art class anyway."

"How so?" Jay asked.

"He doesn't help anybody. Briana's grandma died, and she was secretly crying, and then stupid Tony stood up and made fun of her." She paused for the briefest instant. "And then, I got up to go help Briana, but Mr. Johnson yelled *at me* to go back to my seat."

Jay exhaled. "Is Briana the kid who was also being bullied?"

"Yeah, Tony is so mean to her, and Mr. Johnson never tells him to stop."

"People are messed up, baby, and it gets worse when you get older. But in times like this, you're better off telling another adult that you trust than taking matters into your own hands. You have a bright future ahead of you, El. Your mom and I, even Gavin, are always going to believe you, so how about you let us take care of these things, and you be a kid for a little while longer."

Eloise sighed loudly. "Okay. How many more days do I have until I come to New York again?"

"I'll be there to get you this weekend, but let me talk to your mom real quick."

She handed the phone over to Maya.

"Me again."

"Hey, so is she out for good, or are you going to try and get her back in?"

"Nope, she's out. I don't want to force her when she's this upset. We'll find some other way for her to continue art in the fall if she wants."

"Yeah, it doesn't seem like she feels comfortable around him, and I wouldn't want her in an environment like that. Still good with me coming in this weekend?"

Maya was silent for a beat; she seemed to be rummaging through something. "Totally. Kira and I still have plans to come up during the third weekend of July, too. I'll text you the actual dates later. I'm blanking right now."

"Sounds good," Jay said, then hung up his phone.

WITH HIS LAPTOP propped up on his thigh, Jay turned to pick up his phone from his bedside table. Searching for Sahar's name, he found her contact card and stared for a moment.

Sahar Peck. Just reading her name entranced him.

He typed in her email address, then sent over the screenplay, his finger hovering over the key for a minute too long as nerves whirled inside of him.

Afterward, he shut off the laptop, set it down, and prepared a text to Sahar. He had her number—it was only fair that he gave her his.

JAY

> Hey, it's Jay from Amanda's. I sent you all the episodes. Feel free to give me your honest, unfiltered opinion, even if you think it's shit. Thanks again for today.

It was 11 p.m. now, and he wasn't sure if that meant she'd be home yet or not. Still, he didn't expect a reply from her. At least not tonight. He was about to put his phone away when it vibrated in his hand.

SAHAR

> I appreciate you clarifying which Jay you are, but I'm chuffed to report you're the only one I know. Lol. & I'm certain it's not shit, though I'm more than happy to give you an honest opinion. I'm not very good at sugarcoating things.

JAY

> Good. I don't want you to sugarcoat.

SAHAR

> I hope you're feeling a bit better.

A sharp stab of something lodged itself in his throat. He *was* —just barely and largely because of her.

JAY

> I am. Hope you had a great show.

SAHAR

Thank you! I've opened this doc with a cup of tea, and I'm already very upset this was shelved because the title alone is such a win.

JAY

Every Speck of Dust?

Frankly, if there was one thing he hated, it was that title. He was awful at coming up with them, and so was Patrick, his best friend and frequent collaborator.

SAHAR

There's a quote in one of my favourite books that features a line like that.

JAY

What book?

SAHAR

The Wolf Lady by Gertrude Mae Dawes.

JAY

I've never heard of it, and I have many questions.

SAHAR

Happy to answer them, but now I'm off to read ep 1.

He looked up the book on the Strand's website, seeing that it was only available for online purchase. He did have many questions, especially if he were to judge by the title and cover, but if this was one of Sahar's favorite books, he wanted to know why. He had to.

He knew what kind of video games she preferred, but a favorite book was like walking into a secret passageway straight into the most sacred parts of a person's mind. He was sure there would be a treasure trove attached to it.

Though first, he'd read it for himself.

THE FOLLOWING NIGHT, as he was getting ready to sleep, he noticed two notifications from Sahar appear on his lock screen. Reaching for the glasses he'd just taken off, Jay put them back on and read the text.

SAHAR

I realized I hadn't actually gotten around to watching your films yet, so after reading the first page (not the full ep yet), I decided to watch Beneath the Sun.

I have multiple bones to pick with you.

He heard her voice in his head as he read the text, and a genuine laugh rose at the base of his throat.

JAY

Haha let's hear it.

SAHAR

Why do you hate happy endings?

JAY

They're unrealistic.

SAHAR

That's a lie. Let's try that again.

JAY

They're rare. Also, that ending is up to interpretation. You're welcome to picture it as a happy ending.

SAHAR

You cut that film right at the airport after that huge fight. How am I supposed to think it's happy or hopeful?

JAY

People can reconcile after fights? A few people have interpreted it that way.

SAHAR

If that's the case, I'm choosing to pretend that he goes back to her. Liam loved Sadie too much to move past what they built.

JAY

You have my blessing to do that. I gather you're not going to be happy with the way Every Speck of Dust ends…

SAHAR

WTF, mate. I just went through a shit breakup. Stop causing me more pain. (Kidding. You're not actually causing me pain. In case that doesn't translate via text.)

JAY

I didn't know that. I'm sorry.

Fuck. Sahar was single. He had a chance.
She could do better than him.
But she was single.

SAHAR

Don't be. He isn't missed. I'm just a hopeless romantic that's all.

JAY

I'm not opposed to romance. It's just this industry…the things that studios want are mostly grim.

SAHAR

I know. I also realize that there's not always a space to be vulnerable with fiction.

JAY

You know I hated film school?

He surprised himself with how transparent he was willing to be with her. Something about Sahar's tender curiosity made it easy to dig into the parts of his past he often ignored.

SAHAR

How come?

Dragging his hand over his short beard, he prepared himself for a mental visit to undergrad.

JAY

Because it did sometimes feel like the content that was often praised was bleak. I took regular narrative writing classes, and I remember this one girl who wrote romance. The class gave her so much shit because it was "too cliche." She held back tears the entire time they were critiquing her, and then the next time she came in, she had the darkest story. They all fucking jumped at the chance to tell her how incredible it was. I don't think any of them realized she was calling them out.

SAHAR

Ugh! This industry!

That doesn't shock me one bit. I hope she's writing the happiest stories now because look at the way things are panning out. Bridgerton is one of the highest-grossing shows on Netflix. Romance novels are also dominating the publishing industry. There's a space for it.

JAY

I don't think I'm capable of writing a romance. Plus, I'm a white man. I don't want to take up that space for women or people in marginalized communities who'd do it much better than me.

SAHAR

I'm not saying you should. But it wouldn't hurt to incorporate it.

He'd try. For her, he'd try anything.

JAY

Maybe.

Thank you for watching, though.

SAHAR

You're very welcome. I plan on watching Cuts tomorrow.

He didn't know what to do with the fact that she'd unknowingly get a glimpse of his horrifying childhood and teen years.

JAY

Cuts is more brutal.

SAHAR

I read the logline. I'll mentally prepare for it. Can I ask you a question?

JAY

Sure.

SAHAR

What made you get into movies? You don't have to answer that if it's too personal. I tried searching for an interview to see if you'd said it somewhere but you haven't. I just really love knowing what pushes people toward their craft.

Except it was personal. If he told her, he might as well give an account of his entire life and why he was so fucked in the head. Yet, the need to tell her whatever she wanted clawed at him again.

He wanted her to know *him*, and more than anything, he wanted to know *her*.

JAY

I had a shitty childhood. Movies and TV were the only way I could escape.

He kept it short but honest, and when the three dots appeared, it instantly made him nervous.

SAHAR

I love that. (Minus the part of you having a shitty childhood.) Was there a specific movie that pushed you down this path?

JAY

Rear Window.

SAHAR

Oh, brilliant! That's my favourite from Hitchcock. Do you prefer writing or directing?

JAY

Do I get to ask you questions about your career as well or is this a one-way Q&A?

SAHAR

Haha you can ask whatever you want. But
answer my question first.

JAY

It depends on the day, honestly. But I think
writing a little more.

What made you go into theatre?

SAHAR

That's good to know. I love words. I wish I could
write.

To answer your question, I was a very dramatic
child who put on shows for her family, so they
finally decided to take me to drama school and
dance classes. You love writing the parts people
play, and I look forward to bringing them to life.

God. He would give anything to see her bring to life one of
his characters.

JAY

Just theatre? Have you done movies or TV?

SAHAR

I haven't, no. I'm not opposed to the idea, but
there's something about live performances with
an audience that fuels me. Speaking of, have
you worked with or know any of the others in
Midnights at Pemberley?

JAY

Yeah, Sam and I have a few mutual friends, so I
knew him before. I watched Detective Vice, so
I'd seen Ethan there. But I'm not familiar with
anyone else outside of visits to the shop.

SAHAR

Declan also did TV and film, but his work is more my cup of tea.

JAY

Lol what does that mean?

SAHAR

He's been in some great PBS series—period pieces, romances, etc.

JAY

Gotcha gotcha. What's your favorite movie?

SAHAR

It's a solid tie between Roman Holiday and The Sound of Music.

JAY

One of those is not a romance...

SAHAR

Yes, I'm fully aware of that, but Gregory Peck and Audrey Hepburn are perfect in it. And it still centers around a love that changes everything. But look, you didn't ask for a top three or anything, and I feel it's imperative to share that my comfort movie is Clue. No romance in that.

JAY

Can you imagine the discourse that movie would've stirred on social media with alternate endings if it aired for the first time today? Granted, I think the time period adds to the charm, but imagine if they'd kept up the secrecy and you had to keep going to different showings to see an alternate ending.

Anyway, solid choice for a comfort movie.

SAHAR

Right!? I was way too young when I first watched it, but I loved it so much. It's a good thing Wills loves it, too, otherwise she would've kicked me out of the flat because of how often I put it on. Do you have a comfort movie?

JAY

Butch Cassidy and the Sundance Kid.

SAHAR

I just burst out laughing because both our comfort films have something to do with crime. Were we criminals in another life?

His mind went straight to Bonnie and Clyde. His mind should *not* have gone there.

JAY

Or detectives.

SAHAR

A better option, for sure. I'm going to put it on and try to sleep. I'll talk to you tomorrow.

JAY

Goodnight.

If he gave his mind the agency to continue wandering, thoughts of Sahar would keep him up all night, so instead, he set his phone down and also tried to sleep.

Jay had an earlier shift tomorrow where he'd maybe—hopefully—catch her before he was off.

3

SAHAR

A quiet, post-Sunday performance night-in was exactly what Sahar needed right now. Cozy matching lounge wear on before 6 p.m., hair washed and braided to the side. Bliss. She was eager to watch Jay's next film and giddy about having something to look forward to—a new piece of fiction that wasn't just for entertainment, but for the sake of getting to know someone better.

When the time finally came after she'd gotten home from work, showered, and cooked dinner, Sahar situated herself comfortably on the sofa before purchasing the film digitally. Balancing a plate of saffron rice with fried chicken and vegetables in one hand, she pressed play with her other before setting the remote down.

She hadn't seen Jay at the coffee shop today, which was a good thing because it probably meant that he either had a short, early shift or a day off—two things she was sure he could use.

Eyes focused on the screen, Sahar forked an asparagus spear into her mouth as the film opened on a panning shot of two neighboring houses. The sound of crows cawing in the scene instantly made her heart drum faster, and she could already tell that this film was about to destroy her.

When she finished the movie and dried her tears, her initial thoughts were about her own dad—how grateful she was that not only was he a good person, but he was alive.

Jay was a gifted director, there was no doubt about that, and the fact that they'd shot *Cuts* exclusively on film made the entire viewing experience that much more haunting. It was like stumbling on someone's old family videos and pressing play to unleash all the terrors they didn't know were being recorded in the first place.

But the question of whether any of it was real or made up pounded in her head.

She read over the words, paused on the screen once more: *In loving memory of Michael Sharp.* A chill swept through her as she questioned if the film's undeniable hero, Michael Swift, had any relation to the person the story was dedicated to.

SAHAR

I failed at mentally preparing myself for Cuts. That was BRUTAL. I'm sending you my therapy bills this month. My heart is in absolute shambles.

She didn't wait for his reply and instead went to get ready for bed after washing her dishes. She had plans to finally start reading beyond the first page of *Every Speck of Dust,* but she'd do that from her bed, despite it still being light out. After tackling her skincare, brushing her teeth, and grabbing a glass of water for her bedside table, Sahar drew the covers and made herself comfortable.

When she looked down at her phone, Jay had replied to her.

JAY

Forward them to me. What'd you think of it outside of that?

SAHAR

I genuinely loved it. Five hearty stars on Letterboxd. The writing was harrowing, and the performances were incredible. That final shot of Brady standing on his porch was so evocative I'm going to have to sit with the emotions for a while. It felt so raw.

She really, *really* wanted to ask how personal it was, but she kept that to herself. Jay had directed the film, but he shared the writing credit with Patrick Sharp. Judging by the surname, she could assume some things, sure, yet even that felt wrong.

JAY

Are you just saying that to be nice, or do you mean it?

SAHAR

I don't sugarcoat, remember?

JAY

Thank you then. It means a lot coming from you.

SAHAR

You're very welcome. I have tomorrow off, so I plan on reading. Did you have a good day today? You weren't at the coffee shop, so I hope that means you took a break.

JAY

I did, yeah. Went upstate to visit a friend's set.

And I'll be off most Sundays for the rest of the summer since my kid will be with me until late August. Did you?

Jay had a kid? A whole child that he shared with someone else? He was someone's dad? It was such...an unexpected thing to think about, and good lord, she had even more questions about *Cuts* now. Once more, *was* any of it personal?

SAHAR

I did! I didn't know you had a kid! Just one?

"You ask way too many questions, Sahar," she berated herself aloud.

JAY

Yeah, just the one. She's 8 and spends the school year with her mom in Philly. I assumed you knew, not sure why? Maybe because Sam knows.

SAHAR

Aww!

What more would she say after that? Specifying her mom's house likely meant she and Jay weren't together, but Sahar wasn't one to make assumptions. Also, she *shouldn't* be making assumptions because this wasn't anything other than the beginning of a new friendship.

She shrugged off the thoughts, opened the file she'd downloaded onto her iPad, and began reading.

INT. BACK AT THE OFFICE - NIGHT

Henry, hunched over at his desk, brushes his fingers over the ransom note again. Katherine is gone. It dawns on him. Over and over again.

MARK
Henry, you have to go home.
We won't accomplish shit if you don't rest.

Henry shakes his head. Mark doesn't get it. No one gets it.

HENRY
I'm going to find Katherine.
I'm going to bring her home.

He snatches the note off the desk and walks off.

END OF EPISODE

The thoughts running through Sahar's mind were agonizing. Was Henry going to find Katherine? Was she alive? Was Mark somehow involved? Fuck, she wanted to keep going, but she'd been so burned in the past that she desperately wanted to spoil herself. The investment she felt in Katherine was inexplicable, strangely visceral. She needed to know.

Oh, this was an abomination. Peeking at the ending instead of experiencing the narrative as it was meant to be consumed was sacrilegious. But she couldn't help it. Desperate times and all that. Sahar searched for the finale and skimmed through.

Dead.

Katherine was dead.

What the actual fuck. *Why?*

Studios wanted heavier content; she understood that, but

refused to accept it. Jay did say he wanted her feedback, so after some thought, she texted him. Again. She'd tell him her honest opinion, lay down how much she cared about these characters already, and question why he'd made the decision to kill off Katherine.

SAHAR

So…

I have some thoughts on Every Speck of Dust. I did something I rarely do, and I read the finale after finishing the first ep.

JAY

That's a crime.

SAHAR

I know. But look, I have a doctor's appointment on Tuesday and PT afterward before work. What time does your shift end? I'd love to pick your brain about this in person.

JAY

3

SAHAR

Shit. I should be done with PT after 3:45 would you be willing to hang around? If not, I have a matinee on Wednesday and can meet you during your lunch around noon.

JAY

I can make Tuesday work.

SAHAR

I'll meet you at the coffee shop?

JAY

Sounds good.

I don't sugarcoat, she had said to him. Well, maybe she should have. Perhaps she should tell people what they want to hear because that way, they wouldn't think she was only palatable in small doses.

Maybe she shouldn't tell him that she strongly believed Katherine shouldn't die in the end. *You want him to run, too?*

Ugh, but she really liked having someone to talk to about films—someone who knew the artistry of writing and directing, too. Someone who was passionate and willing to listen.

Absentmindedly poking at a bruise on her thigh, she thought about what she'd say to him. Maybe she'd start by asking why he wanted to tell this story in the first place. In addition, picking his brain in person would help her see his perspective and get a better understanding of the story he wanted to tell. Still, if Jay wanted to get this screenplay out there again, he'd have to change the story substantially.

She'd heard whispers of how scrapped content generally never resurfaced again. But Sahar already wanted to *see* it. She wanted him to have a second chance.

And for reasons she couldn't quite understand, *she*, too, felt tethered to this story.

～

SAHAR WALKED DOWN to the coffee shop, where Jay was already standing outside, waiting for her.

"Hi," she said, her voice sounding far more chipper than she wanted it to.

A barely-there smile played on his face. "Hey. Did everything go well with your appointments?"

Jay could be dry at times. Prickly, but he was generally courteous with Sahar. She wondered if it was his default with everyone or...

"Yeah, routine stuff. Would you want to walk to Bryant Park? Or we could stay here."

He eyed the coffee shop. "I'd prefer to be away from here," he told her.

Nodding, she led the way as they swerved around people and pigeons.

She wanted to ask why he chose this coffee shop of all places, because although she knew that artists often had side jobs in this grueling industry, she couldn't imagine working anywhere near the Theatre District if she wasn't doing a show. It was a tourist trap, and Jay was the last person who seemed to get a kick out of crowds.

Exhaust smoke from a passing car wafted unpleasantly through her nose, and she paused, clearing her throat. "Hey, so question," she said as they reached a hectic intersection. "Why Amanda's of all places? I would imagine you'd rather work somewhere quieter."

A huff of laughter rumbled out of him. "It's a long story. I'll tell you when we don't have other people breathing down our necks."

Huh. He didn't seem upset by her asking, but a long story made her waver. She gave him an understanding smile before the pedestrian signal indicated that they could continue walking.

New York City was always loud and bustling, yet Sahar always appreciated the pace. It was a stark difference from LA, where people lingered. It was also vastly different from London, even with their similarities. Here, most people had places to go and people to see. And thankfully, they *moved*.

She could feel Jay's towering presence over her, never quite noticing how tall he was behind the counter at Amanda's. For a brief second, it overwhelmed her, how steadying being beside him felt.

Two seats became vacant right as they entered Bryant Park. "Willa likes to joke that the universe always leaves empty chairs for me as an apology for what happened to my ankle," she said with a low laugh.

Sahar sat down, and Jay followed on the other side. "What happened to your ankle?" he asked.

"I had a horrible sprain in secondary school. High school, as you lot call it here. Didn't take proper precautions because I had a production of *Sound of Music* I wanted to be part of, so I made it worse. Every now and then, it likes to remind me when I've over-exerted it."

The look he gave her almost made her want to laugh. If Sahar didn't know he had a kid, she would've questioned it at this point. It was the type of gentle scold that, at the same time, held a plethora of concerns. "Do you take better care of it now?"

She narrowed her eyes. "Yes, I do. Anyway, we aren't here to talk about my ankle. We're here to talk about Henry and Katherine."

Shifting his large frame in the chair that was far too small for him, Jay looked her in the eyes before saying, "Let's hear it."

Sahar took a breath, collecting her thoughts. "Okay, so I read the first episode, and it made my heart burst. I don't know how you managed to give me so much right from the start, but I was all in. *That's* why I skipped ahead and read the ending."

A bee flew between them, buzzing along the table, and Sahar leaned back in fear. Clearly aware of her sudden discomfort, Jay carefully brushed it away and gestured for her to keep talking.

"Thanks for that," she started again. "Anyway, that final line, Jay. It reads, 'I'm going to find Katherine, and I'm going to bring her home,' but in the end, she's just gone. Dead? Her body is found after everything, and that's it? Can you tell me what led to that decision?"

Jay's face fell a bit. Sahar couldn't read his expression.

He swallowed, his Adam's apple bobbing. "I thought about it—Henry finding her, realizing that she's been trying to get out all along. But it felt too easy. It felt too...I don't know, convenient. I was also at a low point in my life when the idea came to me, so it wasn't exactly easy to see a happy ending."

Sahar blinked, once, twice.

Who hurt this man?

"That's entirely understandable. And I don't want to disregard the idea of realism, so I hope this doesn't come off that way. But I think the death dismisses Katherine's strength as a woman. I read up to episode three last night, and the bits we see of her while she's trapped... She's just as determined to survive, and she wants the Logan brothers gone as much as he does. She's no damsel in distress, Jay."

"She doesn't die at their hands," he countered.

Sahar leaned forward a bit, chair creaking underneath her. "And I think that's the problem. From what I gather by skimming the finale, she dies from an untreated wound, which I completely understand is reasonable in a situation like this, but you're telling me that when she snuck off during the raid, she didn't find a pharmacy to hold herself over until she could properly see a doctor?"

Jay's eyes went somewhere else. His mouth curled in thought.

Sahar remained quiet.

"Yeah, I...uh, I realize now I did the one thing that countless critics always seem to hate, which is when a man's character development is tied to the loss of a woman. Though I'd argue that the focus here is on Katherine's worth and how much he loves her, I can see where it feels forced. Plot over character."

Sahar smiled. She hadn't expected him to hear her this intently.

Sighing, Jay dropped his gaze to the pigeon wobbling beside their table. "I wanted this to be a story about endurance. I want these characters both to overcome all this bullshit and set themselves free, but why does that seem too easy in fiction? That wouldn't be the case if it happened in real life."

His cadence fell at the last sentence, and a sharp stab of sadness punctured her heart.

Once more, with feeling, who hurt this man?

"Real life might not be happy, but aren't people allowed to hope? To watch something and maybe for a few hours believe that life *can* be like that?"

He didn't say anything. He merely looked at her.

"So, Katherine survives. But I think in order to make it feel earned, we have to push it far beyond what I have. We need to keep elevating the stakes. Henry has to come to a point where everything is too painful, and he's not sure how much more he can take."

Sahar nodded. "He grows a beard, loses himself a bit... that'll make finding one another hit even harder."

Jay tilted his head, running his fingers along his own beard. It momentarily bewildered her. Something about the intensity in his dark eyes, his angular features, and the curve of his lips—nope. She would *not* go there.

"He grows a beard. Loses himself, what else you got for me?"

"I'll think about it once I actually finish. The next few weeks will likely get chaotic while my sister's visiting and with the

Tonys, so I don't know when I'll be able to resume without constantly having to pause to do something else. I planned on reading the entire thing yesterday, but at the last minute, Miles realized he could take guests for this fundraiser at Clyde's company, so he asked us to join. But really, Jay, this story is great so far. Like really fucking amazing. I think if you change that ending, there's something special here. Will you try resubmitting?"

"Do you think I should?"

Sahar sat up straighter, crossing one leg over the other. "Of course, I do. I think you have a real shot here. Never underestimate a happy ending in 2024. People need it."

He took a breath. "Maybe. But I don't know how much I have left in me."

The small puncture she'd felt earlier grew exponentially more painful. "If you need me to metaphorically hold your hand and cheer you on every step of the way, I'll do it. Ask Willa. It's my expertise."

"I might take you up on it."

"You should. In fact, you better. I fear I'm now too attached to these characters not to know what they're doing every step of the way."

Jay's mouth curved upward. "Sounds like a plan," he said, adjusting his position in the chair again.

4

JAY

Sahar's warmth and the steady smile on her face made it easy to believe that the world wasn't a gushing cesspool of literal shit. Beside her, it was surprisingly effortless to believe that he wasn't failing.

"For a second there, I had hope after the strikes last year," Sahar noted. "I'm still shocked things are getting scrapped, but it shouldn't be surprising in this industry. I really hope people like you don't give up, Jay. We need original stories now more than ever."

Jay swallowed the rigid lump lodged in his throat. One hundred and forty-eight days of the Writers Guild of America strike and one hundred and eighteen days of SAG-AFTRA, but AI still hadn't burned to the ground.

People were being replaced left and right by soulless robots, and it made him violently angry every time he thought about it.

"Yeah," he managed to say.

A weary expression crossed her face. "Have you seen improvement from any of your peers?"

He shook his head. "No. At least not from the people who'd already been struggling. Some colleagues were thankfully able to bounce back, and I know that there's progress happening behind the scenes we won't be seeing for a while, but it's still so jarring how disposable real people are these days."

"I follow a few journalists who've been writing about our show, and I keep seeing that smaller outlets are closing down because they can't compete with the changes in the algorithm and AI articles."

Worrying at his bottom lip, Jay said, "And it's those very journalists who are always so supportive of indie filmmaking, too."

Sahar closed her eyes for a beat and then squared herself. "Okay, listen, the biggest fuck you to AI is going to be getting the best story out there. Henry and Katherine are going to be on my TV screen soon, and the world is going to love them as much as I do. I believe in you, Jay. I believe in this story. These rewrites could be good for you," she paused for a beat. "Us, really, because as I said, I'm selfish and *want* to see it myself. I want to be insufferable about it all over social media, and tell everyone I know."

She beamed, and he wanted to bottle the look on her face like a jar of fireflies for the nights when all he could see was darkness.

Jay let out a small laugh, one he didn't realize was bubbling inside him. Sahar was like the sun. He understood at that moment that this was why he always appreciated seeing her at the coffee shop. It was how she'd quite literally kept him tethered to the light during that one horrific day when he almost quit.

"Have you always been this optimistic?" he asked.

She smiled softly. "My mum claims I was the happiest baby." Thinking over the next words she was going to say, Sahar tilted her head and shrugged. "But it often works against me. I try to force things to work, come off as too much, and things slowly backfire." Her voice broke a little by the end. He wondered if someone had said that to her.

No part of Sahar was too much; in fact, he could tell that she was holding parts of herself back. Like all the joy and vibrancy she showed in his presence were a mere fraction of the real her.

He was positive that if he continued to watch her shine as she'd just allowed moments ago, he wouldn't know what to do with himself.

"You could never be too much for me. You're like sunshine. People need you," he returned, astounding himself with the overt declaration.

Sahar laughed. It was sarcastic, but a sound he'd happily still get drunk on. "You know people loathe summer, right? That's not a compliment."

"I didn't say summer. I said sunshine. There's a difference. Also, plenty of people love summer."

She scrunched her face in thought. "Okay, you saved it there a bit, but still, people get tired of sunshine. It overstays its welcome."

Had an actual human being looked into those big, beautiful brown eyes, claiming that she overstayed her welcome? What kind of a fucking moron wasn't willing to perpetually orbit around her?

Leaning forward in the uncomfortably small chair, Jay looked her in the eyes and said, "Well, *sunshine*. You're welcome near me any day."

Sunshine. The fuck. Did he really call her that out loud?

It flowed so easily from his lips that it was both strange and familiar at the same time. But what was she to him other than maybe a friend and now an unofficial (read: official in his dreams) writing partner? He shouldn't have been calling her anything other than her name.

Sahar. *Sunshine.*

He'd read somewhere that in Arabic, her name meant "dawn," and he'd never known another person whose name matched their personality so seamlessly. Sunshine might not always be present at dawn, but he'd argue that it was the ideal time of day—the most hopeful, the most picturesque.

He chanced a glance at her amid his whirling thoughts. She was smiling leisurely, her features soft and warm, actual sunlight glimmering on her, brightening her dark red hair. He could gaze at her for hours, count the small freckles dusting along her nose, and lose himself in the stories present in her eyes.

"I'm honored," she said, and he could tell that she meant it, even as he sensed that she didn't fully buy into his statement. She dropped her forearm onto the table then and said, "Do I get to ask again about why you chose Amanda's now that we're alone?"

Jay sighed, thinking about how much he could say to her without disclosing the sob story of his and his sister's past. "In short, my dad is a piece of shit and he put Alex—my sister— through some things that fucked with her mental health before her Broadway debut. I was bartending for a while, but the later hours made it hard to be present for both Alex and Eloise, my daughter, so I applied to the coffee shop. Alex was in the production that ran before *Midnights at Pemberley* came to the Hyacinth, so it was just a matter of convenience. Then I got the manager's job, strikes, and well...shit industry."

Sahar's expression was empathetic, and there was no trace of pity in her eyes, only a look that said she wasn't judging him or his family for any of it.

"Is your sister doing better these days? That must be so hard, especially with how demanding our industry can be."

He nodded. "A lot better, yeah, though she has her days."

"That's good to hear. Is she in anything now?"

"*Hatchard's Academy.*"

Jay caught the stark change in her entire demeanor. A shadow of unease flashed in her eyes. "My ex is in that."

"Who's your ex?" he asked.

"Martin Tucker."

He couldn't remember if his sister had told him anything about him. "Do I need to worry about him?"

"In terms of what?"

Did he hurt you? Did you love him? Did he break your heart?

Jay shook his head. He wasn't sure why he had asked the initial question. It wasn't entirely about Sahar either, and Alex wasn't a kid anymore, but he still worried about his sister constantly after everything she'd been through. "I don't know. The way your expression changed tells me something's off about him. I don't think my sister has mentioned him before, so I don't know, should I be concerned that she's in this show with him?"

"Oh, no, I don't think so. He's more someone who'll use anyone to get to the top, and he hates sharing the spotlight. Now that I think about it, he probably got with me to see if he could get closer to Ethan and Declan, but they both kept him at arm's length. Unless your sister has some high-profile connections, he's simply a leech."

A drop of relief washed over Jay at once. "Alex keeps to herself a lot. She had a few good friends in the last show, but I don't think that's the case here."

"If you want to warn her, feel free. But on a more positive note, it's lovely that both you and your sister are in the industry somehow. You said your dad is a piece of shit, but what about your mum?"

He was about to answer when she shook her head abruptly. "I'm so sorry if that's too personal. I didn't think, Jay."

"No, you're fine. Our mom is great. She was on Broadway, too, before she met him. Now, she teaches music theory." *Don't tell her how he broke her spirit and forbade her from ever stepping foot on a stage again. Don't tell her how you're scared you'll end up just like him, even though you know you'd never.*

Sahar smiled again, breaking him free from his maddening thoughts. "I'm glad your mum is great. Did the stage not call to you?"

Tapping his thumb along the circular table, he exhaled a low laugh. "Not even a little."

She was looking at him with such curiosity that it made his chest tighten. "Someone's gotta give us performers the story to tell."

He swallowed, thinking once more of how he wanted to write a character just for her. "You're a storyteller, too, now," he said.

Her lips quirked upward. "You've made me a monster. I can't wait to read the rest tonight if I'm not too tired after work. Speaking of. I should get going."

"I'll walk you back," he added, rising from his seat.

Standing up, Sahar adjusted the strap sitting across her body. "Do you live in the city?"

"No, I'm on the Island. You?"

"Willa and I are in Queens."

"Nice. Did you two meet on the show?"

Sahar shook her head, dodging two pigeons in her path by veering closer to him. "We were in a production of *Macbeth* together back in London. Clicked instantly and moved here together six years ago. But *Midnights* is our first show together since then."

"Is this your first principal role on Broadway?"

She confirmed with a nod.

"I've been meaning to see it. Time keeps getting away from me."

Sahar let out a sardonic gasp. "How dare you take so long?"

"I know. I'm sorry. I'll be there one of these days. I promise."

She turned to him, another bright, slow smile rising on her lips. His breath hitched.

"You don't have to. I'm teasing."

"I *want* to," he underscored.

Jay knew very little with utmost certainty, but he knew that Sahar Peck was someone he wanted to keep close in his life. How, he wasn't sure of that part, but there were layers to her that he prayed to unfurl, secrets he hoped to excavate, and smiles he wanted—no, *needed*—to keep.

5

SAHAR

"Sahar? You're quiet today. Is everything okay?" Willa asked, glancing at her from the mirror in their shared dressing room. Sahar hadn't told her she had met with Jay to talk about the screenplay. She hadn't told anyone, including her sister, who was set to visit soon for the Tony Awards.

Sahar faced Willa through their reflections. "Yeah, I'm fine. I just can't stop thinking about how...never mind." She had no business thinking about Jay's circumstances. None whatsoever.

Willa turned in her seat. "Hey, it's me, babe. You can talk to me about whatever's on your mind. Is it the prick? Has he done something again?"

Sahar shut her eyes briefly. "No, no. It's Jay, and some things he told me today. I got the sense that...I don't know; I could be making assumptions here, but something about the look in his eyes made me feel like he's a bit broken. He told me some stuff, and with the way he talks about people, it's clear that he's constantly taking care of others, but who's looking out for him? Or at least, I don't know. Maybe someone is. I just can't shake it."

Willa looked confused for a beat. *Yeah, hi, Sahar; it would have helped if you'd started from the beginning.*

"Wait, he told you all that at Amanda's?"

Shaking her head, Sahar added, "No, I met up with him for a bit at Bryant Park after PT to talk about his screenplay."

"Ah, well, that makes more sense. Do you reckon he...?" Willa's words remained suspended in the air as a rap on the door demanded their attention.

"Come in," Willa called out.

Sam barged in, phone in hand. "Ladies," he greeted, then turned to Sahar. "Work wife, want to get on Instagram live with me? People have been asking about you."

Sahar chortled. "I'll be there as soon as I'm ready."

Willa spoke again after Sam left. "I forgot what I was going to ask, but did you find out anything about his daughter's mum?"

Shaking her head, Sahar said, "It didn't come up, and I already felt so invasive asking him twenty-one questions. Why am I like this?"

"You mean a person who cares about genuinely getting to know others? Why aren't more people like you is the better question," Willa replied, positioning her blush brush on her cheeks.

Sahar blended out her makeup with a sponge. "I don't know, Wills. Few things make sense right now, including how I do— well, anything."

Willa's hand dropped to Sahar's shoulder with a squeeze. "I'm here to work through whatever you want. Always."

Acknowledging her gesture with a smile, Sahar finished off her makeup so she could join Sam for a few minutes. She lined her lips, added the nude lipstick she'd typically wear for the first half of the show, and completed the routine with hefty spritzes of setting spray.

She still had about thirty-ish minutes before she needed to

get into costume. Leaving their dressing room, she strode off to Sam's, two doors over.

It was wide open, permitting her to avoid the action of knocking. "I'm here. Let's roll," she signaled, joining Sam next to him in an empty chair.

"Yes!" Sam bellowed. He picked up his phone, opened Instagram, and went live. "I didn't realize we haven't been on together in a minute until people started asking yesterday."

"How long has it been?" Sahar questioned.

"A few weeks," Sam answered.

"Shit, really?"

"We've been busy bees," he added before they noticed that people had started watching.

"Hello, hello—thou ask, and thou shalt receive," Sam motioned toward Sahar.

Sahar let out a chuckle. "Hi, my loves. I've been made aware that it's been a minute since we've done this."

Sam pointed to a comment that read, "*Sam, please never do a Shakespearean production,*" and laughed out loud.

"I'd never. Don't worry. No one would even hire me."

"Do people know that even though you're British, you've lived longer in the States?" Sahar asked.

"I don't know. Is this something I've talked about?" he asked aloud to the camera, as though people would respond. "But yeah, my family moved here when I was fourteen because of my dad's job, so I never got the West End theatrical experience. There is no Shakespeare in my acting history."

"Meanwhile, I've been in almost every Shakespearean play except for *Othello,*" Sahar noted.

"What was your favorite?"

"*Macbeth,* obviously. Playing a witch with Willa. What more could I ask for?"

Hearts filled the phone screen. Sam motioned to another

question that specifically asked Sahar what she was currently reading. She'd grown so accustomed to sharing the books and movies or TV shows she was watching that she realized she hadn't talked about books in a while. Briefly, she wondered if anyone had watched *Cuts* or *Beneath the Sun* since she had posted about them during the last two days.

"Right now, I'm reading a secret project written by a friend, so that's been taking up most of my free time. No new books so far, but I'm more than happy to take suggestions. You all know I'm always game for historical romance."

"Priya keeps trying to get me to read some," Sam commented.

"And you should listen to your wife," Sahar emphasized.

"I fear the only book I'll be reading for the foreseeable future is some dinosaur series Ravi's currently obsessed with."

Sahar gave him a big grin. "You're not going to share the title with the class? Maybe some people want to read it to their five-year-olds, too."

"Way to embarrass me, mate. If I remembered the title, I would've already said it."

She punched his shoulder playfully. "Post it when you get home."

"You got it." He pointed to a question that read, *What are you two listening to right now?*

"The National, as usual," Sahar answered. "But I'm also eagerly waiting for the new Glass Animals album."

"Taste," Sam replied, then answered for himself. "I've been listening to a lot of instrumentals lately. Dec reminded me of the *Interstellar* score, so I've had that one on replay again."

Sahar bobbed her head. "Hans Zimmer can do no wrong." She pointed to Sam's phone. "Speaking of the ill numpty, Dec's requesting to join."

Sam frowned sympathetically and then clicked on the accept

prompt. Declan came into the frame from his living room. He'd been out with a bad cold since Saturday.

"How are you feeling, baby boy?" Sam asked.

"Decccccc," Sahar elongated the c.

Declan shut his eyes dramatically. "Like death and decay," he answered.

"Bro, how'd you get so sick?"

He shrugged. "No idea, man. But I'm mostly just congested today, so I'm hoping the worst of it has passed. Scale of one to ten, how much do you all miss me?"

Sahar scrunched her face, gesturing with her hands. "Like an eight. It's way too quiet."

"Ten. Thank the lord it didn't happen while Ethan was off on his vacation. I couldn't survive without both my boys."

Sahar turned to him. "What am I, chopped liver?"

Sam and Declan both laughed. Momentarily, as though on cue, Ethan ran in. "I heard Dec," he mentioned before stepping into the frame. "You realized you wouldn't be seeing me for three days, so you got yourself sick by stressing about it so much? Is that what happened, sweet Cinnamon Toast Crunch?"

They all laughed. These three and their endearments toward one another. They'd never use such saccharine shit with their wives or girlfriends. It was hilarious and adorable.

Trailing off for a split second as the laughter settled, her mind wondered how Jay was around his friends.

"That's it. That's what it was. I should get sick more often. You're so nice to me when I am. Is this how you felt when Willa was gone?" Declan mentioned with a wink.

Ethan shook his head lovingly. Sahar peered up at him, remembering how quiet and sad he'd been when Willa had gone back to England for her brother's wedding. Outside of their interviews, he'd been so dejected. Lost. She hadn't realized

Declan and Sam hounded him about it, but it made sense that they would.

What would it be like to have someone miss her like that? To have someone for whom she wasn't too much, but everything instead. Someone who craved her company the moment she was no longer with them.

"Okay, I'm leaving. I just wanted to say hi to the sick peanut."

Declan blew a kiss through the camera. Ethan did the same and then left Sam's dressing room.

"Okay, sweet cheeks, we gotta go get ready. They're going to call fifteen minutes any second now." Sam said.

Declan pouted. Sahar did, too. "Feel better!" she added.

Waving, Declan left the Instagram live, and after, Sam and Sahar said bye to the viewers watching before promising not to wait too long until they went live again.

Sam turned to her before she got up. "Hey, are you okay? Dec being gone isn't the only reason it's quiet around here. You've seemed off the past few days. Is it the breakup? You know, I'm here if you need anything."

Sahar trusted Sam like she trusted everyone at *Midnights*, but she wasn't going to tell him that she was tamping herself down because it'd occurred to her that she could be the problem in all her relationships.

She dismissed the truth. "No, no. I've just been more tired."

He tilted his head like he was trying to read her. "You sure that fucker didn't hurt you in any way? You say the word, and the three of us will beat his ass for you."

Giving him a genuine laugh at the sentiment, she nodded once more. "I'm grateful, but no need to duel in my honor."

"Okay, fine. I'll take the hint. But also, what's this project you're reading from a friend? Do I get to know?" he added with his signature smirk.

She could tell him this. It wasn't like Sam would go parading it around. "You know Jay from Amanda's? He's written a limited series, and I got him to let me read it. It's incredible."

"Oh, shit. Yeah, his work is fucking deep. Ethan, Dec, and I watched *Cuts* together, and all three of us were in tears."

Sahar agreed. "Mate, I watched it Sunday night and straight up wept."

"He's a really good guy, too. I've hung out with him a few times, in large gatherings, sure, but he's down-to-earth and mellow. There's not a pretentious or fake bone in his body. Plus, Patrick, the other guy who wrote *Cuts* is a fucking ace. I know him a bit better, and he and Jay have been best friends since they were really young."

These very words coming from Sam made something flurry inside of Sahar's chest. She wasn't entirely sure why, but it mattered to her that both Sam and Ethan respected Jay. It was important for her to hear that he was indeed a good person because it meant that maybe she wasn't awful at reading people.

Plus, she liked Jay a lot. She was growing to care about his friendship, his opinion, and his company, too. Something else poked her heart—a barely there hint of an emotion she couldn't quite translate, but she liked it. Whatever it was, it felt...safe.

Sahar brushed her fingers along her jeans and then rose from the chair she'd been sitting on. "It makes me happy to hear that. That's the vibe I get from him as well."

Sam smiled. "I'll see you out there."

Sahar left the room and went back to the dressing room she shared with Willa. Ethan was leaning against the vanity, eyes fixed on his girl, who was fully in costume now.

He spotted Sahar, smiled, pressed a kiss on Willa's head, then walked out, patting Sahar's shoulder on his way out.

"How'd the live go? I meant to watch, but Anna called me, so I got sidetracked talking to her, and then Ethan came in." Anna was Willa's sister-in-law.

Sahar shut their door and then moved to the wardrobe. She took her first costume for Jane out. "Delightful. Dec got into the chat. He called Ethan out about missing you," she said, wiggling out of her jeans to change into the first layer of pantyhose.

"Ha! Ethan was just telling me."

"I can't stand how adorable you two are."

Willa scrunched her nose. "He's the best."

Sahar proceeded to add another layer of pantyhose. "You deserve it all, babe."

"So do you," Willa returned. "Please tell me you know that?"

Sahar shrugged, reaching for the third pair of pantyhose after aligning the second. She wasn't sure what she deserved these days. But she wanted it. All the romance novels she read, the attempts she'd made at finding love—she wanted it more than anything. She was a bloody hopeless romantic through and through, but too damn unlucky to experience it for herself.

Was she solely meant to read about it?

She'd told Willa that she was swearing off men, and this time, she meant it. Sahar could no longer dive deep into something she wasn't one thousand percent sure about. She couldn't give her heart freely anymore—it was too fragile and fractured now—the next person could be her undoing.

She couldn't survive another heartbreak, and *that* she was sure about.

6

———

SAHAR

The Tony Awards were here, and the most exciting part of the day was sharing the experience with her favorite people: the brilliant cast that had become her chosen family, and her older sister, Amina, visiting from London.

They'd just finished the day's show, where their performance of the titular "Midnights at Pemberley" track was recorded to air during the awards.

Back in their dressing room with some time to kill, Willa and Amina were talking about how they both sworn they'd never date someone they worked with, but their self-made rules went down the drain the second they fell in love with their current partners.

Sahar looked at her phone, staring at the text that had come in from Jay earlier in the day. *Good luck today!*

Since it was Father's Day, she assumed that he'd be with his daughter, and she wouldn't be seeing him at the coffee shop. What she hadn't considered was that he'd take the time to acknowledge her Tony nomination.

Sighing, she looked up at Amina and Willa. "Do you say

Happy Father's Day to someone who isn't your dad but does have a kid?"

"We said it to Sam," Willa said.

"Yeah, but that's Sam."

"I'm not following," Amina added.

Sahar took a sip of her coffee. "Do I say it to Jay or not?"

Willa flashed her a toothy smile.

Amina cocked an eyebrow. "So, that's who you're texting."

Sahar rolled her eyes. "I'm not texting him. He just said good luck, and I'm debating if I should say Happy Father's Day. There's nothing complicated here."

"You're the one making it complicated with your question, you twat," Amina bit back with an affectionate sneer.

"I hate you."

Willa reclined in her seat. "I would."

"Yeah, you sure?" Sahar muttered.

"Positive," she said, then turned to Amina. "Too bad you missed him today, Mina. The man's fit as fuck."

"That's because you have a glasses kink," Sahar retorted.

"You're telling me you don't think Jay is objectively attractive?"

Sahar tried not to give in to the whirling thoughts in her mind. Of course, she thought he was attractive. Anyone could see that. But admitting to finding him attractive was another added intricacy to her already convoluted thoughts. "Okay, yes, he's fit. Happy?"

"Over the moon," Willa replied.

"It's all good. I'll come back one of these days when you two are working just to see this specimen who's got my no-nonsense sister tripping over her words."

"I'm not tripping over my words," Sahar argued.

"If that helps you sleep better at night, feel free to keep telling yourself that, boo. But also, you're allowed to have feelings. Especially today of all days, my Tony-nominated little queen," her sister rebutted.

Willa's mouth quirked at the edges. "Did you write a speech?"

Sahar grimaced. "No, and before you start with me, I'd straight up stand at that podium and reject the award if I won it over Jodi Holbrook. I'm *still* haunted by her performance in *The Ongoing Train*. She has it in the bag, and if she doesn't, ooh boy, the theatre league will hear my wrath."

Both Amina and Willa laughed.

"See, you can't even disagree because you know I'm right. Your guy deserves it. Naomi does, too. But I'm up against that goddess extraordinaire, and my name next to hers on the nomination list is already a win."

Scowling, Amina said, "Why'd you drag my arse here if you had no hopes of winning? What am I supposed to brag about at the office?"

Sahar playfully kicked her foot. "And here I was thinking you wanted to support my first nomination out of the goodness of your heart and your unyielding pride in my glorious talents."

"Or I just really wanted five days off work," Amina joked.

Sahar stuck out her tongue. "Twat."

"I'd still give the award to you if I had a say in it," Willa said.

Sahar blew an air kiss at her. "Because you're an angel."

"No, because you're *that* good."

"It's rather unfair that my work bestie was transferred. I miss this," Amina noted, looking from Sahar to Willa.

"Please do not remind me. I've been so emotional about the end of this show's run, and it's not even close. But wait, didn't you say Paulette would be back?"

Amina sighed. "In a year. If she chooses."

"You know she would. Wasn't it hard for her to take the job

in the first place? I thought she did it because she needed the extra pay in all the training she'd be doing."

"Yeah, but she's got so much potential, that one. If something else with better pay opened up, no one would fault her for taking it."

Christian peered into the room, eyes lit up. "We're all taking a celebratory pre-show shot on the stage."

They all stood up.

"I'm coming to take a group photo of you all," Amina chirped excitedly.

Smack dab in the center of the stage, shot glasses were spread across a folding table. Their entire cast and crew gathered around, different conversations blurring together.

Sahar and Willa drew forward, and Ethan handed them both a plastic shot glass.

Jeffrey Henderson, their director, and his wife, Greta, stood near the edge of the stage.

After everyone had raised their drinks upward, Jeffrey spoke.

"Whatever happens tonight, I couldn't be prouder of each of you." He meant those words, too; no one could deny how pride painted his entire face at the moment. It was also on full display in Greta's eyes.

"When Greta came to me with this idea. I didn't think we could pull it off at first. It took a while to get here, and the best parts of it are because of every person standing on this stage. You all gave me the chance of a lifetime to direct this show. Thank you from the bottom of my heart. Cheers to Pemberley."

"Cheers to Pemberley!" echoed through the stage. Heads tipped back, shots gulped down. The clear liquid burned through her lungs. The sounds of joy and celebration enveloped her. This moment was the win, as Jeffrey had deemed it. No matter what happened tonight, this show was a part of her. A piece of her she'd carry forever. If she didn't already have a *Pride and Prejudice* tattoo, she would've gotten one for *Midnights.* Come to think of it, she still could.

Amina bounced closer, sticking her phone in front of Sahar. "Look at this. Isn't it gorgeous?"

Sahar let out a low gasp.

It was. Amina had captured the moment in stunning clarity, shot glasses in the air to toast, bright, beaming gazes on each of their faces. The backdrop of the stage behind them.

It was, in every way, a perfect photograph.

"Mina! This is everything."

Pride burst from her sister, too. Sahar looked more like her mother, with olive skin, dark hair, and dark eyes. But she and her sister had the same exact smile when something thrilled them.

She looked around the room, acknowledging the chance she was given to be a Tony Award-nominated actress. She thought of the first few dozen auditions she'd gone to. The way casting directors looked at her, butchered her name, and made a decision before she could even prove her talents. And now, she was a lead in a Jane Austen musical, performing alongside one of the most gifted Black actresses in the industry. Naomi Driver was a force to be reckoned with, an unmatched voice accompanying her brilliant acting chops.

Laura Tiu, Innilla Jani, Lea Driver, Declan McNair, Willa Davidian—they were each people who had, in some way, at one point, been considered less than in this industry because of their race or ethnicity. Hollywood loved to pretend it was inclusive, but that was seldom the truth. Yet, at the Hyacinth Theatre, in *Midnights at Pemberley,* they were stars. All those rejections led to this moment—the joy, the sadness, the sleepless nights, and all the hard work.

It was worth it. Here and now.

But the industry's bleakness came to her again. And *oh, shit.* She had forgotten to text Jay back.

SAHAR

> Thank you, thank you! & Happy Father's Day to you.

Putting her phone in her back pocket, she willed herself fully back in the moment.

LATER THAT NIGHT, after the celebrations, Sahar and Amina spoke to their parents.

"Happy Father's Day, Dad!" They both belted into the phone when he accepted the FaceTime call.

He let out a small laugh. "Thank you, girls. How was today?"

"Sahar, we're so proud of you! He spent all of yesterday gloating at dinner about you," her mum said.

Sahar did a small bow over the video call. "Did you lot have fun today?"

"It was great, yeah. Your uncles and I all decided we're getting Man City season passes again."

Sahar and Amina looked at each other, bursting into a fit of laughter.

"We knew you couldn't stay away! Sahar said it. 'The man can't go a season without games.' Cheers, Dad. You deserve it," Amina declared.

"First thing I'm doing is visiting when my contract is over, and you're taking me to a game," Sahar added.

"One hundred percent, my girl."

"You really win the best of both worlds. You get one engineer daughter just like you and another football fan."

Their father reddened with pride over the camera. "Luckiest dad in all of England. In the entire world, if you ask me."

"As are we," Amina said.

They talked for a bit, a little about the awards and how many *Midnights at Pemberley* took home. How exciting the ceremony was for the two of them to experience together.

Sahar counted all her lucky stars that night. How truly fortunate she was to have parents as loving as Iman and Andrew Peck, a sister as brilliant as Amina, and friends as amazing as the *Midnights* cast. She wouldn't trade it for the world.

7

___

JAY

"Dad!" Eloise called out. "Can you please braid my hair?"

Closing the door to the washer and dryer, Jay stepped back out into the living room and walked toward the bathroom, where Eloise was standing on a pastel pink step stool. He let out a low laugh at the sight of his newly showered daughter wearing her Spider-Gwen costume from last Halloween.

"Did you not have anything else in your closet, kiddo?"

The same brown eyes that he saw in the mirror every day looked back at him—the same glint of mischief his mom had told him he also possessed when he was young. "I wanted to make sure it still fits," she exclaimed, handing him her hairbrush. She'd already detangled her slightly wavy, brown hair.

Standing behind her, Jay gently smoothed her hair back, careful to leave her bangs intact. She'd gotten them earlier this year, and Maya had shown her how to blow-dry them into shape.

As he divided her hair into three sections, Eloise said, "It's so hard to make braids at the back of my head. I can only do it when I want pigtails, but I only want one right now."

Jay gave her a smile through the mirror while he crossed one chunk of hair over the other. "It's okay, baby. You'll get the hang of it in no time."

A small part of him hoped it wouldn't be too soon, that she'd need him and Maya for as long as possible. He never understood parents mentioning the passage of time as much as they did until Eloise was born. He had blinked, and the newborn baby he was terrified of crushing when he first held her was now eight. He would blink again, and she'd be nine. Finishing up the braid, he reached for the small yellow hair tie in her hand. Jay took it from her, secured the pigtail, and dropped a kiss to the top of her head.

She thanked him with a giggle, then hopped down and out of the bathroom.

Switching the light off, he stepped out and strode over to the kitchen. The drawing she'd given him for Father's Day was neatly placed atop the island. Jay picked it up, turned on his heel, and magnetized it onto the fridge, tracing his finger over the detailed video camera she'd sketched.

He wasn't sure how long he'd been standing there, looking at her old drawings, when she popped up beside him. "Dad, you should take down some of my old drawings. They're not nice!" She'd changed out of the Spider-Gwen costume and into a pair of gray sweatpants and a white T-shirt to match him.

It was so damn adorable.

He pointed to one of the earlier pieces she'd ever drawn for him: the two of them as stick figures, holding ice cream cones in their hands. *Daddy and me,* written in her handwriting, spelling confirmed by Maya. It'd been the first artwork she'd given him for Father's Day. "Nah, they're all perfect to me. This one's my all-time favorite."

Laughing, she squealed with disgust. "It's ugly! I can draw better than stick figures now."

Jay gave her a sincere smile. "It's not about its imperfections; it's because that's the first Father's Day drawing you gave me. It's special. And progress is important. It's part of the journey. You think I like my first movie?"

"You don't?" she asked.

He shook his head. "When I first released it, I was proud of it. Then, I learned new techniques and refined my process, so I started to dislike it. Now that a few years have passed, I see that it was meaningful in its own right to show myself how I can improve. It was important to understand what my strengths and weaknesses were. Plus, some people have said that it's one of their favorites, even if I don't exactly get why. That's how art works, baby. You never know what people will connect with."

Smiling, she seemed to be processing his words.

"Did your dad keep your old drawings?" she asked.

No. He was a dick before I even learned how to walk. "Well, first, I wasn't as talented as you are, so no," he said.

"But you just said: progress is important."

Jay bent down, meeting her at eye level. "Yeah, but my dad didn't think like me," he admitted, sparing her the ugly truth about how vicious her grandfather truly was. Someday, if she wanted to, she'd be old enough to learn more about what he'd done, but today wasn't that day.

"Was he nice?"

No. He was the worst person I've ever known. "Not exactly, but that isn't important. What *is* important is how many scoops of ice cream do you want?"

"How many scoops do *you* want?" she returned, emphasizing the word *you* giddily.

"I feel like it's a three-scoop night. Beach days always warrant an extra scoop, don't they?"

Eloise agreed with an emphatic nod. "Yeah!"

She grabbed two spoons from the drawer, then lunged onto the island's barstool. Taking the ice cream from the fridge, he loaded their two bowls—coffee for him, strawberry for her—and sat down.

"Dad?" she said before taking a bite.

"Hmm."

"You're the best dad ever." She said it so plainly, so matter-of-factly, so sincerely that he couldn't help but believe her.

Jay harbored countless fears and never-ending doubts—messing up parenting at the top of the list, but if the floor-boards cracked open and swallowed him whole, right at this very second, at least he'd know that he'd somehow done right by her.

And he wanted to be even better for Eloise. Always.

"I love you times infinity," he said.

With a big smile and way too much ice cream in her mouth, she repeated, "I love *you* times infinity."

That had been their thing. When Eloise was four, she had learned what the concept of *a scale of one to ten* meant, proceeding to ask him then how much he loved her at that level. He'd replied none, because ten simply wasn't high enough. He'd said infinity, and in her adorably shocked state, she'd said, "You love me times infinity?"

I love you times infinity, Jay had confirmed, because that was exactly what he had meant, and she said it back to him.

He'd been knee-deep in student loans, struggling, and in the world's worst rut the day Eloise was born. February 16, 2016, 8:32 in the morning. He wasn't with Maya in the hospital room because she only wanted her mom, but Jay had been right outside when he heard Eloise's near-howling cry. Tears had fallen the second he saw her sweet little face, and his entire life changed the first time he held her, promising to himself then and there that he'd pick up all the discarded pieces of himself and patch them up one by one for her.

With her mouth full of ice cream again, she mumbled, "Why are you staring at me?"

Because I can't believe how lucky I am to have a kid as amazing as you. He smiled, dodging the question. "Slow down, or you'll get a brain freeze."

She swallowed abruptly and then winced, shutting her eyes.

Trying not to laugh, Jay suggested, "Press your tongue to the roof of your mouth."

She did so and lightly tapped her foot along the chair's wooden leg like some sort of reflex. Once it was gone, she scooped some more and said, "Are we going to play *Shrek* after?" They'd been playing all the old *Shrek* games that he was shocked still worked from Alex's old PS2 console.

"How are you not tired?" Jay asked.

"It's summer!" she exclaimed.

"That doesn't answer my question."

Eloise squared her shoulders. "Sleep is for the weak."

"Where'd you hear that toxic nonsense? Sleep isn't for the weak; it's what every human body needs."

"Some boy at school."

"Well, that nameless kid is wrong, and you can tell him that the next time you see him again."

She giggled with her mouth full of ice cream again. "Okay, okay, sleeping is important, but can we still play a little?"

"Yeah, but on one condition."

"What?"

"I get to be the Donkey this time. You know, in honor of Father's Day and all."

Some sort of a dramatic cackle unleashed from her throat. "But I get to do the hero-time quest?"

"Always," he confirmed.

With a big grin, she scarfed down her last bit of ice cream and then ran to start the game in the living room.

Jay took a spoonful of his, recalling the text Sahar had sent him earlier. A simple *Happy Father's Day,* yet it had meant so much.

Looking at the time on his stove, he realized that the awards would be over by now. Jay opened Google to search for the results. Glancing through, *Midnights at Pemberley* had taken quite a few accolades home. It also looked like Ethan won, too. But when he located the category Sahar's nomination was in, the winner hadn't been her. It was an actress named Jodi Holbrook. Sure, he hadn't seen Sahar's performance—yet—but he wanted her to win.

Was she upset? Did it ruin her day? Did she care about these things? Her sister was in town for the show, too. He remembered her telling him that a few days ago.

He exited out of the article and texted her. What would he even say? What was appropriate?

JAY

Hey, I hope you're not too upset by the outcome of the awards. If it's any consolation, I would've given it to you if I had any say.

"Ready, Dad?" he heard Eloise say from the couch where she was already seated.

Nodding, Jay stood up and took their bowls to the dishwasher. "Coming."

His phone buzzed after a few seconds.

SAHAR

Ha! And I would've politely rejected. I'm not at all upset. I was rooting for Jodi. Her performance was the best thing I've seen this year!! It's an honor just to be nominated alongside her.

A low laugh emanated from him as he read the words. He was again so taken aback by how easily he appreciated her outlook. Sahar was passionate about the industry, and it was often evident, but especially in these moments where she championed her peers.

JAY

Ah, good then, I suppose. I'm glad you're not upset.

SAHAR

All good here, really. I appreciate you checking in, though

He wanted to keep the conversation going, but he replied *anytime* and put his phone down, joining his kid on a night of battling fairytale characters.

8

***

SAHAR

With a few short days with her sister and only one day off to actually hang out, time had gotten away from Sahar. When they weren't working, it was one event after another. Lovely days, but still tiring.

It'd been almost two weeks since the Tony Awards, and she was now at Ethan's, cat-sitting for the weekend while he and Willa were on holiday.

She hadn't had time to read beyond episode three of Jay's screenplay, but now that her schedule was a bit more clear, she could finally resume.

And currently, the fourth episode of *Every Speck of Dust* was destroying her. Sahar admired a compelling flashback in an already thrilling episode that filled the present-day gaps and took viewers on an emotionally gripping journey. It always made her feel closer to the characters. When well-placed and thoughtfully executed, it usually ended up becoming one of her favorite episodes of the season.

INT. THE OFFICE - LATE AT NIGHT

Henry's eyes are fixed on Katherine. A pen in between her teeth, humming something to herself. They're the only ones left. Slowly, her gaze rises up to meet his.

KATHERINE
Whatcha thinking about over there, Palmer?

Pause

HENRY
I...

Silence.
He can't hold it anymore.

HENRY
Earlier today, you asked me what my perfect world would look like.

She's quiet. Katherine swallows and sets the pen down.

HENRY
In my perfect world, you and I would be together.

A long beat of silence passes.

KATHERINE
Henry...

HENRY
(Smiles, just barely)
You're good, Stephens. No need to respond. You and I both know this line of work is too dangerous for any of that.

KATHERINE
Yeah.

Fuck. Tears welled in Sahar's eyes, cascading down onto her face. Why was she crying? Why was her heart thumping so rapidly?

In my perfect world, you and I would be together.

It was two in the bloody morning. That was it. That was why she'd been crying—delusion and exhaustion.

Sahar read the words over and over again. The tears kept coming.

What part of it was hitting her so hard? Was it Henry's longing? Was it the knowledge of Katherine's fate prior to Jay saying he'd alter the ending? Was it her own profound desire to experience what Henry and Katherine feel for one another?

How she wished she could consume fictional content without fixating on every part of it—to love and appreciate things a normal amount.

Shutting her eyes, she slid further down on the sofa, setting her tablet away on the brown oak coffee table beside her. She covered her face with her hands, loathing her mind for its inability to let go of things easily. Wiggling, she tried to make herself more comfortable.

Maybe her period was right around the corner. Or maybe it was the knowledge of how sentimental today was.

Back in May, she and Willa had made an agreement that if Sahar dyed her hair red (which she did), Willa would have to publicly post photos of her and Ethan for his birthday. She was now upstate with Ethan for his birthday, where she had *finally* upheld her end of the bargain and posted the photos, publicizing their relationship in *her own* way. It'd also always been a dream of Willa's to go inside a treehouse, and before they'd left,

Ethan had told Sahar that he planned to surprise Willa with one in his parents' backyard.

Perhaps that was it—the further proof that love was real and not something she only ever read about. It was the love her parents had. The love her grandparents knew. It was the relationships her friends were in. It was a man so irrevocably in love with his best friend that he had built a treehouse to make her childhood dreams come true.

And maybe that was why reading Jay's words was so evocative. It *felt* real somehow.

But again, why on earth was she crying?

She should text Jay, tell him all her thoughts. He would appreciate that. She was sure of it. *No. It's 2 a.m.—the only thing you should be doing is trying to sleep,* her mind bit back. *Or, you could go for a late-night treat. There's no problem sour belts won't solve.* Yes, that was it.

Kicking the covers aside, Sahar bounced off the sofa and strode toward her William Kilburn floral tote from the V&A museum that hung on a dining room chair. Rummaging through it, her fingers swam along her travel makeup bag, sunglasses case, crumpled receipts, and deodorant before she felt the edge of the reusable silicone bag she'd tossed a bunch of sour belts into. She slid a green-apple-flavored one into her mouth. Crisis averted. Sour candy was the cure to all emotional woes. So were everything bagels. Or, coffee ice cream, but there wasn't any at Ethan's.

Tulip wobbled in from where she'd been sleeping, jolting Sahar and making her yelp.

Jesus. She'd momentarily forgotten that she wasn't alone in the flat. The orange cat meowed and circled around Sahar's ankle. "You want a late-night snack, too, or are your emotions also screwing with you?"

Tulip blinked. Sahar blinked back at her. And then she

wobbled away the same way she came in. "Okay, so no late snacks for you, I guess," Sahar said aloud.

She popped another sour belt into her mouth, deciding she might as well go to the bathroom before trying to sleep.

When lying back down on the sofa, the words came to her again. *In my perfect world, you and I would be together.*

Over and over and over again.

Fuck.

9

JAY

He could hear running from inside the house as he stepped through the back door and into the laundry room. Then, as he entered his mom's kitchen, Eloise charged to his side with full force. "Dad! Dad!"

"Hey, kid. Did you have a good day?" He was about to crouch down to hug her, but she hurriedly grabbed his hand and dragged him forward.

"Yeah, we found a new teacher to give me more art lessons. Can I go, Dad? Please?"

"Slow down. What art lessons? Where?"

She pivoted, looking at him like he was asking the most absurd, unheard-of questions. "Grandma will tell you all about it!"

The screen door was already open, and Eloise pulled him out into his mother's backyard, where she was hunched over, tending to some newly bloomed, coral hybrid tea roses in her garden. Three barn swallows huddled around the feeder hanging from the branches of their sugar maple tree, as a light breeze served as a welcomed change from the city's mugginess.

His mother tipped her gaze in their direction. "Hi, honey."

"Hi, what's this about a new art class?"

She stood up, dusting her pants. "Do you remember Kathy Sinclair? You went to high school with her son, Mason."

Jay searched his brain, but neither of the names rang a bell. "Nope."

"He was a lanky kid, blond hair, very sweet. Kathy was a doll, too. We did some PTA stuff together. They'd moved to D.C. but recently moved back?"

"I don't remember most people from high school, Mom. What about them?"

She sighed but continued, "She used to teach art at the community college. Anyway, Ellie and I ran into her at the grocery store this morning, and Kathy mentioned that she now has her own studio where she teaches beginner, intermediate, and advanced students. Your daughter blurted that she'd just left her art class back home, and Kathy suggested coming to her. You should go check it out. She's an incredibly kind lady."

Jay looked from his mother to Eloise. His daughter's big eyes widened even more, donning the expression she often wore when she really wanted something. With that look, he'd never been able to say no.

"You really want to go?" he double-checked.

"Yes! I liked art class a lot, but hated that shitty man. Can you at least talk to her?"

He glared at her. "Language."

"Horrible man," Eloise clarified.

"You know it'd only be for the summer. Is there a commitment?" He aimed the second part of the question at his mother.

She shook her head. "No commitment. Pay can be weekly or monthly. Seasonally, she can come and go whenever. And classes would be twice a week."

"Okay, I'll run it by Maya. Did she give you a card?"

"Ellie has it in her backpack."

He veered his gaze back to Eloise. "Alright. Say bye to grandma and grab up your things."

Eloise ran to his mom's side and hugged her. "See you tomorrow, Grandma!"

"See you, love bug," she replied. "You don't want to stay for dinner?" she asked Jay.

"I promised her we'd get shrimp tacos. You're more than welcome to come with us."

"No, it's okay. Spend time with your kid. But don't forget about Sunday. I'm making moussaka."

He stepped closer to where she stood and placed a kiss on her head. "I won't. And is El still staying over on Saturday?"

"Yes, Iris and her granddaughter have confirmed the sleepover."

Jay bobbed his head. "Cool, cool."

Since he didn't have to pick up Eloise after dropping her off that day, maybe he could finally see *Midnights at Pemberley*. He made a mental note to add it to his to-do list.

Talk to Maya. Revise episodes three and four. Call the art teacher. Buy tickets.

Jay walked back into the house and into the kitchen as Eloise came down the stairs with her belongings. He opened the garage door for her, and she called out another enthusiastic goodbye to his mom.

"Do you want to go home for a bit first or have an early dinner now?" he asked.

She thought about it, maneuvering her way around his mom's parked car. "Um...early dinner," she returned.

He agreed. "Food it is, then."

"How come you were late today?"

"I had a meeting," he answered candidly.

He and Patrick finally had the time to catch up in person to discuss some of the changes in the screenplay before Patrick had to go to work. But Jay didn't want to say who the meeting had been with, so Eloise wouldn't get upset about the fact that she hadn't seen her godfather in weeks. Patrick had been caught up with a few commitments, and she'd be seeing him on Sunday anyway when he came to dinner.

"What kind of meeting?"

"We talked about a TV show we're working on."

When they drew closer to his white Honda CR-V in the driveway, Eloise jumped into the backseat. He shut the door after she buckled her seatbelt, right as he caught a pesky mosquito landing on his arm. He swatted the demonic insect with his other hand and flicked it off with his middle finger.

She spoke again as soon as Jay got into the driver's seat. "It's not fair that I can't watch your movies."

He glanced at her through the rearview mirror and started the engine. "My movies aren't meant for kids, baby. You can watch them when you're older."

"But don't I get to see them earlier *because* I'm your kid?" she whined.

More like the polar opposite, he thought. *You're not allowed to watch them until you're forty. Maybe even older. Better yet, never.*

He set the car in reverse, pulling out of the driveway and onto the open street. "Nope. They're sad, and I don't want you to be sad."

"Why do you only make sad movies?"

Because life is fucking unfair and sad movies sell. Sad movies are an outlet—a punching bag to release all the pent-up anger and pain.

"Why are we asking so many questions today?"

"Because I want to know," she answered plainly.

Jay sighed. "Sometimes, when bad things happen, the only thing we can do is tell those stories so that the people watching feel a little less alone." *Nailed it*—an honest and appropriate response.

Eloise stayed quiet for a beat. Jay continued to drive.

"What kind of bad things happened?" she asked eventually.

Jesus Christ. I hope you never know, kid. "Why don't we talk about happier things? Did you get any fun snacks at Trader Joe's?"

"Yeah, the shortbread cookies with raspberry filling inside and uh, popcorn. Bad things like in *A Series of Unfortunate Events*?"

Apparently, she had no intention of moving on from this topic, despite his attempt to change the subject.

"There's a downside to your reading level being higher than your grade. But a bit, yeah. Minus the constant deaths of guardians, I suppose."

"Well then, I think I'm old enough," she declared.

Jay gave her another look through the rearview mirror as he stopped at a red light. "How about you let your mom and me determine that?"

"Can I watch when I'm ten?"

"Maybe." He hoped that answer would do the trick because any sort of staunch objection today seemed only to pique her curiosity further.

She pursed her lips in thought. "Fine. Can we watch *Barbie* again when we get home?"

"Definitely," Jay confirmed, switching his foot to the gas pedal again.

ELOISE LOOKED up at him after they'd sat down and finished ordering drinks at Bahama Breeze. "Dad, can I order the food for us?"

Jay nodded. "Of course. Remember to tell them about your pineapple allergy, though."

She bobbed her head up and down, kicking her feet excitedly across the booth from him.

When the waiter returned and looked at Jay, he gestured for Eloise to talk.

"Hi! Can we, um...have two of the shrimp tacos, please? But with no pineapple chutney," she enunciated, reading the menu. "I'm very allergic to pineapples."

"Of course, and for you, sir, would you like the pineapples on the side?"

Jay shook his head; he wouldn't eat them if Eloise couldn't. "I'm good, thank you."

The waiter jotted the order down in her notepad. "Alrighty. We'll be back out with those orders shortly."

"Good job, El!"

"How come you don't get pineapple? You're not allergic."

"Solidarity," he answered.

Eloise smiled, giddily taking a sip of her strawberry lemonade. And then, she perked up, dropping her mouth open in shock, her eyes leveled at his wrist. "You aren't wearing the bracelet I gave you! Did you lose it?"

Jay looked down, remembering that he had left it beside his watch near the sink yesterday. "I took it off last night to shower and forgot to put it back on."

"Phew," she said dramatically, leaning back in the booth like the mere thought took years out of her life.

When kids at school started making friendship bracelets for concerts or something, Eloise made them for her family, too. She'd given Jay one that simply had her name on it with navy and pale blue rubbery beads. He'd worn it proudly every day, except at the coffee shop, to ensure nothing would happen to it. There, he usually kept it in his pocket with his wallet and keys.

Eloise, on the other hand, basically wore five bracelets on her left hand at all times.

"I'll never lose it. It's precious to me," he promised.

A sweet smile made its way onto her face, bright and beaming.

It was moments like these that always made his chest constrict. His childhood was shit, but his present was nearly perfect because of her. Once more, he thought of how lucky he was. He thought of how he and Maya got along so well that when it came to Eloise, they almost never argued.

Jay's earliest memories were full of either neglect or blaring altercations, one curse word after another. A father who was almost always either at work or causing fights. A father who never once spent time with his son. Doors slammed often in his house. Yelling was a constant.

Until recent years, his mother's eyes were perpetually swollen with tears.

Maybe Sahar was right. Life, for most people, was too sad to solely create heavier content. Perhaps people could benefit from small glimmers of hope in the fiction they consumed.

"Is the bracelet as precious as my ugly, old drawings?" Eloise asked, pulling Jay out of his thoughts.

He gave her a playful glare. "What'd I tell you about calling your drawings ugly?"

"That progress is important."

"Exactly."

With a closed-mouth smile, she looked at him through her lashes. "Fine, fine." She took another sip of her drink.

"Now, hypothetically, if I *did* lose my bracelet, which I haven't," he promised, gesturing with his hands, "would you be able to make me another one?"

Gavin, Maya's husband, had some sort of a brown one that said "badger" because it was his favorite animal. Jay was mostly asking out of curiosity, wondering if one day, when he had someone, whether Eloise would be able to make something for her.

For Sahar, his mind whispered.

"Yeah! But it would have to be later because I left all the letters and beads in Philly."

He bobbed his head, grabbing his Coke for a sip.

When their food arrived, Eloise proceeded to ask twenty-one more questions about why he only made sad movies. After talking to Maya about the art class later that night, they spent the rest of the evening watching *Barbie* for the eighty-seventh time.

Eloise fell asleep on his shoulder, and as he carried her to bed, she woke up briefly to say, "I want to make movies, too, Daddy."

Jay nearly lost his mind at the sleep-born statement, every fear he ever possessed materializing into phantoms that danced before his eyes. He prayed wordlessly that she didn't mean it— that she'd grow up and realize life as a pediatrician like her mother guaranteed a far better future than the unpredictable industry he was mercilessly chained to. It had been his choice to go into entertainment, sure, but every single day, he wished for the brain and the passion to pursue a different career.

If only he loved writing and directing a little less. If only he were better at biology or math or *anything* else.

MUCH LATER THAT NIGHT, as he sat in bed, reviewing episode four, Jay realized that most of it would need to be rewritten. He took his phone from the bedside table to text Sahar. They hadn't talked in a few days outside of the coffee shop, and this could be a segue back.

At least, he hoped it'd be.

JAY

> With the changes in the beginning, I think episode four needs a major rewrite.

She answered almost right away.

SAHAR

> As long as you don't touch the line that made me cry...

A line made her cry? As in, real tears, or was she being hyperbolic? He was about to ask when three dots appeared again.

SAHAR

> I mean, it's your show. You could do whatever you want, of course, but please don't touch the flashback.

JAY

> What line made you cry? And the flashback is safe. You have my word.

SAHAR

> "In my perfect world, you and I would be together."

Something in Jay unlocked.

That'd been the first line he'd written for the series.

It had come to him while he was on the train, snow falling out the window, blankets of glittering white covering the naked trees—the city sparkling in the dead of winter. He wasn't sure what it meant or how he'd use it, but he knew he needed it.

JAY

> Did you actually cry? Real tears?

SAHAR

Yes. And don't ask me why. I almost messaged
you about it, but it was 2 in the morning.

Did she miss her ex-boyfriend? Was that why it made her cry? *But she'd told him he wasn't a good person.* Regardless, he had no right to ask. Maybe it would be a good thing if she wanted her ex back. Or maybe she had someone else she was interested in.

Every probability Jay calculated ended with Sahar being untouchable. Someone else's.

JAY

I'm honored it made you feel so much.

Maybe one day, he'd tell her how important that line was to him—how this moment would stay with him, even if nothing came from this story again. And oddly, that would be okay, too.

Maybe Sahar was the only audience he needed.

Her investment was becoming crucial to him.

SAHAR

Henry and Katherine are everything. I keep
thinking about them, and you're entirely to
blame.

JAY

Well, you're the reason they're getting a happy
ending, so I'm glad that's the case.

SAHAR

I love getting what I want 😊

Side note: I'm almost done. I have the last act left, and all of this hurts so much more after I've read the whole thing. Henry's spiral in the penultimate had me straight up clutching my chest. It was so rugged and vulnerable and raw.

God, he said aloud. This woman was dangerous for him. He was a moth to her flame. The fact that she cared about these characters as much as he did made him feel...lighter.

She didn't owe him any of her support, so the fact that she was giving it freely made him feel like his insecurities could temporarily get lost. Kick rocks. Step on LEGO.

JAY

His breakdown is a scene I plan on keeping, even with the changes. I hope it'll hit twice as hard if we push him a little more and have him see Katherine again on top of all this shit.

SAHAR

100%. It's so important. And it's also a brilliant culmination of all the little ways he kept cracking before. I kept thinking to myself, he's going to do it. He's going to break the laptop. And then he did it!?!? Jay, I swear I gasped out loud, and Willa came into the room because she thought something had happened.

He couldn't believe that someone appreciated his words this much. *Sahar, of all people.* How she saw every little detail he wanted the audience to see, how she could read the underlying emotions of the characters, even without the performances that would eventually elevate the words on the page.

JAY

That scene was cathartic to write, too.

> Do you want me to send you updates on the rewrites? I can shoot over the first two episodes.

SAHAR

> PLEASE.

> And I can imagine. I've always wanted to break a laptop lol but like then miraculously get everything back.

JAY

> There you go. You see the vision.

> And you got it.

Setting his phone down on his bedside table, Jay kicked off his socks and lay down fully. Adjusting his pillow, he lifted his arm above his head and stared at the ceiling.

He was glad he had bought tickets for *Midnights at Pemberley* while he and Eloise were watching the movie. There'd only been a few seats available for a Saturday matinee. Most of them were too far, and if he were going to support Sahar, watch her in her element, then he'd go all out. He'd be as close as possible. He chose the nearest he could, third-row orchestra.

She deserved that.

10

JAY

When Sahar and Willa came in on Saturday morning, Jay had been on the phone in the breakroom. So in tune with Sahar's voice, he could hear her husky laugh while the aggressively irritating hold music played on a loop. He wanted to go out to say hi, but a part of him was stupidly nervous about seeing her before the show.

He had a couple of hours left until he was off anyway; he'd text her from inside the theatre.

Only the universe decided that the two hours should feel painfully slow, loud, and demanding, with people screaming left and right.

He hated weekends. Loathed. He had yelled at a man who tried to hit on their new hire, Sally, and then ten minutes later, he had to kick out another for attempting to steal the vinyl records on display along the shop's wall.

Sometimes, hell on earth was smack dab in the middle of a coffee shop on the corner of 45th Street.

It was days like today when he most ached for a film or TV show of his to do well enough that he wouldn't need a second or third job. Now that Alex was doing a lot better mentally, he could start applying for other positions, too. He should start looking again. Get the fuck out of here and onto something better.

But then, how would he see Sahar's glowing face almost every day? At what other place would he get the chance to hear her laugh?

Jay shrugged off his thoughts, looked at the time on the bottom of the register, and then went back to the breakroom to finish the week's schedule. He rearranged some hours, glared at the chart for another fifteen minutes with his eyes freezing constantly, and then clocked out when their other manager, Nora, came in to take over.

Because he refused to go somewhere nice while smelling like coffee, he'd brought a change of clothes with him. He went into their small employees-only bathroom and switched into a pair of dark-wash blue jeans and a white, short-sleeved button-up, then reapplied cologne. He left the work clothes in his locker to take home with him tomorrow, beelining out the door before anyone could stop him.

Hell. He could still smell the coffee beans, but he hoped it was at least somewhat less potent than before.

With his shift ending at one thirty, he trekked the short distance to the theatre. Too many fucking people. Not enough space to walk. He blew out a grunt, trying to move away from a group of teenagers who were literally bouncing all over the already crowded sidewalk. Catching his opportune moment, Jay hovered closer to the brick wall and bolted in front of them, another audible grumble flinging out of him in sheer frustration.

With a few short strides, he veered to the relatively calmer street where the Hyacinth Theatre was located. Its architecture was already decadent, but with *Midnights at Pemberley's* marquee maroons intermingling with the structure's brownstones and shades of rust, the location came alive in a uniquely time-bending way. For a couple of hours, 2024 was 1813.

He observed the character posters along the brick walls, one of its principal stars, Ethan Everett, and another of Naomi Driver. Then, he spotted hers. Sahar's was an exhilarating shot of her in some sort of dance move he didn't know the name of—her one hand up, another behind her. She wore a bejeweled scarlet bodysuit and vibrant red lipstick, with her hair falling gorgeously along her back.

Adorned in red, but pure sunlight still. Her smile, even through a photograph, was overwhelming. He would have stood there all day, staring, but he continued walking forward, passing the poster of Sam Butler as Bingley next.

Jay sped to the end of the line where attendees stood, moving slowly ahead with them. He opened his phone to check in on his mom and Ellie, letting her know that he was putting his phone fully on silent, but he'd check during intermission in case they needed him.

He stepped through the metal detectors, scanned the ticket with his phone, and then went to his seat. He'd remembered the theatre's interior from when Alex's previous show was here, but with a completely different set design on the stage, it felt like he'd come to a different place. The stage was modeled to mirror the grand estate of Pemberley, embellished with gold railings. It looked like something that would have to open or slide up during the show's duration.

The maroon wallpaper surrounding them featured a floral damask motif. He didn't remember paying attention to them before or if they had changed for *Midnights at Pemberley*, but it matched the show's theme pristinely.

Since photography was allowed for another ten minutes, he snapped a quick photo from his view and texted it to Sahar.

He set his phone down on his lap, not expecting a reply from her until maybe intermission, if she even checked her phone then. Yet, he was surprised when his screen brightened. His heart did a little sprint at the sight of her name, signaling not one message, but two.

It was like every logical part of his brain went into some inexplicable trance around Sahar. He pressed send before he could second-guess the last word.

At least he didn't freak her out.

He placed his phone in his pocket and looked around. There was some sort of sultry instrumental tune playing that he'd just noticed must've been part of the show. The theatre was slowly filling up with more people, and a warning through the speakers announced that photographs were no longer allowed.

Three women sauntered over to the stage, and he recognized one of them as Willa. The other two he wasn't sure if he'd seen at the coffee shop or not. He then spotted Sahar and Naomi, and shortly after, Sam, as Bingley, walked out and enthusiastically deemed Pemberley open to the public, kickstarting the first official number.

He might've been seeing things, but he was almost positive that Sahar noticed him because her already massive smile grew tenfold during a specific ensemble track. And the woman didn't believe she was sunshine in human form?

Sure, theatre actors had to smile and come alive, but that wasn't the point.

The point was, Sahar stood out to Jay unlike any other performer he'd ever seen, and the intensity of that realization jarred him. She was so fucking enchanting, moving across the stage with a honed grace that made him want to topple over. He'd heard bits of the tracks while listening to the Original Broadway Cast Recording album, but her voice was something else entirely live.

The show itself was surprisingly engaging, too. He'd only ever seen one version of *Pride and Prejudice*, and *Midnights at Pemberley* was like its rebellious, wild little sister. It heightened all the emotions of the contained longing from the book and set everything on fire.

Jay was also surprised by Ethan's range, well and truly—he knew that Ethan was gifted as an actor, but he hadn't seen him in a theatrical production. There was a pained look in his eyes during one scene in particular where, for a split second, Jay wondered how his capacity would bring to life the role of Henry Palmer in *Every Speck of Dust*.

If that story even crossed beyond the pitching process again. *If if if.*

During another number, Sahar and Naomi had left behind their more modest costumes for leotards and more skin. When Sahar came into view, his breath caught in his throat, thankful that loud applause and music would allow him to hide it from the people sitting beside him.

What dumbass part of him thought it was wise to willingly spend a little over two hours gazing at the woman he had a thing for?

He felt like such a jackass, gawking at her perfect body. But *fuck*, she was unreal, breathtaking, and beautiful in every way. He watched her character, Jane, timidly flirt with Bingley, and when Sam's hand slowly caressed her forearm—the spot where he noticed her crow tattoo was now covered—jealousy shot through Jay's spine.

He wanted to know what her skin would feel like under his fingertips.

He wanted to ask her about her crow tattoo and learn of its importance.

He wanted to tell her that he had one, too.

Then there was the flower tattoo that peeked out on her shoulder when she wore tank tops. He could only see parts of it —a hydrangea or something similar, if he had to guess.

Just then, Sam—er, Bingley—moved Jane into a secluded corner and brushed his lips across her cheek. *Fuck.* Five seconds ago, Jay would've killed for a chance to simply touch her, and now, he'd give everything to have his lips on her.

Coming here was a bad, dangerous idea. He was a goner. What if he faked an illness and left during intermission? Shit, though, he wouldn't do that to Sahar. She was so supportive of his writing, and he needed to be there for her, too.

He flicked his eyes toward Darcy and Elizabeth, who'd been arguing in the middle of the stage. Better. *Focus on them.*

But Sahar, every part of his mind, body, and soul called out. He turned his gaze again, and his heart nearly flared. Jane was sitting on Bingley's lap, giggling quietly—the two of them worlds away in character, lost in a daze.

Now, Jay wanted her on his lap, her arms wrapped around his neck, her lips at his ear, his arms vining her waist. He wanted to be the one making her laugh.

Who the fuck was he, thinking like this? What was this woman doing to him? Why couldn't he have been an actor like his mom and sister? Then maybe he'd have a chance to play pretend with her—satisfy all his selfish desires, and then leave them at bay. But that wasn't how acting worked, either.

He looked down for a fleeting second, and she was moving farther into the wings with Sam, their eyes glued to each other, bodies close. A more upbeat melody began to play, and the entire ensemble returned, Sahar and Sam included.

The lights dimmed, and Elizabeth came center stage. The intimacy of the lighting hinted that he likely wouldn't be seeing Sahar for the rest of this number, so the flames in him temporarily cooled. The scene passed—a heated, extraordinarily well-directed moment between Elizabeth and Darcy—then, the curtains closed, and the lights came on.

Intermission.

He pulled his phone out of his pocket, spotting a text from Sahar.

SAHAR

Christian and I were supposed to have lunch during our break, but he's not feeling well. Would you like to join me instead? If you don't have plans afterward! No pressure.

No pressure. Maybe he could make up an excuse. *Sorry, I have to get home, Ellie's waiting for me.* But she wasn't. She wouldn't be waiting for him all day and until tomorrow morning. He had no reason to say no except that he was sure spending more time with Sahar would result in falling head over fucking heels in love with her.

As if he'd ever say no to her.

JAY

Sure thing. You're excellent, btw!

SAHAR

Aw, thanks, Jay. I saw you, told Sam, too. Seriously, thanks for coming. Meet me outside the stage door after? It might be a tad crowded, but it's usually not as intense as it is during a night show.

JAY

Sounds good.

The rest of the production flew by during the second act, and when Sahar came out in a wedding dress, Jay was sure he'd somehow ascended, leaving his corpse in the orchestra seat, row D.

He knew that the show was now a Tony Award-winning musical, and he fully understood why. It was a clever, captivating adaptation with sensational performances from the whole cast.

He was partial to one of them, sure, but the overall artistry was undeniable. Jay trekked out with the crowds and stepped out to where a few people had already been huddled at the stage door. He dodged the masses, finding a secluded area that afforded him some breathing room, but still somewhere Sahar could spot him. Propping his foot up against the brick wall, he leaned back.

Jay peered down at his phone, keeping himself busy by jotting down some ideas in his notes app.

Flesh out the flashback with silence stretching out between H and K. Talk to Pat about the finale's third act.

He exited the app and checked his emails, deleting a few spam messages before noticing a screening invite he'd circle back to when he could read beyond the subject line.

The low chatter nearby grew to cheers, prompting Jay to whip his head back toward the stage door. And there she was, popping out with her glimmering smile, waving to everyone standing by to meet her. Denim shorts hugged her hips, and a white racerback tank bared her gloriously toned arms and shoulders. Her hair was down, stage makeup still on, and her olive skin glowed in the sunlight.

She said something he couldn't catch to the fans standing by, then quickly signed a few Playbills and eyed him.

When she bopped over to his side, Jay lowered his foot down from the position he'd supported it in and angled his body toward her. Before he could catch what was happening, she had outstretched her arm and reached up to hug him.

Circling his arm around her waist, he welcomed the feel of her close to his body. It was the quickest hug of his entire life, and he wanted nothing more than to hold on—keep her near, breathe in the scent of her citrusy perfume, tip his head a fraction, and kiss her.

Fuck.

"Thank you for coming," she said before parting from him.

He smiled at her. "You're welcome. You were a fucking star. Do you have to stick around more?"

She shook her head, ushering him forward by walking. "We usually don't during matinees. I have such little time, and I need food. A lot of them are lovely and understanding."

"In that case, did you have somewhere you wanted to go?" Jay asked.

"Honestly, no, I just started walking." She let out a small laugh. "I could go for anything. The one thing I'm blessed with is zero food allergies. Do you have any?"

"I don't."

Jay looked over at Sahar, her lips pursed in thought. "We could go to Sam's favorite Japanese restaurant nearby, Summer Nori?" she suggested.

"Yeah, I know it. Works for me. I'm buying," he said quickly.

"No, you're not. This was *my* idea."

"Should've called it first, then," he added with a wink.

Sahar cocked an eyebrow. "I did when I asked you to come with me. The person who invites pays."

"Never heard of that rule, so it's not valid."

"Jay."

"Sahar," he parroted.

She opened her mouth to say something, shook her head, and then closed it.

They rounded the corner in companionable silence, the comfort of her smile filling his heart with an ease he wasn't sure how to cope with. A few short steps, and they were inside the restaurant, greeted at the front desk by a hostess, who he assumed also knew Sahar.

Of course, they would.

Of course, he wasn't the only service worker Sahar was unbearably kind to. Why would he ever think he was special? She knew the names of every barista at Amanda's, too.

They all knew her.

That was the beauty of *her* light.

He wasn't the lucky one. They all were.

11

SAHAR

"Yup, your usual booth is free," Carly said, then gestured for them to follow her, guiding Sahar and Jay to a spot toward the back of the restaurant. Sam came to Summer Nori so often that the staff typically kept some of the more secluded tables open for the *Midnights* cast. "Okay, also, I love this bag strap. Where did you get it?"

Sahar looked down at the embroidered orange tapestry and answered eagerly. "Pom Pom London. I'm obsessed with their bag straps. Someone needs to ban me from buying them in every color and style."

Sahar was never one to gatekeep quality products; she preferred to scream openly about them instead. And she had done so extensively, enabling Willa to buy her first bag, too.

"Ooh, I'll have to check them out," Carly exclaimed before setting the menus on the table. "Your server will be here with drinks shortly."

When she and Jay were left alone, her eyes darted straight to his mouth, his lips twitched at the edges, trying to conceal a smile.

"What?" she asked.

He shook his head, eyes narrowed behind his glasses. "Nothing."

"Spit it out."

Crossing his arms, he leaned forward. "I just find it fascinating that everyone lights up around you," he said, amusement unambiguous in his gaze.

Sahar wasn't sure what to make of the statement.

Tell that to my exes, she wanted to say.

"They do not," she countered.

Jay's knee bumped into hers underneath the table, sending a spark of electricity shooting through her. "They do," he affirmed.

Suddenly, she couldn't read him.

The conviction in his tone was believable, but she couldn't accept the truth behind his words. She didn't have that sort of effect on people. People like Sam did. Ethan hated social media until Sam opened him up to more Instagram lives. Sam could crack anyone's tough exterior with a single look and a dumb joke that you couldn't help but laugh at. His genuine kindness and sprightly nature *ensured* that people wanted to be around him.

That wasn't the case with Sahar.

"Have your glasses fogged up? Do you maybe need a cloth to clean them with? You might be seeing things."

He clicked his tongue. "Did that right before I left work, but thanks for offering."

The server brought them both waters, and Sahar took a sip from her cup, eyeing him. Shaking her head, she looked down at the menu, avoiding his gaze. It was too much, too soon to sit in front of him while he claimed that she was a source of light for other people. Too much to let her mind ponder the likelihood that *he* could also be one of those people she presumably had that effect on. Too much even to admit that *she* would *want* that.

She looked over at him once more, but his head was down,

fixed on the menu. That was when she noticed his left hand now resting on the table, a blueish beaded bracelet next to the black-leather watch circling his wrist. She hadn't seen it before, but she could make out some of the letters, *E L,* before it curved. *Eloise,* she assumed. Fuck, that was precious. His daughter probably made it for him. Her mind wandered again, latching on to how attentive he was. How caring. *Ugh.* Sahar darted her eyes back to the menu.

Food, food was good. Food should be the focus.

They ordered a few things—appetizers and sushi rolls to share—before talking again.

"Is Christian okay?" Jay asked afterward.

She nodded. "Yeah, he didn't sleep at all last night because his tooth's been bothering him, so he went to the dentist at the crack of dawn for a filling. He wanted to sleep off the pain before the next show."

Jay's eyes widened. "And he's performing like that?"

Shrugging with a grin, Sahar said, "Oh, yeah. We'll generally only call out if we're sick, so no one else is infected, but Ethan's back now, and since Christian's no longer on as Darcy, and he's back in the ensemble, he doesn't have to do as much singing. If he did, he might've had to."

"Ah, that makes sense."

"Since Eloise is with you, I'm going to hope you won't be picking up more shifts. Proud of you if that's the case," she added.

He let out a low huff. "Yeah, no. At least not the super last-minute ones."

"Good."

A conversation about how they couldn't believe it was already July occupied them until the waiter returned with their food.

"Oh, *The Wolf Lady* was finally delivered to my doorstep this morning. No idea why it took so long, but I'm intrigued to read it," Jay said before biting down on edamame.

Sahar nearly choked on her shishito pepper, and it wasn't because she couldn't handle its spiciness. "Okay, but you can't judge my taste for it. There's a lot of nostalgia connecting me and that book. I haven't read it in over ten years, and it might not hold up. I just think about those characters often."

"I won't judge your taste, even if I question it."

Sahar popped the salmon roll into her mouth and chewed before speaking. "Twelve-year-old Sahar and thirty-one-year-old Sahar aren't the same person."

"I would hope you wouldn't be," he said matter-of-factly.

She scrunched her nose and flashed him a toothy grin. Something about Jay made it easy for her to be...well, herself. The same person she was around all her closest friends. And she liked that. She liked having another friend in her corner.

But maybe she shouldn't be herself. Maybe she should tone it down.

"Can I ask you something?"

Jay nodded.

"What'd you *really* think of the show?" she asked, taking a piece of calamari.

His expression looked puzzled for a beat. "I told you. I thought you were a fucking star," he repeated.

She smiled, shaking her head. "No, not me, though I appreciate the compliment. I do. I mean the show in general. I'm curious what *you* think, as someone who's in the industry but not so much into romance."

Jay sat up straighter. "Okay, first, I never said I hated romance. Let's make that clear. But I thought it was incredible—the production as a whole. I can see why it's so loved and how it swept the Tony Awards."

"Have you read Austen?" she asked.

He bobbed his head up and down. "Yeah, *Pride and Prejudice* was part of my curriculum in high school. And I took a British literature class in my undergrad where we had to read *Sense and Sensibility*. Other than those two, I haven't read any others."

"A follow-up question, then. What's your favorite book, or at least one of them? You technically know one of mine."

There was something thrilling about dissecting his brain and understanding him more intimately. She couldn't remember the last time she had asked someone what their favorite book was. Sahar wanted to know everything about Jay.

Stroking his beard, he pondered. "Um...you know, I've never thought about it? Maybe *The Outsiders*? Or *And Then There Were None*?"

Sahar perked up. "Jay, what do I have to do to get you to write me a whodunnit?"

A laugh burst out of him, low and rumbling. "Oh, I want to. Believe me. I'm just not sure I could."

She narrowed her gaze. "You absolutely could. The majority of your characters have that stoic humor in them that could translate well into satire with a few shifts in how the dialogue is structured. A lot of the conversations we get between Henry and the chief, George, made me think of it."

He pushed his glasses up the bridge of his nose. "You think so?"

She nodded rapidly. "Yes! Next one, a whodunnit. Please and thank you," she declared.

A slow, sweet smile rose along his lips. "Okay," he said.

Sahar tilted her head to the side. "And maybe a romance sprinkled into it?"

She caught him trying not to roll his eyes.

"We'll cross that bridge when we get there."

"Hater," she mumbled, putting the last of her salmon roll into her mouth.

Jay grabbed a piece of calamari and leaned closer to her. "What was that?"

She chewed. "You heard me."

"I'm not a romance hater, sunshine."

There it was again—that endearment. *Sunshine.*

No one had ever called her that before. She thought he was joking when he first said it. But this was now the third time Jay had called her that, shortly after he'd deemed her someone who brought some sort of light to people.

Was he like this with everyone? Why did it make her insides feel all mushy—rearranged and right?"

Stop being such a hopeless romantic. He's just being nice. It doesn't and shouldn't mean anything.

Sahar dismissed the unwanted thoughts. "I'm teasing. I know you're not. Plus, you're giving me what might be my favorite romantic relationship in a while, so thank you for that."

"Henry and Katherine?"

"Mhm," she agreed.

"You really care about them that much?" he asked.

She took another sip of her water. "I really do. I'm a big romance reader, but I haven't been able to read for the past three months, so they're currently filling that void in my heart."

She couldn't tell him that the reason she'd stopped reading was that, instead of making her happy, romance novels were now making her feel weird and more dejected. They were a reminder of the fact that all her previous beliefs about love were untrue and unattainable.

"Why haven't you been able to read?"

Sahar thought of ways to dodge the truth, but Jay was looking at her as though he knew there was a legitimate reason behind her reading slump.

"For starters, I tried playing *Halo 2* again because Ethan and

Dec got back into it, and I hate it. I don't know why I keep trying."

"I've never even tried," he noted.

"You're better off. It drives me bonkers. I'd much rather go back to *Dread Quest*. Speaking of, is there an official release date yet?"

She briefly recalled the moment he'd first shared the *Dread Quest* code with her a few months ago, telling her about how his friend developed it, and how he was certain she'd like it. She hadn't thought of it as a big deal then, but now, she wondered if his decision to share the game with her meant something more.

His eyes lit up a bit. "Yeah, September 27."

"Ooh, excellent. I'll have to tell the boys and Naomi. She's also into gaming."

Jay glanced at her for a beat, took a sip of his water, and then spoke. "Gaming, soccer, movies, TV, romance novels...what are you not into?"

Sahar mulled over the question. "Camping. I love the outdoors temporarily, but I need a clean bed and bathroom at the end of the night. Gambling makes absolutely no sense to me. I spook easily, so no horror or anything with legitimate jump scares. Though I'll watch a slasher film occasionally if I know what's coming."

He dipped his chin up and down, taking in her words. "Same to all of that, though I don't spook easily. And now we need to discuss knowing what's coming. Sahar, that ruins the whole purpose. You might as well not watch," he rebutted.

Oh, she must've destroyed him when she'd told him she read *Every Speck of Dust* out of order. Sahar failed to hold back a grin. "See, I'd argue against that because knowing what's coming doesn't change the execution. I know that every romance, if it's properly categorized, will end with the two main characters getting together, but how we get there is where the story's magic lies."

"That's different. That's being aware of the formula. But when you straight up find out the twist in *The Sixth Sense,* it defeats the point of letting the story unfold as it's meant to."

Sahar's smile grew. It was fun riling up Jay. "Did it hurt, Jay? When I told you I looked at the final page before reading the entire screenplay of *Every Speck of Dust?*"

"Yeah, as a matter of fact, it did. Teaches me never to send you something that's complete," he bit back, his tone grumbly but gentle still.

She pushed her plate to the edge of the table and circled her water cup with both hands, bringing it closer to her while she slouched further back into the booth. "Does it make you feel better if I say it's because I have trust issues, and I wanted to ensure that I wouldn't be sad?"

He tilted his head in an unreadable expression. "I get that. I still think you're wrong."

"Fair. I'm wrong about many things," she added, hating the way she admitted the last part.

"Nah, I'm sure your reasons for other things are valid, except for this. What was it that caused the trust issues? *Game of Thrones?*"

Sahar guffawed. It was fascinating how the series always came up as a point of discussion when considering finales. "Sort of? I wasn't as attached to the characters, but in general, I find that in recent years, there seems to be a need to subvert expectations and shock the audience. It's one thing to execute a great plot twist, but it's another to take something out of thin air to cause conversation. And I see that complaint from countless critics, too. Beyond that, I like being able to see the seeds coming to fruition, yet it seems like some series would rather take the finale to places that honor the plot over the characters."

Twisting her lips in thought, she added, "Life is sad as it is. I choose darker video games, sure, but these days, I want movies and TV shows that won't rip my heart out by the end. I want to *trust* creators. Plus, I have no shame in admitting that I'm a hopeless romantic. I can stomach heavier content, but when I'm exhausted and everything hurts, I'm going to turn to *Singin' in the Rain* or *While You Were Sleeping* and not *12 Angry Men*, even though it's one of my top ten films of all time, you know?"

Jay twisted a piece of napkin around his fingers, bending and folding. "I'll forgive you for calling *12 Angry Men* one of your favorite films."

Sahar gestured a bow with her hand. "And look, if it's any consolation, it's something I do on very rare occasions. I don't always spoil myself. I'm not a total monster."

His lips broke into a genuine smile, eyes crinkling at the corners. She wondered what it'd be like to see all of his edges soften.

She wanted to ask about his daughter's mother. What their relationship was and whether they were together, though she figured they wouldn't be if she lived elsewhere. Did she even have the right to know this information? Were she and Jay at that level in their friendship? Was she into film, too? Maybe she could start with that.

"So, uh, your co-parent, partner?" Sahar phrased it as a question. "Is she in the industry as well?"

He shook his head. "Maya is a pediatrician. She couldn't be farther from this industry. She's also not my partner."

Sahar opened her mouth, then closed it, wondering if there was anything else she could know. "How does that work? If I'm allowed to ask that."

"Co-parenting?" he specified.

She nodded. "Yeah, like, are you two on good terms?" Sahar shook her head. "Sorry. Wow, I realize that's really personal."

His lips curved into an amiable smile. "You're good, don't worry. We're on great terms. We were young and careless when she got pregnant after a one-night stand. We tried to make something of it for Eloise, but neither of us had feelings for each other, and we're better off as friends. She's married now, and Gavin's great. They get Eloise for the school year. I get her in the summer. On holidays, we alternate. I go over to Philly every two weeks, sometimes three if my schedule is shit, so I can see her for a weekend."

"Wow, that's incredibly healthy."

"Few things in my life are, but at least this is."

His honesty struck a chord, deep and puncturing. There were countless details about Jay that she wanted to know more about.

What did his father do to terrorize him? Was he still in the picture? Was his sister truly okay? She could sense the shadows looming around him—how suffocating they must be, forcing darkness to follow him home unrelentingly. Who held his hand at night when his demons came knocking?

He was a good person. She was sure of that—positive, now more than ever. And she wanted him to be happy.

She wanted to keep asking him questions, but instead, she said, "I appreciate you taking the time to see the show. I really hope you didn't feel pressured or anything."

"Not at all. It worked out conveniently. Eloise is staying over at my mom's tonight. She has a playdate."

Sahar's lips quirked upward. "That sounds lovely."

Jay smiled, his eyes sparkling in a way she hadn't noticed before. Though she'd seen it elsewhere, it was the same look that Sam got in his eyes when he showed her something Ravi did.

Sahar opened her mouth to say something, but their waitress interrupted them with the bill instead. Rapidly swiping it toward him, Jay added his card to the plastic slot and returned it to her with a courteous smile.

She shook her head at his swiftness, stifling a laugh. "Thank you."

Jay winked. Something in Sahar came alive in response, like sudden bursts of fucking fireworks.

Stop. No. She couldn't. She refused to let her silly heart ruin the start of what felt like a solid friendship. Sahar knew how to flirt—how to touch and tease and pleasure a man. She knew all the words to use to get someone's attention. But she couldn't, not with Jay. She *needed* to commit to being alone, to dancing on her own for a long while until she could be trusted with her choices.

Until she...until she was also right for someone else.

The last conversation with Martin came to the forefront of her mind again. *You're a joke, Sahar. A selfish whore. I wanted to break up with you way before you did. If you didn't have your body, no one would even want you.*

It was the most cruel he'd ever been. She'd laughed at it then, but she'd be lying to herself if she said the words hadn't tormented her.

She heard Jay call out to her before her eyes focused back on the present. "Hmm."

"Where'd you go?"

Sahar tried to smile, but her lips felt locked in place. She willed herself once more. "Sorry, remembered something."

Jay cocked an eyebrow.

"It's not important," she emphasized.

His curiosity morphed into concern. It made the present knot in her chest tighten. "You sure?"

She nodded, now reprimanding herself internally. "Yeah, all good. Promise." She changed the subject with another question. "So, before I get back to work and you head home. When can I expect a new episode?"

The worry in Jay's expression remained. She wanted to break it, pull out a smile, or the sweet sound of his quietly deep laugh.

"I'll have some time to work tonight. So maybe tonight or tomorrow."

Sahar smiled. Good, back to writing. It excited her. It was a safer topic, guaranteed to result in compelling conversations that wouldn't cause her to spiral. He should never wink at her again. Her insides were incapable of handling it properly.

They stood up to leave. Sahar turned back to face him. "What does Eloise think of Dad's job?" she asked.

Something indiscernible flashed in Jay's eyes. It resembled fear, but she couldn't quite place it. "Please don't ask me that. Last night she mumbled something about wanting to make movies like me, and I almost had a heart attack."

He held the door open for her, allowing her to walk out first. The afternoon sun was blazing, and instantly, thick humidity enveloped them in its muggy hold. "Why is that a bad thing? That's wholesome, Jay. My dad's a software engineer. So is my sister. Frankly, I wish I weren't the black sheep who chose acting."

Jay vehemently shook his head. *So it was fear.* "I don't ever want her to know how treacherous this industry is. I'm a man, at least. I have advantages. It'd kill me if she faced even a fraction of discrimination."

Sahar stopped in front of the restaurant, pivoting to face him.

He bobbed his head forward. "I'll walk you back to work."

"You don't have to do that," she contested.

"I want to."

She turned to continue walking before she spoke. "Mate, I hate to break it to you, but she'll face discrimination in every single field—even if she wanted to be a pediatrician like Maya or a teacher or, I don't know, the manager of an all-women's clothing store. This world is shit, and unless there are drastic changes, as women, we're always going to have to fight harder. I haven't seen your daughter, so I'm not sure if Maya's a woman of color, but if she is, take it from someone who knows what it's like to be half, we're all a bit fucked."

Despite the bustling city's sounds, she caught Jay's deep breath. "Maya's Latina. And I know. Trust me, I'm aware, but Hollywood is still so vile, even when they pretend they're making progress."

Sahar looked up at him. *Wow, she hated this.* It was like seeing him that one morning, hunched over in front of the coffee shop. Grumpy Jay was one thing, but sad, concerned Jay was gut-wrenching.

"Were you like this when your sister dove into acting?"

"A bit, yeah. But I was also more optimistic back then. I hadn't seen the worst of it yet."

Sahar tried to smile, but her heart ached. This industry really was shit, and it was getting worse by the second these days. Come tomorrow, they could get another disappointing announcement about yet another thing taken over by AI.

They drew closer to the theatre, and the uncertainty of when she'd get to see him again outside of the coffee shop sent a drizzle of sadness falling over her. She faced him once more; the look in his eyes continued to tug on the knot inside of her. She needed it to let up.

"Try not to worry about it right now. She's got a few more years before she can actually do something about those dreams of hers. And hey, when I was eight, I wanted to be a veterinarian, so things could definitely change."

She must've said the right thing because a glimmer returned to his expression. "From your lips to God's ears," he said.

"Thanks for coming to the show again, really, and for keeping me company at lunch," she added.

"It was my pleasure, Sahar."

She inched forward and wrapped her arms around him. He hugged her back, and for a heartbeat, she thought she might levitate.

They parted as quickly as they had collided.

"Happy writing. I'll talk to you soon," she said.

Cordially, Jay inclined his head, turned, and walked away.

She opened the stage door and went inside.

12

SAHAR

Sahar sprinted toward Ethan's dressing room, making the safe assumption that it was where Willa would be. She needed someone to knock some sense into her, and what better person than her level-headed best friend and flatmate?

Willa might be sickeningly in love, but unlike Sahar's sappy, romantic nature, she was always more practical.

The door was open, so she knocked quickly and walked in. Willa and Ethan had been looking at something on his iPad when they swung their heads in her direction with near-perfect synchronicity.

"Hi, sorry to interrupt. Wills, can we talk?"

Willa stood up. Ethan shot Sahar a concerned glance.

"Sorry, E. I'll try to get your girl back promptly."

Ethan gave her an *all good* nod. Sahar watched as Willa's fingers slowly slid out of his hand. The two of them had no concept of personal space when they were friends, let alone now when they were openly dating.

It was adorable, sickening—*affectionately*—and a pivotal reason why Sahar had finally understood that what she had with Martin was far from love. Watching Ethan and Willa fall for each other months ago was proof that the things she believed weren't solely fictional, even if they felt impossible for *her* to attain.

Willa looped her arm into Sahar's as they headed toward their dressing room. "Did lunch with Jay not go well?" she whispered.

Sahar let out a deep sigh. When they entered their dressing room, Willa plopped herself down on her chair. Sahar hung her purse behind their door and began pacing as much as she could in the small space.

"I need you to remind me that working on myself right now is more important than anything else, and I need you to confirm that I'm terrible at picking men, and I'm probably just extra riled up because I'm on my period and maybe haven't had decent sex in a while, so that's what I need."

Willa was looking at Sahar as though she were speaking in another language.

"Okay, slow down. What happened?"

Spinning on her heel, she said, "Wills, please just confirm all of these things so my silly brain can grasp it and move on."

Momentarily, Willa studied her, then shook her head. "First, you're not terrible at picking men. How they present themselves to you in the beginning versus how much of their true selves they show later isn't the same thing. Second, yes, working on yourself is important, but need I remind you that's a decision you made yourself, and there's no time frame on it? Third, sure, you probably do need a good shag, but that's not what's causing all of this," she gestured with her hand. "Sahar, what happened with Jay?"

Sahar let out another heavy sigh. "Nothing happened except we had a nice time, then he winked, and it was the hottest wink I've ever seen, and he's been so kind that for a split second there, I *thought* about shagging him, which I absolutely *shouldn't* do because he's lovely and I like spending time with him."

Willa's eyes were...sparkling? "No," Sahar opposed.

"I didn't say anything," Willa objected.

"I know that look."

Willa bit down on her teeth.

"What?" Sahar questioned.

Trying to suppress a grin, her best friend said, "I'm trying to think of what to say so I don't make this worse."

Groaning, Sahar grabbed her water bottle from the vanity and took a big swig.

"Sahar, look, Jay's kind of been into you for a while now. Don't think I don't notice the way his face softens the moment we walk into the coffee shop. And I can guarantee *I'm* not the reason for it because when it's just me and Ethan or Christian, it's not remotely the same. It's *you*."

She stared up at their bland, monochrome ceiling. Sahar wasn't oblivious to the way Jay looked at her. She'd noticed it often but kept it tucked away. She was attractive. They all were. To top things off, she actively went out of her way to start conversations with him. If Willa had done the same, he'd probably be interested in her, too.

"Wills, it's not—he's not..." she tried to say.

Willa interrupted her. "Babe, he *is*. Ethan's noticed it, too, and I'm sure if you ask Christian, he'd also verify. And I don't know whether this will make you feel better or worse, but Jay is a significantly better person than your exes. All the initial red flags I noticed in Martin are nonexistent in Jay."

"You don't know that," Sahar countered.

"Actually, I do. There are stark differences between Jay and Martin. Not to mention that Jay and Sam have a number of mutual friends, whereas if we compare that detail directly to

Martin, literally no one in our trusted circle knew him or anyone he was associated with."

That much was true, but it wasn't helpful. Far from it. She couldn't let herself go down this road.

"Just tell me it's a bad idea. *Please*. Yes, he's a good guy. You're right about that, and I like being around him, but I can't have my stupid brain fly away with thoughts about kissing him."

Willa stayed silent for a beat.

Sahar wanted to scream.

"I can't keep messing up everything I touch," she whispered, barely audible enough for even Willa to hear, but she did.

Willa rose from her seat and came closer to Sahar. "Hey, you don't mess up everything you touch. Jesus Christ, I could kill that man for making you think like this. Sahar, you're one of the best people in this entire world. You bring so much light every-where you go."

That was what Jay had said, and the fragments of her heart that believed the absolute worst wanted desperately to cling to those words.

But beliefs could change.

"Jay's...I don't know. He's special. I want to keep him in my life. His words have been comforting. There's something about the way he tells stories, and amid everything, they've been help-ful. I don't want to make things weird."

Willa nodded with understanding. "I get that. Completely. You know I do. The best advice I can give you then is to take things one day at a time. Dodge romantic thoughts of him if you have to. Be his friend. But, Sahar, take it from me: if it starts to get too loud to ignore, then maybe there's a reason those feelings are there. Life is precious. A wise person once told me that being too cautious could stop me from experiencing something extraordinary, and *she* was right."

That supposed wise person had a lot of love in her heart and wanted to see her two best friends get together. She had more faith in their relationship than she had in her own.

Trying to smile, Sahar said, "That wise person's advice wasn't meant to be volleyed back at her, but I hear you, Wills."

"Wasn't it? She's the one who took care of me while I was drunk, so I'm here to look out for her now. One day at a time," she promised.

Sahar swallowed, trying to take in Willa's words. "One day at a time," she repeated, then added, "I'm sorry if I start screaming at the TV more because I'm ignoring my feelings through video games."

"Yell as much as you need to. I'll love you the same anyway."

Sahar felt a genuine smile curving along her lips. She couldn't be totally awful at picking people when she'd chosen Willa as her platonic soulmate. She couldn't be too much if Willa stayed beside her through everything. Sahar wanted to believe that desperately, but she also knew that sometimes, people were different around significant others. Maybe she did something around her exes that she didn't do around Willa or her other friends. Maybe she—*Ugh.*

Willa booped Sahar's nose with her finger, and then sat down to pin her hair back again for their wigs. Sahar would do the same.

She was grateful that all of this happened during a two-show Saturday because performing was exactly what she needed to wear out her body and quiet her mind.

13

—————

JAY

J ay thought of Sahar during the entire duration of his train ride, and in his car from the station as well. He called his mom, wanting to see how Eloise was doing, but she'd been too busy playing with her friend to want to talk to him.

He had tomorrow off, which meant he wouldn't be seeing Sahar, and since she was off on Mondays, it'd be three days from today. On Tuesday, his shift was set to end at three, and she wouldn't be coming in until around five-ish anyway, so he'd *maybe* see her on Wednesday before her matinee performance. There was no other justifiable reason for him to be around her, even though he wanted it more than anything.

He wanted her to keep asking him questions. He wanted to answer them all.

When Jay was finally home, he hopped into the shower, scrubbed off the smell of coffee, dragged a pair of sweatpants on, and sat at his kitchen table.

Flipping open his laptop to write, he hoped that the time spent with Sahar would maybe inspire him with the episode he'd been working on.

Jay thought back to the moment when she'd disappeared from him, her mind undoubtedly wandering to a place he wasn't meant to follow. He had counted the seconds ticking by, deliberating when he should say something.

A minute had passed when he finally nudged her.

Sahar had been far away, even when she came back to him.

He blinked, once, twice, trying to focus on the screen. Reading some parts over and over again, he eventually decided to delete a good chunk of the dialogue that no longer served the narrative and started writing with a fresh perspective. He considered how Sahar viewed Katherine's bravery, and because the scene dealt with her wounds, it felt easier to flesh it out more.

All at once, the words began pouring out of him.

It was as though the characters had full control of his brain, and they were the ones in the metaphorical driver's seat.

Pausing for a few minutes, he stood up and shuffled to his fridge to grab a can of Coke. Water felt too dull now that he was making progress. Snapping it open, he took a few sips while walking back to his seat.

By fully attempting to focus on Katherine's unease as she was captured, Jay learned that her determination did, in fact, stem from her mother's stories and the influence she continued to have on her daughter long after she passed. He berated himself for not realizing that Katherine would've been twice as resilient as he initially thought because her motivations weren't just for her—they were for her mother, too. She wanted to fight against all the people who believed she should never have been made a detective in the first place. That was what Sahar must've seen when she determined that Katherine's death would be a disservice to her character journey and all that she had fought for.

He typed away at his keyboard and, for a fleeting moment,

felt proud of the series coming to life in front of him. He was sure now that telling the story with a new ending in mind was the right way to move forward. It allowed the characters to guide him as opposed to how he'd originally written it—a product to sell. There were parts of the initial draft that were undoubtedly sincere, but even then, Jay knew at the back of his mind that he was composing what he thought producers *wanted* to read.

And from day one, he should've been writing for himself instead—for Sahar, too, who he still couldn't believe was a part of this journey with him.

Jay continued to write for another two hours, pausing briefly to eat dinner, then resuming until he couldn't see straight.

He took off his glasses, rubbing his eyes with his thumb and forefinger. Blinking a few times, he then looked at the digital clock across from him on the stove. It was nine-forty-five. Staring fixedly at the time, he debated whether he should send the revisions to Sahar now or wait until he was able to edit tomorrow morning. He mulled it over briefly. Really, he should wait. But he wanted an excuse to talk to her.

Sighing, he decided it'd be better with an early morning reread.

He closed his laptop and trekked toward the front door, crouching down by the shoe rack. He skimmed through the three unopened packages piled on the floor, looking for the one in book form from the Strand. That was where his copy of *The Wolf Lady* would be. Locating it, Jay tossed the wrappings and order confirmation slip in his recycle bin, then headed toward his bedroom. He could at least start reading until he fell asleep.

As he sat on the edge of his bed and unclasped his watch, his phone vibrated beside him with a call from his mom. Jay answered, knowing it'd likely be Eloise.

His daughter should've been exhausted after a full day of

activities, but she was as chipper as ever when she exclaimed, "Hi, Dad."

"Hey, kid. Did you have fun today?"

"Yeah, a lot of fun! Grandma let us play the *Shrek* game, and I beat Mary twice! But then she beat me during the last round."

Jay smiled. "Nice. Did you pass that level that was hard in the beginning?"

"Yeah! Aunt Lexie helped us before she went to work."

"That's cool. I'm glad she was able to help you two."

"What did you do?" Eloise asked.

Swinging his legs over the bed, he leaned back against the headboard. "I went to work, and then I had lunch with a friend," he answered.

"Did you have fun?"

"I did."

"Yay! We both had fun. When are you coming to Grandma's tomorrow?"

"I can be there whenever you want. I'm off the whole day."

"Can you come early so that you can help me with the next level?"

"Sure can," he promised.

She squealed again. "Yay! Okay, I'll see you tomorrow. Grandma set up beds for me and Mary. We're going to sleep in a fort in the living room."

Jay let out a small laugh. "That sounds perfect. Sweet dreams, baby. I love you."

Eloise nearly screamed, "I love you," then hung up. He set his phone down and after shifting his pillows around to find a comfortable position, he opened *The Wolf Lady* to its first page.

He texted Sahar after finishing the first chapter because even though it was too early to tell, he couldn't figure out why this was one of her favorites.

JAY

> Okay, I read the first chapter of The Wolf Lady. I can't for the life of me figure out what got you hooked.

He knew that Sahar wouldn't respond for a while, so he continued reading, squinting to fight the tiredness in his eyes because he was determined to keep going.

After a while, his phone buzzed beside him, and he looked down at her name, lighting up his screen.

SAHAR

> Once again, I must remind you of the nostalgia of it all. But okay, here's the full story: I stumbled upon it accidentally in the library when I was 12, and I picked it up because I thought it'd be an easy read (since it's short and all). My parents had a rule that I had to read 3 books a week if I wanted to keep up with dance. I loved it so much I begged my mum to let my rereads count for the 3. I read that book 3 times in the same week because I was so obsessed, Jay! It's the farthest thing from a love story. I realize it's not on brand for me, but the way they just hold hands and walk away (spoiler?!), and I don't know. I think about whether they've made it. I think about what they're doing now—how all those events must have changed them and shaped their lives as adults. There's a sequel, but I was always scared to read it because what if it ruined that last scene? I just really wanted to protect them. They were just kids, a little broken and sad and lonely, and I wanted them to be happy. I think that's why it's stuck with me, despite how long it's been.

Jay laughed, not in a mocking way, but because he could hear Sahar through her text. He could feel her passion and sincerity. He understood it—the need to protect damaged, lonely kids. That fully made sense, and maybe if he hadn't been tired, he would've picked up on its theme.

JAY

Jesus, that's precious.

I'll continue reading.

Three dots appeared right away.

SAHAR

You don't have to! If it's not gripping you please don't force yourself. I'd hate for you to feel like you've wasted time. Give me Henry and Katherine updates instead.

JAY

I want to. I'm now curious to see where it goes. And I've written a good chunk. Once I reread it tomorrow and ensure it makes sense, I'll email them over.

SAHAR

😬 looking forward to it.

Jay liked the text and smiled to himself. He'd find any excuse known to man to continue talking to her, but now that he knew the crux of why the book affected her, he was more interested in reading it with that perspective in mind.

He could see traces of it in the first three chapters, sprinkled chunks of fractured kids trying to find themselves amid all the pressure and cards stacked against them. Whatever scene got to her the most, he wanted to understand the importance of that, too.

~

JAY STAYED up reading *The Wolf Lady* last night, breezing through it even though he'd been exhausted. It was short and intriguing, and by the time he reached the end, he could fully tell why it had impacted Sahar. It was heartbreaking and messy, yet consistently hopeful throughout, and the ending cemented what growth often looked like in the face of grief for young people.

He could probably give the book to Eloise when she was older. Maybe she'd like it, too.

Jay then spent the early morning looking over and polishing the sixth episode before emailing it to Sahar. He got ready and drove to his mom's house. When he parked, he entered the house through the garage door. Stepping inside, he found his sister leaning over the kitchen island, munching on Lay's chile limón potato chips.

Alex perked up, popping another chip into her mouth before wiping her hands on what he assumed was a wet paper towel. "Hi, stranger. I feel like I haven't seen you in months."

Alex was being dramatic. It'd only been two weeks, exactly on the dot. He drew closer and hugged her. "How've you been?"

"Good, good. The usual. You?" She nudged the bag of chips in Jay's direction, offering him some.

He shook his head in a wordless *no, thank you.* "I'm good. Same old. Where are Mom and Ellie?"

With two more chips in her mouth, Alex's lips quirked upward, and she pointed to a crystal vase in front of her. "Mom found this in the garage yesterday, and Ellie wanted to put flowers into it, so they're in the yard picking some." With a content smile, she added. "It's really nice to have her here, Jay. The house feels more alive when she's around."

The corners of his mouth curled into a smile. It was true—Eloise had that effect.

Immediately, the steadfast vestige of sadness inside him

made its presence more pronounced. *It's temporary. She'll leave soon.*

He knew that if Maya lived close, they would've made accommodations to alternate custody weekly, giving them both equal chances to spend time with Eloise. He missed the days when he and Maya both lived in LA, and later, when Maya lived in Jersey. When they'd been closer in proximity, sharing their time with Ellie had been incredible. He'd never fault Maya for moving to Philly because of a better job, but he hated that it took them farther away from him.

Sighing, he walked over to grab a clean glass from the cupboard, filled it with ice from the fridge, and headed back to the filter by the sink for water. "Yeah, it does," he replied finally.

Fuck. It was only July, but summer had a way of slipping faster than it arrived, and while Eloise wasn't gone yet, he already missed her. *It's temporary,* his mind repeated.

If he thought about it further, it'd make him miserable.

Chugging the water in his hand, he considered deflecting with another topic, yet this one was also sure to increase his frustration. It was also now or never because he wanted to ask Alex about Sahar's ex, and he'd have to do it while his mom wasn't within earshot. Both for his sake and Alex's.

She'd been looking down at her phone, checking some sort of notification, before she took another chip between her fingers.

Jay set the glass down. "Hey, so, question. The lead in your show, Marvin, or whatever? Is he still a dick? You haven't gotten close to him, have you?"

Alex arched an eyebrow. "Martin? No, I'd befriend the giant rats at the subway station before I'd befriend that guy. He has no interest in us little people anyway. Why?"

He again wondered what a woman like Sahar had seen in a man like that.

"No particular reason. A friend of mine dated him, and I got curious," he said. "Wanted to make sure he isn't trying anything with you."

"Who's your friend?" Alex asked.

He considered withholding the truth, but there was no point to that. Alex had always been honest with him. He could do the same. "Sahar. Sahar Peck. She's in *Midnights at...*"

"Pemberley?" Alex interjected. "Since when are you friends with Sahar?"

Jay gave her a puzzled glance. "You know her?"

"Not personally, no. But I know *of* her, the whole cast, really. I follow them on socials, and they're delightful. The rapport they seem to have in their Instagram lives is nothing like what we have going on at *Hatchard's.*"

Damn it. That made him so sad.

He knew Sahar loved her co-workers, and he could see that they were all close, but he also knew that was a rarity in most workplaces. It was the opposite at Amanda's Coffee, too, because even while he liked the majority of the people he worked with, he wasn't friends with any of them outside of the shop.

Still, he wanted his sister to have what Sahar had. The unmoving shine in her eyes every time she brought up one of them in conversation was a type of joy Alex also deserved to experience.

"She's great, yeah. A bunch of them come to the coffee shop. That's how I know them," Jay finally said.

A slow, mischievous grin materialized on Alex's face then. "She's gorgeous, too. Get it, brother."

He narrowed his eyes. "It's not like that."

"Maybe not, but I bet it could be. You're a far better man than Martin is. I never understood why someone like her dated someone like him. She's twice as talented and way, *way* too stunning. Granted, I don't know her, but her social media presence says a lot. Her entire feed is full of photos of all her friends. She's always hyping everyone up. Meanwhile, I'm ninety percent sure Martin doesn't even know half of our names in the ensemble."

That sounded exactly like the Sahar he was getting to know. Jay didn't have any social media accounts, save for Letterboxd, which also didn't count as one; yet, it didn't shock him in the least that Sahar used her platform to prop up others.

"Well, fuck that guy," Jay emphasized. "I'm glad you're aware of him, though. I got worried for a second when she told me he was in your show."

A melancholy smile appeared on Alex's face. "You don't have to worry about me as much, Jay. I'm feeling a lot better about most things. I still have my days, but if everything I went through taught me anything, it's that I'm not going to trust people as easily as I trusted Dad when he came back."

Her transparency eased the ache in his chest. "Is therapy going well?"

Alex nodded. "Really well."

Good. This was good. His sister being on the right track toward healing was comforting. And Jay was grateful that even when Alex shut herself off and broke because of their deadbeat sperm donor, she felt safe enough to come to him about whatever she needed.

He was about to ask if she'd seen *Midnights at Pemberley* when the screen door to the backyard opened, and Eloise waltzed inside with his mom.

"Dad!" she screeched.

Jay bent down, flinging his arms out, and Eloise ran into his embrace. "We found so many flowers," she said excitedly. He gave her a big squeeze before letting go.

"Yeah? All in our backyard?"

Eloise bounced her head up and down. "Every single one. Grandma's garden is so big now! There's always a new flower!

Even on the cactus!" She spun to face his mom. "Grandma, can we please play video games before lunch?"

Jay looked over at his mom, trying to mimic his daughter's doe-eyed expression.

Setting the flowers down on the island, she opened a drawer and pulled out garden scissors before saying, "Yes, I'll clean up some of the dirt off these flowers and cut them properly, then you have come to help me arrange them. This was your idea, little lady. I want to see *your* bouquet."

Eloise bolted into the living room. Jay stood up and followed.

He plopped down on the couch while Eloise enthusiastically set up the game. Alex and his mom chattered about the flowers in the kitchen. After Eloise turned everything on, she sat beside Jay on the couch. "The level is so hard. We tried it four times yesterday!"

Jay looked over at the screen to where a giant gingerbread man was standing against some sort of wall. "Okay, remember how I explained the logistics of a game to you? Before you start, look at your surroundings. Think of everything you could use and how you could use it. If you need to pause and let your mind catch up, you're better off doing that than trying to speed through."

"It's a lot."

He nodded. "You're nearing the end, so it'll start becoming more challenging now."

Eloise looked attentively at the screen, considering his advice.

Jay leaned closer to her. "I think it's also freaking you out that you can't see what's coming for you, but you have an advantage here. You're not trapped like the character."

She faced him. "It is."

Eloise then squared her shoulders and pressed play. Jay cheered her on. "There you go. Keep going. It's gotta be timed or something," he said. She meandered through the level seamlessly, jumping and hopping enthusiastically in her seat as she played. And then, she did it. She actually freed the thing, beating the level entirely.

"I did it! I did it!" she celebrated, running around the living room, doing some sort of a happy dance in the process.

"I hear the excitement. And just in time to help me with the flowers," his mom called out from the kitchen.

"Thanks, Dad!" Eloise nearly screamed, then she ran to the kitchen.

At that exact moment, his phone vibrated in his pocket.

SAHAR

> I just finished reading the revisions for ep 4 and I'm W R E C K E D. Everything hits so much harder with the drawn-out silence and the beats that came before. The way you had Henry stumble on his words before THE confession came out!??? I straight up cried. Again. Jesus, mate. Warn me next time.

Jay smiled to himself as he walked back toward the kitchen. Nothing might come from this story. Even if he changed the majority and pitched it again, the powers that be might not be interested in it. It might stay shelved in his archives indefinitely. But Sahar's admiration for it—her full understanding of his vision could be the very reason why he'd persevere and why he wouldn't give up on writing, even when he thought about it at least once a day.

She was single-handedly giving him the confidence necessary to see that his words weren't complete shit.

JAY

> Your stamp of approval means everything to me.

He almost called her *sunshine* again, but managed to delete the word before sending it.

After putting his phone away, he slid his forearms down and leaned against the island, watching Eloise and his mom pick and choose flowers to add to the vase. He thought about the flower tattoo on Sahar's shoulder again, still wanting to know what kind it was—wanting to know if there was a reason behind it. Shaking his head, he cast away the thoughts, focusing intently on the present.

Eloise picked up two yellow daisies and added them to the vase, next to the white rose that was already inside. Next, she carefully added what appeared to be a lavender plant. Another white rose and another daisy. She repeated the pattern until all the flowers sitting on the marble were inside the crystal.

"I hear florists make a pretty penny these days, El. You might have another talent on your hands," Jay said.

His daughter grinned at him. "I want to make movies, silly," she said.

The coils in his chest twisted. Not again. He didn't want that for her. She deserved a happier life.

Alex must have caught the look on his face because she eyed him suspiciously, then turned to face Eloise and their mom. "All I can see here, clear as day, is that we're a creative bunch."

"I'm proud of myself," Eloise declared.

Jay stepped to the opposite side of the island and carried her. He was so fucking proud of her, too. "As you should be, baby," he declared.

A smile spread across his mother's face. "You should try to draw this arrangement in art class."

As she excitedly peered at her work, Jay pushed her other declaration to the back of his mind.

"Will Mrs. Sinclair let me?" she asked him.

He shrugged. "You'll have to ask Mrs. Sinclair in case she has something else in mind for you. But we can also take a photo of it, and you could draw it on your sketchpad at home."

"Okay," Eloise replied.

Then, his mom lovingly swatted them away. "I need you all out and away from my kitchen while I cook. Go make yourselves busy until I need help setting up."

"Can we play one more level, Dad?"

Jay nodded. "We can start it. Sure."

He set her down, and she skipped to the living room.

Alex tapped his arm as they walked behind Eloise. "What was that look back there?"

"She keeps mentioning wanting to be in this industry, and I don't want that for her. She deserves better."

His sister gave him a weary glance. "Apple doesn't fall from the tree. Plus, she'll have you if she's serious. You'd show her everything you know. She wouldn't be alone like you were."

"The apple should tumble toward the pediatrician's side of the tree."

Alex rolled her eyes. "The apple does what the apple wants. Stop freaking out about everything when it comes to Eloise," she whispered. "I know you think you're going to screw her up somehow, but you'd never. Look at everything you've done for me."

"I don't freak out about everything," he clipped back, as they drew closer to the living room.

Alex gave him a sardonic glare. "Yes, you do."

He didn't bother arguing as they stepped closer to Eloise. All three of them sat on the couch, and Ellie handed Alex a controller. "Third one is charging, Dad."

"All good. I'm happy to watch," Jay responded and kicked his sneakers off, settling comfortably on the forest-green sectional. He wasn't in the right headspace to play now, anyway. But he took Alex's words into consideration—*look at everything you've done for me.* Watching the two of them affectionately bicker over which character they wanted to play as, his mind eased for a while.

He'd do it all a thousand times over.

For both of them.

Leave LA for New York, work at a job he hated to be near their place of work, and answer every phone call, no matter what he was doing.

14

SAHAR

After her alarm clock blared for the third time, Sahar finally stopped snoozing and opened her eyes fully. She rolled onto her back and stared up at the ceiling. Her blackout curtains still drawn, her bedroom dark.

Her mind was right where she'd left it before she'd fallen asleep—on Jay's words. In his made-up world. If Sahar could curl up into them and blanket them around her, she would. How and why did such a simple line have such an immense hold on her?

She should be over it by now. Last night, she had read the rewrites for episode five, yet she was still hung up on the words from four. She'd thought about them while performing; she'd ruminated on them when Willa and Ethan forced her to join them for dinner after work, and she'd fixated on them again in the shower.

In my perfect world, you and I would be together.

It wasn't some poetic masterpiece, but it felt so intimate and tender that her heart ached every time the words crossed her mind. With every new addition to the story, Henry's confession grew in gravitas, while Sahar's feelings grew more clamorous. More confusing.

Maybe it was the fact that no one had ever said something like that to her. Or, maybe it was knowing the words had been born from Jay's mind.

She wondered what it had been like for Willa when her feelings for Ethan dawned on her all at once. How the two of them must've felt when they first shared the stage as Darcy and Elizabeth, forcing their real emotions to bleed into the characters. She saw it, yes, and felt the chemistry it evoked as an outsider, but to experience it herself? Such longings felt foreign.

Love felt foreign.

Sahar wanted to know what it'd be like to experience the sensation of feeling like her heart could burst out of her chest because the person standing in front of her was *that* important. She wanted to experience love in its most overwhelming form. She wanted someone to be so compelled by her that they felt as though they'd explode if they didn't utter the words aloud.

She'd known fractions of love—there wouldn't be heartbreak if she hadn't—but the more she read and the more she observed other people, it became clear that she'd never known *real* love before.

None of her relationships were worth fighting for, yet she had fought anyway, tried too hard to be worthy all the time, and destroyed herself in the process.

She groaned aloud, pulling the covers off her. *No more thinking.* After brushing her teeth, Sahar strolled to the living room, determining that video games would be a far better outlet right now. She took her controller from the TV stand and walked to the sofa, tossing herself down lazily.

Browsing through the games on her PlayStation 5, she decided on *FIFA 23.* Frustration from football was far better than frustration from romantic feelings. She could hear Willa's slippers along the floorboards, stepping out of her bedroom and into the kitchen, as Sahar chose her player and started the game.

"Crap. I forgot we're out of milk. We need to go to the shops." Sahar heard Willa call out.

Sahar kicked a goal in her game, paused, and spun in her seat to face Willa. "Yes, we do. Can you please check the pantry and let me know if we have any bags of orzo left? I kept meaning to check last night but forgot."

She watched as Willa opened the cupboard where they kept their rice and pasta.

"One bag," Willa said, holding a finger in the air.

"Okay, maybe I'll get one more, so we don't have to go back when I want it. I planned on making salad for us tomorrow," she started, and then followed up with, "Are you staying with Ethan tonight?"

"No. I think we should have a girls' night instead."

Sahar let out a small, knowing pout; she knew what Willa was doing. "Wills, you can go hang out with Ethan. You don't have to stay with me just because I'm having some questionable feelings these days."

"Ethan will be fine. And your feelings aren't questionable. They're normal."

"Okay, then we have to do something *you* want to do," Sahar proposed.

Willa's eyes went wide. "What if I want to get another ear piercing, even though I said I was done?"

Sahar grinned. "Yes. Yes, let's do it. I'll get one, too! What time does Max's Tattoos and Piercings close?"

Swiping open her phone to check, Willa searched for the answer before speaking. "Seven today. I can ring them and see if they have spots open? But they also said we could do walk-in last time."

"Call, just in case."

Willa nodded and pressed her phone to her ear. Sahar turned back to her game, only for a daft move from a midfielder to force her into a state of further irritation until she heard Willa confirm and hang up. *Good.* Something exciting.

"We got it," Willa exclaimed. "I'm making tea. You want some?"

Sahar propped up a thumb. She could hear Willa turn on the kettle and skip back into her room. A defender intercepted her goal and she nearly howled, stomping her socked feet down onto the floorboard. "Oh come on, you fucking twat!"

She hollered another rush of curse words out, then threw the controller down beside her. "Fine, universe, I get it. Today's not my day," she sneered aloud.

Switching over to *The Golden Girls* was now the guaranteed stress-free solution.

Once the show was on, Sahar treaded toward the kitchen, opened the fridge, and stared inside at its contents.

Eyes frozen, she must've been standing in front of the fridge longer than she realized because Willa had returned to the kitchen and was talking to her.

"Huh?" Sahar uttered.

"I asked if you lost something in there."

Sighing, she closed the fridge. "My sanity, apparently." And then, she remembered what she'd wanted, opening it back up to fetch the bowl of yellow cherries she'd left inside the night before.

She placed them on the countertop between her and Willa, popped one into her mouth, and opened the rubbish bin to spit the pit inside.

Willa didn't say anything about her sanity comment, and Sahar was partly—*very*—glad. She *needed* to snap out of this bizarre headspace—focus her mind elsewhere.

Absentmindedly, she glanced down at her phone in her

other hand, noting the date. That was when it clicked that Willa's birthday was on Wednesday. "Wills, shit, your birthday is coming up! Any plans since your parents had to postpone their trip to the end of August?"

Willa made a face, reminding Sahar how much she hated talking about her birthday. "Nope. And I told Ethan the same thing. He's not allowed to do anything after taking me to the treehouse on *his* birthday."

Sahar guffawed. Oh, delusion. It was adorable on Willa. "And we all know he's not going to listen to you, but go on."

"He better," Willa countered.

"Let the man shower you with all the affection and gifts. You deserve it, Wills. You've spent too many birthdays alone. And then, afterward, you should let us girls take you out to brunch."

Willa shook her head. "Nope," she repeated.

Sahar discarded another cherry pit with its stem. "Please, Wills, I'm sad and have confusing feelings. Let's shift the attention onto you."

Willa's brows furrowed. "Sahar, that's so evil. How dare you make me feel bad?"

"Because you're the best flatmate and friend anyone could ever ask for, and I want to celebrate you. I also know you hate seeing me sad, and I know you know that not celebrating *you* would make me sad."

Affectionately, Willa rolled her eyes. "Okay, fine. Only because seeing you sad makes me contemplate homicide, and I currently love my life a bit too much to go to prison."

"Finally, a win," Sahar screeched. "I'll text the usual girl group?"

Willa nodded, stepping in front of the tea kettle as it signaled its boiled status with a pop. "Okay, but only brunch. Casual." She took out two red polka-dotted mugs and placed them on their countertop.

"I got you, babe."

Prepping the text, her thoughts harassed her again. Sahar knew that at some point, Willa was going to have to move in with Ethan. It was only a matter of when. They were already closer than she'd ever been with her exes, and Sahar knew that would be the next best step. She wanted that for them. She cared about their relationship so much that the milestones mattered to her, too.

Still, a microscopic part of her was already a little sad because while Sahar knew she'd never lose Willa's friendship no matter where she lived, losing her as a flatmate was going to be one of the harder changes to get used to.

The realization made her more grateful that she could soak up these little moments they had before that time came. The fact that Willa was so adamant about spending the day with Sahar simply because her headspace was wonky was proof that she'd never find another friend like her.

Her eyes flicked to the TV—a scene featuring late-night cheesecake shared at a kitchen table—prompting her to look back at Willa. "Wills, when we're in our seventies and retired, can we ditch our husbands and move in together again?"

Willa snorted a laugh. "One hundred percent. Yes. But we need to find two other people to move in with us, so we can fully embrace our Golden Girls era."

"Priya and Carmen?" Sahar suggested—Sam and Declan's wives, respectively.

Tea kettle in her hand, Willa grinned. "That sounds like heaven on earth."

∾

WILLA HAD INITIALLY PLANNED to get her tragus pierced, but at the last minute, she opted out of it and went with a flat, just like Sahar.

The two of them also decided to get matching floral studs.

After leaving Max's Tattoos and Piercings, they grabbed dinner at Leo's Pizza near their apartment. The humidity hadn't eased, yet the twilight afterglow showing off around them was more than welcome. She snapped a quick photo of the cotton-candy sky while they waited for their food, letting the chatter around her blur into noise.

It wasn't until she heard the words, *Deadpool and Wolverine*, and turned to see a billboard behind her that she realized she didn't know Jay's stance on the Marvel Cinematic Universe. It was an industry detail that often came up with renowned directors voicing their apprehension toward the superhero genre, so where did Jay stand on it?

She could text him to find out. Another harmless conversation starter, nothing to worry about. Sahar opened her phone to do so.

SAHAR

> You know what we haven't talked about? Where do you, Mr. Writer and Director, stand on the MCU?

They carried off their pies from the pick-up section and walked back home. Willa was humming a song Sahar didn't know, and the night had turned out to be quite lovely in that way only time with your best girlfriends could be—safe and comfortable.

Jay responded almost instantly.

JAY

Lol I generally prefer DC adaptations, though I find it's significantly hard to top what Nolan achieved with the Dark Knight trilogy. But I don't dislike the MCU. I preferred it more during the Infinity saga than I do now with Phase 4. Or 5. Whatever number we're in.

Unsurprisingly, his opinions matched her own.

SAHAR

I fully agree. I'm sticking around for Spider-Man, but I'm a bit tired of keeping up.

JAY

Knowing you, No Way Home probably wrecked you.

Knowing you. He did know her, didn't he?

Sahar giggled. Willa pivoted to face her. She shook her head as if to say nothing. Except, it didn't feel like nothing.

It felt like—the beginning of everything.

No. Stop.

SAHAR

Wrecked, ruined, permanently damaged my whole soul, you name it.

JAY

It was a near-perfect movie.

SAHAR

I emphatically agree.

Fuck. The urge to keep texting Jay overwhelmed her again. Potential feelings aside, she liked talking to him. She wanted to pick his brain as much as she could, about anything and everything. Whatever he'd give her.

But she couldn't. She shouldn't be the one who was always chasing people. Why couldn't he keep conversations going instead? *Probably because he doesn't want to. You're good to him when it comes to his writing. That's all.*

Her phone lit up with another message from him.

JAY

Did you have a good day off?

Oh, maybe he does care. Take that, brain.

SAHAR

I did. Thanks for asking. Spent the day with Willa. Did you?

JAY

Yeah, I was with my family all day yesterday and most of today.

SAHAR

That sounds lovely. I'm so glad you're able to get Sundays off now. Were you off today, too?

JAY

Yeah, I need at least one weekend day away from the city crowds. And I switched some hours with another manager, so I have the next three Mondays off.

SAHAR

I'm guessing they wouldn't let you choose Saturday for a weekend.

JAY

Your guess would be correct.

SAHAR

Pity. You deserve Saturdays off, too.

JAY

Says the woman whose job requires her to put on two (incredible) shows on Saturdays.

SAHAR

Right, but I love my job.

JAY

Every single part of it?

The question made Sahar stop in her tracks, conveniently realizing that she hadn't spoken to Willa since Jay started texting her. When had they drawn closer to their flat?

"When did we get home? Jesus."

Willa chortled. "I figured I'd interrupt and warn you when we were about to get out of the elevator so that you wouldn't trip over the raised floorboard."

Sahar let out a groan. "I'm sorry. Jay texted."

"I figured he'd be the one to hold your attention."

"I hate this," Sahar added.

Willa pulled their lobby door open. "There's nothing to hate about it. Let it happen to you."

"I let too many things happen to me," Sahar countered.

Willa swung her arm into Sahar's. "And I've always admired you for it. Your massive heart is going to take you far someday."

"Or it'll destroy me."

Willa squeezed Sahar's bicep. "My vote's on the former. You'll see."

Sahar didn't say anything. They went up to their floor quietly, and Willa opened the door to their place with another comforting smile. Setting the pie down on their kitchen table, she disappeared to the bathroom.

Meanwhile, Sahar sat at the edge of the sofa and typed her response back to Jay.

SAHAR

With Midnights, yes, I love every part of it. But I know it's rare, so I'm trying to soak up every minute of what I'm sure will be the best job I'll ever have.

Three dots appeared and disappeared for what felt like over a minute.

JAY

That's really good, Sahar. I wish my sister felt the same way. She and her coworkers aren't as close as you all seem to be.

Please keep that between us.

Fuck. It pissed her off to no end to read those words because so much of a job's joy and safety started from the top, and Martin was only ever capable of ensuring that Martin was satisfied. They'd also heard whispers about the director of *Hatchard's* being a shady scum, so that likely didn't help either.

SAHAR

I won't tell a soul. But I'm sorry, Jay. She deserves better.

She wondered if Alex was on social media. Sahar wanted to know her. She hoped she had a friend like Willa she could vent to when the days were frustrating. Lord knows she and Willa wouldn't have survived the earlier years of living in the city if they hadn't moved in together. Though she was glad Alex was close enough to confide in her brother, at least.

JAY

She does.

SAHAR

Is my asshole of an ex part of the problem?

JAY

She's not fond of him, but I don't think he's one of her bigger issues.

SAHAR

I also hope you can leave the coffee shop soon. I realize it's impossible sometimes not to have multiple jobs in our industry, but you deserve your dream job every day.

JAY

It's not all bad. At least Henry and Katherine can be happier because a specific redhead from said coffee shop demanded they get a happy ending.

Sahar laughed out loud.

SAHAR

She didn't demand. She nudged. Gently.

JAY

If that was gentle, I'd hate to see what the opposite looks like.

SAHAR

Very funny. That's the thanks I get.

JAY

I am forever indebted to you.

SAHAR

See, much better.

JAY

Speaking of, I'm making some very minor tweaks to episode seven while El's asleep. I might send it over to you after work tomorrow.

SAHAR

Yes, excellent!

More words to look forward to, tiny pieces of Jay's mind sprinkled onto paper for her to read. How had his story become so special to her? What was it about his writing that made her feel so seen?

She was nothing like Henry or Katherine. Frankly, she was a lot like the one secretary at the agency—Robin. Loud, happy, and hopelessly optimistic.

Except, rather these days...

Maybe she was like Henry—broken but determined. Maybe she was more similar to Katherine—angry and guarded.

Or, maybe, despite all her efforts to swear off men and relationships for a while, she could no longer deny how captivated she was by the one whose words awakened some indescribable form of comfort in her soul.

Sahar tossed her phone on the sofa. This shouldn't be happening. She couldn't be trusted with her feelings. Her feelings would push Jay away. Even if Willa was right and there was a part of him interested in her, she was certain that it didn't go beyond the physical.

He'd get to know her more, and she'd be too much for him, too.

She needed to work on that part of her before she could let someone in again. Standing up, she went to the kitchen sink, washed her hands, and averted her attention back to the pizza. And Willa. Willa, who was holding a slice, and grinning like a mad woman. It could be because of the pepperoni—her third favorite thing after Ethan and pickles—or it could be because she knew that Sahar was losing it.

~

IT WAS two in the morning, and she couldn't sleep. Again. So while Sahar was initially saving the sixth episode to reread at some point tomorrow, she decided she might as well do it now.

Sahar wanted to wait to text Jay in the morning, but fuck it, like most people, he probably had his phone on silent. It wasn't like she'd wake him up with a single text. She'd do it now.

SAHAR

> I just finished rereading ep 6. Henry's slow descent is actually my undoing. And good grief! I loved those bits of Katherine remembering her mom's words and how they're driving her survival. Like I know that the Logan brothers need her, so they aren't going to harm her, but because we're past the halfway mark now, it's natural to feel concerned since it'd be understandable to see her almost give up. I love love love the fact that she's pushing through.

She exited her messages app and browsed through social media. Scrolling mindlessly through her phone, her mind trailed back to Jay.

Sahar wondered what kind of a partner he'd be to someone.

How kind he was.

She thought of his hands—how massive they were—what his fingers could do...

Martin berated her every time she wore high heels because she'd pass his 5'10 frame, but Jay must've been at least 6'2 or 6'3. It didn't matter. What mattered was that she wanted to know what his body would feel like pressed up against hers for longer than a few mere seconds. How his lips and tongue could move, and how his beard could burn... *Nope.*

When his name appeared in a banner on top of her phone screen, Sahar's heart palpitated inside her chest.

JAY

Thank you so much for saying that. I hoped the changes in this episode would work. Why are you awake?

Because apparently my brain really wants to know what your fingers could do outside of typing.

Stop.

SAHAR

Can't sleep. I could ask you the same question.

JAY

Neither can I. Though I just finished ep 7. Ellie stayed up a bit longer than usual, so I got a later start on writing.

SAHAR

Aw, was everything okay? Or she just didn't want to sleep.

JAY

She wanted to watch Barbie. Again. And then once more asked me about what it takes to be a filmmaker, so I came very close to another heart attack.

She chortled, turning over to her left side.

SAHAR

Way to make her think her dad's being very dramatic with his thoughts.

JAY

I have to embarrass her somehow, don't I?

SAHAR

Is that in the handbook?

JAY

No clue. They forgot to give me one at the hospital.

SAHAR

Well then, if you're winging it, I think you're doing pretty well. If you're that concerned about ensuring her future is without its struggles, you're doing something right.

JAY

I sure hope so.

SAHAR

I know so.

JAY

Do you have a good relationship with your dad?

SAHAR

I do. He's a goofball and the sweetest man I know.

JAY

How does it feel being far from your parents, from the kid's point of view? It's gonna kill me when Ellie goes back home to Philly.

Her heart broke then. She couldn't imagine what it must've been like from his perspective, or how it had been for her parents.

SAHAR

I'm so sorry, Jay. I can't imagine. I never thought of it from a parent's point of view until now. But I suppose we all leave someday, don't we? It was tough adjusting at first, but I talk to them almost every day. Being older probably helped them. I'm sure Eloise misses you a lot, too.

JAY

> I almost hope she doesn't so it's easier on her
> than it is on me.

God. Sahar wanted so desperately to be beside him now—to hold his hand and tell him everything would be okay. But would it be? She had no clue how he felt; how could she comfort him through it?

Another text came as she was about to answer.

JAY

> Do you ever plan on moving back to London?

SAHAR

> I don't know. When I'm not in a long running
> show, I go back at least twice a year, but I think
> I was meant to live here in NY.

> Is there a way you could visit Eloise more
> frequently than every two weeks?

JAY

> I'm going to have to do everything in my power
> to. I need to get out of the damn coffee shop,
> but it pays the bills.

SAHAR

> Not sure how good I am at manifesting things,
> but putting it out there again that I believe this
> show can succeed, snag some Emmys, and get
> you deals left and right. It's what you deserve.

JAY

> The way you love this show never fails to stun
> me. Thank you.

SAHAR

I really do love it. Always remember, when everyone's screaming your name, I was its biggest fan first.

JAY

I couldn't forget that even if I tried, sunshine.

Sunshine. The fourth time. Fuck.

What if she took advantage of the moment—asked him a thousand questions like what his favorite songs were, and if he ever cried? She wanted to know his favorite color and whether he preferred lakes or beaches. She wanted to know his favorite food. His earliest memory. She wanted to make sure his terrible father could never come near him again. But before she could ask anything, another text came through.

JAY

Can I ask you something personal?

You can ask me anything, she wanted to say. Her hand cramped texting like this, but she refused to stop. Not now. Not when things were getting interesting. She rolled to her side, holding up her phone against the mattress.

SAHAR

Only if I get to do the same.

JAY

Of course.

Why were you with someone like Martin? You clearly deserved so much better than him.

Fuck.

She typed and deleted her response multiple times. *You don't know that I deserved better. According to him, I was the problem.*

According to all of them, it was always me ruining things. You think this now, but come tomorrow, you might see what they have. Unless I change and shrink myself down to become more palatable.

SAHAR

Because I was a hopeless romantic, and I ignored all his red flags.

JAY

Was?

The fact that he caught the tense change made her feel both better and worse.

SAHAR

Lol yeah. But next question, please. I really don't want to talk about him.

JAY

Understandable. I'm sorry for bringing it up.

SAHAR

Not at all. What about you? Is there anyone in your life?

Please say no. Please say no. Please say no.

JAY

Nope.

That was drier than Jay's usual response, but a preferred answer nevertheless.

JAY

One more question. This one isn't personal. Promise.

SAHAR

I don't mind if it is, I just don't want to talk about that asshole.

JAY

Fair enough.

What's your favorite ice cream flavor?

SAHAR

Coffee.

JAY

Really?

SAHAR

Yeah, why?

JAY

Nothing. It's mine too.

Heat suddenly rose in her belly.

SAHAR

Not sure why that's comforting, but it is.

Why would you actually say that to him?

JAY

The fact that our favorite ice cream flavor is the same?

SAHAR

Yeah.

JAY

It is. You're right.

SAHAR

What are Henry's and Katherine's?

JAY

Mint chocolate chip and pistachio, respectively.

Grinning at the response, Sahar turned over to lie on her back again.

SAHAR

Did you think of that on a whim, or did you already know those answers?

JAY

Ice cream is very important to me, Sahar. It's a detail I take into careful consideration for all my characters.

SAHAR

I'll bet you never say no to Eloise when she asks for some for breakfast.

JAY

Don't tell Maya.

SAHAR

We all have a weakness. I respect that yours is apparently ice cream.

JAY

What's yours?

SAHAR

Everything bagels and sour candy.

JAY

Should've told me that earlier. I would save a bagel for you every day.

SAHAR

You're not there every day.

Lord. Why would she say it like that? It sounded weirdly romantic in her head, like she noticed when he was gone. *Of course, she noticed.* But still.

She groaned, hating herself a little bit.

JAY

I could still have one waiting for you. Just say the word.

SAHAR

How about instead of every day, maybe every time you're there?

JAY

Deal.

Still not tired?

Was he growing tired of her? Wouldn't he just stop responding if that were the case?

SAHAR

No. I'm going to be miserable tomorrow. Are you working?

JAY

Yeah, I am.

SAHAR

You should sleep. You have to be up earlier than me.

JAY

I would if I could.

What do you hate? What bores you? I'll start talking about it, and maybe you'll fall asleep.

LOL

Baseball. It doesn't make sense to me. Opera. Car commercials. (it's such a weird fucking thing to advertise as if people who are looking for cars are going to rely on ads to tell them which one to get?) The texture of those white styrofoam cups, who's willingly buying and drinking something out of them? Walnuts—you can't convince me that shit was meant for human consumption. Every other nut, sure, but walnuts? I'm good. The coffee shop, unless you're there.

Unless you're there. Unless you're there. Unless you're there. Fuck, she wouldn't be able to sleep at all now.

It's a good thing you're a modern man and don't have to attend any operas to be part of high society. I'm afraid you wouldn't have made it before the birth of television.

Your thoughts on walnuts slightly concern me, but we won't push It today. The rest are all valid.

I most definitely wouldn't have made it back then.

And yeah, best not to get me started on fucking walnuts.

Want me to send you some renowned opera tracks? I can make you a whole playlist.

JAY

I would rather you make a playlist of all your
favorite songs and send me that instead.

SAHAR

Bold of you to assume I don't have one already.

She opened Spotify on her phone and sent him a playlist
titled "The Way Back Home."

He replied after a minute or two. In the meantime, she
quickly ran to the bathroom and back.

JAY

All of these are your favorite songs?

SAHAR

Mhmm, I have a playlist for almost everything.
I'm half tempted to make one for Henry and
Katherine.

JAY

Please do.

Also, there are a lot of songs by The National on
here. Favorite band?

SAHAR

YUP. Team sad dads forever.

Expect that playlist soon. I'm already on it, and
first up is The National's "I Need My Girl." The
song screams Henry.

JAY

Listening now. It really does.

SAHAR

I don't want to blow my own trumpet, but you're
about to find out that I'm quite gifted when it
comes to making playlists.

JAY

I'm already thoroughly impressed.

She kicked her blanket off one leg. Heat and desires, continuing to battle inside of her.

SAHAR

Okay, but we've got to backpedal. I didn't ask you my question. I just kept piggybacking off you.

JAY

Ask away.

SAHAR

I actually don't really have one, but I want to ask something, so give me a second. Need to think.

JAY

Make it a good one. I'm in an obliging mood.

Well, fuck, if you weren't literally taking care of a child, I'd ask you to come over. Spend the night. Maybe that way, I'd get you out of my system.

She tried to think of Martin's flaws. How she was certain that he'd never be excited to share the spotlight in the way Ethan was with Willa. How he'd never admit to being better because of his partner, the way Sam always beamed when talking about Priya's influence on him.

Martin wanted to shine on his own. He wanted the sole spotlight.

But if she wanted to know how Jay would be in such situations, she needed to be subtle. She needed to phrase it correctly. She couldn't outright ask him, so she typed and retyped a few variations before settling on, *What do you think is the most important characteristic in a person?*

JAY

Honesty and empathy. I grew up with a selfish, heartless dad who lied through his teeth. There are few things that make me angrier than finding out someone's belittling someone or lying about something.

SAHAR

I wholeheartedly agree. This might be way too personal, but have you ever talked to someone about your dad?

JAY

Like a therapist?

SAHAR

Yeah.

JAY

When I was a teenager, yeah. But not as an adult.

She felt like she'd just crossed a line.

SAHAR

I'm so sorry if that was too much on my part.

JAY

Stop apologizing every time you ask me something personal. I don't mind telling you things you want to know. That said, I also went to a few sessions with Alex when she was older because she wanted me there.

Smiling at his words, she took a breath, remembering the plotline of *Cuts.*

SAHAR

You're a great brother for doing that. I'm guessing parts of Cuts were drawn from experience?

JAY

Yeah. Pat's dad was the one who passed. Mine's the abusive piece of shit.

SAHAR

Jesus. He's not around anymore, is he?

JAY

No. We have restraining orders against him. The very last time, he hospitalized my mom. He wasn't allowed near any of us, and then the piece of shit tried to get close to Alex, manipulated her into thinking he'd changed, and wanted to "be a better dad to her," but the second she publicly came out as bi, he said he wanted nothing to do with her. There aren't enough shitty words for him.

Fucking hell.

SAHAR

I'm so sorry, Jay. That must've been so traumatizing for your sister to go through.

JAY

She's doing better. We all are.

SAHAR

Still, none of you deserved that.

JAY

SAHAR

I hope bringing this up didn't rile you up more. I'm very concerned about how you'll be at work tomorrow.

JAY

Hahaha, don't be. I went through a horrible bout of insomnia three years ago. It's nothing compared to this.

SAHAR

😩. That sounds awful. Is this a bad time to admit that this is so out of the norm for me? I have a secret talent that I can actually fall asleep anywhere.

JAY

Please elaborate.

SAHAR

The floor, a plane, the world's tiniest bench, a chair. It's a gift? Maybe a curse? Haven't quite decided yet.

JAY

And your body is fine with that?

SAHAR

Sometimes ...

JAY

You just gave me another reason to worry about you, and you expect me to sleep?

Sahar Peck, you're a bloody disaster. She yanked her blanket off entirely. Too hot. Too riled up. Too frustrated.

SAHAR

I'm sorry! I'm just going to stop responding, and maybe that'll do the trick.

JAY

Nah, that'll just force me to make up replies in my head.

SAHAR

One of us has to be the strong one here. Both of us can't worry about the other.

JAY

Well, I guess we're stuck here because it's not gonna be me.

Something about the words *we're stuck here* made her heart beat even faster.

SAHAR

I have the luxury of at least going to work later.

JAY

Okay, let me ask you one more question, and then I'll try to sleep.

SAHAR

Go on.

JAY

You have all Mondays off, right?

SAHAR

Correct.

JAY

I have a premiere on Monday the 22nd, two weeks from now. A friend of mine, it's his movie. Would you like to come with me?

Sahar opened the calendar on her phone to ensure she had no plans that day before responding.

SAHAR

Ooh, what's the movie? And sure, I don't have anything scheduled on that day.

JAY

Franklin Street.

That sounded familiar. Where had she heard that title before? She exited out of the chat and opened the IMDb app, searching. The poster jogged her memory.

She went back into her messages.

SAHAR

Oh! Sam and Priya recorded an original song for this movie. I got a snippet of the demo, and it was glorious.

JAY

Ah, shit, they did? That makes sense. I know Sam because of Pete. I met him at his party a few years back.

SAHAR

Small freaking world. But cool, I'll be there!

JAY

Excellent. Alright, sunshine. Try to sleep.

SAHAR

You too! Goodnight!

A part of her brain wanted to ruminate over why he'd asked her. A logical part assumed it was because they were building some sort of friendship within the industry. Another, also equally logical part could accept what Willa and everyone saw, which was that Jay was interested in her. Whatever that looked like for now, the beginning wasn't a problem. It was the middle.

The last time she'd gone out with Martin flashed before her eyes. *No.* The real reason she broke up with him—the hurt that kept tearing into her mind at random intervals. The way Martin had looked at her, like she was some sort of rat, crossing his pristinely trimmed and manicured path with its filthy claws.

She swallowed the lump in her throat and read Jay's text over again. *Alright, sunshine. Sunshine. This was the fifth time now.* Why was she even counting?

Heaven help her, she could hear the word fall from his lips, soft and honeyed still through his deep bass.

If she fell for him—if she allowed herself to jump as quickly as she often did, his eventual resentment would shatter her. It'd be the very thing to guarantee that she would never bounce back. She was sunshine to him now, but everyone drew the curtains closed at some point. Everyone longed for rain and cold weather when the sun overstayed its welcome.

But good lord—she wanted to just—*give* herself up to him, even if it would all be fleeting. Yet, maybe, if there were no commitments, there'd be no heartbreak. Except, she'd read the stories before; she knew how the words *one time* could actually be synonymous with forever. But maybe they were wrong. Life didn't always imitate art or vice versa. It didn't have to.

Human beings had choices.

And at the moment, what she should have been choosing was to focus on falling asleep.

15

___

SAHAR

Two guests ahead of her at Amanda's Coffee were ordering with Dahlia, as Jay had his back turned, right arm moving, likely writing something.

Today, July 10th, was Willa's birthday, and they had a two-show Wednesday, plus a girls' brunch planned for tomorrow afternoon. Eager to add on to the gift she'd homemade, Sahar had texted both her and Ethan to let them know she'd be getting coffee.

She glanced around the space, forcing her eyes away from Jay's broad shoulders and back. He had no right to look *that* good from behind. Most importantly, she had no right to *stare.*

Sahar had always noticed the vinyl records hanging on the side wall, but she'd never really looked at them before. From where she stood, she could make out Robbie Williams' *Life Thru a Lens,* The Beatles' *Abbey Road,* and Death Cab for Cutie's *Narrow Stairs,* among others. Upon detecting movement in front of her, she averted her gaze back to the registers, and as though on cue, Jay did the same.

He eyed her, an amused smirk on his lips and a tilt of his

head, gesturing for her to come closer. "Hey, you. Where are the others?"

"Hi. Just me today. It's Willa's birthday, so I've volunteered to make the coffee run."

"Ah, well, the usual then?"

"Yes, please. And add one iced Americano, plus an Earl Grey. I'm getting them for Ethan and Christian, too."

"Everything bagel?" he asked.

She bit back a bigger smile, and her heart did a little gallop. She assumed he'd forget about that particular detail. "Not today, but thank you."

"You got it, sunshine."

The endearment was so low on his lips that she was sure no one else could hear it. She wasn't even sure he realized he'd said it. Sahar opened the digital wallet on her phone, getting ready to pay when his hand hovered over the keypad.

Looking up to face him, her eyebrows rose.

"It's on me," he said, and the numbers below her phone disappeared.

She shook her head. "You can't keep doing that. Plus, it's not just mine," Sahar objected.

He winked. The bloody bastard gave her that specific wink again, and her insides turned to molten lava.

"As a manager, I think I can do whatever I want," he said, nudging her to follow him to the area where he'd make the drinks.

"I know for a fact that's not how it works. Jay, come on."

"Tell Willa I say, 'Happy Birthday.'"

Walking and talking concurrently, she suggested, "At least let me pay for Ethan and Christian."

"Next time," he returned, adding shots of espresso over ice.

"You said that last time," she argued.

He plucked out a cardboard carrier from the stack, set it

down, and then finished making the iced Americano before placing it inside. "This time, I mean it."

"How do I know that?"

"Trust me," he said, then began working on Christian's Earl Grey next.

She did. And that was the scariest part. Not about future coffee payments, but with everything else.

It was terrifying how quickly she was growing to trust him.

The faint jingle of the shop's door opening caught Sahar's attention, and she watched as Jay's eyes flicked over her head. There was unmistakable recognition in them. She looked over her shoulder to where he'd given someone an upward nod, spotting a young woman, maybe in her early twenties, walking over to them.

A sweet grin rested on her pretty face.

Up close, Sahar could see the same shaped eyes, hers more hazel in color, and thick lashes with an acutely similar bone structure to Jay's. She had to be his sister—Alex. There was no denying the relation between the two.

"I didn't know you were coming in," he said, pouring a splash of oat milk into what Sahar was sure was her lavender latte.

The petite woman shrugged. "Wasn't planning on it, but I accidentally picked up mom's phone instead of my own this morning, not knowing mine was in my bag. I wanted to drop it off, so you could take it back when you pick up Ellie."

She turned to Sahar then, a sincere smile on her face. "Hi! I'm Alex," she said, pointing her thumb in Jay's direction, "his sister."

Sahar smiled back. "I've heard such great things about you. It's so nice to meet you, Alex. I'm Sahar."

"Oh, not to be weird, but I know who you are. I'm a huge fan of *Midnights at Pemberley.* I was rooting for you all during the Tony Awards."

Sahar's eyes gleamed then veered back to Jay, who'd just finished adding Willa's drink to the carrier, with the words *Happy Birthday* written on the plastic cup in lieu of her name. "I like her," she said aloud.

Alex smiled. So did Jay.

Sahar took the tray in her hand. "Thank you for everything, Jay."

"Anytime," he said while simultaneously taking his mom's phone from his sister and setting it in his pocket.

"Mind if I walk out with you?" Alex asked Sahar.

"Sure, I can wait with you while you get whatever."

Alex shrugged. "Oh, I'm good. Nothing is more tragic than the fact that my brother works at a coffee shop, but I have way too much anxiety and acid reflux to take advantage of it."

Oof. That was tragic indeed. Sahar was so glad she didn't have to live without coffee. Caffeine aside, she loved the taste too much.

"See you, I don't know when," Alex commented.

Jay bobbed his head at them both.

Hatchard's Academy played two streets away from *Midnights at Pemberley.* When they were out of the coffee shop, Sahar turned to Alex. "I hope my asshole of an ex is nice to you."

Alex guffawed. "The only person he's nice to is our equally shitty stage manager and the director when he sometimes comes in."

Sahar was sure disgust oozed out of her face. "I'm so sorry."

"It's not your fault. You know, he tells people he dumped you, but everyone knows it's probably the other way around. No one believes him."

It was Sahar's turn to guffaw. "Yeah, I'm the one who finally saw the light. But it doesn't shock me one bit that he's doing that. I expected as much from him."

"You dodged a major bullet there."

Sahar agreed. "Oh, I know."

Alex looked like she wanted to say something, but stopped herself.

They'd been drawing close to the Hyacinth Theatre already.

Sahar wanted to ask what it was, but figured it was best not to.

Instead, she said, "Hey, Aisha Sharma is in *Hatchard's* too, right? I know she was recently in *Here on Earth,* but her run ended?"

Alex bounced her head with a smile. "She is! I've known her for over a decade now, so having her come onto *Hatchards* is exactly what I needed. She started two days ago, and we literally swapped dressing rooms just to be in the same one."

Small freaking world. Or industry, rather. Aisha was Priya's cousin, and they'd met at Sam's birthday last year. She remembered Jay saying his sister didn't have many friends at *Hatchards,* so it was lovely that Aisha had gotten the gig. Sahar had read something about one of their stars stepping down, which must've been the role Aisha had booked.

"She's such a sweetheart," Sahar said. "Plus, few things are more comforting than having a trustworthy person in our line of work."

"She really is," Alex affirmed. "And I agree. I was miserable without her. So, I'm personally glad Lydia Nolan got pregnant and had to leave. To be honest, everyone's happier away from *Hatchards.* But you know how it is, necessary experience and all."

Sahar gave her an understanding smile. The unsettling thought of her contract at *Midnights* ending rushed back to the forefront of her mind again. She'd been doing so well without that particular fear.

"Tell her I say 'hi!'" she chose to say next.

"Absolutely."

Once they were at the Hyacinth's stage door, Sahar faced her fully. "It was so great to meet you, Alex."

Alex's lips curved into a genuine smile. "Same!"

Sahar leaned forward, balancing the drinks with one hand and giving Alex a hug with her other arm.

Somehow, even though she'd known Alex for mere minutes, it had felt longer than that. Maybe it was a Callahan family effect—an inherent kindness and warmth woven into their ways of communicating. Their father, excluded.

"See you around, Sahar."

"See you!"

When Alex walked away, Sahar spun on her heel and headed inside. One of their guards, Zayn, was already standing in front, holding the door open. She gave him a fist bump and beelined toward Ethan's room, knowing Willa would be there.

"Christian, boo, I've got your tea," she called out while passing his and Miles' dressing room.

"Coming," Christian replied.

Walking into a bustling dressing room, Sahar's excitement doubled at the sight of her co-workers. Miles and Declan were inside, too, heckling Ethan about something.

She placed the tray of drinks on the vanity and ran over to Willa, giving her the biggest squeeze. Willa had spent the night at Ethan's, so this was the first time they had seen each other since yesterday's show.

"Happy Birthday, you fucking goddess. I love you to the moon," Sahar declared into their hug.

"I love you more. Thank you," Willa giggled, tightening their embrace.

After parting, Sahar added, "Jay wouldn't let me pay again. He says, 'Happy Birthday.'"

Willa gave Sahar a look. She knew exactly what it meant, and it wasn't something they were going to talk about here.

Declan turned to Ethan then. "Why don't we ever hug like that on our birthdays, and why don't you ever call me a *'fucking god?'*"

Ethan playfully slapped Declan's exposed, rock-hard abs. "Is that what you're itching for when you refuse to wear shirts?"

"Obviously," Declan agreed.

They all laughed at the exact same time. If there was any moment where Sam should've been recording, this was it. For the past two months, when Sam went on Instagram live, Declan would stubbornly put on a shirt to spite him for telling everyone he walked around shirtless, even though he'd more than earned the reputation.

Sahar reached into her tote then and pulled out a wrapped box, handing it to Willa.

"We agreed to no gifts," Willa protested.

Sahar shrugged. "I agreed to no such thing."

Willa sighed contentedly. "Why are you like this?"

Funny, she'd just said the same thing to Jay.

"Want me to open it now?"

"Yes, because I'm very proud of it."

Smiling, Willa opened the present and pulled out the item covered in bubble wrap. Tears welled in her eyes when she took it out and saw what was inside.

"Sahar," she whispered.

A gratified sense of joy ribboned itself around Sahar.

Willa turned to Ethan to show him the Polaroid-style photograph of the two of them from their time as Elizabeth and Darcy. Sahar had taken it while they were backstage. Willa was mid-dip, smiling earnestly at something Ethan had whispered to her.

"Sahar, this is so fucking thoughtful," Ethan said.

"I can't stand how cute you two are," Christian added, peering at the picture from the corner of Ethan's shoulder.

Declan pretended to wipe a stray tear from his eye. "My babies, all grown up."

"I'm a year older than you," Ethan asserted.

Grabbing Ethan's face, Dec squished it. "Still my baby boy."

Willa burrowed herself in Sahar's arms again.

"Do you like it?" Sahar asked.

With full-blown tears in her eyes, she replied, "I love it with my whole heart."

Sahar held on tighter. "That makes me so bloody happy."

Another squeeze. "We should start getting ready," Willa said. She kissed Ethan on the cheek, then reached for her drink from the vanity.

"Sahar, thank Jay for us, please," Ethan added.

"Will do," she promised, taking a sip of her own latte.

Once they were inside their dressing room, Willa set the framed photograph in front of her and smiled at Sahar. "I'm seriously obsessed. This is so wholesome."

"I'm so glad you love it, babe. You deserve the happiest birthday."

"Between you and Ethan, I'm the luckiest."

Sahar beamed, remembering the text Willa had sent her this morning about Ethan surprising her with a sold-out vinyl of The National's High Violet 10th Anniversary Edition. "I still can't believe he managed to track it down for you."

"I know. Sixteen record stores? He said he wanted to make sure he checked everywhere before caving and ordering it from a reseller. And then he freaking found it. I could bloody well explode. I still can't believe he's real sometimes."

Sahar gave her friend a toothy grin. "Oh, he's very real, and

I'm going to repeat it again, but you deserve all of this and more, Wills."

"Speaking of things we deserve. So, like you're never going to have to pay for coffee again? Also, please literally text him right now and tell him I say 'thank you very much.' I don't want you to forget."

Taking a deep breath, Sahar tilted her head. "Wills, he's so... So—*ugh*. I don't know. I also met his sister as I was leaving, and she's delightful. I feel like a mess. Speaking of, I should try to find her on socials."

"Oh, I love that. Immediately getting along with a sibling is a good sign."

"You say that as if it were some official meeting."

"Might as well have been," Willa declared, then started pinning her hair back to prep for her wig. Sahar should do the same, but first, she was going to text Jay.

SAHAR

Two things: first, your sister is an absolute doll, and second, everyone says thank you for the drinks. Willa is sitting next to me right now.

She set the phone down and got started on her routine. One Bobby pin, then another, her phone buzzed, but she refused to look at it.

Not yet.

Once she finished pinning her hair back and priming her face for makeup, Sahar glanced at her messages again.

JAY

You're all very welcome. And I'm glad you think so. Alex would be psyched to hear that.

Sahar opened her Instagram app and searched for her. She wasn't able to find her with her name and last name, so she went to Aisha's account to search from her list. And there she was, only instead of her last name, there was another: Alexandra Daphne. She was already following Sahar, and Sahar immediately followed back.

Another message from Jay popped up.

JAY

P.S. You'll have ep 8 in your inbox soon.

The most excellent news.

SAHAR

I CAN'T WAIT!

A smile curled at the corners of her lips, and this time, she didn't fight it.

16

SAHAR

They'd reached that point in the summer where the heat was now unbearable. It was especially suffocating inside the cramped subway car where Sahar, Willa, Ethan, and Christian were pressed together like sardines, legs spread out for balance.

Willa was arguing that because they'd taken her out for her birthday, it was someone else's turn to choose a post-workday activity. The car jerked, moving each of them a bit and opening up a vantage point for seated passengers. Sahar's eyes immediately focused on an older woman in front of them, her gorgeous silver hair in some sort of elaborate coiffure, ruby red lipstick, with a black pin-up-looking dress. She looked like Mrs. White. The thought of what to do came to her at once.

"Ooh, what about a classic *Clue* night? It's been a while since we've had one of those. What do you say, Wills, would you play?" Sahar asked excitedly.

Willa and board games were seldom a match, but Sahar knew that occasionally, *Clue* could be an exception.

"*Clue*, yes," she answered.

Christian took a big gulp from his water bottle. "Hold up,

though, I just remembered that Miles and I have tickets for *A Quiet Place: Day One.* I'll have to see if we can swap them for tomorrow instead."

"Okay, yes. We also need one more person to make it a total of six. I refuse to play with less," Sahar said. "It *needs* to be exciting. Is Clyde free?"

The car stopped, and the doors slid open. The four of them jumped out and power walked away. Christian nearly yelled his response. "Clyde's on a work trip in Boston for the weekend."

A person with a massive backpack bumped into Sahar's shoulder while they ran by her. She massaged the spot as an infant sobbed uncontrollably in their stroller up ahead. *Mood, kid.* It wasn't even noon yet, and the 42nd station was already roaring with tourists.

They stepped out into a bustling Times Square, a gorgeous day greeting them in spite of the muggy thickness and summer crowds. The faint breeze was, at the very least, helping her dress unstick from her body.

The four of them sprinted through the crowds silently until the sight of Amanda's Coffee, nestled at the end of 45th Street, brought him back to the forefront of her mind again. *Oh.* He'd invited her out, couldn't she do the same?

"Maybe I can ask Jay? Would that be cool with you lot? He might not even be able to come because his daughter's with him," Sahar suggested.

"Yes!" Willa answered too quickly.

Endearingly, Sahar rolled her eyes.

Ethan and Christian agreed with collective *sures* as they strode hurriedly through the busy crosswalk.

Christian swung open the door to the coffee shop, stepping aside to let everyone in first.

Jay's eyes flung toward them.

Ethan and Willa stepped to the register Molly was at, while Sahar went straight for Jay.

"Usual?" he asked, fighting a grin.

Sahar nodded. "Quick question: any plans tonight?"

"None outside of writing. El's staying at my mom's again for another sleepover."

He added in her order, and the keypad lit up with a number. *Good. He let her pay this time, keeping his word.* She tapped her phone and walked to the other side with him.

"Okay, so we're having a *Clue* game night, but I refuse to do so without six people. Wanna be our sixth? It'll be me, Wills, Ethan, Christian, and likely Miles."

Nodding, he seemed to be processing her invite. "Sure, what time?"

"Right after the show. When does your shift end?"

"In two hours."

"Oh, shit. You okay hanging around? You're welcome backstage if you'd like."

She noticed Willa moving closer from her peripheral. Once she was near, she propped her chin on Sahar's shoulder. "Please come. Sahar and Ethan scare me when a game's involved. Christian and Miles only enable. I need an objective third party who will be a little more mellow."

A barely there smile spread over his lips. "Yeah. Okay. Sounds good. I've got some errands to run, so I can meet you all afterward at the theatre."

Sahar took her drink from the counter, popped her straw in, and sipped. "Excellent!" Turning to Christian next, she asked, "Did Miles confirm?"

"Yes, ma'am. He'll be there."

Willa and Ethan grabbed their drinks from Molly, said bye, and walked toward the door.

Sahar looked back at Jay. "Just in case, I'm going to give our guards your name and information. If you finish your errands with too much time to kill, go to the stage door and come inside. You can at least wait indoors and away from the heat."

He acknowledged with a nod.

She could feel his gaze follow her as she walked out the door—wanted to turn back, *badly*—but she let the giddy anticipation of seeing him again be enough. This could be fun. Really *fun*. You could learn a lot about someone based on how they reacted to losing a board game. *Monopoly* could tear houses apart. *Clue* could, too.

And oddly, this wasn't as nerve-wracking as being alone with him. It'd also likely be a better outcome than her birthday last year, where Martin ruined a DnD party with his prissy attitude.

No matter how Jay behaved, she was sure it wouldn't be worse than Martin.

17

WILLA

The original plan had been to go over to Willa and Sahar's place, but Ethan had convinced everyone they should go to his instead because his dining room table was bigger, and he'd just bought a bunch of snacks. It worked conveniently because he also had a better variety of alcohol, and they'd ordered pizza from another favorite spot of theirs that was closer to his apartment in Manhattan.

After eating, they quickly set up the game table while Sahar threw the colorful character pawns in a bowl, and then went around the group. She stepped in front of Jay first. "Everyone, close your eyes and choose."

He regarded her first, a spark glinting in his gaze. Willa wondered if Sahar noticed it. Jay shut his eyes, dug his hand into the bowl, and picked Mr. Green.

Sahar moved to the others, Miles next, who chose Colonel Mustard. Willa rummaged inside the bowl, her longer nails making extra clicking sounds, and got Professor Plum. Ethan picked Miss Peacock. Christian took out the red totem for Miss Scarlet, leaving Sahar with Mrs. White.

"We all know the rules, yeah?" Sahar said.

"Yes, yes, let's go," Miles replied, chomping down aggressively on a hot Cheeto and gesturing for everyone to take their seats.

Christian took a swig of his beer. "And no one's allowed to help their partner win."

"Say my name, man. I'm the only one here who'd help their girl," Ethan bit back.

Puffing his chest, Christian jokingly stood in front of Ethan. "I was talking to you, double E."

Willa smiled and sat down. "Don't worry, Christian. I know there's no room for love in a game with him."

Miles barked out a laugh. Sahar smirked in their direction.

"Okay, but wait, what are we playing for?" Ethan asked.

"Does everything have to come with some sort of bet?" Willa contested.

"Yes," Sahar, Miles, and Christian all said at once.

Jay remained quiet. The poor guy. He had no idea what he was in for with this lot.

When they were all seated, Christian spoke. "The person to the left of you does whatever you want for a week." Pausing, he added, "Within reason, of course."

Sahar looked toward Jay. He gave her a wink. Ethan planted a quick kiss on the side of Willa's head.

Miles popped a few pieces of Old Bay-seasoned popcorn into his mouth as Christian began the game as Miss Scarlet. It got too loud too quickly with everyone but Willa jumping at each other's throats. Jay was also quieter than their wild circle, but he still participated.

Ethan had gone around the table with no one able to counter one of his guesses, and then, when Sahar finally did, he let out a loud grunt. "You'd suck at playing poker, Sahar. You don't hide shit. I knew it was going to be you," he said.

Shrugging, she let out a loud laugh. "Who says I'm trying to be subtle? I'm more than happy to gloat when I know you're about to lose."

Ethan shook his head, annoyed. Willa sardonically patted his shoulder. "There, there."

"Whose side are you on?" he fired back playfully.

She tried suppressing a laugh. "My own? I didn't think there were teams here, babe."

"And he claimed he wouldn't help his girl," Christian remarked.

"Shut it," Ethan returned, and then he handed the dice to Jay. "Your game."

The closeness between Jay and Sahar was unmistakable. How Sahar watched him with a look in her eyes Willa had never seen before with her other exes. How he watched *her*. He rolled the dice, decided to stay in place at the conservatory, and made a guess.

His body tilted toward Sahar, and his eyes spoke a distinct language with hers.

Jay was asking Sahar to show him a card—a play Willa knew well—but his body language, lax and languid, was a luminous sign of familiarity. A comfortable ease, stretching between them. She leaned closer to him, her hands concealing the card, angled underneath the table for his eyes only.

He glanced back at Sahar to confirm that he'd seen it, and she gave him a playful shrug, a smirk rising along her lips. Miles and Ethan jotted something down on their detective notes sheet. Willa probably should, too—the conservatory, wrench, or whatever. But Willa didn't care about winning.

She cared about the sight before her. The stark difference in how Jay looked at Sahar compared to how Martin looked at her. How, even though he was probably grumpier by default at the coffee shop, Jay fit in seamlessly around this table. He had an edge about him, but something comforting, too. He wasn't silently judging any of them or calculating how he could one-up them outside of observing the game.

But more importantly, he wasn't expecting anything from Sahar. Willa could tell as much and more from how he looked at her. From the ease in her friend's posture while she was around him. Sahar wasn't second-guessing her every move around Jay. She wasn't a shell of herself.

She was lively and open and free.

"I got it!" Miles nearly screamed. "I know who the killer is."

Christian threw a light punch at his shoulder. "Keep it in. You're wrong ninety percent of the time we play."

"This time, I'm right," he argued.

"If he wants to get himself eliminated, who are we to stop him?" Sahar added.

Ethan agreed. "Though I also want to get Sahar eliminated, I'm with her on this."

Sahar sneered at him, crumpling up her napkin and aiming it straight for his head.

Swerving, Ethan dodged it, and it fluttered lightly onto the floor.

"Control your man, Wills," Sahar joked.

Willa shrugged her shoulders. "Weren't we all ganging up on Miles? Why are you two fighting?" she asked, reaching for popcorn from the plate in front of her.

"She knows what she did," Ethan replied.

Wait, no, actually, now I'm lost. What did she do?

Willa let out a laugh. "Which was?"

Sahar took a sip of her whiskey sour and answered, "It's likely because I moved him out of the billiard room a few rounds back, and he's being a bitter numpty about it. But I'll be the bigger person here, E. Miles, hold that guess," she said.

"This is bullying," Miles retorted.

"It's not bullying if we're looking out for you, you idiot," said Christian.

Miles grimaced, fighting a smirk. "Fine, but I swear, if I lose because *you* stopped me, you're buying me lunch all week."

"Yeah, yeah," Christian agreed.

It was Willa's turn again. She landed on a six but opted out of moving from the kitchen. She made another random guess: Professor Plum, in the kitchen, with the wrench. She had the Professor Plum card; she knew that wasn't it. Again, she didn't care. Christian to her left couldn't show her a card, but Miles carefully showed her the kitchen.

Sahar giggled, making Jay's eyes dart longingly in her direction. The spark in his gaze might have been the most precious thing she'd bear witness to today. He'd turned to her like the sound of her laugh was his favorite song, and it just came on the radio. She was like sunlight cascading through a stained-glass window to him. A rare jewel. A monument. A renowned work of art. Something to stop and stare and marvel at.

"Oh, I've got this in the bag," Sahar singsonged.

Miles' brows shot up. "See, I knew you were cheating. You just wanted me *not* to beat you all."

They all laughed.

"It's not cheating just because you're bad at the game, boo," Sahar said.

Christian took the dice and rolled. He was in the study, taking four out of his five steps. He went into the hall.

Pursing his lips in thought, he guessed, "Miss Peacock, in the hall, with a revolver."

Ethan groaned, annoyed that his person would be moving from the ballroom to the hall. Miles couldn't show Christian a card to counter his guess, and neither could Sahar. Jay, however, had something, so the rest of them closed their eyes until he was done disputing Christian's guess from across the table.

Next, Miles rolled, landing on a three.

He took his totem, went in through the secret passageway into the study, and dramatically cleared his throat. "Accusation time, butternut squashes. Watch and learn. Mrs. White, in the study, with the revolver," he bit out.

He was surely right about Mrs. White and the revolver, but Willa was almost positive that someone must've had the study.

Miles closed his fingers over the confidential envelope and opened it. "Motherfucker!"

"That's what you get for accusing me of cheating," Sahar said, then threw a piece of hot Cheeto at him. With his ridiculously honed reflexes, Miles caught the crisp in his mouth.

Chewing and talking at the same time, he accepted his loss. "Fine, good luck without me. Where's Tulip, E? I'm going to bond with her."

Ethan shrugged. "Check the master bedroom. She usually hides there when people are over. If she's not there, check the guest room."

Miles got up and walked over to the bedroom, calling for Tulip with *pspspsps.*

They played two more rounds until the game came back to Sahar. First, she'd rolled and landed at a six, moving her totem out of the study; afterward, she landed on a three, putting her inside the library. If Willa was actually paying attention, she'd wager the library was now the objective. And if Sahar won, like some cosmic interference, her winning wages—whatever they may be—were tied to Jay.

Everything about this outcome was *already* glorious.

"Hey, Miles. Get your ass back in here. I want to see your face when I win," Sahar bellowed.

Willa turned to Ethan. "You think she's got this?"

"She'd never risk the loss," Ethan returned.

Jay was looking right at her, pride and excitement split evenly along his habitually stoic demeanor.

Miles walked back in with Tulip cuddled in his arms.

"Mrs. White, in the library, with the revolver," she declared, then turned to face Jay.

He shrugged his shoulders. The rest of the table couldn't give her anything either. Sahar picked out the contents of the envelope and flashed them on the table, indicating her win.

Grabbing her glass in hand and taking the final sip, she declared, "Victory tastes divine."

Sahar averted her gaze to Jay. "I feel like I can't even ask you for anything. You're changing your whole story for me."

That's right. His screenplay. Sahar's new favorite story. She wondered if anyone else at the table could tell what was happening, and knowing how they'd all reacted to her and Ethan, she assumed they *did.*

"Rules are rules. Your wish is my command," he promised.

Precious, Willa thought again. *These two.*

"I'll have to think about it," Sahar replied.

Miles shook his head then. "Nope, we need to go another round. Sahar can still be a winner, but someone else deserves a shot."

"And I'll probably win again," Sahar said.

"Let the record show that if Sahar hadn't taken me out of the billiard room early on, I would've had this," Ethan added.

Sarcastically, Sahar pouted and lowered her voice. "Sure, mate. If you need to believe that in order to sleep better at night, go on, keep telling yourself that."

Willa looped her arm around Ethan's neck and pulled him closer to kiss his cheek. "You're still a winner to me, babe."

He smiled, squeezing her thigh underneath the table.

"Aw, man, I miss my fiancé again," Christian said, looking at them with his head tilted.

"I also miss Dan," Sahar agreed. "Only one day of hanging out wasn't enough. He needs to be around more."

"End of September can't get here soon enough," Christian said.

Sahar faced Jay. "Dan's in LA filming a series. He's also a director."

Jay looked at Christian then. "Wait, it's not Dan Westley, is it?"

Christian's eyes grew wide. "You know him?"

Adjusting his glasses, Jay smiled. "Yeah. We worked on a short film together for a class project in NYU, and then again, for shits and giggles a few years back."

"Huh, it must be amazing to be off social media and not realize how many mutual connections you have," Sahar noted.

Willa sighed. "Oh, I'm so envious. I wish I could get off social media."

In a reassuring gesture, Ethan squeezed her thigh again.

"This is so rad. I need to text him and tell him," Christian said, then picked up his phone to do so.

Miles gently put Tulip down and came to where Sahar sat. "You can text him after," he said to Christian. "Let's get back to the game first. Everyone, switch seats," he added.

"It's not my spot that's lucky, mate. I'm just *that* good," Sahar volleyed.

Willa's eyes darted back to Jay. Once more, he was looking at Sahar like she hung the moon. As though he couldn't believe she was real—beside him. Did he realize he wore that look often around her? Did he know that a softness eclipsed his prickly edges every time she was around?

"Move," Miles repeated.

"Fine. Is that good with everyone else?" Sahar asked around.

They all nodded, dispersing around the table for different seats. Willa purposely wedged herself between Ethan and Christian, leaving another chair empty between Miles and Sahar, so Jay could sit next to her again.

While it was obvious he was growing comfortable around each of them, Willa also figured he would prefer to be beside Sahar. And her hypothesis proved to be true when he inched closer, whispering something in her ear. A quick conversation about how cute Tulip was sprawled on the floor distracted the others in a way that gave Jay and Sahar their own private moment.

Whatever he said must've been intriguing because Sahar's expression openly exhibited elation. There was an understanding between them, another small but significant detail that was theirs and theirs alone. Sahar turned, whispering something back.

His eyes crinkled at the edges, a smile reserved just for Sahar curling along his lips. It was impossible not to notice the effect she had on him. His arm had been resting on her chair, and Willa wondered if Sahar could tell—if she was aware of how Jay gravitated toward her with every tilt and movement.

She was the sun to Jay, and he tipped toward her light like there was nowhere else in the world he'd rather be.

Willa didn't know him well enough, but she knew Sahar. And the version of her she saw with Jay was the very same version of the woman who'd been her flatmate for six years now and her friend for an even longer stretch of time. She was bright and beaming, and in the company of someone who cherished the pieces of her she used to tuck away out of fear.

Jay respected Sahar enormously. There was no question about that. There was also no question about his intentions or motives either. Unlike Martin, he wasn't in this room to gain something. Jay wasn't sitting beside Sahar because she was a gorgeous woman he could later brag about to his friends.

He was here because the woman beside him asked him to come, and he couldn't say no to spending time with her.

Willa was sure of that, now more than ever. There was something special here. Awe-struck wonder sat at the center of his gaze, love letters and sonnets stretched to fill the small space between them.

18

SAHAR

After ordering their rides home, the five of them stepped out of the elevator and into the lobby of Ethan's apartment.

"Wills, want me to come and hold your hand at the dentist's tomorrow?" Sahar asked.

Miles swung the outside door open and held it. Willa walked out first, turning to face Sahar. "At nine in the morning? You love me that much, yeah?"

"I'd wake up at six in the bloody morning for you."

"You would. Honestly? Yes, please. Ethan offered, but I refused to let him. There are few places less romantic than the dentist's office."

"I'll be there then," Sahar declared.

She moved beside Jay, who'd been texting someone.

"I hope our chaotic little circle didn't scare you," she said to him.

The sound of his low laugh made her heart squeeze. "Not at all. You let me win that last round, didn't you?"

Her expression morphed into a half-gasp, half-smile. "I

would never. I zoned out for a bit halfway through because exhaustion got to me."

Jay smiled back at her. It felt so natural to be on the receiving end of his softer side. His warmth and the ease that she'd felt all night. Sahar was losing it, one look at a time. He was getting to her. If she weren't careful, if she didn't force herself to stop, she'd fall for him. She'd fall so hard and so deeply, no one would be able to pull her back up.

But *ugh*, he was making it impossible to stop. Impossible not to appreciate his every gaze and every move.

She thought of the way his knee bumped hers underneath the table, his denim jeans rough against her bare leg. A clandestine move. A deliberate choice. She thought of his whispers against her ear. His nearness. The scent of his cologne. How she wanted to tilt her head, and see if he'd taste like the whiskey sour, too.

If Henry and Katherine played Clue, do you think she'd let him win?

Is this you admitting that she would be better than him?

Oh, absolutely.

He'd asked her that question, sharing his characters with her in a way that felt so intimate—so vulnerable. Sharing his characters as though they were fragments of *them*—Jay and Sahar. She wondered, at that moment, if by admitting Katherine was better, he was talking about Sahar. It was a selfish, self-inserting, silly thought, but she couldn't help but think of it. The others had been gawking over Tulip—rightfully so—but she and Jay had been in their own little world. In *his* little world.

Sahar hugged her light cardigan tighter. The breeze and the goosebumps prickling her skin made the sticky summer night feel momentarily more frigid.

Her eyes flicked back up to Jay's as they stood, waiting. He held her gaze, warm and right.

More goosebumps. More butterflies. More uncertainties.

God, she couldn't do this again.

She couldn't. She couldn't. She couldn't.

He didn't run when he saw you throw the crisps at Miles, a reasonable part of her mind said. *He watched you and Ethan bicker, and he didn't tell you to calm down,* it added.

Another louder voice countered. *Yeah, but you aren't with him. It'd be different if you were his girlfriend. It'd be different when he feels embarrassed to be seen with you.*

Sahar could feel herself shrinking again. She looked away. She grew quiet.

The mosquito bite on her arm reminded her of its presence, so she picked at it, scratching gently. Willa had asked Jay a question about the syrup Amanda's Coffee used for her Irish cream latte preference, and it kick-started a whole topic on ingredients.

Sahar was grateful she could keep to herself for a beat.

A moment to collect herself.

A moment to still the butterflies.

A moment to contain every small flame trying to spread inside of her.

19
______

JAY

"Dad?" Eloise said, drawing his attention from the air-fried broccoli he'd been picking at on his plate.

Jay set his fork down and looked up at her, trying not to let the slight concern in her small voice make him nervous. "Yeah, baby."

"Would you ever live in Philadelphia with us?"

Jesus.

Of all the questions, he wasn't expecting that one.

A heavy lump grated in his throat. "I'm not sure, sweetheart. Maybe."

Eloise's face fell, the sorrow in her eyes breaking him. "The summer is almost over, and I'm just going to miss you a lot."

Jay closed his eyes, inhaling a deep breath. "We still have a little over a month, baby. But how about I promise to come visit more?"

"But what if your job doesn't let you?"

"I'll make sure it does," he reassured. "You're always going to be my priority, Ellie, you know that, right? Your mom and I would move mountains for you."

A faint smile crept up her lips. "You can't move mountains. It's impossible," she mumbled.

"It's a metaphor, you little nerd. It means there's nothing we wouldn't do for you."

Eloise twirled the spaghetti she'd requested for dinner with her fork. "How come you don't have a Gavin?"

Jay choked on a swallow. "A what now?" He knew exactly what she was asking, but Christ, why was she suddenly so inquisitive, and how on earth was he supposed to answer that?

"You know, like Gavin is for Mommy. Someone to marry."

"Maybe I don't want to get married," he said.

Eloise's eyes widened. "You don't?"

Okay, so that didn't work. How did he get himself in an even weirder bind? He thought about the answer some more.

"I mean, I do. I would, if I found the person I want to marry, but I haven't met her yet."

There, good save. Or is it?

But you have met her, his brain whispered.

And he already wanted Sahar more than he'd ever wanted anyone else.

"How do you find one?"

Jay blinked once, twice, three times. "Why's this topic suddenly a concern of yours?"

"I don't want you to be alone when I leave."

Put a dagger straight through my chest, kid. It'd hurt less.

He smiled, trying to conceal the sadness in his voice to give her little brain some semblance of comfort. "I don't want you to worry about me, baby. I'm fine."

"But you live all by yourself."

"Plenty of people live by themselves. It's normal when you're older."

She pouted, the expression in her gaze breaking him further.

"But what if you want to play video games or watch a movie and there's no one?"

It was a parent's job to worry about their kid, not the other way around. "That's what friends are for," he answered, trying to ease her with a different approach.

"But when you find someone to marry, can I meet them, too?"

Picking up his glass of water, he gently tapped her nose. "Your approval is the most important one I'll need, so, of course, I'll introduce you."

Her lips quirked upward, but the sadness in her eyes still lingered.

"Hey, how about you go get into your PJs, and we can play a whole level of the new *Shrek* game?"

Elatedly, she stuffed her remaining dinner into her mouth and bolted to her room while still chewing.

Thank God!

He flipped his phone back over from the table to quickly check his texts, surprised that there was one waiting for him from Sahar.

SAHAR

Finished reading ep 8 during intermission, literally lost my mind at Henry finding the letter from Katherine in his desk drawer. It hit me the first time, too, but the fact that you leave it at a cliffhanger here is going to make people FLIP. Also, please write the actual letter, Jay. I know you feel like it's better without the audience knowing what's inside, but can you at least show it to me!??!?

Jay laughed out loud. She was so fucking precious.

JAY

> Maybe we can show the audience a snippet of it. But the full letter will be for your eyes only.

Her eyes only. He could think of countless other things he wanted for her eyes only.

SAHAR

> YES! Try not to make me sob, though.

JAY

> I'll do my best.

Walking over to the sink, he quickly washed the two dishes he and Eloise used for dinner.

Jay had parts of the letter written; it was something he'd done even if the audience might not see it, but he hadn't dug into the whole thing. Like the ending, it was one of the more demanding parts of the story.

Katherine's romantic feelings were less explored than Henry's, but there, nonetheless. Jay often felt the urgency of them; he knew the weight of her pain and the depth of her strength, but he hadn't explored her headspace as intimately as he had Henry's.

Eloise ran over to the TV and turned on the gaming console. Jay sat beside her. "If it's easy, Dad, can we play two levels?"

He looked at her for a beat. Wide-eyed and eager with excitement. Maybe it wouldn't be the most awful thing in the world if this little firecracker followed in his footsteps. He was *sure* of the fact that her brain was a more thrilling place than his, anyway. Her capabilities would be boundless—her imagination, unmatched. More than anything, he *hoped* that there'd still be a space for real human beings and their inimitable minds by the time she was old enough to tell the stories she wanted.

She could change the world if she wanted to, and if he did miraculously get to a place where he succeeded in the industry, then he'd *ensure* that her journey would be easier than his. Suffering and hard work should never be mutually exclusive. She could work hard without her spirit breaking at every turn.

Pulling her close to him, Jay placed a kiss on the side of her head. "Yeah, baby, we can."

Two levels proved to be too much, but they still made solid progress in getting halfway through the second. After talking to Maya through FaceTime, Jay put Eloise to bed, sat at his kitchen table, and looked for the letter file.

He read over what he'd written so far.

Henry,

When you said that in your perfect world, you and I would be together, I couldn't say anything back. Even if you hadn't deflected or mentioned the risks our jobs entail, I don't know if I could've formed the words then and there. We've sat side by side in this office for three years, and in the beginning, I couldn't see through my grief. When Andy died, I never thought I'd find love again. I didn't think I could ever trust another person with every part of me. I'd lost the two most important people in my life. My mom and the man I was supposed to marry. I never thought I could open my heart to another person, but there you were, every single day, trying to make me laugh when all my wounds were still cut wide open.

I don't know if I'll actually give this to you. I think you know how I feel by now—you're better at reading me. You once swore you knew all my smiles. So maybe you know now. I really hope you know now. I think I'll leave this in your desk anyway. You rarely open that second drawer because everything you need is in the first one. By the time you find it, hopefully, this Archer case will be behind us, and we can maybe go get lunch again.

That was all he had, but Jay needed a hook. He needed something more poignant and profound—something emotionally evocative that Sahar would be proud of. Outside of *Cuts,* Jay rarely ever wrote from personal experience. He wrote the stories that came to him, but they were seldom things he'd experienced himself.

What would he say to Sahar if he wrote her a letter? How honest would he allow himself to be if she wasn't going to see it? He could do it—for the sake of a creative exercise and nothing more. Then, perhaps Katherine's point of view would come to him.

He remembered the significance of writing something by hand sometimes, how words could flow when he put pen to paper for the sake of notes or messy, untamed ideas.

He went over to the bookshelf anchored to a wall in his living room and pulled out the notebook he often used. Taking out a G2 Pilot .32 pen, he started writing the first word.

Sunshine.

That singular word encapsulated so much of who Sahar was to him that he almost hoped it'd be enough to divulge it all. It was too bad Henry rarely called Katherine anything other than her last name—sometimes, her first.

I thought you were the most beautiful woman I'd ever seen the first time you walked into the coffee shop. I spotted you right away, and I'm pretty sure I stopped breathing. I didn't take your order then; I was too nervous to. You came once more, then another time, and by your fourth visit, I'd finally plucked up the courage not to hide in the back. You had the brightest smile on. I could still drown in it. It's the one you wear every time you walk into the coffee shop.

But there was one day in particular.

He didn't want to think of that day. That godawful, horrific moment where he was so close to a panic attack that he could taste the bitter nausea in his throat even after all this time.

20

———

JAY

Five months ago. February

"Hello? Jay, are you listening?" He heard Nora ask before he managed to unfreeze his eyes from the noisy, barely functioning broken printer in the breakroom.

Every word out of every person's mouth sounded like nails on a fucking chalkboard today. She'd been saying something about Veronica.

Who the fuck cares?

"What about Veronica?" he asked, pretending to be invested, willing himself to pay attention because it was his job.

The job he was five seconds away from quitting.

"If Veronica keeps calling out, we're going to have to let her go. I've already warned her three times. I don't buy for a second that she's sick, and this is the fifth time she's done it on a Sunday."

A static sound came through his ear first, then Gillian spoke from the walkie-talkie. "Um, Jay, will you please come to the registers? A customer wants to speak to the manager."

Fucking hell. He blew out a heavy sigh.

Stepping out of the breakroom and into the front of the shop, he saw a man there, roughly around his height. A massive line behind him, too.

Dahlia was running around, trying to make drinks at a rapid speed. Harrison, too.

"What's the problem here?" he asked, utilizing every morsel of strength he had to keep his tone in check and not hurl an insult from the get-go.

A disgusting sneer was plastered on the man's face. "As I was telling this lovely little lady, I find it difficult to believe you're out of bagels and can't find me one. Don't think that a pretty face at the register can stop—"

Nope. This motherfucker.

"Was she not speaking English when she said that what's out is out, and we aren't a factory mass-producing bagels?" At this point, he didn't even care that his rage was palpable.

The customer's sneer deepened. "Excuse me?"

"What part of that was hard to grasp?" Jay bit back.

"Do you have any idea who I am? The type of clients I represent? You and your bitchy employees better show some respect."

A low, frustrated grunt ripped out of Jay as his fingers balled into a fist. Today of all fucking days. Swallowing back every curse he wanted to use, Jay gritted out, "I don't care who you are. You'll respect my employee and get out of this coffee shop before I kick you out."

"You're all rats here. Filth," the man spouted. "Put your money elsewhere, people," he announced to the remaining customers. And then he stormed off like a petulant child.

Jay could tell that Gillian sensed his agitation, so he willed himself to calm down and logged in at the register beside her. "Next guest," he called out.

A woman stepped forward, smiling with compassion. "I've worked retail. I get it," she said simply.

Jay didn't say anything. He couldn't. Everything in him was tense and tight.

She continued. "Can I just get a small vanilla latte with soy milk, please?"

"Sure, and your name?"

"Elena," she said.

Jay swallowed a lump in his throat.

February 11. The day that fucker hospitalized his mother. His mother, who was also named Elena, who deserved everything in the world, but instead, she got a son with an unstable career and rage consistently burning inside of him, as well as a daughter with a heart too big not to forgive.

His mother, who never expected anything from him, yet he was sure he still disappointed her anyway.

Blinking away the combating fury and pain, Jay wrote the woman's name on the plastic cup. His hand was shaking. She could probably see it.

After paying, she still kept her smile. He bobbed his head, attempting to show that there was a human being somewhere inside of him and not a monster fighting for control.

Except his hand wouldn't stop shaking. His chest tightened. And the bustling sounds of casual conversations were more akin to banshees screaming.

For a split second, his head spun.

It was too fucking loud—too overstimulating.

Gillian was speedily managing the line. He felt like he was moving at a snail's pace.

A customer stepped forward, a teenage boy named Lucas. He only wanted an iced tea.

There was one other person waiting afterward. He'd leave her for Gillian.

What was the point of writing and directing and fighting to create when he couldn't even captain the ache perpetually docked in his chest? What was the point of working at this dead-end job when he was miserable here, and he could be miserable elsewhere—in Philly, closer to Eloise at least? What was the point of chasing some silly childish dream to make movies because they were there for him when he was desperate and lonely and sad and needed an escape? What was he trying to accomplish, and if he hadn't already, shouldn't he consider it a sign that it wasn't in the cards for him?

Fuck all of this. Fuck the dreams. Fuck the hope. Fuck the pain.

He'd never been scared of the dark because he'd only ever known darkness. Light and joy were only ever around for three months out of the year—in the summer, when Eloise was with him. Sometimes, on the weekends, when he'd visit her.

Nora walked out behind him; the lines had been miraculously cleared. Two seconds of reprieve. It was all thanks to Gillian, Dahlia, and Harrison holding down the fort.

"Gillian, you can take your fifteen," Nora started, then she turned to him. "I heard you yelling out here, but I was on the phone. Jesus, Jay. I get that some people deserve it, but you have to try to keep your cool."

"That *was* me keeping my cool. Consider it a miracle I didn't curse him out," he argued.

An exasperated exhale left her lips. What was he exhausting her, too? There was actually no point to any of this. On this day, of all days, it felt like a huge fucking sign. It was time to go.

Another disappointing thing to call his mom about. *Hey, so I know today usually marks a tough anniversary for you since it's the day Grandpa died. And that asshole who should've been your loving husband simultaneously hospitalized you, but I also quit my job because I'm not man enough to make a name for myself.*

The tightness in his chest wouldn't let up. He was done. He was out. He was too damn tired and too damn weak.

Shaking her head at him, Nora turned, walking back into the breakroom. Jay opened his mouth to call out after her and say the words, but the shop's bell chimed.

And then he heard her voice—her *laugh*.

Drawing his eyes to where Sahar had just walked in, Jay breathed again. Big brown eyes and wavy, long brown hair falling freely, she had on an oversized rust and orange plaid coat.

Sahar stopped mid-conversation and looked right at him—the tail-end of her laugh still dangling at the edge of her voice. "Hi, Jay."

Sunshine. Sunshine. Sunshine.

It'd been a dark, gray morning. It'd been a horrible afternoon. It'd probably be a godawful night. But none of it mattered. Not at this second.

Not when his name falling from her lips sounded like solace.

Salvation, serenity, sweet, sweet sunlight.

Fuck.

Swallowing, he conjured a smile for her. "Hey, Sahar, Willa —the usual?"

"Hi," Willa waved.

Sahar answered for them. "Yes, please. You alright?"

He knew that was the British way of greeting, but a part of him still felt like she cared. Like she sincerely wanted to know. Like she wasn't just being polite. The smile on her face, still big and bright—*sunlight.*

This was how it always was with Sahar—she always acknowledged him. The other baristas, too, but *they* were the ones who bonded over football and video games.

He let out a low sigh. "Typical Sunday," he replied candidly.

She gave him an empathetic pout. It was the most adorable thing. "Ah, I'm sorry, mate. I hope the day eases up."

"Thanks," he said, the slight quiver in his voice still present. He hoped she didn't catch it.

But she must've because her eyes held a bewildering gaze. She looked like she wanted to say something, but she smiled instead. They moved to the other side of the counter after they'd paid.

Maybe he'd stick around for a little while longer here.

PRESENT DAY

It's terrifying being open like this.

Setting the pen down like it burned him, Jay shook his fingers and wrist. Writing the letter to Sahar took more out of him than he thought it would.

He felt pathetic. *Christ,* he needed to pull himself together. He could never say any of this to her. She'd probably laugh in his face. *No, she wouldn't.* She'd let him down gently instead. Sahar was too good and too lovely to ever be crude like that.

He tore the paper from the notepad, folded it into a square, and stared at it. What on earth was he supposed to do with it now? Where was he supposed to put it? Throwing it away felt wrong. Placing it somewhere where anyone could stumble upon it felt invasive.

And then it came to him. Standing up, Jay strode to the small table near the door where his keys and wallet were. He tucked the folded piece of paper inside his wallet, leaving it there for now until a better place came to him.

When he sat back down at the kitchen table, he willed himself to focus on Katherine's letter instead.

If we get through this, then I'll meet you at the spot where we had our first case together. You know the one. That's where I'll be.

His chest ached, and a hollow part of him ignited with an inexplicable sense of hope. How did he ever kill off Katherine in the first place? How had he allowed the story to end so somberly when he should've given them a happy ending instead?

It'd been so hard to tell this story before, but now, so much of it was beginning to make more sense. So much of it was starting to feel...right.

21

SAHAR

After she'd followed Alex on social media last week, Sahar had replied to a story about *Hatchard's Academy*, mentioning that if Martin was ever out, she'd want to come see the show again for Alex and Aisha. *If* it happened to be during their Thursday matinee, which Sahar could attend before going into work at night.

Last night, Alex had sent her a direct message saying Martin would be out from Wednesday to Saturday, which also worked in Sahar's favor because she had a PT appointment at noon that Jenny squeezed in for her at the last minute.

And since the *Clue* night, Sahar had begun feeling more comfortable hanging out with Jay. She'd mentioned the show, asking if he was free to join her. He was.

Stepping out of the Hyacinth Theatre after PT, she looked around the street, taking in the city's pulse in the early afternoon. Quiet, but loaded with the comforting boom that perpetually pounded from every building and passerby. An impact that could only be felt in the more secluded streets wedged in between the roaring Theatre District.

After a minute, she spotted Jay walking toward her, and the

black T-shirt clinging to his body made Sahar suddenly more aware of the thick humidity crawling up her back.

She strode forward, meeting him in the middle of the empty sidewalk, hilariously right in front of the promotional shot of her as Jane. The corners of his mouth hooked up in a beguiling closed-mouth smile, once more contrasting how Martin would approach her like she was the fucking guillotine. Not that she and Jay were anything but friends. Still, she liked the way he moved toward her—head held high, eyes locked on hers like there was nowhere else in the world he'd rather be. And with that, she was once more confronted with the reality that the sight of Jay outside the coffee shop was becoming a rare beat of comfort she wanted to pocket for safekeeping.

Winding his arm around her as he drew closer, he gave her a cursory side hug while simultaneously turning both their bodies back in the direction he came from.

"How was your shift?" Sahar asked, her body itching to be closer to his.

A grunt toppled out of him in response.

She laughed. "That bad?"

"I wouldn't even know where to begin. Was PT okay?"

His hand hovered over the small of her back as she stepped in front of him to avoid a group of people falling over each other in their path. Bending back while power-walking, she answered him with a "Yeah."

They rounded the corner, passing Summer Nori, and her heart thundered at the memory of their first time having lunch together. She looked over at him again, overwhelmed by his sharp, dangerously tempting features.

"Did you think of what I owe you?" he asked, deep baritone coated with a softness concocted specifically to travel through her bloodstream.

"I thought we decided it didn't count for us because you're

giving Henry and Katherine a happy ending for me. Plus, the letter," Sahar said, amusement spreading across her face.

Jay clicked his tongue. "Nah, that's not part of this. You gotta think of something."

You. Your mouth. Your hands. Every square inch. "Let me think about it," she returned.

Nodding his reply, he nudged her toward the queue for *Hatchard's Academy.*

The feeling of being here *with* Jay, knowing Martin wouldn't be anywhere in sight, was a bloody treat. Sometimes, the universe was good to her.

She was so excited to see Alex and Aisha perform—so jazzed to watch the show when she didn't have to deal with Martin's ridiculous comments afterward, like how he'd heard someone cheering too loudly during the bows and immediately assumed it was her. *It wasn't.* She knew better than to whistle and holler when he made her feel like shit for it. All his friends could do it, but God forbid Sahar had the same agency.

Jay broke her out of her thoughts with a whispered, "So, how are we embarrassing Alex?"

Sahar chortled. "She wouldn't hate it, would she?"

"Nah."

"I can whistle?" she offered.

A smirk rose along his lips. Everything in her came alive, immediately and all at once. "Hell yeah. So can I. And we've got to call her Alexandra. She'll love it."

"By love it do you mean she'll hate that part?"

"Absolutely. But deep down, she'll appreciate it."

Jay could whistle. Jay didn't hate the fact that she could.

～

THE SHOW WAS BETTER than she remembered it. The understudy for Martin's role was an ace, but more importantly, Alex and Aisha were incredible. They would've been perfect for the *Midnights at Pemberley* ensemble.

Standing in a secluded corner near the stage door, she and Jay waited for Alex to join them for lunch. Aisha was meant to as well, but cramps forced her to rest in her dressing room until the second performance.

Alex hopped out after a few short minutes and walked toward them. She hugged Sahar first, then her brother, and when they were face to face, her mouth flattened into a line. "So...uh, you know how I do that thing where I reply to texts in my head, but then forget to actually reply?"

Grumbling, Jay whipped his head in her direction. "What'd you do?"

"I completely forgot that Mom had offered to come down and have lunch with me today since Hayden and Jess took Ellie and the kids to Coney Island. I thought she'd meant next Thursday until she texted me asking what I wanted to eat."

Oh fuck. Spending time with Jay's sister, whom she was now following on social media and casually getting to know, versus meeting his mum was *not* on the day's agenda. Scratch that, it wasn't on the *month's* agenda.

Sahar alternated her gaze between the siblings.

"Sahar, I'm so sorry, will you still come? Our mom's super chill," Alex offered.

What's the big deal? You're not Jay's girlfriend or anything. It'd be more awkward if you were. It could be fun. See how he is with his mum.

"She really is." The look on Jay's face was nearly begging her to say yes. It'd be hilarious if it weren't so adorable.

Giving herself a moment to think, she said, "Sure. Mums

love me." *But will Jay's?* Her mind pestered. *Does it matter? Yes. Ugh.*

"I don't doubt it for a second, sunshine," Jay added, elation splayed across his entire face.

Sahar's eyes went wide, wondering if Alex caught the endearment and what she'd think of it.

She said nothing, but an identical smile to Jay's cascaded onto her face.

It definitely won't be casual if you blurt that out in front of your mother, she thought. *Maybe he's affectionate and has an endearment for everybody.* Jay? Of all people, the Jay she was getting to know would *not* be walking around calling everyone by a pet name.

Diverting, Sahar pivoted her attention back to Alex. "Well, show stopper, what do *you* want to eat?"

A blush crept up her cheeks. "I did want Raising Cane's, aka the only good thing about Times Square now. But Mom won't eat fast food. Any other suggestions?"

"There's a Spanish restaurant nearby, isn't there?" Jay aimed at Sahar.

"Yeah, Lucia's. It's a little closer to the Hyacinth," Sahar supplied.

Alex answered. "Ooh, I'm down. I'm sure she will be, too."

"Text her and tell her to meet in front of the coffee shop instead. We can walk with her," Jay said. "And hit send," he punctuated.

Alex looked down at her phone, and then up again, pointing to a woman walking toward them. "We can just tell her ourselves," she noted.

Sahar glanced at the blonde woman as she stepped toward them. *Oh.* Alex was a carbon copy of her mum, except with darker hair. A low wave of anxiety crashed over Sahar, small yet obvious, nevertheless. She'd briefly met Martin's mum at the opening night of *Hatchard's Academy,* but outside of a quick hello, she hadn't bothered to actually speak to her during the rest of the night, even as Sahar made the effort. His dad had been sick at home, so Sahar had brushed off Mrs. Tucker's indifference, thinking maybe she would've preferred to have been there with her husband instead.

Looking up at Jay, he had his eyes tethered on hers, a glimmer resting at the center of his gaze.

She smiled at the woman who was now hugging her daughter.

As his mum turned to face them, Jay's arm hovered over her back. "Mom, this is our friend Sahar," he introduced.

Sahar extended her right hand forward, and the older woman did the same. "Hi, it's so very nice to meet you!"

Joy spread across her face, and something about the look in her eyes reminded her of her own mother's warmth. Of Alex's kindness on the first day they met. "Lovely to meet you, Sahar."

"I'm an idiot. I completely forgot that I made two different plans," Alex interjected.

Their mother rolled her eyes fondly. "In that case, where were you all off to?"

"There's a Spanish place nearby we can go to," Jay said.

Nodding, she gestured for them to lead the way.

THEY SAT at a small booth nestled toward the back of the restaurant, surrounded by red brick walls and cushy leather seating. Jay sat across from Sahar and next to his mum, while Alex was beside Sahar. After ordering and some small talk about Alex's inability to text properly, their mother, whom Sahar learned was named Elena, mentioned that she'd worked with the director of *Midnights at Pemberley* back when they were younger and she was on Broadway.

"Oh, that's wicked. I can't believe you know Jeff. He's my favorite director I've had so far."

Jay's mum smiled, but the heartbreak in her eyes was unmistakable. Sahar hadn't known the full extent of her story apart from what she had just told her, so it felt far too private to ask why she'd left the industry behind. Still, she wondered if it was tied to her ex-husband. "Yeah, he and Greta have been inseparable since they first met at Juilliard. Everyone knew they'd make it big. And *together*," she underscored.

"They really are a dream to work with," Sahar agreed.

Alex popped a fried chicken croquette into her mouth from beside Sahar. "Better than the deadbeats running my show," she bit out.

"Alexandra," their mother chided.

"You hate them, too."

"Yes, but we're in public."

Jay let out a low grunt.

"I didn't say it loud enough for anyone to hear," Alex rebutted.

Smiling, Sahar looked back at the older woman, changing the subject. "So, I have to know: which of them was the bigger troublemaker?" she joked.

Elena laughed, taking a sip of her lemonade. "That little menace sitting next to you. She had so much energy as a kid. I never knew what to do with her."

Sahar held out her hand to Alex in a high-five gesture. "So was I, apparently."

"She once brought home a box of stray kittens from God knows where and insisted that we name them all Alex," Jay added.

Chewing on her paella, Alex mumbled, "Don't pretend you didn't get sad when we couldn't keep them."

"Sure, but I didn't want to name them all Alex."

"That's because you suck at naming things. We can all thank Maya that Eloise is an adorable name."

Sahar nudged his foot underneath the table, catching his attention. "So you weren't being humble about being bad at names and titles."

"I most certainly was not," he said, a subtle smile flirting with the corners of his mouth as he kicked her foot right back.

Eyes fixed back at their mum, Sahar added. "What about Jay? Was he quieter?"

"Definitely more than Alex. But he got in trouble in different ways. Getting him to do homework was a chore all throughout his school years. And he had a picky eating stage that drove me crazy."

Sahar's jaw dropped. "Really? The homework, I can imagine, but you don't seem picky at all," she aimed at him.

"I wasn't picky," he argued.

"You refused to eat anything but mac and cheese for two whole months. I couldn't even sneak in a single vegetable, or you'd refuse to eat it."

"When?"

Pursing her lips up in thought, she answered after a few seconds. "I want to say you were about five or six."

"I don't remember that," Jay supplied.

"Yeah, you got better with food as you grew older, but your palate consisted of very little. It was deeply concerning for a while."

He leaned back in the booth, taking a fry in his mouth. The side of his knee brushed against Sahar's, and whether intentional or not, the familiarity made her heart flutter. Every single part of this lunch should've been awkward, and yet, it wasn't. Not even a little. Was this how he felt with her friends the other night? *She hoped.*

"Thank God Ellie isn't picky since none of you ever get Taco Bell with me."

Disgust parked itself at the center of Jay's face. "Why would I go to Taco Bell when I can get better Mexican food five minutes away from my house?"

"Best of both worlds. Live a little."

He rolled his eyes.

Sahar laughed.

Elena's voice echoed through the siblings' bickering. "Enough about you two. What about you, Sahar? Do you miss England while you're here?"

"Loads, yeah. I miss my family and my mum's cooking. There are some decent Persian restaurants here, but they don't compare to her dishes."

"Oh, I'm sure. This one refuses to eat any Greek food that isn't mine," she said, pointing to Alex.

Alex agreed. "Only in Greece, if we get to go together."

"Were you born there?" Sahar asked Elena.

"Yes, my family immigrated to the States when I was seven."

Smiling, Sahar added, "I love that. My uncle's family now lives in Greece. I've always wanted to visit."

"It's a magical country, though I haven't been back in many years."

Again, it wasn't her place to wonder whether it was because of her ex-husband, but she couldn't help but think that it might be. Every sad, heartbreaking look felt like it was somehow linked to him. It contrasted with her own family's relationship because one of the first things her father did when marrying her mother was visit Tehran to see where she'd grown up. He had also been the one to insist that both Sahar and Amina have Iranian names, allowing their mother to choose.

"I hope you get to go back soon. You, too, Alex," she said finally.

Alex grinned.

Jay tapped his knee against hers again, like their own secret little language.

Hi.

Hi back.

Fighting back a smile, she attempted to calm the emotions threatening to escape from the cage she was desperate to keep them barred in. She wanted to ask his mother a thousand questions—get to know *him* more. Their whole family.

Elena bit into a croquette, eyes fixed on her son. "Have you heard from Ellie?"

"No. She forgets I exist when there are other kids around. I texted Hayden, though. He says she's doing great and sent a photo."

"You're so dramatic. She doesn't forget you. And show us!" Alex declared.

It registered to Sahar at that moment that she had no idea what Jay's daughter looked like. Opening his phone to the photograph, he slid it across the table between Alex and Sahar.

"Her smile kills me," Alex announced, voice slightly pitched.

Of the two little girls, Sahar could safely guess which one was Eloise, but she didn't want to assume. "Is she the brunette?"

Jay nodded.

Alex brought her thumb and index finger to the screen, zooming in. "I die for her. Isn't she the cutest?"

"Aww, she really is." Gazing up at him, she added, "She has your eyes, Jay."

He pushed his glasses up the bridge of his nose. "Hopefully not my eyesight."

Sahar's smile morphed into a sympathetic pout.

"Do you have plans after this?" his mother asked him.

He shook his head. "No, I'm heading home. Why?"

"If you'll be home then, I might pop into Astoria to see Donna."

Jay nodded, his knee still brushing against Sahar's underneath the table. "You should. I'll pick up Ellie when they're back."

"And I must go back to a job I hate," Alex started, paused, then said, "Sorry, I know I should be grateful in this economy, but I'm miserable."

A low sigh fled from Jay, accompanied by an empathetic glance from their mother.

Sahar pivoted her gaze to the girl beside her, resting her elbow against the table. "You're allowed to complain if it's sucking the life out of you. We can't always win in this industry."

"Yeah," was all Alex managed to say.

A comfortable silence lapsed between them as yet another spark of gratitude flickered in Sahar.

She loved her job.

She loved her friends.

And for a heartbeat, she allowed herself to wonder what it'd be like if present company also remained a part of her life.

22

SAHAR

They'd agreed to meet in front of the Hyacinth, from where they'd go down to Stonewall Theatre together. She'd been texting him from the subway station, but when Sahar turned the corner on 45th Street and spotted Jay, her heart did a little trot.

Since the *Clue* night last Sunday and the lunch with his mom and sister on Thursday, she'd spent every day trying to veer away from any and all wishful thoughts that wedged themselves into the forefront of her mind.

His smile, his voice—the way his eyes held hers. Every text conversation they had afterward. His mouth, his body—the way his knee would brush against hers underneath tables.

Stop fighting it. Give in.

He'd swapped his glasses for contacts and wore an all-black dress shirt and black jeans. *He looked good.* Too bloody good. To be fair, Jay always looked good, but it all felt different now. She could spot the bracelet that Eloise had made him next to his watch, and it was so freaking precious that he continued to wear it, even with business casual attire.

Drawing his eyes away from the building on the other side of the street, Jay caught her nearness. His gaze darted to her with a shimmer that his glasses often hid.

Sahar wanted to hug him, wrap her arms around his large frame, and feel the warmth of his body against hers. And not in a fleeting embrace. No, she wanted to hold on. She wanted to inhale the scent of his cologne, cedar and something musky she couldn't place, along with the bit of coffee that clung to him. As a palpable reminder of work every time he left, Jay probably hated that part. But it worked for him. It worked for *her*.

Given everything that had transpired in the past week, she wondered if the day felt different for him, too. This wasn't a date—not the conventional kind—but she was his plus one, wasn't she? That had to count for something.

The way he looked, *leaning* against the wall. No one should look *that* good in the simple act of leaning.

Striding closer, she didn't second-guess herself. Sahar inched forward, circling her arms around his neck. He wrapped his arm around her waist with a tight squeeze, making everything in her burn from his touch.

They parted too quickly again.

She wanted to keep holding on.

"Hi," she said.

The smile tugging at the corners of his mouth deepened. "Hi."

A stillness extended out into the air. An intimacy. A comfort. Something visceral she could feel all around her.

"I'm not late, am I? Were you waiting long?" Sahar added.

He shook his head amiably. "Not at all. I got here about five minutes ago." Jay's eyes mapped her frame before he spoke again. "You look really nice."

A blush heated her cheeks. "Yeah?"

"Yeah," he repeated, his smile wider. Then he added, "Subway or a ride?"

"If I get a say in the matter, ride, please. Bad ankle and heels are seldom a wise combination. I didn't want to ruin the outfit with a tote and extra shoes." Courtesy of Willa's styling, Sahar wore a pair of light-wash, high-waisted straight-leg jeans, a white silk cami, and a dark purple, oversized blazer, with four-inch white pumps.

Pulling out his phone, Jay nodded with understanding.

And while she was wearing said four-inch heels, he was still taller than her. His body, toned and lean. *Stop ogling him.* His beard was more of a scruff now, and so wildly hot as it accentuated his bone structure.

God, he was *fit*—so devastatingly attractive. Yet, it wasn't only the physical with Jay—it was knowing what went beyond his edges. It was the glimpses she had into his heart. His goodness. His patience.

"How was work today?" Sahar asked, brushing away thoughts of her attraction to him aside.

"I didn't go in. I'd taken it off, so I spent the day with Ellie, then came straight here when I dropped her off at my mom's."

"Bet she loved it."

He beamed at her. "She demolished me in a game of chess twice, so I'm sure she did."

"Did you say chess?"

"I did."

"That's brilliant. My uncle tried to teach me once when I was like fifteen, and I almost cried because I couldn't fully process the rules."

A low laugh left his lips. "Are you one of those people who has to get something right the first time, or you'll get frustrated and feel like a failure?"

"I think you can safely guess the answer to that."

He could probably guess the answer to many things about her.

Jay had sent her the letter from Katherine two days ago. She'd wept over it and texted him right away to thank him. It was easy to gush over his words. It was seamless communicating with him when the topic of discussion wasn't the sparks detonating between them. But he had to feel it, too, didn't he? How intimate it all felt now? How, despite the sticky heat and makeup, the red staining her cheeks was an effect of how he looked at her.

"There are a few things I can't guess," he said finally, his voice low with gravel.

Jay and Sahar stood so close together that onlookers would surely mistake them for a couple. All she had to do was move a fraction, and her shoulder would be touching his.

Something had shifted.

A warmth stretched between them.

Their gazes locked.

He was staring. So was she.

"Like what?" Sahar asked.

He inhaled, eyes narrowing in thought. She heard the engine of a car approaching, shifting both their attention off each other and onto his open phone.

Blowing out an exhale, he veered toward the silver Kia Odyssey. Jay opened the door for her, guiding her inside with his hand at the small of her back. The goosebumps, the butterflies —every ember inside of her came alive. Again and again and again.

Her burning question was left lingering in the air as they mostly sat in silence inside the Uber. Everything else would come later. *Maybe.*

. . .

Midway through the film, she realized that the random chap beside her kept leering at her. It was discomforting, so she readjusted her position, scooting closer to Jay.

Catching her movement, he quickly averted his gaze from the screen and noticed what had been happening. He eyed the man, explicit irritation coating his glare, and dropped his hand possessively to Sahar's knee. The chap's head immediately swerved toward the film.

Encouraged by their slight predicament, she took it one step further, placing her hand atop his and sliding her thumb across his knuckles. Jay looked down, then back up at her. Their eyes locked again. An inhale, an exhale. He smiled, scattering warmth and comfort all over her.

She smiled back, then turned toward the screen.

At the after-party held at the Bill Hotel across from the theatre, Jay's hand remained stabilized at the small of her back. He'd spotted his friend, Pete, the director, first and wanted to introduce Sahar to him.

"Jay!" Pete bellowed. He was a cheery man, perhaps somewhere in his early forties.

The two of them clapped each other affably on the shoulder.

"Man, I'm so proud of you. You've done such an unforgettable job with this one," Jay declared. And then he turned, introducing Pete to Sahar. "This is Sahar; she's the sole reason I haven't lost my damn mind with my latest project. Sahar, Peter. Pete and I are old friends from undergrad. He was also one of the executive producers of *Cuts.*"

Sahar's eyes lit up at the mention of *Cuts.* She'd think back on how fondly Jay introduced her later. Pete reached for her hand, shaking it with a hearty grip. "It's so nice to meet you. And Jay's right. The film is so very lovely. You should be so proud!"

He held his hand to his chest. "Ah, shit. *You two.* Thank you.

And it's so nice to meet you, Sahar. You look so familiar." He eyed her as though he were attempting to figure out how.

"She *is* a Tony-nominated star whose face is on buses around the city," Jay said.

Pete's eyes widened, putting two and two together. "*Midnights at Pemberley!*" he declared.

Sahar blushed, giving him a closed-mouth smile. "Yeah."

"With Sam," Pete added, looking around the small, reserved ballroom that had been crowded with people. "My wife and I came to one of the pre-shows."

"The very one, yeah. Did you?"

"We'd been in such a hurry that day, we couldn't stick around. Otherwise, I would've made Sam introduce me to everyone there. But thank you so much for coming tonight. It means so much to me," he said. "*Both* of you."

Sahar smiled. Jay gave him another pat on the shoulder. "Proud of you, man."

When Pete walked away to talk to someone else, Sahar turned back to Jay. "Well, he was a delight."

"He's such a good guy," Jay confirmed. "And he's been working so hard for so many years. He deserves all the attention for this movie."

"It was phenomenal. And that ending? You *know* what made it so special, don't you, Jay?"

He tried and failed to fight against the smile curling up his lips. "They each make it back to Franklin Street?" he questioned, surely knowing it was the exact answer Sahar was looking for.

"Wounded and battle-worn but *together*. A whole family torn apart, but back from the trenches where they belong."

Draping his arm over her shoulder, he pulled her to him. It felt so natural, so familiar.

She squeezed his waist. "Admit I'm right."

The low laugh diving out of his mouth landed right into her belly. "You're right, sunshine. You know you are."

She scrunched her face giddily. "I know. I just wanted to hear you say it."

His jaw flexed, he was biting the inside of his cheek. She wanted to press her mouth to the crooked smirk his lips created. *Fuck.*

Quickly looking away, she spotted Sam and Priya amidst the crowd, animatedly talking to three people. They noticed her and Jay, then parted from their friends and walked toward them.

Priya stretched out her arms to Sahar. "Hot damn, you regal beauty. Purple looks so good on you! I'm obsessed."

"Look who's talking! But I'll pass the compliments to my stylist," Sahar said, hugging her back.

"Wills?" Priya specified.

Sahar nodded. "You know it."

"Our girl is so good."

"The best."

Then, Priya turned to say hi to Jay. Sam gave Sahar a questioning smile, but mostly behaved himself. She was screwed if he started suspecting that she was interested in Jay.

Priya looked from Sam to Jay. "There are drinks right at that table," she pointed. "Would you two be the dolls that you are and get us some?"

Smiling, the men both obliged.

Priya nearly screeched when they were out of earshot. "Sahar, what the actual fuck? You two are so hot together."

A blush flared Sahar's cheeks. "So, I'm about five seconds away from kissing him and jumping his bones. Can you tell?"

Priya chortled. "I mean, he probably wants to do the same. Don't think I didn't notice how he had his arm over your shoulder and then down at your back as you walked toward us."

"You know I'm trying so hard not to rush into something, but it gets harder by the second with him, Pri," Sahar added.

"He's a total catch, babe. Physically and everything in between. Sam has a lot of respect for him. If he knew you were into him, he would've been plotting how to get the two of you together himself."

Sahar blew out a sigh. "Oh, lord. Of course, he would. *Please* don't say anything. *If* he asks after today, dodge it."

"I'll do my best. My husband and self-control do *not* go together. The only reason he didn't intervene in Willa and Ethan's relationship was because he knew those goons were always together, and it was only a matter of time. If he knew you were into Jay, he'd be planning shit left and right to get you two in the same room. And respectfully, I'm too exhausted to host anything for the rest of the summer."

Priya must've noticed them coming back. "And with that, I say, to hell with trying so hard. Take what you want." She drew closer and wrapped her arms around Sahar's neck. "I'll bet he's waiting for your move." And then she spun them both to face the guys with a huge smile, as though they weren't just talking about Sahar wanting to shag Jay.

23

SAHAR

The Bill Hotel's entrance wasn't as crowded as the rest of the streets in Manhattan were, but it was still loud —full and alive. The air was thick and muggy and uncomfortable, and yet... All she was acutely aware of was every emotion inside of her demanding to be *felt*. Expanding. Spreading. Impossible to ignore.

It was wild how nights like this, specifically in the summertime, always felt like a thousand things at once. Enigmas and answers. Permanent yet simultaneously fleeting. *Hopeful.*

And she knew that Jay felt it, too. She could see the same tapestry of emotions woven into his gaze.

Sahar knew, without a shred of doubt, that if she leaned forward and kissed him, he wouldn't push her away. He'd welcome it. He'd probably taste like the gin and tonic she'd also had.

It might not last, but it could still be lovely. It could heal you, even if another part of you dies. Maybe just for tonight.

Tonight and before, Sahar knew that most of her longings stemmed from how Jay had been with her. How he'd introduced her to his friends and colleagues like she was someone worthy and special, instead of the afterthought she had been to Martin.

Jay wanted the people who didn't know her name to remember it. He'd even corrected someone who'd misheard or simply didn't care enough to retain that Sahar and Sahara were two different names.

His meticulous attention meant something.

It meant *everything*.

His hand, at the small of her back. The way he leaned a little forward every time they spoke. His arm, around her shoulder. The way he held her gaze every time he looked at her.

He'd said he'd take her home first, make sure she got there safe, but what if he didn't have to leave her?

What if he stayed?

Sahar flicked her eyes from the ground and up toward his gaze. Jay was already looking at her.

"Jay," she whispered.

A delectable hum reverberated from his throat, emboldening her.

Stepping closer, she brushed her fingers along his bicep, down to his forearm, and up again. Slow, sweeping slides as he watched her, his eyes tracking every movement. "Willa's gonna be at Ethan's tonight. Would you like to come over for drinks? Maybe a round of *Dread Quest* or..." she trailed off, pale-pink nails still grazing gently across his skin.

Jay brought his thumb and forefinger to her chin, tipping her eyes up from his arm and onto his face. "Or what?"

Biting down on her bottom lip, she desperately wished it were his. Here. *Now*. "I think you *know* what."

"Maybe I want to hear you say it." Jay's already deep voice had dropped an octave lower, desires playing on his face like a kaleidoscope.

Warmth enveloped her, compressing the small space remaining between them. Sahar briefly scanned the entryway they stood in. If they were anywhere else, she would've flung her arms around him and kissed him. But she wanted to have him outside of Manhattan, somewhere quiet and not as bustling. Though maybe they'd end up in some passerby's photograph, immortalized as a tangible memory if they didn't last beyond this point of endless possibilities.

Looping one arm slowly around his neck, she leaned fully into him. "Maybe I want you to kiss me," Sahar whispered in his ear.

Jay wrapped an arm around her waist, clutching her firmly, as she caught the word *fuck* harnessing deliciously in his throat.

"Or that," she agreed, her tone a bit more cheeky, looser.

He darted his eyes from her to the oncoming car that'd pulled into the lot, letting out another low curse. "Ride's here."

Sighing, she released her hand from his neck, but Jay didn't let go of her waist. Instead, he once more guided her to the car and opened the door.

While inside, Sahar laced their fingers together, squeezing. He welcomed her gesture by lifting their hands to his lips, and the tender press of his mouth to the back of her hand made her heart swoop.

The car's obnoxiously loud air conditioning and Fleetwood Mac's "Go Your Own Way" blared through the speakers, the lyrics making her momentarily second-guess it all. Jay, Martin— her present and her past. Her future.

What was *she* meant to learn from all her former relationships? Why did so much heartbreak always find her? Over and over and over again. And had Jay ever gone through heartbreak as numbing? Had he lain awake at night, questioning why he wasn't ever enough for someone? Had he ever wondered if he was too much for people to handle?

Someone honked their horn repeatedly, pulling her out of her thoughts. She looked up at him again. His gaze hadn't left hers. As though catching her mental spiral, he mouthed the words, *"You okay?"*

Sahar nodded. She needed to be. She *wanted* to be.

Late-night text messages and quick conversations at the coffee shop were no longer enough. She wanted more of him, however ephemeral their moment would be.

She wasn't in love. He couldn't break her heart after one night, no matter how great a kisser he turned out to be.

He couldn't shatter her spirit this early on.

After arriving at her apartment and getting out of the Uber, they'd been quiet in the elevator, his hands in his pockets. Tension rose with every floor. She fumbled with the keys for a split second before pushing the old, white wooden door open. Inside, Sahar kicked off her heels and footed them away toward the front of their shoe rack.

Turning back to Jay, she locked her eyes with his. "Do you want something to drink?" she asked.

"Not exactly," he said, mere millimeters away from her.

She smirked, narrowing her eyes. Every fragment of her magnetized toward him. Pulling. *Begging.*

Sahar closed the distance between them, and Jay's hand flew to her cheek, cupping her face as he pressed his lips to hers. It was slow at first, luscious. Staggering tugs and gentle sweeps.

Jay kissed her like she was air—a lifeline.

Hope. Sanctuary. Something sacred etched in his every move.

It was electrifying, so very right in a way that surpassed the workings of her wildest imagination. Their breaths grew heavier, heat rising between them like rapid fire.

He wrapped one arm around her waist, walking her backward against the door, where he pinned her body with the lightest of thuds.

They stayed pressed to each other for a brilliant beat—kissing, tasting, savoring. His tongue waltzed with hers like they'd been partners for years, trained and honed so intimately that there was no routine too complex for them to master.

She bit his bottom lip, and he groaned in response.

Tucked in between the wood and his large frame, her world burned hotter than the summer heat.

Jay's lips traveled down to her jaw, toward the curve of her neck, where he placed an open-mouthed kiss at her pulse point, making her entire body scorch. A low moan bounced from her throat when he bit down and sucked at the same spot.

Sahar felt him hardening against her, and her nipples tightened in response, everything in her demanding for more. *Leave a mark. Please.*

His kisses grew needier, matching her own wants in an equal race they were both set on winning.

Another slow sweep of his tongue along her lips, a bite and a kiss like it'd been a constant with them. Sahar slid her fingers into his shirt and dragged them up along his torso where hard planes of muscle clenched beneath her touch. She wanted to press her tongue along the ridges there, bite down, and chase the sting with kisses every time.

He seized her mouth again, once, twice, three times. Familiar. Frenzied. Freeing.

Dropping his forehead to hers, he blew out a heavy breath. "God, Sahar. I want you so bad."

She crawled her hands around his back, ready to yank the bloody dress shirt off him. There were too many layers between them. "Is that not what's happening here?" she asked, dropping a small kiss along the bridge of his nose.

Jay sighed, something unreadable appearing in his eyes. Palming her cheek with the most delicately mind-melting touch, he said, "But what is *this*? I can't just fuck you and walk away. I've wanted you for too long now."

Oh. She wasn't sure what she expected him to say, but it certainly wasn't *that.*

"I don't... I don't know," Sahar tried to say. "I don't want it to be a one-time thing, but I'm also not sure *what* I want." A flicker of sadness squared itself in his gaze.

She drew her fingers out of his shirt and curled them around the nape of his neck.

Meet him halfway, her heart and body pleaded. *Try. One more time.* She ran her fingers into the short strands of his hair, holding his gaze. "What I *do* know is that I like you, Jay. So, whatever this is, it's certainly not meaningless. Can we just... figure the rest out later?"

He placed a quick peck on her lips. "Yeah. We can." Another kiss, deeper this time.

Parting, Sahar added, "I'm also on the pill, and I trust you, so whether you'd like to use a condom or not is up to you."

He nodded, locking his eyes with her once more before skating his lips back down to her neck, toward her collarbone.

Lifting his hands underneath the shoulder of the purple blazer she wore, Jay tugged it off and set it down on the small, glass-top gold table near the door. He lowered a strap down and kissed her bare shoulder blade in a slow, deliberate manner, making her heart do some sort of delicious twist. He repeated the same dizzying motion on the other side.

Between the subtle scrape of his scruff and the softness of his lips, Sahar was sure that being kissed by Jay would swiftly become a safe harbor she'd always return to.

A moan tumbled out of her when his tongue darted back

into her mouth again. He pushed up against her—the brief stroke of friction already substantial. Her head fell back against the door as his hands wrapped around her backside, kneading her ass.

And then, he stopped.

She heard the vibration coming from his back pocket. "I'm so sorry. My phone's always on do-not-disturb, and the only people that bypass that are family."

"No, no, of course, take it."

Steadying his breathing, Jay plucked his phone out and answered.

"Mom, hey."

She couldn't exactly make out every word coming from the other end of the line and felt wrong for listening, but when Jay's face fell, hers did, too. Something about a fever and everything's fine, she deciphered.

"Why didn't you call me sooner?" he said, frustration obvious in his tone. A few short seconds, and then an "Okay, I'll be there soon."

When he hung up and placed his phone away, Jay looked at her, distress eclipsing what had been fervent longing in his eyes.

Delicately, Sahar cupped his cheek. "Is everything okay?"

He leaned into her touch. "Ellie has a fever. She's fine, but... I had a feeling she was off before I left, and I figured she was just tired. I don't know how I didn't notice it."

"The poor thing. I'm so sorry, Jay, but please don't berate yourself for not catching it earlier. Fatigue doesn't always signal an incoming illness."

A heavy sigh left his lips. "She fell asleep, but I should be there in case she wakes up."

Sahar tried to give him some sort of reassuring smile, but his sad eyes made it nearly impossible to get through. "Of course. Text me when you get there and let me know how she is, yeah?"

He inched forward and pressed his lips to her forehead. "Okay. We'll talk soon?" he phrased it like a question.

Brushing her nose along his, she touched her forehead to his. "Yeah," she promised.

And then he left.

24

JAY

When Maya assured him she wasn't worried and that Eloise would be fine, Jay calmed a bit. He knew logically that kids were tiny germ magnets and that colds weren't all that shocking, but still. For an agonizing few minutes, his mind attempted to put all the blame on himself, state how he should've noticed that something was off about her, and that if he hadn't been so selfishly preoccupied, he most definitely would have.

During the uncomfortably long train ride, he'd called the two other morning managers and had his shift for tomorrow covered. Then, to distract himself, he emailed Patrick updates on the rewrites.

Coming in through the back door from inside their garage, he walked in on his mom and sister drinking tea in the kitchen.

"You didn't have to rush over here, honey. I told you she's okay," his mom said.

"Is she asleep? Did you check her fever again after you gave her Tylenol?"

She set her glass mug down, irritation making its way onto her face. "Did you forget that I raised two perfectly healthy children?" she countered, matching the attitude he didn't realize he was projecting in tone.

"Mom," he bit back, his voice once again unintentionally harsher than he intended.

She arched an eyebrow. In all thirty-four years of his life, his mother never yelled at him. But with a single look, she knew *exactly* how to guarantee that her kids grasped their mistakes.

Alex answered for her. "Obviously, she did."

Shutting his eyes briefly, he took a breath. "I'm sorry. You know it freaks me out when something's wrong with her."

"And that's why I told you to come here instead of going home, so keep your tone in check."

He drew closer and placed a kiss on the side of her head. "I'm sorry," he repeated. "I love you."

"Love you more. Did you eat? Are you hungry?"

Jay sauntered over to the kitchen sink and washed his hands there. "I'm fine. Thanks, though."

"Was the final cut of the movie good?" He heard Alex ask.

"Yeah, it was. I think you'll like it. Sahar did," he answered.

He dried his hands on the dish towel hanging from the stove and turned to go see Eloise.

"Nice," Alex declared.

Their mother didn't say anything, and he was glad for it. Apart from stating that she thought Sahar was sweet after their initial meeting, she hadn't mentioned the unplanned lunch. A part of him hoped that it meant his feelings for Sahar weren't obvious *then*. But to hell if they were now. Or tomorrow.

He walked out of the kitchen and up the stairs, finding the door to the guest bedroom where Eloise usually slept left ajar. He peeked inside first, then quietly tiptoed in. She was asleep, thankfully. Placing his palm gently on her forehead, he tried to see whether she was still feverish. He found her a little hotter than normal, but she wasn't burning up.

Jay stood there for a moment, staring, trying to convince himself that she was indeed fine. As he was about to walk out, her eyes fluttered open. She blinked once, twice, three times, trying to orient herself. "Dad?"

Leveling himself with her, he squatted beside her bed. "Yeah, baby. I'm here. Do you need anything?"

"Are we home?" she asked, croaking.

He brushed his fingers gently over her hair. "No, we're still at grandma's. But I'm staying here, too, tonight."

"Okay," she said, wincing. She tried to swallow. "Can I have some water?"

Jay eyed the glass of water next to her bed, noticing it was empty. "I'll go get more for you. Is your throat feeling okay?"

"A little scratchy."

"Does anything else hurt?"

"No," Eloise replied drowsily.

He placed a kiss on her forehead. "Okay. I'll be back with your water in a sec."

Jay beelined back into the kitchen, filled the glass with water from their filtered dispenser, and headed back. His mom and sister had dispersed, likely to their own rooms. Or, maybe at the front porch.

Walking back into Eloise's room, he found her sitting up. He passed her the water cup, and she took a few small sips before giving it back to him.

He set the glass down and tucked her back underneath the mermaid-themed comforter.

"You're gonna be here in the morning?" she asked again.

"Yeah, baby. I'll be right downstairs on the couch."

"Can you stay in here? Until I fall asleep?"

"Of course."

He sat on the mustard-yellow velvet armchair in the corner of the room and watched as Eloise dozed off. His stomach was still in knots. When she was fully asleep, he picked up his phone, remembering to update Sahar.

JAY

I'm home. Ellie seems okay. Thanks again for coming with me today.

She answered almost immediately. It was comforting, helping the knot in his chest slowly uncoil.

SAHAR

I'm so glad to hear she's okay! And thank you for inviting me.

Jay thumbed at his sternum. He wanted to keep talking to her, but a part of him felt weird, guilty, and oddly nervous.

A text message from Patrick appeared just as he was about to type something to Sahar.

PATRICK

Yo, you up?

JAY

Yeah, what's up?

Instead of answering the text, Jay's phone buzzed with a call from Patrick. Stepping out of Eloise's room, he went downstairs and out into their backyard. He shut the screen door only, so he'd still hear Ellie if she called out for him.

"I'm on my way home from the train station, so I thought I'd call. I read the new episode, and, man, this is your best work yet," Patrick declared.

Jay let out a sigh of relief. "Yeah? All good on your end?"

"Hundred percent. I think I had like three small notes. I can't wait to see what you do with the finale."

"We're still collaborating on that one, aren't we?" Jay asked.

"Yeah, yeah, of course. But I'm not touching the Henry and Katherine bits. That's all you. I'm almost done with my parts for Henry and George. Theirs is the arc I wanna nail down. You take us home with the very last scene."

He fixed his eyes on the orange geraniums his mother had planted as he sat on the cushioned ivory bench, overlooking the garden she'd continuously honed. The automatic motion lights had turned on, and cicadas sang louder. Mosquitos would also start eating him alive any minute now. "Sounds good. I'm gonna try to finish this weekend when El's in the city with Maya."

"I can aim for this weekend, too. How was *Franklin Street*?" Patrick asked from the other end of the line.

Leaning forward, Jay drew his fingers along the velvety petals. "Really solid. The final product is excellent."

"Yeah? Shit, that's awesome. Pete deserves it. And how was Sahar?"

He straightened himself, Sahar's name drawing his attention away from the flowers. "Normal, how was she supposed to be?" Jay questioned.

Patrick barked out a laugh. "Bro, c'mon. I've known you since we were ten. I *know* when you're into someone," he emphasized.

Sighing, Jay opted for a different response. Another truth. "Ask me again when the only thought in my head isn't my kid's fever."

"Aw, shit. Ellie's sick? Give my angel goddaughter the biggest hug then."

"Will do."

"Alright. I just parked. Talk soon."

"Night," Jay replied.

He set the phone down beside him on the wooden deck and raked his hand through his hair.

Fuck. The night wasn't supposed to end like this.

TUESDAY

SAHAR

Morning! I just wanted to check in and see how Eloise is doing.

JAY

No fever, thankfully, but she's sniffly and lethargic. Thanks for checking in. I took today and tomorrow off to be with her.

SAHAR

Aw, poor little darling. I'm happy to hear she doesn't have a temperature, though. You alright?

JAY

I think so. Maybe. I've stopped blaming myself if that's what you meant.

SAHAR

That's exactly what I meant because I had a feeling you would be.

JAY

We should talk about what happened. But it doesn't feel like a text conversation.

SAHAR

Yeah, definitely an in-person one. We'll figure it out.

JAY

WEDNESDAY

SAHAR

Checking in on Eloise and also on you.

JAY

She's much better today. So am I. How are you?

SAHAR

I'm so happy to hear that! And I'm solid.

JAY

Will I see you tomorrow? I have a later shift that got switched around.

SAHAR

You will!

JAY

Want me to snag a bagel for you when I get in?

SAHAR

Not a bagel, but maybe one of the strawberry rice krispie bars, if they're available? They keep selling out by the time we arrive.

JAY

You got it, sunshine.

Dahlia's trying to get Adriana (the lady who bakes them every morning) to sell them to us year-round.

SAHAR

Dahlia would be my hero. Is it working? They're bloody divine. I want to try the regular if she's the one baking them, but I fear the strawberry might've ruined me. And I'm not that big on sweets usually.

JAY

No, she keeps saying they're special while they're seasonal. But Dahlia's persistent.

SAHAR

She does have a point there.

JAY

I suppose. Do you think they cure colds?

SAHAR

I have a feeling they might.

JAY

I'll have to check with Ellie to confirm. Thanks again for checking in.

SAHAR

Anytime

25

SAHAR

A dull ache in her ankle woke up Sahar ahead of her alarm. She'd felt an odd discomfort yesterday, chalking it up to the usual overexertion instead of something serious. But now, it was a bit more pronounced.

Yet, more apparent than the irritation in her ankle was the anxiety ballooning inside of her. Sahar wasn't one to pride herself on many things, but she'd appreciated the strength she typically had to combat her fears. She was good at bouncing back. She excelled at compartmentalizing and rationalizing.

But with each passing day, it was growing harder and harder.

It was especially challenging given how she was diligently trying to fit into some mold that'd maybe be more palatable to others, even while it meant shutting parts of herself off. It was particularly frustrating to continue upholding these walls because she *liked* Jay. She liked him a lot more than she thought she would, and all she wanted to do was jump right in.

Forget slow. Forget figuring things out. Forget what it meant to be afraid of love and welcome the possibility of heartbreak as part of the whole ordeal.

But *ugh,* she couldn't do that with Jay. After checking on him and Eloise, she'd started to feel like she was bothering him. It was the polite thing to do—she knew as much—yet her mind insisted that it wasn't her place.

Sahar groaned in frustration and looked at her phone. Six in the bloody morning. She sighed, sinking deeper into her bed as she thought of how his mouth felt roaming over her skin. How needy his hands were.

Grumbling, Sahar kicked off her apricot-colored comforter and got out of bed. She brushed her teeth and took care of her morning skincare before walking out into the kitchen. Opening the fridge, she stared into it. Willa spent the night at Ethan's, so Sahar would be going to work with Christian.

Christian would be a safe buffer. Christian also wasn't aware of everything that had happened. And if he was, he was blessedly staying quiet.

She shouldn't have agreed to allow Jay to hold the strawberry Rice Krispies bar for her. She should've just let it be. Brushed it off. *Overthinking doesn't become you, Sahar. Enough.*

She picked out a white peach from the fridge, washed it, and took a big bite. Tea, later. She'd keep busy today, meal prep for lunch and dinner—hold off on a workout because her ankle was being strange—and then go into work.

When Christian texted her that he'd be in front of their flat in five minutes, she got ready to leave the house.

Their too-tight subway ride to the theatre was quiet, and when they got to the coffee shop, everything was suddenly too loud. She spotted Jay making drinks, and he appeared to be so stressed and pissed off that she wasn't even sure she wanted to be here.

Except, a barely there smile rose across his lips as he saw her, and he gestured her over to where he stood.

"Hey, you two," he started. "It's been a shit show today. I'll have your orders in a sec, don't bother going to the register."

Christian tried to argue.

"Bud, I'm serious. The registers are acting up, and the baristas are all irritated. It'd be much easier if I just put it on my tab."

"When are you off?" Sahar asked.

Jay poured her drink into the to-go cup. "In an hour, but I don't even know if I could leave if we're still in this mess, so we'll see."

Christian gave him a sympathetic glance. "Shit, sorry, man."

While letting the tea bag seep in, Jay signaled with his finger for them to wait a second. He quickly strode to the back somewhere and returned with a brown paper bag. He handed it to her—the Rice Krispies, she assumed.

"You're the best," Sahar added, a huge smile on her face.

It prompted his mouth to twitch upward.

He then placed Christian's cup into another for an extra layer of heat protection before giving it to him. How the man could drink hot tea when the world was on fire was the real mystery here.

Sahar took her drink next. "Thanks a million. Godspeed."

Jay nodded sincerely and walked over to another barista.

Okay, universe, when I said I was nervous to see him, I didn't mean for you to meddle and make sure he has such a hectic day that he's barely a functioning human.

"I don't know how anyone has the patience to work in customer service," Christian said as they were out the door.

Sahar shook her head, knowingly. "Jesus, right? It takes a special kind of human. I feel like I'd throw drinks across the wall and then run out crying."

Come to think of it, Jay's position at the coffee shop should've served as proof to Sahar that the man's patience was far more enduring than even her own. *If he could manage this level of chaos every day, couldn't he deal with her?* But he hated his job. She'd never want him to hate her. She also didn't want to be someone who was synonymous with chaos.

Her mind dove straight into a spiral again.

Not watching where she was going, she almost tripped over a small pothole, the heel of her white Veja trainers stopping the fall. Her ankle stung emphatically when she twisted her foot to step out.

What the hell was happening today?

"You good over there?" Christian asked.

"Bloody fucking pothole," she cursed.

He moved closer, holding the back of her elbow to help steady her.

One step, then another—oh, hell, the pain grew far more pronounced. Christian let her go when she straightened herself.

Okay, okay, you're fine. You just need to sit for a bit. This had to happen on the day when Jenny, their physical therapist, was out?

They walked the remaining short steps to the theatre, signed in, and went into their respective dressing rooms.

Willa was already in her seat, applying eye shadow. "Hi!"

Sahar smiled and slowly sat down on her chair. "Hi, babe."

"You alright?" Willa asked.

Sahar nodded. "My ankle is being a little bitch, but nothing out of the ordinary."

Willa shot a concerned glance in her direction. "You sure?"

"Positive. I think I misstepped yesterday, and I almost tripped just now, so it's probably trying to calm itself down."

She left out the part that it'd been bothering her *all* morning.

It was Sahar's day to choose the music, so she opted for the playlist titled "Where the Waves Crash." The women got ready mostly in silence until Naomi came in to show them a cat video she couldn't stop laughing about, and Miles stole Willa for a beat to run through a choreography that was brewing inside him.

For the entire cast, the titular number, "Midnights at

Pemberley," featured the most singing and dancing. The rest of the scenes Sahar was in were relatively more mellow. But right as she stepped on the stage in her dance heels for the "Bennet Sisters' Interview," it hit her.

Performing today would be a bad call.

Her ankle had no plans to ease up on her.

Shit. The smart thing to do would be to say something, stop entirely, and let Willa go on after Intermission. But Sahar didn't want to disappoint people. Was it really that awful, or was fixating on it simply making it worse? Perhaps that was it.

She could push through. It'd be fine.

It was not fine.

But time was at least passing. During "Stubborn Bastard," Sam, as Bingley, came forward to her and pulled her onto his lap. This was where they'd lose themselves in each other while Darcy and Elizabeth fought center stage, followed by Declan's entrance as Wickham. Sahar willed herself into character, thankful for the chance to sit. Thankful for the few minutes before "Midnights at Pemberley," which would surely make matters worse.

After Intermission, she would only have to return to the stage for a quick scene at the end of "The Letter," before everything began with "Jane and Bingley's Wedding." Sahar walked carefully to her dressing room, avoiding her friends on the off chance that someone might pick up on what was happening.

She sat in her chair and propped her foot up on the stool that sat in the middle of her and Willa's seats for anyone else who'd visit the room. Did she slam her ankle into a wall while walking to the bathroom half asleep? How had it gotten so irritated? She'd wrapped it earlier in the day, but she took off her shoe and tightened it again.

The pain made her wince.

Oh, she couldn't do this. But it was too late to make a fuss of it now. She'd deal with it the second the curtains closed. For now, she'd talk to Sam. If nothing else, he could make some of the movements easier on her.

Sahar rose from the seat and slowly limped to Sam's dressing room. The door was open while he was lying on the couch, eyes fixed on the ceiling.

Sam sat up the moment he saw her. "Yo," he acknowledged.

Sahar tried to smile, but she couldn't even fake it. Sam must've caught her expression because he rose off the couch entirely.

"Sam, I need a favor."

He stepped closer to her. "Of course. What's up?"

"My ankle. I'm... I think I'm having the flare-up from hell."

Sam's eyes filled with worry. "Shit. Are you okay? How long has it been happening?"

"Since I got in. I should've called it the second I realized it was getting bad, but I've probably pushed it too far now, and it's too late to say anything."

Sam nodded automatically. "What do you need from me? What can I do to make sure our numbers are as easy as can be?"

"Can you lift me off the ground? As much as possible during the improv bits in 'All For You?'"

"Yes, yeah. Of course. Do you want to talk to Dina? We can maybe get a prop chair, something for you to lean on?"

Sahar shook her head. "No, it's okay. I'll put all my weight on my right ankle when we stand. As long as I don't move too much, I should be fine."

Sam agreed. "And you'll get it checked out the second we finish?"

"Yes."

Sam gave her a sympathetic look. "You have to be careful, Sahar. Our bodies are the one thing we always have to be on top of. Better to miss one show than mess yourself up completely."

She nodded. "I know. I've been having a rough few days, and I didn't want to miss a show on top of everything else."

"I get it. I do."

Sam motioned for her to sit on his sofa and forced her to put her leg up on his chair. "Stay here until you have to go out," he said, then his eyes widened with an idea. "You know, you could probably disappear during the 'Midnights at Pemberley Reprise' and come back out during bows. It'll be jarring at first, but we could make it work, I think. Want me to talk to Dina?"

Sahar pondered the idea. "Yeah, maybe."

Sam held up a finger as if to say hold and ran out of the room.

Five minutes were called, but for Sahar, that meant at least fifteen.

In a few short seconds, Sam returned to the room with Dina.

"Sahar, Sam filled me in," Dina started. "I think we could make it work if you want to sneak away during the reprise."

Sahar nodded. "Maybe we could have Willa step in just for the choreography part of it? She won't be in costume, but we'd have one less ensemble member."

"Willa could still probably make the ensemble bit work anyway because you four leave the stage during their solos. Someone get her in here. Willa," Dina bellowed.

It was convenient that Ethan's dressing room was right next to Sam's because if she were in it, she'd hear.

"Wait, who called me?" Sahar heard Willa's voice from the hallway.

Dina popped her head out of the door. "We're in Sam's dressing room."

"What's up?" Willa said, walking in.

"We need to have Sahar sit out of the final reprise. Do you think it's possible for you to quickly step in as her—stay in costume, we have to make do, and then step back out for the ensemble solo."

Willa's head cocked toward Sahar's on the sofa. She had every inkling of what was now happening, and Sahar knew her well enough to understand the depth of concern appearing on her face. "Yeah, I think that's possible. I'll just have to fill Miles in, and we're set."

Sahar groaned and leaned her head back. She hated herself for this. In an effort not to make things difficult, she managed to add ten times more trouble. Their voices disappeared in the background for a beat before Willa stepped beside her. "I had a feeling something was off with you. I wanted to ask, but I thought maybe it was an emotional thing you didn't want to talk about. How are you feeling?"

"Like shit for countless reasons," Sahar answered.

Willa placed her hand on Sahar's shoulder. "Why didn't you talk to me?"

"I didn't think it'd get this bad. I've been all over the place, Wills. I hate this."

"We'll talk afterward, yeah?"

"Yeah."

Readying herself to go back on stage, Willa smiled and walked off.

The duration of the show was all a blur. Sahar thanked every lucky star looking out for her that she had the type of friends who immediately worked around her blunder and made everything possible. She just hoped that whatever came out of this wouldn't be too bad.

She couldn't deal with that. Not now.

SAHAR WAS SUPPOSED to stay off her ankle until Sunday.

Fuck everything. She would be missing three days of work and four shows. How could she have allowed a small irritation to get this bad? She and Willa spent over two hours at the emergency room last night until the doctors determined that it was a bad flare-up and thankfully, nothing more serious.

Ethan had picked them up and dropped them off at home, and Sahar spent the entire night moping. She hated every part of this. Willa had also advised her not to play any video games because Sahar was susceptible to kicking and stomping when she got frustrated. *Cool, great.*

What on earth was she supposed to do for three whole days? Four, technically, if she counted Monday.

She took about five naps, foot elevated and all, and that passed some time in the morning. Maybe she could play a crossword or word search; those didn't make her angry often. Sahar searched for one on her phone.

A text from Jay popped up shortly after.

JAY

> Willa and Christian just told me what happened.
> I'm off in two hours. Want some company?

Oh, shit. Yes, please.

SAHAR

> I'd love it, but you should go home to Eloise.

JAY

> Maya's here for the weekend. They're having a
> girls trip in the city.

SAHAR

> In that case, sure. I feel like I'm losing my mind,
> so company would be nice. 🫠

JAY

Can I bring you anything?

SAHAR

Just yourself.

JAY

Come on, sunshine. I don't want to come empty handed.

SAHAR

There's Leo's Pizza near my place. If you want to pick up a pie, I won't say no.

JAY

You got it. What kind?

SAHAR

I'm a classic girl, but if you want pepperoni or something, I don't mind just taking it off!

JAY

Cheese it is.

SAHAR

Her nosy brain needed to know how she came up in the conversation, so Sahar FaceTimed Willa, knowing she'd be doing her hair and makeup at this point.

Willa turned on the video, a hair grip in her mouth. "Yes, my darling, how are you feeling?"

"Losing it, mum. Save me."

Willa smirked. "I'm sure someone will at some point."

"Oh, so you know why I'm calling you?"

Willa let out a laugh. "Did he text you? Wait, hold on. Ethan's in the room. Want me to kick him out?"

"All good. He can intrude on my love life."

"I'm flattered," Ethan said, his voice coming from a distance.

Sahar shook her head. "I need to know how I came up and what you said to him."

"Didn't say anything. His whole face dropped when we walked in without you. So, while we ordered, he asked if I was getting your drink, too, and I told him you'd be out for the next three days because your ankle was acting up. And I shit you not, Sahar, he looked like a bloody sad puppy that'd been kicked to the curb. He stumbled on his words, asking if you were okay. I reassured him that you were fine, but very likely miserable because you hated missing work. And then he thanked me for telling him and said he'd check in on you during his break."

"He's coming over to keep me company. Eloise is in the city with her mum for the weekend."

Willa's smile expanded. "I almost lied to him, but I made the momentary executive decision to be honest because it's what you'd do for me."

"I'm glad you told him. I don't think it means what we think it means. But it would be nice to maybe talk. Who knows."

"Did you not hear the part where I called him a sad puppy? You do not get *that* concerned for someone if you're not inter-ested in them. And *especially* after the kind of night you two almost had."

"You have a sap's brain now. Your eyes can't always be trusted."

Willa turned to Ethan off-camera. "Back me up."

He came into the frame. "She's right. I'd recognize a sulking man in love anywhere."

"And were you there?" Sahar asked.

Ethan let out a chuckle. "Nah, but I trust my girl. And I've seen that look in him enough times when you're not there to know by now."

"You freaks in love don't count as reliable sources."

"Actually, we're the most exemplary sources now," Willa countered.

"I'm hanging up," Sahar declared.

"I want updates," Willa added.

"Yeah, yeah, love you, bye," Sahar said, then hung up.

Freaks. Stupidly in love, gorgeous freaks.

She wanted what they had. The certainty. The trust. The deep, overwhelming love.

Realizing that she was still in her pajamas, Sahar changed into a pair of ribbed, baby blue drawstring shorts and a matching tank top with a built-in bra underneath. Thank heavens, because she wasn't about to wear anything with an underwire.

26

JAY

Jay felt like an idiot.

He kept wanting to text Sahar last night and talk to her. He wanted to apologize in case he'd been short with her at the coffee shop because of the afternoon havoc. He'd thought about it all day, but he could never tell what the right move was. He didn't want to push or assume. He just—*fuck*.

But when Willa told him that Sahar was injured, Jay's heart had immediately plummeted in his chest.

Then, he didn't think twice about checking in. Nor did he question whether he should be there for her. There was no other option.

If she wanted him, he'd go to her. He'd do anything.

Holding their pizza in one hand, Jay knocked lightly on the door. "Coming," he heard her call out.

Sahar opened the door with her signature smile, flaming red hair loose and wavy, her face somehow prettier than ever.

"Hi," she said before slowly moving aside for him to walk in.

Jay let her guide him back into the place where he'd almost had all of her. Pathetically, his breath hitched at the memory.

"Hi, sunshine. What happened?"

She gave him a small, sad shrug. "The universe decided to be a little shit because for five seconds things had been going too smoothly for its liking?"

Limping toward the living room, she nudged him to follow. He set the pizza down on the coffee table and pivoted to face her.

Jay opened his arms in her direction. "Come here."

Sahar curled herself into him, and delicious notes of orange blossom from her shampoo or perfume drifted into his nose. Squeezing her close, he cradled her head in his hand.

"Thanks," she murmured, her arms tightening around him.

He tipped his head to the side, pressing his mouth to her temple in a featherlight kiss. "For what?"

A heavy sigh descended from her lips and echoed inside his heart. *Fuck.* "Last night was shit. This morning's been shit. I needed a hug."

A part of him hoped that she meant from *him,* specifically. Because Willa could've hugged her, couldn't she? Any one of her castmates could've.

"I got you," Jay whispered.

He held her for a few seconds, letting her take as much of him as she wanted. Knowing he could be here for her eased him, too.

When she eventually let go of him, her pretty brown eyes were glassy, heavy-lidded. Blinking, once, twice, Sahar forced a smile up at him. He didn't want her to do that. She didn't have to smile if she didn't want to. He was about to say something before she spoke. "I forgot to grab us drinks when I got plates and napkins. Would you mind?"

"Sure. Where do you keep them?"

"In the fridge. Ginger ale for me and whatever you want. I think we have Dr. Pepper and Coke." She pointed toward a small hallway. "And we keep our alcohol on a little mini bar right before our rooms."

"What about your water?" he asked.

"You're going to drink water? That's boring."

"I've only had caffeine today. My head will explode if I have more."

"Fair. Filter by the sink, glasses in the cupboard right next to it, and ice in the fridge dispenser."

Jay followed her instructions, grabbed the drinks, and sat beside her on a light gray sectional couch. Sahar had her leg elevated on another chair, a fluffy pink pillow propped underneath. Now that his headspace was *slightly* more clear, he noticed what she was wearing, and the small space between them contracted. Light blue sweat shorts and a matching top, her long legs exposed. Lord help him.

She spoke after a few moments of silent eating. "You said Eloise is in the city with her mum?"

He nodded mid-bite and chewed prior to answering. "Yeah, Maya's sister and her daughter are also here from D.C., so it's a girls' weekend. They're seeing *Hatchard's Academy* tonight for Lex."

"Fun! Does Eloise like musicals?"

"Oh, yeah. She loves them."

A genuine smile tilted up her mouth, and his heart did a small backflip, thumping repeatedly in a plea to catch that look again.

He eyed the crow tattoo on her forearm, wanting to ask about it once more. Wanting to tell her about his—how it'd been one of the first things he noticed about her after her perfect smile. But he swallowed the desire, shoving it aside for now. "How's your ankle?" he asked instead.

She let out a low sigh. "The pain's not unbearable, but I'm really disappointed I can't perform."

"I get that. But your health should come first. You can't control it."

"I could have, though. If I'd called out yesterday when I first realized I was having a flare-up, I could've probably saved myself from being out for three days."

"Why didn't you?"

Sadness docked itself in her eyes, and she looked so small. So broken. His heart plummeted once more, proving that he wasn't strong enough to see her dejected like this.

"I didn't want to disappoint people. My mental health has been shit, and I didn't want my body to give out on me, too."

God. Setting his empty plate down on the wooden coffee table, he shifted his body to face her more comfortably. "How can I help?" he asked, not knowing what else to say.

Rounding her lips, she exhaled another heavy sigh. "Can you rewind time?"

He inched closer, tucking an errant strand of hair behind her ear. "I'm serious."

"Distract me with your brain, then. How'd *Every Speck of Dust* come to you?"

Jay took a breath, remembering the specific day off from work when he had stared at his empty document, wondering if he should once and for all abandon it. Years of trying had left him drained, more alone than he'd ever felt, and completely void of ideas. It'd been the dead of winter, but he'd decided to take a drive to the beach. He'd thought that maybe, if he felt the cold air against his skin, then he'd feel less numb and a little more alive. It'd been a stupid idea given the downpour he was later met with, but still.

Sahar was gazing at him, her sparkling brown eyes filled with the transfixing wonder that made him want to consistently *try* a little bit harder. It was a look he wanted to bottle up and open every time he felt the piercing ache of self-doubt consume him. Would it ever stop astounding him that *she* cared as much about his work?

"I think Henry was always with me," he started to say. *He had been, hadn't he?* He was part of a short story Jay had written when he was fifteen, and then, he'd added him into *Beneath the Sun* as a background character. The short story version of him would never see the light of day since he was a mere exercise. An escape from his fraught household.

And yet, Henry's existence always felt visceral—real and vital for some reason.

Katherine appeared shortly after, right as he watched massive waves crash into the shore. He wasn't sure what their story would be at the time, but he knew their fears—their struggles. There were crosses they both carried, perhaps parts of Jay's own pain bleeding through...

He looked back at Sahar, her pink thumbnail between her lips as she waited for him to answer. "I was having a lousy few days, and I went down to the beach. I remembered Henry from *Beneath the Sun*. Katherine came to me afterward, and they stayed with me. But I was on the train one morning, heading over to the location in Jersey where we were shooting *Cuts*, and..." he paused, trying to push down the lump in his throat.

He'd never told anybody this part of the process, not even Patrick when he first pitched the series. "That line, the one that you said made you cry—'In my perfect world, you and I would be together'—I heard that line, from Henry's point of view to Katherine, and I had no idea what it meant, but I wrote it down in my notes app anyway."

Jay caught the sound of Sahar's breath hitch, and he wanted to fucking cry. The perpetual light in her eyes held him steady. "And I just kept thinking about them—the longing to find someone who was missing. It all came suddenly, but in broken fragments that I wanted to piece together."

He paused, staring—trying to find the strength to keep going through her eyes. "But in truth, you brought out the version I wasn't capable of finding on my own."

His name fled Sahar's lips in a whisper.

Her hand was so close to his that if he simply moved an inch, he could glide his fingers over hers, smooth the pad of his thumb across her knuckles. But they hadn't talked about what happened yet. Their friendship was complicated now. Maybe even a little fragile.

Sahar looked down to where his eyes had been. She crawled her hand toward his, and he rolled his palm over, slowly lacing their fingers together. Instantly, every part of him warmed from her touch, one by one, each cove filled to the brim with her light.

Neither said a word.

The conversation taking place in the silence felt like the most seamless exchange he'd ever had. Somehow, Sahar heard all that he wanted her to hear. Every word he said aloud and the ones he couldn't find, too.

He had told her something sacred and watched her collect every detail for safekeeping.

Hope coursed through his veins again, and it was all because the woman sitting in front of him didn't want one more thing making her sad. She wanted to watch another woman make it back home, and he'd give her that every single time.

"When I first read that line, I couldn't understand why it made me cry so much," she said, brushing his fingers with her thumb. "I blamed it on my period, but then I kept thinking about it. I kept thinking of Henry's desperation and longing. I *think* I finally get it now."

A smile began curving up her lips.

Desperate to have a little more of her, Jay lifted his other hand and cupped her cheek. "Tell me."

Sahar sighed. "You said it yourself in the script, 'He can't hold it anymore. He doesn't want to.' The exposition. The confession itself. It all feels so...monumental in its simplicity."

Pausing once more, she leaned into his touch. "There's something so human about bottled up secrets becoming too much for us to carry alone. He's kept it in during every case, every moment they've been alone together, and I just...it's so easy to *feel* the depth of his love for her."

His mind raced around the words she'd said, fighting tooth and nail with him to *just fucking tell her. Tell her you can't hold it anymore. Tell her you want her.* "Bottled up secrets," Jay repeated, sweeping his thumb gently across her cheek. The words left his mouth before he could lasso them back in. Better this than anything else, he thought.

Her lips opened then closed again before she said, "I know the feeling."

He was about to lose his fucking mind. *What feeling? Tell me. Please.* Choosing his response carefully, Jay settled on, "What are you bottling up, sunshine?"

Sahar tried to smile, but the light in her eyes was still switched off.

"At the moment? Or in general?"

Jay wanted all of it—every part of her, every secret, every confession. He'd give anything. "Let's go with 'at the moment.' Start small."

She let out a low, honest laugh. It wasn't the reaction he was expecting, but he'd take it. Bottle it up. Sanctify it. With her other hand, she traced idle circles around her knee. Jay's eyes trailed there, aching to touch her. She had a bruise right underneath, and another he could see near the inside of her thigh. He wanted to press his mouth to them. He wanted to relieve all her aches.

If only she hadn't been injured. If only she still wanted him.

"What I'm bottling up at the moment might be even bigger

than the general. I don't know why I asked for the specificity. I made it worse for myself."

He stayed quiet, trailing his fingers to her jaw.

You do it then, his heart begged. *Tell her everything.*

"What if I tell you something?"

Sahar moved her head up and down. "I'd like that."

"I've felt what he has. Every time you've walked into the coffee shop," Jay confessed. "Every time I see you. Every message you send. I didn't before, but I know how Henry feels now."

There, it was out there. He'd already told her that he'd wanted her for a long time, but this confession felt bigger, more intimate.

Jay couldn't read the expression on her face.

"You say that now," she uttered suddenly.

He blinked, unsure of what to say. *No, fuck that.* He'd already done the hard part. "Now, tomorrow, the next day," he countered.

She looked like she wanted to cry. He blamed himself for it, his heartbeat waging a war inside his chest.

Time slowed for an instant, the fan from the AC unit turned back on, and white noise dispersed, filling the space between them.

Closing her eyes, he could see her fight against something— the reason for the walls bricked in front of her. The explanation for the bridges she wouldn't let him walk over.

Sahar released a heavy sigh. "If this were a year ago, I would've jumped headfirst. But I can't let myself do that now. What happened the other night, Jay, I—" An inhale, an exhale. "I like you. *A lot.* I'm growing to trust you in ways I've never trusted anybody else, and that scares me, but I... I don't know how to move forward without mucking it all up."

He understood her. Fully. No matter how fiercely his body

demanded or how intensely he craved to know more about her, he would give her all that she asked for. He'd back away.

Moving his hand away from her face, he set it down against his thigh.

"I didn't mean to upset you," Sahar added. "I just...I think if anything is going to happen between us, it shouldn't be impulsive."

He managed to smile. "You didn't upset me. I get it. Completely."

Her lips curled up slowly. "Can you...can you keep holding my hand? And tell me something else about the story. Something that won't make me feel as much?"

Jay squeezed the hand he was holding onto and thought of what he could tell her.

Shifting in his seat, he tried to get more comfortable.

"Hmm, okay, so honest to God, other than *Cuts,* which both Pat and I drew inspiration from our dads, I've never really modeled a character after someone I know in real life. Not in *Beneath the Sun,* definitely not in *Fraudulent Causes*—the movie that was cut from the studio recently—and nothing in any of the stuff I've worked on with other friends. But you know Ramona? The woman who works at the Spirit Halloween store they go to in episode eight?"

Sahar nodded.

"I had an awful third-grade teacher who's the reason I hated school and everything pertaining to it. She hated Halloween and was terrified of clowns. Her name was also Ramona."

She bit back a laugh. "So you have her working in a Halloween store where she's constantly miserable? That's so vindictive."

Jay shrugged. "The woman told my mom I'd amount to nothing, so take that, Ramona."

"Oh, hell. Make it worse, Jay. Throw in a scene where a

bunch of teenagers come in while they're all dressed in clown costumes and spook her."

The smile she gave him was dazzling. He let out a laugh.

"This is why you never piss off writers. They'll immortalize you in the worst way. The fact that you kept her actual name is pure genius," she declared.

Jay agreed. "She looked like a Ramona, too, you know? I can't explain it."

"Oh, I can totally see it. I now have a clear picture of her in my head," Sahar said.

She looked down at their clasped hands and gave his another squeeze. His eyes flicked up to her. Sliding her head back against the cushion, she let out a low grumble. "I hate this. I hate that you're here, and I'm fighting against how much I want you."

He shut his eyes, taking a deep breath. Maybe if they spent more time together, she'd feel more comfortable around him. Maybe she'd feel safe enough to unload all her burdens on him —let him be the one to tend to her wounds.

"It's okay, sunshine. I can be patient. But look, I have a shorter shift tomorrow, and Eloise doesn't come home until Sunday night. Since Willa's going to be out all day because of a two-show day, would you like to join me in my neck of the woods? If you want a change of scenery, that is."

Sahar smiled. It was shy and unfamiliar to him. "You're not obligated to hang out with me, Jay. Plus, I wouldn't want you to change your plans for me."

But *he wanted to.* He *would* change his plans for her. He didn't even have any plans outside of writing.

"My only plan was to try finishing the finale, but I've been stuck on it for two days, so maybe you could help me?"

Sahar's lips curved upward. "Do I get any credit for all these brilliant ideas I'm giving you?"

"Of course you do. EP, sunshine."

She shook her hand. "I'm one hundred percent joking, by the way."

"I'm not," he protested.

Another foreign expression crossed her face. "What are you stuck on?" she asked.

"We could discuss that tomorrow," he answered.

A barely-there smirk rose along her lips. "How would that work out?"

"Simple, I'll drive into work tomorrow, come pick you up, and we'll drive back."

She tilted her head. "Don't you usually take the train?"

He nodded to say yes.

"Well then, why would you drive?"

"So you won't have to do much walking?"

Sahar smiled. "Jay, I can walk a few steps in and out of a train station. I just shouldn't stomp and kick my feet with intense choreography."

"I've driven to work before, Sahar. I promise it's not a big deal. Please let me."

"Okay, but I get to take the train back, and then I'll Uber home from Jamaica to avoid the subway."

He was about to protest when his mind told him not to push. "If that'll make you feel better, then sure."

"It will."

"You got it."

She drew forward to grab her ginger ale from the coffee table, but he did it for her.

"Thanks," she said, then took a sip. She held onto it with her other hand, repositioned her leg propped on the pillow, and inched closer to him with the rest of her body. "I'm not allowed to play any games, but wanna watch *Clue* with me?"

He wanted to wrap his arm around her shoulder. She was so close that he could.

"I'll take anything that isn't *The Incredibles* right now," he replied.

A sweet huff of laughter left her lips. "Is that what Eloise has been making you watch?"

"Yup. She's deemed it her 'sick comfort show,' and we've watched it four times since Tuesday."

Her smile was so fucking adorable, he didn't know what to do with himself. She meandered with the remote until she found *Clue*.

They lapsed into a companionable silence, hands tightly entwined together.

27

SAHAR

Tightening her ankle brace after she'd iced it, Sahar stared at her open wardrobe, trying to figure out what to wear.

What did one wear to spend the entire day potentially writing at someone's house that would be comfortable, cute, and weather-appropriate?

Sahar was generally decent at picking outfits when she wasn't thinking about them, but now that she was—and thinking of Jay—her entire closet blurred into a colorful, indistinguishable blob. An unfolded batch of clean laundry sitting in a woven basket also eyed her from the corner of her room. It'd been four days of her saying, *I'll get to it today,* but remembering it only in the dead of night when she was comfortably settled in bed.

"Wills," she called out. When it came to clothes, Willa was better under pressure, and the blazer and denim jeans outfit she'd styled for the *Franklin Street* premiere had already been a hit.

Stepping into Sahar's room with two cups of tea in her hand,

Willa grinned at her. "Brought you tea. How may I be of service?"

Sahar reached for the mug. "I don't know what clothes are. I'm nervous. I'm stressed. Help me, Obi-Willa, you're my only hope."

Willa barked out a laugh. "That's my new favorite nickname. How is this the first time you've ever used it?"

Sahar blew out an exhale. "Maybe because I've never needed you more?"

"Are we feeling dramatic?"

Groaning, Sahar replied, "Extremely."

Willa set her mug down on Sahar's bedside table, then drew closer to her wardrobe, swaying hangers left and right. She eventually pulled out a simple black cotton midi-dress and held it out for Sahar to approve.

"See, this is why I need you," Sahar declared.

Hanging the dress facing forward, Willa walked back for her mug and took a sip of her tea. She eyed Sahar again, sympathetic understanding resting in her gaze. "Are you feeling up for this?"

Sahar circled her fingers around her own mug. "I'm so nervous, Wills. I almost want to text him and tell him that I feel worse and don't want company, but I don't want to do that to him," she said, pausing. "But also, I *want* to be around him. I can't help it."

Willa gave her an empathetic smile. "It's not like you to be anxious or apprehensive. That's my brand."

"That's because—" sighing, "I don't think anyone's made me feel like this before," Sahar said, setting the mug down on the nightstand. She closed her eyes for an instant. "He makes me feel... mushy and soft. It feels like there's stardust or some other flowery shit constantly collapsing inside of me when I think about him. Everything about Jay feels," another pause. "Bright and lovely, and little by little, I'm losing it."

"Aw, babe. Those are some real lovey-dovey emotions you're feeling."

Sahar let out a groan and leaned against her cream tufted headboard. Willa set her mug down again and joined her on the other side of the bed.

Turning to face Willa, Sahar first readjusted the position her ankle had been propped in. "I'm not nearly as close to Jay as you were to Ethan before everything happened between you two. I think we have a long way to go before we understand each other that closely, but he already means so much to me, Wills. I fully understand why you were hesitant to lose the friendship you two had, and I'm sorry that I assumed it would've been an easy thing."

Willa smiled. "Yeah, but your honesty helped me see that sometimes the scariest things are the ones worth chasing. Sahar, I've said it once, and I'll say it again, just because you've had shitty boyfriends doesn't mean you're incapable of scoping out good people. It also doesn't mean that you have to swear off love to learn some sort of a lesson. Please, tell me you get that by now."

"But the patterns have to mean something, don't they?" Sahar whispered.

"The only thing it means is that you've opened your heart time and again. The patterns aren't trying to teach you some twisted lesson."

Sahar sighed, burrowing her head against Willa's shoulder this time. "I don't know what I want to do, but I know that I want to keep him in my life. It's that simple. I can't imagine a world where Jay isn't there."

Resting her head on top of Sahar's, Willa added, "Something tells me he feels the same way about you."

"So WAIT, you were born in Buffalo but grew up in Sleepy Hollow, and then you all moved to Long Island when you were ten?" Sahar asked Jay while they were seated inside his car. It smelled like some sort of a tree, which she assumed was coming from the green, circular-looking air freshener placed in a small nook underneath the head unit. Being in his car was unsurprisingly comforting. Easy. There was a booster seat in the back, too, a Man City hat for kids, a small cream cardigan—reminders of his life outside the coffee shop. The dad part of him she knew very little about. The part of him she *wanted* to know.

He nodded. "Correct. Though technically, my apartment is in Huntington."

"Huh. Fun fact, I always thought Sleepy Hollow was made up? I think I learned it was a real place when I looked it up in primary school or something."

Jay let out a small laugh. "Where did you grow up?"

"London."

"So where does your loyalty to Man City come from?" he asked.

Sahar laughed. "My granddad was born in Manchester, so my dad grew up as a Man City fan, and he passed it down to us. Me, rather. My sister isn't as invested."

"Nice. Did your parents meet in London?" he asked.

Reaching over to the cup holder, she grabbed her coffee to take a sip. He'd also brought her a strawberry Rice Krispies bar that she was saving for later. "Yeah, in uni."

Smiling, he looked at her from the driver's seat. "I hope it means they're happy and still in love."

A big grin spread across her face at the thought of her parents. "Yeah, they're real cuties. Too bad their daughters have shit luck." *And that part you should've left out.*

"How so?"

"Wait, wait. I'll answer after. How did *you* become a Man City fan? I just realized I don't know this."

He smiled contentedly, his expression telling her that this part of his past wasn't so dark. "Patrick's dad. He watched all the games with Pat and his brother Hayden. They invited me over once my family moved in next door, and it sort of stuck."

Something in her heart squeezed and ached simultaneously for him. "That's so lovely. I'm thrilled to know their family has superlative taste."

"Back to you and that shit luck you were about to tell me about."

She sighed. "My sister Amina married her childhood best friend, then divorced him a year later because he realized he didn't want monogamy. And me, well—"

"What about you?"

The traffic ahead made him slow down and look right at her.

"You know all there is to know about my failed endeavors in love," she said, turning her gaze toward the road. She caught him doing the same through her peripheral.

"I don't know anything other than your ex is in *Hatchard's*, and he's a piece of shit."

"That should tell you everything."

He clicked his tongue. "That's where you're wrong, sunshine. You're good at hiding what you don't want people to see, but those pretty brown eyes of yours tell a different story."

Trying to withhold a smile, she turned back to him. "You think my eyes are pretty?" she asked, a hint of cheekiness in her voice to contrast the shock it sent to her bloodstream. *Had any of her exes ever commented on her eyes before?*

It was always her body with others. Sometimes, her smile.

Occasionally and stereotypically, her accent if they were

American. If she recalled correctly, no one had ever called her eyes pretty.

"I think a lot of things about you are pretty," he answered candidly, chancing a glance at her as he took his foot off the brake. "But that's not why I want to know everything about you."

"Further details would bore you, so they're better kept under lock and key. But thank you," she said.

Another irritating halt in the road slowed him down. "No detail about you would bore me."

"Get me drunk enough, and you might get them then."

Tilting his head, he cocked an eyebrow at her. "That adds up. You like me better when there's alcohol in your system."

She let out a loud laugh. If nothing else, the fact that their conversations could be unfiltered like this made her feel better about everything.

"I like you without alcohol, too. I just seem to think less when it's present."

"That can be arranged," he declared with a wink. *That bloody fucking wink.*

Sahar grabbed her coffee again, taking another sip. In all fairness, conversations mattered, and if Jay were willing to give her parts of him, then maybe, just maybe, it'd be easier for her to give parts of herself back. "Okay. Answer this question, and I'll answer whatever you want. Have you ever had your heart broken?"

"Straight for the jugular, I see."

"Are we surprised?"

Dropping his gaze toward her first, Jay sighed. "My last serious girlfriend. Her name was Lillian. About five-ish years ago, I think. I really liked her, but I was closed off, so I'm mostly to blame. She tried to fight for us, and I just sort of didn't." He punctuated the last word with a tinge of regret.

"She was moving away for her residency, and the idea of

being far away sort of snapped me back in, so I was willing to do the whole long-distance thing. We'd been in LA at the time, but understandably, she didn't think it was worth it anymore."

Sahar's face fell. She wasn't sure how to respond.

"If she wanted to give things a try today, would you?"

He eyed her for a second, then looked at the road again. "No, I wouldn't. We were two completely different people back then, and I'm sure that's still the case today. Plus, her dad hated me."

That made her double-take, wondering if she'd heard correctly. "I'm sorry, what? Why?" Protectiveness made her voice grow louder.

He's not asking you to fight his battles for him. Relax. Shifting her body, she eyed the road, too.

"She comes from a long line of medical professionals. Everyone in her family is a specialist of some kind, so I was just some loser making movies who needed to grow up."

Her pupils blew wide. "Did he say that to you?"

Jay replied with a slow nod.

"And did *she* defend you?"

More traffic allowed him to look at her again. "Yeah, she did. I don't think it's something that got to her in the beginning, but it would have eventually, you know? We would have probably clashed over her stability and my lack thereof on certain occasions."

Sahar felt herself growing angrier. *Relax. He's not yours to defend.*

"Does Maya's family give you grief over that, too? Since she's a pediatrician."

He shook his head. "Nah, Maya's family is great. Granted, we aren't together, but they've never cared. Lillian's family, unfortunately, always did. He hated me the day he met me. On top of that, I had a three-year-old from another woman. His judgments used to bother Lillian as well."

Jay's hand was resting on the gear shift, so she reached forward and held on, incapable of not doing *something*. Then, for a fleeting second, she wished for him to lace their fingers together—lift her hand up to his lips.

It was moments like this that made everything with Jay feel more fragile as she remembered how irritated Martin would get when she'd initiate physical contact at a moment when *he* didn't want it. How, especially toward the end of their relationship, he would look at her with an irritated glare when he wasn't in the mood for her touch.

He looked down at where her hand covered his and flipped his palm over, allowing her to lace their fingers together.

See, Jay isn't like Martin, a small voice in her head whispered.

"Was there anyone else after her?" she asked.

"No, a few women I'd been interested in weren't willing to get involved long-term with a man who had a kid."

Fuck. That one hurt.

"I'm sorry," she managed to say.

"It's all good," he returned. "What about you?"

"I'll answer that in a sec, but how long were you in LA?"

"Four years. Maya did her residency at USC. I went with her, watched Ellie when she was at work, and then worked freelance in film when she was off."

"That's so sweet. The kid really scored with good parents."

Smiling, he waited for her to speak next.

He'd opened up to her, and now, she owed him some parts of her truth. "I've had my heart broken a few times."

Jay held her hand tighter. "Was Martin the worst?"

"Maybe?" she phrased it like a question. "A lot of them were the same. He was just great at apologizing and fooling me over and over again, so he was more like my last straw."

"How long were you with him?"

"A year and some change. We met at an audition before I got

cast in *Midnights* and ran into each other after I got back from the Boston tryouts."

Eyes back on the road, Jay said, "I looked him up, so I'd recognize his name and face to make sure he's never cast in anything I'm a part of."

She laughed. "He's got a decent singing voice, but he's a mid-level actor, sadly. Sam had actually auditioned for his role in *Hatchard's* and for *Midnights* around the same time, and he got both but chose *Midnights.* Martin was bitter because he auditioned for all three major roles in *Midnights* but didn't get call-backs for any of them."

"He's certainly not getting a call back if I'm there."

"I appreciate the loyalty."

"Always." The word left his mouth so seamlessly, so sincerely, that her heart burst. Sahar wasn't sure about many things, but she knew that Jay's benevolence wasn't a mask to get in her good graces. He knew pain and suffering well, and while it was clear it hardened him, it hadn't shredded his humanity. Instead, it had deepened his empathy, and she could tell as much by the stories he'd written. From the way he spoke and behaved. The way he *cared* to get to *know* her.

She looked up ahead toward the sky. Dark clouds seemed to be rolling in, but rain hadn't been on the forecast earlier. "Is it going to rain?"

Jay ducked his head a little, squinting to see. "Shit, it might."

"Fuck."

"Not a fan of rain?"

"I am, but it depends on my mood. Are you?"

He nodded. "Yeah, I prefer the rain."

"Do you run hot?"

Laughing, he gave a quizzical look. "Yeah, why?"

She shrugged her shoulders. "Just curious."

"You run cold, don't you?"

"How'd you figure?"

"I saw you eye the AC the second you got into my car, so I put it down for you. You're also holding a jacket, and it's eighty-eight degrees out."

The observation made her smile. "Okay, well, first, the jacket is for later. Second, good catch. I've got nothing to counter."

"How's your ankle?" he then asked.

She moved it a bit under the dashboard. "It really is better. I don't feel a thing right now."

"Is that the painkillers talking?" he asked, concern hanging onto his voice.

"No, honestly. It felt better this morning, and the swelling's gone down significantly. I took painkillers as a precaution."

"You can elevate it again once we're at my place. Or, use my dash if you'd like."

"I'm good right now. Promise."

For the remaining duration of the car ride, they discussed the most random things, getting to know each other through favorite foods and drinks, and letting the playlist she'd curated for *Every Speck of Dust* drive them to his place.

28

JAY

He'd sent her the beginning of the finale the night before, and Sahar had read the back half of the episode while he'd gathered drinks and snacks for them, as well as a pillow to prop up her ankle.

When he finally sat beside her on his gray sectional, her eyes were fixed on the remaining few words on the page. Something about his laptop propped up on her thighs made for an image he wanted to sear into his brain.

EXT. WOODLAWN BEACH - TWILIGHT.

"So this is the final scene, yeah?"

Jay nodded.

"What's stumping you?" she asked.

Sighing, Jay pushed his glasses up the bridge of his nose. "I can't settle on how to close the shot or even how to approach the scene. It feels like we have too many stories that end with two people looking out into the distance together. Lord knows I've done that before. Yet, a kiss doesn't feel right either. But I want something that makes the reunion after all that time apart palpable."

Sahar rounded her lips in thought. Jay kept his gaze on her.

"I think Henry would be in a state of shock," she started to say. "He wouldn't be expecting her there, would he? But even while she's standing in front of him, I think he'd take a second to react—to really process that Katherine's right there—real and whole. It'd be a quiet sort of shock while contentment starts to spread through him."

Processing her words and her presence in front of him, the very same contentment she spoke of rolled through him. He took the glass of water in front of him and drank.

Swallowing, Jay's eyes flicked back to her. "I think he'd hold her and never let go again."

Sahar's expression was picturesque. "Yes! The kind where they linger in each other's arms," she specified, releasing an exhale. "There's something so healing about hugs, and I don't think we give enough credit to them. Plus, it feels so right for Henry and Katherine."

Jay agreed. "At this point, I don't even know if it needs dialogue. If we have two great actors, every word I could write would be reflected in their performances."

She nodded, her eyes full of contentment. "Exactly."

He looked at her then, Sahar's eyes were glistening, something indescribable squared in their center. He had to tell her. "Sahar, I— I have a confession to make."

"Go on."

"I wanted you to be the one to choose the ending. It wouldn't feel right to me if it wasn't exactly how you pictured it. It's why I kept lagging. Why I wanted us to talk."

A loud guffaw burst from her lips. "So, you lured me here under false pretenses?"

"I lured you here to give you the ending you want."

The amusement on her face was coupled with another look he couldn't quite place.

Fuck. He wanted to hold her again, envelope her in his arms, and stay like that for a few hours, letting the sweet, citrusy scent of her perfume permeate itself into his skin. What if he just did it? She said she wasn't ready, though. The fact that she still might want more of him at some point needed to be enough for the moment.

Blinking, Jay tried to unfocus his gaze from her, but their eyes were locked in a conversation his mind hadn't caught up to yet.

She handed him his laptop; he took it, shut it off, and set it down beside him on the couch.

Divert. Keep talking about Henry and Katherine. Concentrate on them.

He had to tell her how much all of this meant to him, how her vision had been his saving grace—the lifeline to this story. "I don't know if anything will come from these rewrites. Quite frankly, I don't have much hope in me that it'll go far. But the last few weeks of working on this with you—the whole writing process," he paused, eyes still holding hers. "It's been rewarding again because of *you*. I don't know how I would've pulled myself out of this rut if you didn't care about these characters the way that you do."

Sahar swallowed. Inching her hand forward, she slid her fingers toward his and laced them together. "I like your words, Jay, and your vision," she added softly. "I know I joke about how they make me sad, but I think we need to feel the heavier emotions to appreciate the happier ones more intimately. I think —*no*, I *know*—that people will resonate with these characters. They'll remember them."

Without thinking, he brought her hand to his mouth and

pressed his lips to her knuckles, entranced by the softness of her skin.

Maybe someday he'd experience the crushing weight of burnout robbing him of his breath again. He knew that this industry only ever gave in small measures. He once had a teacher tell the whole class that when you love what you do, you don't work a day in your life. But what she'd failed to understand was that when your passion morphed into deadlines and expectations, love was sometimes left on the back burner.

Jay loved writing, and he loved directing, but he was so fucking tired of fighting to make a name for himself. It was a lie to say that creative labor was for one's own amusement because while that notion was certainly true to some degree, art was also meant to be shared. It was meant to exist outside of a single person's mind so the world could feel a little less lonely.

A heavy downpour hit the ceiling, echoing the sound of rain throughout his entire apartment and breaking him out of his thoughts.

Lightning flashed through his living room window, and a booming roar of thunder followed. Sahar jerked in her seat. "Fuck, that was loud."

The storm grew harsher and heavier. Reaching for his phone from the coffee table, Jay checked the weather app. It had been updated to reflect the current forecast, showing nonstop rain until three in the morning. *Shit.* He flipped his phone in Sahar's direction to alert her.

She grimaced. "Oh, hell."

He drew closer, taking her hand in his again. "Sahar, stay. Please. I'd hate for you to leave like this unless you'll let me drive you."

"I absolutely will not. I'd worry about you driving back."

Taking a breath, she looked around his apartment. Her eyes

landed back on his and then flicked down to where their hands rested.

"Then stay. I'll make us dinner. We can write a bonus episode for your eyes only. Whatever you want," he whispered.

"I can't," she whispered back, her voice so low he barely heard it.

"Why not?" he asked.

She didn't respond; she merely stared at him.

He wasn't sure how many seconds passed as the sounds of their breathing mingled with the rainfall.

A heartbeat. And then her lips parted, the words "fuck it" spilling out. In one fell swoop, Sahar's mouth was on his. He thought he was imagining it. Soft and stunning, but no, this was real. Sahar was kissing him again. Incapable of holding back how desperately he'd wanted this, Jay kissed her right back.

He palmed her cheek, and her hands landed on his shoulders. Sahar deepened the kiss until his glasses slid down his nose, killing the frenzy.

"What happened to *not right now*?" he asked, his breath still caught somewhere in his throat.

Sahar curled her lips inward. "You'll laugh at me if I tell you."

"Never," he affirmed, skating his hand up and down along the thin fabric of her dress.

She shook her head, pressing her lips back on his.

They kissed slowly for a beat, taking each other in. Over and over and over again.

"Your ankle," he mentioned, remembering why she was here and not at work.

"We can be careful," she hummed.

He tugged on her bottom lip, biting down gently. "You're not going to tell me what changed your mind?"

She lowered her head, placing a kiss at the jut of his throat. "Questions later. Right now, I only want you."

A low groan surged out of him. The sensation of her mouth moving against his was more intoxicating than he remembered.

She cupped his cheek, soft and warm.

God, please no emergencies this time.

Drawing his hands to her shoulders, he drifted his fingers slowly over her collarbones. "Then tell me how you want me. Show me all the ways you want to be touched. Tell me how you like to come. Let me give you everything you want and deserve, Sahar."

Her breath hitched as she looked at him. "Jay," she whispered.

Inching closer on the couch, he settled his lips along her neck, pressing an open-mouthed kiss to her soft, sweet skin. "Tell me," he rasped.

"Whatever you want."

She was being agreeable, tactile, and too damn closed off. He didn't want her like this.

He wanted the woman who'd waltzed into his coffee shop and screamed about the abysmal call the referee made at the Man City game the day before. He wanted the woman who didn't hesitate to tell him his story was too sad, and she wanted a happy ending instead.

Tracing her lips with the pad of his thumb, Jay held her gaze. "I want you to talk to me, sunshine. I want full transparency. In case you didn't hear me the first time, *I want* to give *you* everything," he underscored.

She swallowed, shutting her eyes for the briefest second. He brushed his fingers to the column of her throat, over her shoulder blades, and down toward her arms, as he watched goosebumps dance across her skin.

"I want all of you. I really want your mouth. But the problem is when I return the gesture, I'd prefer if you'd come outside of mine because I don't like how it feels."

"I'm not sure I understand where the problem lies. I have no issue pulling out," he said.

"Martin, he uh—"

Jay's pupils blew wide. He understood it immediately then. Her reservations about talking to him, the unease in her voice, the speedy willingness to do what *he* wanted. "Did that fucker make you feel like you were a problem because he refused to pull out?"

Sahar nodded, skating her fingers over his forearms. "Said it wasn't fair, and he didn't want it if that was the case."

Rage burning through him, Jay huffed. "His fucking loss." He slid his hand to her upper thigh, fingers fanning wide. "You want me to go down on you? That's what I'll do. *Happily*. No questions asked. No bargaining necessary. What else?"

She looked right at him, awe and disbelief running laps in her gaze, then pulled her bottom lip in between her teeth, thinking. "You can touch my hair, but please don't pull. My scalp is super sensitive, and it doesn't help that I have pins in it almost every day."

"Understood. Anything else?"

"That's it."

Placing his fingers underneath her chin, he nudged her to look at him. "I'm going to pick you up now and take you to my room. Then, I'm gonna make sure you've forgotten every other person you've been with. Sound good?"

Her lips parted, eyes dazed. "Yeah."

29

SAHAR

Air left her lungs, and a deliciously captivating warmth materialized all over her. Sahar wasn't prepared for this side of Jay.

He circled one arm around her back, another under her knees, and lifted her off the sofa.

"You know I can walk, right?"

"Ssh," he sounded.

"It's just a few steps," she reiterated.

Jay's lips plunged onto hers, kissing her hard as he walked. *Got it.* "Is that your way of telling me to stop talking?" she teased in between kisses.

"Keep talking. Stop protesting," he specified.

"Noted."

Kicking his way into his room, Jay carried her over to his bed and set her down gently. Sahar propped herself up on her elbows, watching him.

He removed his glasses and placed them on his bedside table, where she also noticed a framed photograph she wanted to pay closer attention to when she wasn't so preoccupied.

Lying beside her, opposite her left ankle, he dropped a

reverent kiss to her mouth. It was slow at first, meticulous. And then another, deeper this time, tongues and teeth colliding. Unrestrained. Messy. *Perfect.*

Fuck. If kissing Jay would always be this magnetic, she wanted to kiss him forever.

"One more thing," she added.

"Name it," he uttered huskily, clutching her waist.

Tugging at his bottom lip between her teeth, she said, "The next time this happens. When my ankle isn't being a little bitch, I want to be on top."

A delicious, throaty rasp rumbled out of him. "Fuck, sunshine. Anytime."

Sahar drew her hands inside his shirt, tracing the planes of muscle she'd thought of since Monday. Dragging the fabric up and over his head, she tossed it behind her.

The sight of his toned chest was the eighth wonder of the world, but it was the ink against his rib cage that made her breath snag. A massive crow, maybe a raven, with its wings spread, flying upward toward his heart. She smoothed her fingers in its path, marveling. "We're going to talk about this," she commented.

He smiled, something comforting and warm. "After. I want to see *you.*"

Anything. Yes. Whatever he wanted. She was more than willing to oblige. He hiked her dress up, roving his fingers voraciously over her legs. It was agonizing, enamoring. The desire in Jay's gaze was kaleidoscopic, unmatched from what she'd seen in other men. The hard length of him strained against her thigh, the feel of his fingers along her knickers—torturous.

He must've caught the bruises on her legs again and the two along her hips because his face fell. His fingers grazed ever so slightly along the one on her hip bone. She remembered how he looked at them last night, how she wanted to say something then, but fear told her not to assume. "I bruise very easily," she started. "Sometimes from the way a choreography pushes a part of my body. If I bump into something while changing. It's nothing out of the ordinary," she assured him.

His mouth dropped to the one along the middle of her thigh, then lower toward her knee, and back up to her hip bone. Gentle, sweet kisses to combat the ever-present throb.

Sahar propped herself on her elbows again. Fuck her ankle for killing the vibe. Still, watching Jay lower himself on the bed, kissing every inch of her, was a sight she could frame. Capture it in a photograph, a black and white film noir filter, with a Polaroid frame, and hang it in galleries worldwide for everyone to see.

When his lips dragged along the seam of her black lace thong, a shiver shot through Sahar's spine. It'd been a while since someone touched her with such deliberate care. He pulled the fabric down, and his jaw dropped, making her dizzy with longing.

"God, you're breathtaking," he professed with a deep groan.

Taking her uninjured leg by her calf, he swung it over his shoulder and looked up at her, his gaze incandescent with flames. *Fuck*—her desire grew tenfold as Jay's lips landed back on her thighs, brushing intoxicatingly up toward where she ached for him.

A flash of lightning and a boom of thunder outside paralleled the fervor rolling through her at the same moment that Jay's lips finally reached her wetness. His mouth moved with precision, his fingers squeezing her hips. *This man.* She'd forgotten what it was like to have someone's head buried between her thighs, how the warmth and feel of a tongue gliding against the most sensitive part of her could thoroughly unravel her.

Sahar hummed his name at the end of a moan, dipping her fingers into the smooth strands of his tousled hair.

Urgency emerged in his gaze as he sank a finger inside of her, making her arch in response. Her breathing grew more shallow, every inch of her body present and alert. *Wanting. Needing.* Utterly entranced.

It was Jay—it was all Jay. The way he revered her. The way he wanted this with as much staggering desperation as she did.

Her muscles tightened.

He picked up his pace.

"Fuck, you're so...I'm—" she breathed heavily, words escaping her.

Jay's eyes flicked back up to her again, the flames in his gaze white-hot now.

"You're fucking perfect," he groaned, the sound deep and guttural before he crawled one long lick up her center.

Her head fell back with a satisfied cry as Jay's mouth continued riding her waves.

Fucking stardust.

Heavy breaths mingled with the downpour outside. Delirious, dazzling sounds composed her new favorite song. She was going to give this man whatever he asked for when she didn't have to move as carefully because of her ankle.

"Inside me, please, Jay," she begged.

He sprang off the bed and undressed at rapid speed. *A masterpiece.*

"Condoms?" he asked, his breathing ragged.

"Up to you. I'm on the pill, remember?"

He inched closer, holding her jaw in his hand. Jay sank a lush, scalding kiss to her mouth, the taste of her still lingering on his lips. "What do *you* want?"

"Just you then," she answered.

Another bolt of lightning, a loud clap of thunder. His gaze flashed with wild longing once more.

Meticulously climbing on top of her to keep her ankle in place, his mouth dipped to the line of her bra, and he pushed the lace aside to kiss her. Slow, sweet movements. Tender presses of his lips and delicate brushes of his tongue. Sahar's fingers drew lower, cresting along his abs, making him shudder in the process.

Jay positioned himself at her entrance, eyes fixed on her. His hand splayed along her torso, and she wanted to scream. No part of her wasn't scorching because of him. She was, for the first time in her life, an inferno. It had always been significantly harder for her to orgasm once, let alone multiple times, but with Jay, she was already halfway there. Then, he slid inside of her, drawing a moan from deep within her throat.

She arched her hips up, wrapping her good leg around him. He dove deeper into her with a slow, achingly delectable rhythm.

"Sahar," he breathed with a thrust. "I almost fucking lost it there," he bit down at her neck, chasing it with a kiss. "Tasting you was—" another thrust, another deep, rugged groan— "ascension worthy."

Fuck.

Neither of them would last long, yet it satisfied her tremendously to know that he could've come just by pleasuring her.

He slowed his thrusts for a split second like he was savoring the moment, collecting it for safekeeping somewhere no one could reach. His mouth dropped to hers in a fevered kiss. Her fingers scratched along his back.

"Jay, please," she begged. What for, she wasn't even sure. She never wanted this to end. Though if it did, ascension worthy was the right way to put it.

A remarkable groan poured out of him. One hard thrust as

his head dropped to the slope of her shoulder. He let her come first again, following immediately after.

Colliding with Jay was euphoric.

Gravity was nonexistent, the sensation of him deep inside of her an indescribable flight.

AFTER CLEANING UP, Jay and Sahar returned to his bed, sitting up against his headboard, neither bothering with clothes yet. He'd also made sure her ankle was comfortably elevated, and her heart once more ached at his continuous means to take care of *her*. It was lovely. It felt safe.

She looked up at him, taking in the sight of his neck, his broad shoulders, the light dusting of hair spread across his chest. *When did Jay have time to work out?* His gaze locked on hers, a smile curling at the edge of his lips, unbidden. Trailing her fingers to the gorgeous crow tattooed on his rib cage, Sahar traced along its wings. "Tell me about this guy," she whispered.

He took a deep breath, something painful and dark clawing up his gaze. Its meaning must've been chained to a sore spot—an open wound. Drawing her lips to his, Sahar kissed him. Languidly. Tenderly. With her whole heart.

His hands in her hair, Jay deepened the kiss before parting from her. "Will you tell me about yours?" he asked.

"Every single one," she promised.

Unclenching his shoulders, he took one of her hands in his and swept his thumb over her knuckles. "When my parents would fight, I used to run outside to our front yard," he started.

God, Sahar could already feel her heart splitting in half. She could see it clear as day: a broken little boy, sitting all by himself, the world taking and taking from him. Too loud. Too dark. Too scary.

"One day, there were two crows, and I had plain toast in my hand, so I tossed some pieces to them." His lips twitched up a fraction, like a portion of the memory wasn't too bad.

"I didn't know anything about them. I think I just wanted to distract myself from the screaming inside. The next morning and the one after that, when I was on my way to school, I saw a bunch of things in front of the door. There were coins and colorful rocks," he let out a low huff.

"The two crows kept coming by me afterward, sometimes together or one at a time. I don't even know if they were the same ones, or if they told their other crow friends. But I started carrying bread with me and kept feeding them until we moved away from that house."

He wasn't looking at her as he spoke. His memories had taken him far away. "Lex wasn't born yet. I think it was just nice to know that something was looking out for me. So, right after I got my BA in film, I got it."

His name fell from her lips in a low whisper, her heart in her throat.

Jay's eyes locked on hers. "You're the only person who knows the reasoning behind it. I usually just tell people it's meaningless when they ask. Crows are badass. That's why."

She wanted to fucking cry. The rain still pounding against his window felt like it was flooding inside of her. No matter what came from this relationship, however long it'd last, Sahar would treasure this detail about him—keep it vaulted close to her heart.

But God, how she wished she had a guarantee of forever. Now more than ever.

Tears pricked in her eyes. "It means the world that you told me. Thank you for trusting me."

He outlined the ink along her forearm, his fingers gliding against her own crow. "What about yours?"

"I've been obsessed with them since I learned about their loyalty and intelligence in secondary school. It wasn't my first tattoo, but it was my first big one." She smiled for a beat, realizing how much more significant it felt now. "Shit, though, I did it when I was here in New York, actually, while I was visiting. I wanted the reminder that wherever I went, I'd have loyalty in my corner."

She lowered her head then, skating her lips over his rib cage to press a kiss along the feathers.

Sahar always believed in love. She fell hard and fast and without reservations, desperately wanting the relationship to last. But she'd never actually believed in soul mates or invisible strings. That stuff felt fictional—fated for other people, perhaps, but never for her.

Yet, everything about Jay felt cosmically intertwined, and nothing scared her more than that. Of all the coffee shops in the world, she had to walk into his. The crow on the left side of his rib cage would always align with the one on her right forearm.

When he'd spotted hers the first time, did he think of his? Did he wonder if the universe was maybe handing him a sign? *There's someone who'll look after you. She'll protect you through everything.* She gazed up at him; he was still elsewhere in his mind.

"Did he steal your entire childhood, Jay? Was there ever a point where you could just be a kid?" she asked.

When he looked at her, his eyes were glassy. The sadness of a lost little boy torrenting right out of him.

"He left for a year when Lex was two, and I was ten. I think that was the only time things were fine. That was also when I met Patrick because we moved next door to his family."

A sigh escaped him. Sahar traced circles along the muscles of his abdomen. "He came back and fucked shit up again. And when I was sixteen, that's when…" he trailed off, his Adam's apple bobbing with a hard swallow.

"You don't have to say it if it's too hard," she noted.

Jay pulled her hand up and placed a delicate, stabilizing kiss at her pulse point.

Let me be your strength, she wanted to say. *Take whatever you want from me,* she wished she could add.

"That's when he hospitalized my mom. It was also the same day my grandpa died. I somehow knocked him out, and we reported it. Mr. Sharp, Pat's dad, was a firefighter. He saw the whole thing. Testified for us. It landed the fucker community service. Nothing else…" he bit out.

Catching the fury swelling in his voice, Sahar palmed his cheek. He wrapped his fingers around her wrist, inhaling another deep breath.

"But we were able to get restraining orders after that, and she was able to finally divorce him. I think the only reason he stopped trying to find ways to destroy her life is because he met someone new. And I fear for that woman every day."

A monster. The person who should've been protecting him caused him the most pain, and then he got away with it. What a vile piece of shit. Her heart was in shambles.

"Is your mum okay now? And I mean, like *really* okay? I wondered when we'd met."

"She wasn't for a long time, but she's been better in the last four years. She found love again two years ago, and we all really like him. He's good to her."

Everything about his mother having a second chance at love made her heart squeeze.

"I hate that he hurt you all so much." She swept her lips along the corners of his eyes, down to each cheekbone, his nose, his jaw. "I hate that he took so much from you."

Jay pressed his mouth to hers in a featherlight kiss. "I don't want to waste another minute with you talking about him. He doesn't deserve it." He roamed his fingers behind her shoulder toward the hydrangea tattoo. "Tell me about this."

"They're my favorite flowers. It's my most recent one. I got it two years ago for my thirtieth birthday."

He touched the January twenty-nine, ninety—written in Roman numerals—on the side of her wrist, wordlessly asking for its meaning.

"Matching tattoos with my sister. She has my birthday. I have hers."

"When's your birthday?"

"September twenty-three, ninety-two. When's yours?"

"October eight, eighty-nine," he answered, kissing her forehead.

Jay pointed to the two hearts on her left arm. "What about these?"

"They're for my parents. Mum and Dad both drew one."

Sahar sat up a bit higher. "Do you want to know about my most personal one?" she asked him.

He nodded, pressing his lips to hers. "I want to know everything."

Slightly, she moved her body away from him to show the words written under her left breast. They were just barely visible under her bra line.

Jay read the words aloud. *"We're all fools in love."*

"It's from *Pride and Prejudice.* Not the book, but the 2005 movie. Charlotte Lucas says it to Lizzie."

Sahar smiled, biting down on her lip. "My ex, a chap named Tyler. I think, of all the people in my past, I loved him the most. He was also an actor," she paused, swallowing. "He dumped me two days before my birthday."

She kept the details of him stating she was only palatable in small doses to herself. She could give Jay so much of herself, every little secret he asked for, but not that—not yet. It would hurt too much. It'd all be too real.

"I was devastated, but I desperately needed to feel something —to continue believing that love wasn't some made-up fantasy. I was rewatching the movie when I heard that quote again, and it made me so proud to believe in love. To know that I wasn't silly for falling. Because really, isn't that the universal theme in all of Austen's stories? That we're all just fools, looking for connection?"

He dropped his mouth to hers, kissing her slowly, reverently.

"I think we were meant to find each other," she let out. *Bloody hell. Shut up. Why would you say that out loud?*

Jay cupped her cheek, and all self-deprecating thoughts were momentarily relinquished. She tilted her head to place a kiss on his palm.

Resting his forehead against hers, he said, "I think so, too."

30

JAY

The vision of Sahar, naked and curled in his arms, consumed him. Breathtaking and ethereal, her pink lips slightly parted. She wasn't kidding when she said she could fall asleep wherever, whenever, at any given moment because that's what had happened after he'd once more dropped to his knees and watched her come undone from his mouth *again*.

She was so devastatingly beautiful. Perfect in every way.

Trailing the pads of his fingers languidly up and down her shoulder, he wondered how anyone could possibly let her go. Her heart. Her mind. Her body. How they'd had a taste of her without wanting more. If it weren't for her ankle, he'd be a dead man walking; she would've wrecked him, he was sure of that. He was already more than halfway there.

He could stare at her for hours, marveling at all the ink scattered across her body. Memorize every dip and curve.

When her eyes slowly fluttered open, he didn't hide the fact that he'd been staring at her. He'd even put his glasses back on to ensure he wouldn't miss a single detail. Every scar, every freckle, every birthmark. Every rise and fall of her chest.

"Hi," she said, voice low and honeyed.

"Hi, sunshine."

"How long was I out?"

Jay pressed a kiss on her forehead. "Not too long."

Sitting upright, her hands ferreted through the sheets. She couldn't find what she'd been wanting, her bra, maybe? Instead, she plucked his T-shirt from somewhere in between them and pulled it over her head. "You know what I really want? That I *know* you'll have?"

The corners of his mouth angled upward. "Ice cream?" he drawled.

Sahar's smile was so luminous, so fucking bright, it could make the sun combust. "Yes."

"I want to make you dinner. How about afterward?"

She brought her fingers to his hair, carding the strands lightly. "But I want it now."

He held her face in his hand and brought his lips to hers in a deep, needy kiss. And then he sprang out of the bed, beelining to his kitchen. When he returned to his bedroom, Sahar had kicked the sheets off, and the sight of her visible, long legs underneath his T-shirt made him ravenous again. *This woman.*

Wrapping his arm around her shoulder as he slid back down onto the bed, Jay handed her a spoon and a pint of coffee-flavored ice cream.

Sahar shuffled in her spot, making herself more comfortable as she shifted to face him. She scooped some up and brought the spoon to him. Holding her gaze, Jay opened his mouth and licked.

"Can you do something unappealing for five seconds because I actually don't think I need to be any more attracted to you than I already am," she voiced.

He threw his head back with a laugh and then watched her

take a spoonful into her mouth, undoubtedly sure that he died right on the spot. "Welcome to the club, sunshine."

Tucking an errant strand of hair behind her ear, he continued. "On the afternoon of the *Clue* night, you walked into the coffee shop wearing some lavender dress, and then you drank from your straw right in front of me, so I spent the rest of the shift yelling at everyone for no reason because all I wanted to do was rip that dress off you and make you scream my name in a thousand different ways," he paused, "I don't know how I would've lasted through the night if you hadn't changed after work."

She brought the spoon back into her mouth, popped it out, and licked her lips. "This is an excellent bit of information. I'm buzzing about how I can torture you with it in the future."

He seized her mouth then, savoring the taste of coffee ice cream on her lips like his own personal serving of heaven. When she deepened the kiss with her tongue, a growl ripped from his throat.

Cursing under his breath, his fingers grazed up her thigh.

She broke their kiss, averting her attention back to the dessert. Another spoonful to his mouth, then back into hers. He would never think about ice cream the same way as his teeth sank into the slope of her shoulder and his fingers clenched her thigh. He was seconds away from begging her to let him drop to his knees again when she pulled his hand up.

"Sahar, please let me—"

Her eyes darkened, and she interrupted his plea by scraping some of the ice cream off the spoon and onto his index finger. His heartbeat collapsed as she brought his finger to her mouth and sucked. Slowly.

Jay's head fell back against the wooden bedpost with a thud, another audible curse lunging out of him. "You're going to kill me," he breathed.

Brimming from somewhere deep inside her throat was the most intoxicating laugh he'd ever heard. Sahar pulled one more lick before she pressed a resounding, needy kiss back onto his mouth.

All at once, the mattress he had for years felt softer with her beside him, warmer and more comforting. Generic cotton sheets felt otherworldly.

He thought back to their two-in-the-morning conversation and how, in the hours when he learned that her favorite ice cream flavor matched his own, he was so sure that Sahar would only be his in his dreams. *And he had dreamed of her that night—his mouth all over her, her body swaying with his.* Except he was fully awake now, and she was carefully twisting herself in his arms, reaching over and placing the pint on his bedside table while her mouth stayed pressed to his.

And for a moment, he felt like his world was actually fucking perfect.

"You're lucky I picked up my work tote before coming here because there was no way I'd stay without my essentials," Sahar said, slowly limping back into the bedroom.

"You know, there are these wonderful things called stores? I would've gotten you whatever you needed."

She gave him a big smile. "I really hope the rain stops by tomorrow. I wouldn't want to be here when your family's back."

He understood her concerns, though he felt differently. "You could just be a friend if you're uncomfortable. No one needs to know there's something more between us."

"You might be able to lie to Eloise, but Maya and Alex weren't born yesterday."

Jay had given her one of his clean T-shirts, and he could catch a glimpse of the underwear she'd changed into, these ones a type of cotton, black with mesh at the sides. He couldn't wait to take them off her again. "So, what if they know?" he asked.

Sitting at the edge of his bed, Sahar blew out a sigh. "I don't know, actually. This is all confusing."

"Does it have to be?" he proposed.

She shook her head, swinging her legs up onto the mattress, finding a comfortable position. Sahar tipped her head to him, the unreadable fear back in her eyes. He hated that look—hated not knowing what to do to help her.

"No, it doesn't, but I *need* to do things differently with you."

Drawing closer, Jay held her chin between his thumb and forefinger. "You're scared of something," he said, trailing his thumb up over her lips. "I don't know what it is, and I hope you'll tell me when you're ready, but God, Sahar, I really wish you weren't."

Uncertainty shot through her eyes, her lips in a straight line. She lowered her head onto his shoulder. "I really wish I wasn't either," she whispered.

Forever was a promise Jay had never offered to a woman. Something always held him back.

But he knew, with absolute certainty, that he could promise forever to Sahar. If she asked for it. If it was what *she* wanted.

"I'M fine taking the train, Jay. I promise. My ankle feels okay, and the drizzle should let up soon."

Standing in the middle of his kitchen, he inched forward and wrapped his arms around her waist. Her arms circled his neck. It was two in the afternoon, and they'd spent the entire morning tangled in each other's arms again.

It hadn't been enough time.

He shut his eyes, accepting that no time with Sahar would ever be enough.

She curled her fingers into his hair. "Want to know what changed my mind about us?" she asked, the steady glimmer he loved back in her eyes.

Jay peppered her face with kisses. "Please."

The blush staining her cheeks red made his heart thrum faster.

"It was coming to the end of the story. Seeing that Henry and Katherine would get their moment. Watching your brain work the way it did, I don't know. It did something to me. I didn't want to miss the chance to be with you."

"Fuck," he grunted, dropping his mouth onto hers in a liquifying kiss.

Sahar kissed him back with equal fervor, her lips and tongue and teeth so familiar that it felt like it'd been ages with them.

And then a knock on his door jolted them. Her eyes grew wide.

Jay walked over to open it, and there were Eloise and Maya, roughly four hours earlier than when he was expecting them.

Eloise jumped into his arms. "Dad!"

Fuck. Sahar was going to feel ambushed—the last thing she wanted. Why hadn't any of them called or texted him?

Maya bolted inside and ran toward the bathroom. "My bladder is on the brink of explosion," she yelled.

Holding onto Eloise, he walked back to the kitchen. "Did you have fun, baby?" he asked.

His daughter screeched into his ear. "Yeah! Aunt Lexie is *so* good."

"Right? She's the best part, isn't she?"

Once he saw Sahar again, he mouthed the words, *I'm so sorry.*

She offered him a small smile, but the discomfort was written all over her face—in her entire posture.

Fuck fuck fuck.

Eloise jumped down from his grip and turned. Spotting an unfamiliar face, she looked back at Jay. He leveled himself with her. "Can you say 'hi' to my friend Sahar?"

Eloise shifted back shyly. "Hi," she waved, her voice low.

"Hi!" Sahar waved back, a bright smile on her face. *Damn, the woman masked her discomfort well.* The rising panic he'd seen in her eyes had momentarily vanished.

"She's pretty," Eloise whispered in his ear.

The ghost of a smile rose along his lips. "I know."

At that moment, Maya walked back into the room. "Hi, sorry. I actually thought I was going to die for like five minutes there, so that was fun."

Eloise gasped.

"I'm exaggerating, mija. Don't worry." With the living room wall right at her peripheral, Maya clearly hadn't seen Sahar yet, so she turned to Jay. "Why do you look so shocked to see us?"

Jay tilted his head toward the kitchen. Maya inched forward and followed his gaze to where Sahar stood. "Oh shit! I'm so sorry."

She ambled over to Sahar, her arms wide open. "Hi, I'm Maya. Eloise's mom. You must be Sahar?"

He was so fucking thankful that Maya was one of the friend-liest people he knew.

Sahar smiled and hugged her back. "It's so nice to meet you," she said.

After they parted, Maya pivoted her attention back to Jay. "Did Lex not text you? My phone's been dead all morning because the stupid plug stopped working, and I didn't notice. I told her to let you know we'd be coming in early."

He shook his head to respond.

"Watch, she probably wrote it but forgot to press send. Ugh, I'm so sorry!"

"How'd you two even get here from the train station?" he asked.

"I drove Alex's car, so we're going to have to pick her up. Anyway, now that I've gone to the bathroom, Ellie and I could drive down to your mom's and hang out with her, so you two can be alone."

Sahar countered. "He was about to take me to the train station, actually. I should get home now that the rain's finally slowed a bit."

"Were you really? I hope it's not because of us," Maya added.

"Not at all," Sahar affirmed, grabbing her bag from one of the chairs at the kitchen table.

"I'll be back in a few," Jay said.

Maya smiled. "Sounds good. It was so nice to meet you, Sahar," she said.

"Likewise!"

Jay knew Sahar's tells well enough to decipher that both her tone and smile were real.

Then, Maya turned to their daughter, who'd been rummaging in her backpack for something. "Wanna show me all the things you drew for art class?"

"Yeah!" Eloise said, forgetting her task at hand. She waved a shy goodbye at Sahar and ran off, dragging Maya with her.

Jay placed his hand on the small of Sahar's back as they walked out the door. "You okay?"

She nodded.

"Maya's sweet. I think I expected her to be angry. Like, she should've gotten to know me before I was allowed anywhere near Eloise."

Ah. That made sense. Jay opened the passenger door for her. "I've known Maya for a decade now. We were friends before we hooked up; neither of us had a thing for each other before or after. I'm sure she wants nothing more than to know I have someone, so she can stop trying to set me up with anyone she thinks could be a fit."

Sahar let out a low laugh. "She does that?"

Closing the door, he walked over to the driver's seat. As he buckled himself in, he added, "I told her about you when she came to take Ellie because she was adamant about introducing me to her yoga instructor's sister, who apparently just moved to New York."

He caught her biting her lip. "Oh."

Driving out of his garage, he looked back at her. "Yeah, and Ellie's a bigger conversation to have. I know that. So, I'm sorry you got ambushed a bit."

"It's okay. Honestly. I think it helps to know that Maya is cool with it. I—"

When she trailed off, he gathered that what she wanted to say was making her nervous, so he reached over and took her hand.

"I've only had this conversation with one other ex, and never this early, but given the circumstances, it's a little different with you."

Jay tightened his hold on her, silently nudging her to go on.

"I don't know if I want—" She cut off again, trying to find her words. "I love kids, and I've always imagined some sort of a family, but it's never involved getting pregnant on my part, so I, uh, don't know if you want more kids who are biologically yours." She swallowed, her voice low. "And if you do, I'd understand if you had to end this now."

He looked at the time on his dashboard and then pulled over on a nearby street, parking the car.

The seatbelt was suddenly suffocating him. He unclasped it, pivoting to face her. "There's nothing in this world that scares me more than being a dad," he said. "Still, to this day." Swallowing the lump in his throat, he continued. "I was so fucked up when Maya told me she was pregnant. I was convinced that if I had any part in the kid's life, I'd somehow morph into the same person my dad was."

Sahar's fingers roamed across his forearm, soothing him.

"It was always going to be Maya's choice first, so when she decided she wanted to keep the baby, I went all in with her. I had to try," he smiled. "Eloise is the best thing in both our lives, and if she's the only kid I have, that's completely fine with me."

Crows cawed somewhere above them, their conversation mingling with his and Sahar's. "I'm glad you told me where you stand, but it's not a deal breaker." He paused, thinking over his next batch of words so they'd come out correctly.

"I'd love for you to get to know Ellie when you're ready, but if that isn't something you're comfortable with, then—this is it, I suppose."

Horror flashed in her gaze. "Jay. Of course, I want that. I just, I need to know that this will—" She exhaled a sigh. "I just need a bit more time."

He palmed her cheek. "Time," he repeated. "Works for me."

And then he turned, pulling his seatbelt back on and starting the engine again.

At the train station, she'd hugged him with a force that shattered him from the inside out. Quiet rain had started to drizzle again. *I'm from London,* she had reassured him. Still. He'd worry.

She'd said she'd call later tonight.

They'd figure things out. At whatever pace she wanted them to.

~

JAY WALKED BACK into his apartment to find Maya sitting alone on the couch, doom-scrolling on her phone.

"Where's El?" he asked, kicking his sneakers off by the door.

She angled her head in his direction. "Showered and immediately crashed, and I just let her. She didn't sleep well last night."

"Is she okay?"

"Yeah, probably the storm. Plus, she was very concerned that you were all by yourself here." She used air quotes around the words, *all by yourself.*

Smiling, he plopped himself on the couch beside her.

"I'd seen pictures of Sahar, so I knew she was stunning, but holy smokes, photographs do not do that woman justice."

A low laugh escaped him. Sahar wasn't just physically breathtaking—it was everything about her. It was her fire and light that made her incomparable.

"I'm pretty sure I'm in love with her, and it's fucking killing me," he admitted.

Maya punched his shoulder with unrestrained enthusiasm. "Fuck yes, Jay! I'm gonna assume she feels the same way?"

He rubbed the spot she'd hit. "I don't know. She's going through some things. I don't know what they are, but I'm guessing they're making it harder for her to fully open up to me."

She folded her knees up to her chest. "You think it has something to do with her ex? Lex told me a bit about him."

"What didn't Lex tell you?" It was lovely that his sister and Maya had always been close, but why the fuck were they talking about his love life?

Maya rolled her eyes. "Relax, it's not like she knows shit with the way you keep to yourself. But she believes you're into Sahar —" she paused, holding up a finger to stop him from countering —"which we now know is correct because you've confirmed it *to me*. She'd just mentioned that Sahar dated the lead in her show and that he's a real piece of work. Your daughter also called him a slimy possum after she overheard Lex complaining."

"That's my girl," he declared.

"Now, answer my question. Do you think it's her ex? Or something deeper?" Maya challenged.

Jay sighed. "To a degree, I'm sure he has something to do with it. But there's something else there."

She gave him an empathetic pout. "Give her time, then. Are *you* able to open up to her? Because I hope you're not expecting her to when we all know how closed off you can be."

He stretched his legs out onto the coffee table, laying his head back on the cushion. "I've told her things no one else knows. She can break me wide open with a single look, Maya," he confirmed.

Maya cocked an eyebrow, then gave him a toothy grin. "Good, good. That tells me a lot."

"You okay with her spending time with Ellie when she's ready for that? And if the kid's okay with it, too?"

"Absolutely. I trust your judgement, and I don't know...I can tell she's one of the good ones. You know my gut," she reminded him.

Jay nodded, taking in her response. Whether a myth or reality, Maya's gut was one to trust; he'd never argue against it.

She told him a bit about their weekend before Eloise woke up and joined them for a quick movie. Later, they picked up Alex and drove to his mom's place for dessert.

Sahar had made it home safe.

Jay spent the rest of the day and evening missing her.

31

SAHAR

Willa came home after work, accompanied by Ethan and Sam, who both wanted to check in on Sahar. They'd ordered food, and she caught them up on what happened, promising that her ankle was indeed okay and she was ready to go back to work on Tuesday.

After the guys left, Sahar had confided in Willa regarding everything she'd felt after spending the night at Jay's, and Willa had suggested for Sahar to be fully transparent with him, vouching that it was the one thing that ensured she and Ethan got off on a healthy start when they decided to risk their friendship for a relationship.

If only being honest with Jay about her specific fears were easy. If only she weren't so terrified that he'd run.

She had a feeling he'd understand because he'd been so patient with her, except her brain heckled that it was because he hadn't fully seen all of her.

He'll also have enough of you someday. A repeat of Martin's birthday is inevitable when you're the problem in every relationship.

Two Months Ago - May

Sahar swallowed, struggling to recognize the woman staring back at her in the mirror. She wore a simple black skirt with a dark gray striped jumper and boots; long brown hair ironed and makeup done as she'd always had it, but someone else looked back at her. Someone lost. Someone numb.

There were knots twisted deep in her belly, growing tighter and more suffocating by the second.

An exhale. An inhale. Repeat.

It wasn't working.

It wasn't normal to feel this much distress over a birthday party—*her boyfriend's* birthday party, of all people. It wasn't normal to wonder what type of mood he'd be in and if he'd remember that they were a couple or if he'd leave her to socialize on her own. If Sahar had been an introvert, she would've lost it. She couldn't imagine what it'd be like if she were like her sweet co-star, Innila, quiet and shy, only opening up to those she was comfortable around.

Sahar was one of the most extroverted people in her circle, yet she still never felt comfortable around Martin's friends.

She spent a weekend with them in the Hamptons, and it had been the single most miserable weekend of her life. She'd faked intense cramps one night to stay behind while they'd gone out to a yacht party. The next morning, she'd done her best to play pretend, and with that, a small part of her died. They were in the same industry; it should've been *somewhat* easy to socialize, but it'd been like pulling teeth with them.

Her eyes stung, forcing her to carefully flutter her lashes and fight back tears. She could do this.

Maybe it'd be different tonight.

Maybe he'd be less stressed.

Maybe he'd be nicer.

Drawing closer to the mirror, she picked a few pieces of fallen stray hair off her jumper. Another sharp inhale.

She bared her teeth, making sure her lipstick hadn't transferred, and then finally, she doused her face with setting spray, letting the mist act as some sort of pixie dust.

She *could* do this.

SAHAR GLANCED down at her phone. It was barely 10 p.m., and time wasn't passing. Martin had only spoken two sentences to her, one of them being a sneering comment about how she'd been late—by five minutes—and another his clipped *thank you* to her happy birthday.

After that, she'd lost him somewhere at the bar. Now seated at the reserved table in the relatively stunning lounge they'd been in, all she wanted to do was leave.

What was the point?

Chelsea—the kindest person in his circle—poked her bicep. "You're quiet."

Swaying the Moscow mule in front of her left and right, Sahar gave her an honest smile. "Exhausted," she answered, a little louder now as Pitbull's "Give Me Everything" blasted in a throwback over the speakers.

Chelsea tilted her head sympathetically and drew closer. "I don't know how you all do it after your shows. I feel like I'd just want to sleep for days," she voiced.

Huffing, Sahar lifted her drink to toast. Chelsea grabbed her pint and clinked. "The things we do for love," Sahar added, hoping the sentiment didn't come across as snarky.

But Chelsea simply grinned back. Her eyes darted across the table where her boyfriend Spencer and Martin were returning from the bar. The six other people who'd been at the bar or on the dance floor followed behind them, lost in laughter. They started sliding into the booth, closing the space that'd temporarily been Sahar's refuge.

Instead of sitting near her, Martin let other people wriggle in while he sat at the very end. She wanted to scream. Why wouldn't he sit next to her? It wasn't like she was *his girlfriend,* of all people.

With agonizing restraint, Sahar turned to Vera, sitting beside her. "I love this top on you, Vera. It looks stunning," she complimented genuinely. It was a gorgeous shade of teal.

The girl brought her hand to the bottom of her chin with a grin. "Thanks! Aritzia," she added.

Sahar smiled back at her. Vera wasn't as genuine as Chelsea, but she was a bit less stuck up than everyone else at this table, including her boyfriend.

Out of nowhere, Martin's buddy Hank stood up and drunkenly slurred a loud toast as the table erupted in howls. Standing up to clap Hank on the back, Martin clearly appreciated the nonsensical speech he'd just gotten over anything Sahar could've said. She would've whistled, but he didn't think it was classy that she could. Likely because *he* didn't know how to, but still.

For a woman who was surrounded by all types of lights eight times a week, the remnants of the smoke machine and the disco lights from the dance floor were making her dizzy. It was too fucking loud when she was this tense. It was unpleasant when her people weren't nearby.

Looking down at the small amount of her drink remaining, she grabbed her glass and took a swig. She needed another if time insisted on lagging.

"Ah! I love this song!" Britney screeched when some mix Sahar couldn't even decipher came on. "We have to dance," she bellowed, then pulled everyone up to the dance floor.

Can the DJ play The National, please?

Sahar looked over at Martin as he declined Britney's offer. *Oh.* Maybe he was going to play nice? Maybe he wouldn't be such a dick to her if they were left alone.

Chelsea tugged on Sahar's hand for her to follow.

"Let me see how my guy is feeling, and I'll be right there," Sahar replied.

Nodding, Chelsea bounced off the cushioned seat and sprang toward the dance floor.

Alone in the relatively secluded corner, Sahar slipped out of the booth and trekked toward where Martin stood, looking at his phone. She wrapped her arms around his neck and placed a kiss on his cheek.

"I love you," she said. "Happy Birthday."

Martin rolled his shoulders, aggressively shoving her off him. "We're in public, Sahar. Calm down."

The churning acid in her belly threatened to rise up her throat. She swallowed, her breath locked uncomfortably inside her lungs.

"Okay, so we're still being an asshole to me? Got it," she noted, doing everything in her power not to cry.

"Don't make a scene," he bit back.

She tried to force out another breath, then reached over the bench and grabbed her bag. She *wouldn't* cause a scene. That wasn't who she was. She'd keep playing pretend, but fuck all of this. She was done. She couldn't keep letting this pitiful excuse of a man make her feel like the smallest person in the world.

"Where are you going?" he asked.

"Like you care."

"Sahar, relax. I'm sorry."

She scoffed, rolling her eyes. "Are you?"

"Stop being so fucking difficult," he sneered again.

Britney came back, dragging Martin to the dance floor. "Last

I checked, it's your birthday, bro—get your ass over there," she hollered.

With two fingers, she pointed Sahar in the same direction.

"I need another drink first," Sahar replied, then beelined straight to the bar.

AFTERWARD, Martin and his friends decided that they wanted to go to some new club that'd just opened up, but Sahar couldn't do it anymore. She made up an excuse about how she wasn't feeling well, went home, and immediately bolted for the shower, where she wept.

We're in public, Sahar. Calm down.

One would think she'd been dry-humping his bones and slobbering all over him like some wild animal in heat. It was a fucking peck on his cheek. The briefest hug. No one was around. What the fuck was wrong with him? And what was wrong with her? Why was she continuing to put up with him?

The once scalding hot water running over her had gone lukewarm.

It's not just him. It's you. You're the problem. He's embarrassed by you. Hasn't he said it enough times? She shook her head violently, fighting the banshees in her head.

You're too loud, they continued. Sahar cried harder. *You get too excited. Everyone's said this about you.*

Hugging her knees tightly, she shivered uncontrollably.

Remember the way you snorted when you laughed at that one joke Vera made while everyone laughed normally? That's why he doesn't want to be seen with you. Her eyes burned. Her heart was too broken. She couldn't shut the voices off. She didn't know how to.

Tyler was right. Martin just confirms it, as have the others.

You're only palatable in small doses.

She cried and cried until the water grew cold enough to force her out.

Then she cried herself to sleep.

The next time she saw Martin, she had to be done.

She had to end things.

PRESENT DAY

Sahar woke up to her alarm blaring. Confused and still tired, she snoozed it three times before remembering that she had a dentist appointment at 9:30 a.m.

She grumbled, pulling her blanket over her head.

Opening her phone up finally, she noticed a text from Jay, remembering that after they'd been messaging back and forth, he'd said he'd call at the end of the night.

JAY

Hey, sunshine. You awake?

She had crashed after her spiral, clearly.

SAHAR

So sorry! I knocked out.

Tell him everything, Sahar. Put it out there. She heard Willa's advice again.

But she wanted to keep Jay.

She didn't want him to run when he saw all of her.

Sighing, she sat up and swung her legs off the mattress. Sahar stretched her bad ankle first, rolling it slowly in the manner Jenny had advised. The pain was mostly gone, but she'd keep the stirrup on for another week while performing.

Her phone buzzed on her nightstand.

JAY

No worries. How are you? How's your ankle?

This sweet, sensible man. A logical part of her brain knew that Jay was patient, honest, and kind. She could accept that he'd wanted her for a while now—it was what he'd admitted to. It was what he'd *shown* her.

SAHAR

Much better, and I mean that.

He answered right away.

JAY

Good good. Will you be back at work tomorrow?

SAHAR

Yes! Will I see you?

JAY

My shift ends at 1, and then I'm meeting Pat to talk about his additions to the finale. When will you get in?

SAHAR

I have PT with Jenny at 4:30, so I'll probably be at the theatre by 4.

JAY

Ah, shit. I need to be home by 6 to pick up Ellie. My mom has a gala she needs to go to.

SAHAR

Wednesday? I'll definitely see you at the shop if you're working.

JAY

I will be. I might have to sneak by the theatre before I leave just to kiss you.

That. His unfiltered longing was comforting. She never wanted it to fade. She hoped it'd continue to grow.

SAHAR

Yes, please!

JAY

Glad we're in agreement. Also, what are you doing Sunday? I realize you might be too tired, but Ellie's having another sleepover with my cousin's kid, and I don't have any plans.

SAHAR

This coming Sunday? The 28th?

JAY

Yeah.

SAHAR

I'm free as a bird. Come over? Are you working on that day?

JAY

I'm not, but I can aim to get to you by the time you're home.

SAHAR

Excellent!

You used too many exclamation marks. Don't bother with a heart. Chill.

With a heavy sigh, Sahar set her phone down. Jay was so fucking good to her, and yet her bloody mind wouldn't let up. How much more did she need to grasp that this man wasn't like her exes? At what point would her mind stop tormenting her with unwanted thoughts about how she shouldn't be too forward because it'd push him away?

What was a bloody heart emoji going to do? Make him run? Of course, it wouldn't. *Still.*

32

SAHAR

With both their unruly schedules and the small distance, dating Jay was unlike anything else Sahar had known. When he was free, she was working. When she was free, he was at home with his daughter.

But he had tried. They both did.

He'd stopped by the theatre to kiss her when he could, and they'd stolen quiet moments at the coffee shop by extending their conversations until it got too busy for him to continue.

And their late-night phone calls were becoming her favorite way to fall asleep.

Still, she wanted more.

She'd missed him.

When Sahar got home on Sunday night, Jay had texted her that he was approximately twenty minutes away. It gave her enough time for a quick body shower and a change of clothes.

He'd wanted to take the lavender dress off her? Well, his wish was her command.

She put on the dress, opting out of a bra and knickers this time around. She was also extremely thankful that she'd finally managed to fold the laundry that'd been taunting her. Jay's bedroom had been so neat, so organized, and while Sahar had far more things in hers, it was at least tidier now. She'd also steamed the dress the night before, giving her another small win.

Most importantly, her ankle wasn't being a nuisance anymore.

A rap on the door alerted her to his arrival, and Sahar tousled her hair one more time in the bathroom mirror before she skipped to the living room.

When they were face to face again, she couldn't suppress the corners of her mouth from twitching upward. "Hi," she said, stepping aside for him to walk in.

Jay's jaw visibly dropped, sending a surge of heat coursing through her. Groaning, he swept her up by her waist and locked the door with his other hand. "Hi."

Sahar giggled, relishing in the desire she felt cascading out of him.

Being with Jay felt right. So right that the mere thought of even poking at their bubble with her truth sounded disastrous.

She just wanted *them*—his body melding with hers, his words wrapping around her heart. Unwavering happiness. Unmarred adoration. Sahar wanted forever.

Planting his mouth at her pulse point, he bit down and simultaneously squeezed her ass as he spoke. "Did you wear this dress because of what I said?"

When Sahar felt his erection against her thigh, a moan and a *yes* fused together.

Jay's mouth landed back on hers in a kiss so deep, she was sure she'd lose her balance. Only, he was the one who seemed to lose balance as it dawned on him that his hiking fingers weren't running into more fabric underneath her dress. *"Fuck me,"* he bit out, his voice delicious and dark and so fucking hot.

Sahar palmed his erection over his jeans. "Oh, I intend to."

His mouth dipped to the sensitive spot behind her ear as her hands quickly undid his zipper.

And then she dropped to her knees.

Looking up at the sight of him, flushed and unguarded before her, Sahar felt the safety net of the trust they'd built.

She lowered his boxer briefs with his jeans, gawking. The red on his cheeks deepened in color as she licked her way up the hard length of him, reveling in the audible hitch in his breath.

When she brought him fully into her mouth and sucked, it was less intolerable than it'd been in the past. Sahar *knew* that Jay would remember her preference. His eyes glazed and heart on full display, she braced one hand around his thigh and circled her fingers around him.

Pumping. Sucking. Licking.

Jay stopped her then, brilliantly breathless. He tipped her chin up with his fingers, his gaze burning through every barricade that armored her. "Sahar," he rasped. "That's enough, sunshine. Inside of you."

She rose to her feet and kissed him, first—an act of gratitude —a surrender of her heart, perhaps. And then she hurried them toward her bedroom.

He stumbled, stopped, and shrugged off his jeans, grabbing them with one hand while keeping his arm fully around her waist. Inside her bedroom, he threw the denim on her floor beside the now-empty laundry basket, sparking a fuzzy warmth of comfort to travel through her. She yanked off his T-shirt, throwing it somewhere in the vicinity of his trousers.

Jay's hands reached for the bottom of her dress again, and he lifted it off her, the stretchy material obliging as if it were as excited for her as she was.

Every curse out of his mouth felt like a prayer—an unfiltered note of praise.

Sahar directed him backward toward her bed and pushed

him onto the mattress. A satisfied grunt blew out from somewhere deep in his throat.

And then, she straddled him.

"You're going to kill me, you know that?" He skated his fingers over her shoulders, down along the middle of her breastbone, all the way to her belly button, before he moved his arms around her ass, bringing her closer to him. "Since you told me you wanted to be on top, the vision of you riding me has been in *every* single one of my thoughts."

She ground on him in one slow, deliberate motion.

Jay shut his eyes, letting another curse fall into the space left between them.

Sitting up underneath her, he brought his lips to her breast, then drew her nipple into his mouth. She moaned, trailing her hands to his hair and rolling her hips against him.

Once, twice, chasing the friction as his mouth worked her breasts.

She curved her hands around his shoulders as she lowered herself on top of him.

"God, you're unreal," he breathed.

He was unreal.

Jay's body was magnetic—on top of her, underneath, wherever—being with him was a dream.

"You—you feel so good," she divulged, tugging on his hair and nudging him to look up at her.

Sahar's mouth moved to his for a messy, *needy* kiss as she rode him faster, the ripples of her orgasm swelling through her.

They came together, his name rolling off her tongue with urgency.

Later, Jay insisted he wanted another taste of her, dragging her up and onto his face, his scruff and mouth and tongue adding a whole new form of pleasure in this position.

. . .

THE WAY he looked at her while they were sprawled in her bed at the end of the night nearly broke Sahar.

No one had looked at her like that before.

His fingers trailed along her forehead, gently moving to her cheek. "I—" he started to say, but the words suspended in his mouth as Sahar bolted upright.

Whatever he wanted to say had to be a fleeting thought. He hadn't seen all of her yet. He hadn't witnessed the parts of her that pushed her exes away. He was lovestruck from multiple orgasms and serotonin running through his brain.

He hadn't seen the aftermath of when it all wore off—the inevitable crash and burn.

Eyes narrowed, he tried to read her. "Sahar?"

Tears threatened to unleash. Her heartbeat thundered in her chest. Sirens outside wailed, and the sounds of people yelling about all sorts of things in the distance rang through her ears.

"Sahar?" he repeated.

Frantically, she shook her head. "We can't do this."

He blinked rapidly, trying to read her. He was always trying harder than anyone else ever had, but she was being pulled away by a current while he was left at shore. *Fuck.*

"Do what?" he asked, his voice even, like he was trying not to push.

She gestured in the space between them. "*This.* Us."

His dreamy gaze turned cold. Bewildered. Sahar was actively hurting him, and she couldn't even tell him why.

She hated herself for it.

Blinking again, he took a breath. "What on earth is happening right now?"

She bit down on her bottom lip, battling the tears that had filled her eyes. And then she jumped off the bed, her entire body shattering.

He rose with her, carefully keeping a distance.

Stop fighting him, a still, small voice inside of her whispered.

"Sunshine, talk to me," he all but begged.

And then she snapped, tears torrenting onto her face. *Sunshine.* "That's just it. *That* endearment. All of this."

Her hands were shaking, like a ruptured fault line, making everything inside of her unsteady.

Jay's eyes widened.

She swallowed hard. "Everything's brilliant now. We're on top of the world. Everyone loves summer in the beginning, but they get sick of it by the time August rolls around." She sniffled, hating how her voice sounded. How *small,* twisted, and torn she felt, saying the words aloud.

Backing up, she leaned against her vanity for support. Jay didn't move.

"They all left because *of me,*" she cried out. "They left because I'm *exhausting.* And it's only a matter of time before this bubble breaks and you get there, too."

He looked gobsmacked.

The light they'd ribboned themselves in turned to tendrils of smoke.

Taking a breath, Jay slowly inched closer. His warm gaze held her, and her heart snapped in two.

How could she mold herself into someone who was worthy of him? What part of her was she meant to change? She didn't even know.

Gently, he tipped her chin up, and even more tenderly, he brushed the tears away from her cheek. "You know why I called you that?" he asked, his voice so soft, she wanted to cocoon herself into it.

Sahar shook her head.

His throat bobbed as he delicately ran his thumb over her cheek. "One day, back in February, you walked into Amanda's right as I was about to turn around and quit." He cleared his throat, like the memory was too painful. God, she felt like shit. Worse than shit.

"I was going to leave this damn city—get a different job elsewhere. I was livid, having the shittiest fucking morning, then you swung the door open with Willa." He swept another tear from her face. "You two were mid-conversation, but you stopped talking, looked at me, and said, 'hi'—specifically to *me,* with the most beautiful smile I'd ever seen."

The glint in his eyes broke her even further.

"The fucking sun came out, Sahar. And I stayed because if I at least got to see you, then I had *something* here to look forward to."

He traced the curve of her jaw with his thumb. "I don't know what was wrong with the men you dated, but there's no way in hell I'm ever going to get tired of your light because I know how dark and grim it gets without you. I can call you something else if you'd like, but I *never* want you to think that you could be exhausting to me."

"I like it when you call me that," she hiccupped, letting the tears fall again. "But it hurts. I don't... I don't know how to make it stop hurting. I always moved on so easily. I kept believing in love and happy endings. I kept leaping right into the arms of undeserving men, and you—you're the one who deserves every part of me. The one who's always deserved it, and I feel too broken to fully give myself to you because I'm terrified of fucking it up."

Pulling her into his arms, Jay held her close.

She wrapped herself tightly around him, pleading internally for the strength to *try*—one more time.

For him. *Because* of him.

"You're not broken," he said, his voice low but full of conviction. She felt the words carefully pricking atop her skin, like they were trying to ink their way onto her body like one of her tattoos. "Tell me what I can do to take the pain away. I'll do anything," he added.

Sahar sniffled, letting more tears fall. "I just want to keep you," she uttered, her voice barely above a whisper.

Cradling her head, he pressed a kiss so transcendent to her temple that she felt it reverberating through her soul. "You have me, Sahar. I'm yours. Only yours."

She pulled away from him. She wanted to tell him what she hadn't even told her sister, Willa, or any of their other friends.

The small, seemingly inconsequential thing that broke her and forced her to reevaluate her beliefs.

Boulders were lodged down her throat, making it impossible to speak. As though he could tell, Jay brought his palm to the side of her neck, sweeping his fingers with a coaxing pattern along her jaw.

Swallowing, she pushed every fear down, then, finally, she looked up at him. Sahar told him about what had happened on Martin's birthday and how he'd shrugged her off. How it had made her feel. How she'd tried to justify it, and that she finally broke up with him the night of Priya and Sam's show because he couldn't even bother to meet with her in person to talk.

She told him how that'd been the night when she realized that the people around her were all irrevocably in love while she was walking on eggshells and no longer recognized herself.

Clingy.

Too much.

Too loud.

And Martin's last words: *Selfish whore.*

The rage in Jay's eyes burned right through her when she repeated the words aloud.

"I know I can be—" she started to say, but with a violent shake of his head, Jay stopped her.

"Sahar, don't you dare try to reason or justify a word out of his mouth. Fuck," he said, gravel grating in his voice. "*Be clingy.* You know how badly I've wanted the woman who's a little loud when she's talking about sports or video games? The woman who took my manuscript and held nothing back when she told me she wanted it to be happier? The woman who's always looking out for others? *I want her.*" His fingers brushed along her shoulders in soothing motions. "I'm always going to want her."

Tears fell from her eyes again. He wiped them away without complaints—no trace of irritation in his gaze.

"You know why they belittle you, don't you?"

Her head shook so lightly that she wasn't even sure she was reacting.

"Because they're insecure little fucks who know they can't hold a candle to you. There's so much empathy in you that it makes everyone around you want to be better. You're so passionate—so fucking bright and loyal that just existing in your orbit makes me want to try harder. *Be better.* And those assholes aren't capable of growing, so they crush you so you won't eclipse them."

He took her hands, bracketing them in his large palms, before bringing them to his lips. "The thing is, your heart is so big that you don't even expect anything from other people. You just keep giving parts of yourself freely. You hold everyone up, even while your hands are shaking in the process. You think I didn't notice that all this time, while you've been propping up my characters and fighting for this story, that something was weighing you down? That *someone* had dimmed your light?"

Taking a breath, Sahar closed her eyes and momentarily wondered if she'd been dreaming. But when she opened them back up, Jay was still looking at her, his gaze the very essence of hope.

He continued. "The people around you—Willa, your family, your friends—*me.* We're the lucky ones," he declared, delicately brushing his thumbs over the tears falling on her cheeks. "And *I* want to make sure I *earn* your trust and your light and your rage and your happiness. *All of you.*"

Wrapping her arms tightly around him again, Sahar nestled herself closer. Jay had already earned all those things. No one had ever come close.

Running his fingers along her back, he tipped his head to her ear, the softness of his lips an immediate fortress. "I know all of this is easier said than done. I know how fucked up our thoughts can be."

Sahar looked up at him, loosening her grip. She tried to smile—to give him something—but she was so numbed by the crying, it came out pained.

Jay looked at his watch, then, taking note of the time, said, "I should get home. I have a 6 a.m. tomorrow. But I need to know you're okay before I do."

No, stay, she wanted to beg. Instead, she peered up at him. Stillness had returned to his gaze.

"I am," she managed to say. "I'm sorry that I..." She stopped, the glare in his eyes telling her *not* to apologize.

He wrapped her in his arms once more. *Home.*

"Thank you," she whispered, hoping, wishing, and praying the words would suffice.

"For what?" he whispered back.

"All of it."

Sahar watched him as he put his clothes back on, frustrated with herself for ruining what would've otherwise been a perfect night. Still, she was grateful for Jay. Grateful to finally have all her baggage out in the open. Suddenly, Jay reached into his back pocket for something, then pulled out his wallet.

Opening it, he took out a piece of paper and walked back to Sahar.

"You asked me to write Katherine's letter to Henry, but I was struggling that night. The words weren't coming. I couldn't get out of my own head, so I wrote one to you instead," he said, handing it to her.

Her eyes widened, and she took it from him, slowly. She ran her fingers along the edges, taking in the warmth as a result of how encased it'd been. Safe in his wallet. Had he just *kept* it there this whole time?

Jay cleared his throat, "I didn't think I'd ever give it to you. I kept it with me because I couldn't—" He shook his head, shutting his eyes. "Keep it. Read it whenever you want a reminder of how important you are to me."

The quiet, hopeful part of her heart that hadn't spoken yet whispered a steady, sincere, *believe him.*

Sitting cross-legged on her bed, Sahar fixed her eyes on the folded letter in her hands.

I wrote you one instead. Jay's words *to* her. These weren't about fictional characters. They were *for* her. Her heartbeat accelerated as she unfolded the lined piece of paper.

She ran her fingers over the first word. His handwriting was neater than she thought it'd be when he wasn't quickly scribbling onto a plastic cup. The fine black ink made her wonder if he had a specific pen preference. If he cared about those little things. Was he hunched over when he wrote it? Did he have a drink beside him on the kitchen table? Was it Coke? Water? Coffee?

Taking a stabilizing breath, she started reading.

Sunshine,

I thought you were the most beautiful woman I'd ever seen the first time you walked into the coffee shop. I spotted you right away, and I'm pretty sure I stopped breathing. I didn't take your order then; I was too nervous to. You came once more, then another time, and by your fourth visit, I'd finally plucked up the courage not to hide in the back. You had the brightest smile on. I could still drown in it. It's the one you wear every time you walk into the coffee shop.

But there was one day in particular. I fucking hated my name until it came from your lips one morning. Your stunning laugh, the glimmer in your gorgeous brown eyes. It brought me back from the hell I was so close to descending to. If I had quit that day like I was planning to, then you wouldn't be a text away. You wouldn't be such a huge part of my life. Henry and Katherine would've been shelved in a drawer, long forgotten.

I'd never know what it's like to hold you in my arms, even if it's for the briefest second.

Maybe one day I'll say all of this to you in person. Maybe you'll let me hold you for a little bit longer. Maybe you'll entwine your fingers with mine, and I'll beg you never to let go. Maybe one day, if I'm lucky enough, you'll let me kiss you. Maybe you'll let me love you and give you everything you deserve.

Your appreciation for my characters is everything, but I'd be lying if I said I didn't want you to see me the way you see them. I want to be a reason for your happiness. I want your light on me at all times.

A few days ago, you walked into the coffee shop, and I could see the Man City jersey under your denim jacket. Before you got to the register, I let myself think of what it'd be like to watch games together. To maybe go to one in person someday. I've wondered how it'd be if we sat on the same couch, playing something together. I'd want to let you win, but you'd hate that, so I'd play fair.

The first time I saw your crow tattoo, I thought it was a sign. I don't even believe in shit like that, but damn, I really hope it is.

I don't think I deserve you. Actually, I know I don't. I don't think anyone does. But if you gave me a chance, I'd fight with everything in me to keep you.

Is it weird if I steal Henry's words? Even if I wrote them myself? Because I don't know how else to say it, Sahar.

In my perfect world, you and I would be together.

A tear dropped on the letter, landing right on the word *perfect*. She brushed it aside and set the letter down on her mattress to stop her sobs from ruining the ink.

And then, she wept. But it wasn't a bad cry. For the first time in her life, it was love. Real, *perfect* love.

SAHAR

I read the letter. I wept through it. Your words continue to be a fortress to me, Jay. Thank you for trusting me with them. I'd call and say all of this, but I think it should be in writing. (I can't give you a letter right now, and I'm too impatient to keep you waiting.)

All this time, I only ever gave myself in fragments—I had no notion of what my perfect world would be like until you.

She clutched her phone to her chest and fell back on her bed, letting her heart flutter from joy. Real, incandescent joy.

33

———

JAY

Jay had read Sahar's message over and over on the train last night. He'd called her quickly when he got home, wanting to check in, and he read it once more before turning in for the night.

She'd told him that she and Willa had made plans to visit Carmen in the afternoon and that they'd drop by the coffee shop to grab drinks before heading over.

It was 11 a.m. now and already too fucking hot outside, but at least, the morning rush was long over. Glancing down at the clipboard that held the daily schedule, Jay noticed that Dahlia had one more break left before her shift ended at one.

"Dahlia," he said. "Go ahead and take your last fifteen."

"Okay!"

The bell at the door dinged, and four teenagers walked in. *Hell.* Molly stepped up to the registers from behind the counter where she'd been getting new cups. "Welcome to Amanda's Coffee. Let me know when you're ready to order," she greeted.

Seconds later, the door chimed again. Jay looked up. *This motherfucker.* It was Sahar's ex. He had a girl with him, someone he didn't recognize.

With Dahlia in the back, their new hire, Clark, was readying himself to make drinks.

Jay should have asked him to take on Martin and the girl, but a part of him wanted to be the one to do it. A part of him wanted to dump the coffee right onto his head or find a reason to kick the grin off of his smug face.

The teens kept Molly occupied with twenty-one questions.

He sighed, irritation ballooning inside of him, as he walked over to the registers. The girl was reading the menu above Jay's head. Martin was looking at his phone. "Ready to order?" Jay asked, his tone dry.

"Is there a special?" Martin asked. What a stupid fucking question from a stupid fucking man. The girl was ignoring him, too.

"Menu's right behind me," Jay said, suppressing an eye roll. He turned to the woman beside Martin then. "Do you have a flavor preference?"

Martin answered again. "I'm not really a coffee guy. She is." *Are you the type of guy who knows how to fucking shut up?* he wanted to ask.

Once more, Jay aimed the question at her. "Do you have a flavor preference?"

"Yeah, can I do an iced vanilla latte, please, with almond milk? Is the syrup sweetened, and can you add less if it is?"

"The vanilla is sweetened, yeah. How does half the number of pumps sound?"

"That works," she replied.

"Small, medium, or large?"

"Medium," she answered.

He added the order to the register and made a note on her cup. Martin placed a bottle of water on the counter. "Better for the voice," he said to the woman beside him.

Jay bit down on his tongue, trying to hold himself back from reacting. She smiled nonchalantly.

"Can I get a name for the order?" Jay asked.

"Martin," he answered.

Ignoring him, Jay looked at the woman.

"Nancy," she said.

He wrote her name down on the plastic cup and set it aside, pressed calculate on the register, and read the price aloud.

Martin paid with his phone and walked away. Nancy thanked Jay.

He nodded courteously.

When they had their back turned to him, Jay gave in to the annoyance that'd stirred inside of him. Is this how he'd been with Sahar? Talking over her? Subtly trying to pass his opinions off as facts? Keeping her quiet? He was attractive; he'd give him that, about three-four inches shorter than Jay, but his pretentiousness made everything about him vastly unappealing. He wanted to say something—punch him in the throat and fuck up his vocal cords for life. He wanted to give him hell for making Sahar feel like she was too much.

At some point, he realized the teenagers had left the shop. He looked over at Martin again, who was glancing at the vinyl records on the wall and telling the woman how he thought the recent craze was overrated; she looked unamused. "I actually think they're cool," she added.

Just then, the shop's door swung open again. Willa's voice came first. "I stand by my opinion. *Mamma Mia 2* is the superior movie," she declared.

Sahar's stunning laugh traveled right through Jay before she stopped in her tracks.

"Sahar?" Martin called out.

Disgust made its way into her gaze as she looked over at Martin and gave him the fakest wave Jay had ever seen.

Then, she turned and strode toward the register. She was wearing a blue denim vest with matching shorts, and *damn*, his girl was pretty. A real, warm smile illuminated across her face when she saw him, and his heart fucking melted. He'd bear Sahar's anger and apologize profusely if she hated what he was about to do next, but he couldn't help himself.

Mine, he wanted to announce, but he would show it instead.

When she was at the register, Jay leaned over the counter, cupped her face in his hand, and pressed a quick, searing kiss to her mouth.

For the briefest beat after they parted, she looked at him like they were the only two people in the coffee shop. Her smile was brighter, and the blush staining her cheeks was a sight to behold.

Mine, he thought again.

Then he shifted his eyes toward Willa, who was looking at Martin with a mocking gaze. She faced Jay and Sahar then. "Get it, cuties!" she hollered. Molly let out a laugh. Jay managed a genuine smile.

Clark called out for Nancy's drink, and Jay glared back at Martin. This time, his scowl no longer withheld that he knew exactly who he was and what he'd done. And like the fucking coward he was, Martin immediately looked down, turning to take Nancy by her shoulder.

The poor girl looked so confused, but she wasn't his problem. Jay dropped his gaze back at Sahar, who hadn't taken her eyes off him.

"You're not mad I did that, are you?"

She shook her head. "Not even a little."

"I, for one, would like to thank you," Willa started. "I'm going to tell my grandkids about what I saw today. You don't need my blessing, but you now have it forever," she declared proudly.

He laughed, adding in their usual orders to the register. "I'll make sure I never fumble it."

Sahar laughed, low and sweet. "No one hated Martin the way Wills did. By the end of our relationship, she wouldn't even acknowledge him if he was in the room."

Willa shrugged. "And I was right for that. It's a real fucking shame he doesn't drink coffee because I would've given anything to see you spit in his drink," she said to Jay. "Though this was glorious, too."

It made him so happy that Sahar had a friend like Willa in her corner. "Oh, orders. Sorry. Anything other than the usual?" he asked.

"Dec won't be home. But another lavender latte for Priya and a hazelnut for Carmen, please," Sahar said.

Nodding, he added that order in as well, then took out his card and swiped it through. He eyed Clark to get on the register while he moved to make the drinks.

"Jay, no! Why are you like this?" Sahar tried to argue.

He shrugged, smiling.

"Jay," she said again.

Molly interjected, facing the women. "Eh, just accept it. He doesn't always get to be nice here."

"Well then, thank you," Willa said.

He bobbed his head, eyeing Sahar again as he started on their drinks.

"I don't know what to do with you right now," Sahar said.

"I can think of a few things," he whispered.

Jay passed Willa her Irish cream oat milk latte.

He made Carmen's next, then Priya's. He was extra attentive to Sahar's. Passing it to her, their fingers brushed, and electricity jolted right through him.

She leaned closer this time, and he obliged, meeting her

halfway over the counter for one more kiss. "I'll talk to you later?" she said, phrasing it like a question.

He nodded. "Course. Have fun."

Thanking him again, they both left. As the door closed and he returned his attention to the shop, he heard Molly say the words, "and then he kissed her while her ex watched." Abruptly turning, he noticed Dahlia standing in the breakroom entrance.

"Not another fucking word," Jay said to them both.

Dahlia's grin widened. "I knew it! I called you being a big ol' softy from day one."

He ignored her. But he didn't hate it. Not at all.

Not today.

How was it going to be August in two days? He thought, eyes fixed on the small calendar magnetized on his mother's fridge.

He heard footsteps from the stairs on the other end of the wall before he actually saw his mom come into the kitchen.

"Hi, hun. Ellie will be down in a second. Patrick was here. They were outside playing, and she ran into some mud, so we've been cleaning her shoes."

Jay covered his yawn while simultaneously nodding, and then he leaned against the island. "I didn't know Pat was coming over."

His mom was putting utensils back into their designated drawer when she looked back at him. "Bonnie made cupcakes, and he dropped some off. They're in the fridge if you want any."

"Ah," Jay said.

She glanced at him, her eyes searching. Had his tone been off? He didn't think it was.

"Is everything okay?" she asked.

Jay answered with a nod.

"Are you sure?" she tried again.

"Do I not seem okay?"

She tilted her head, just barely. He *was* okay. He was more than okay. He'd never been better, given how the early afternoon had been.

"No, you just seem...*different,*" she replied.

Blowing out a sigh, he felt the prickling sadness he often did when he looked at his mom. Thinking of everything she'd been through and how he was too young to stop it. How he didn't fully understand what was happening in the early days. How she never stopped taking care of him and Alex, even when all her wounds were wide open.

He leaned back, eyeing the stairs on the other side of the wall, then he lowered his voice. "I've been seeing someone."

An enormous grin curled along the edges of her mouth. "Sahar?" she asked, the glint in her hazel eyes mirroring Alex's when she was excited about something.

"Was it that obvious?"

"Extremely," she confirmed. "There was nothing platonic about the way either of you looked at each other. But also, you were lighter in a way you haven't been for..." She paused, dejection grounding itself on her face. "A really long time. Maybe ever. It kills me because I know life's forced you to consistently be on edge and to constantly take care of others, but for a split second, you were... at ease. I certainly hoped I wasn't just seeing things, but I didn't want to pry."

He hated the fact that she was aware of the crosses he carried. He hated knowing that she likely blamed herself for them, too, when it was never *ever* her fault. Clearing his throat, his eyes snagged on a fallen leaf from the orange roses at the center of the island. Jay dragged his finger to it and brought it closer before looking back at his mom. "Yeah," he managed to say, brushing the leaf back and forth over the marble countertop.

"Do you love her?" his mom asked.

Jay nodded, still playing with the leaf. "Deeply," he answered. He loved Sahar in a way he didn't know he was capable of.

"And I hope you're comfortable confiding in her?"

"I've told her everything," he admitted.

He looked up at her again, the happiness in her gaze unmistakable. He tried to smile back at her, but the ache in his chest compounded.

"Then what's the problem, honey?"

His throat tightened. The ever-present fear of whose son he was made its way to the forefront of his mind, materializing like some Goliath that was only visible to him.

"Am I like him? Is it...possible that I could ever—"

Anger leaked from her voice, but he knew it wasn't aimed at him. "Jay, stop. Look at me."

He did.

"The only part of that man you inherited is your height," she punctuated.

Stepping closer to where he stood at the end of the island, she continued. "Listen to me carefully, sweetheart. You had this same fear when Ellie was born, and as I told you then, I'm telling you now: you have choices. You are *not* going to wake up one morning possessed to a point where that gentle heart of yours is replaced by a monster's. That's not how this works. You're an incredible father, and you'll be an incredible partner to Sahar."

He sighed, trying desperately to take her words in. "Thanks."

She squeezed his arm. "I need you to do everything in your power to actually believe me. You deserve to be happy, my darling. You both do. And I look forward to seeing her again," she added.

Agreeing, Jay bobbed his head up and down. He was about to say that he wasn't sure how to tell Eloise, when they heard her stomping down the stairs. "Grandma! I decided to wear my Converse instead, so the Vans can dry."

"Sounds good," his mom replied.

Jay shifted his attention toward the foyer where Eloise would step in from.

"Are we going straight to art class, Dad?" she asked him.

He glanced at the stove's clock. "Nope. We've got three hours."

"Good, because I have some things to discuss," she said.

Jay's eyes widened, and he turned to look back at his mom. She gave him an *I have no idea* shrug, then bent down to hug Ellie. After, he reached his hand forward for her backpack. She handed it to him with a dramatic huff.

"Alrighty then," he noted aloud as she strode out of the kitchen and toward the garage door.

He had three full weeks left with Eloise, and every part of him was crushed under the weight of sending her back to Philly. Alex was right. Everything was brighter when his little girl was home. He'd promised her he'd visit more often, and he was going to make good on that. God, how he hoped that *Every Speck of Dust* would perform better—be the one thing that'd *maybe* let him leave the coffee shop so he could be in his kid's life more.

Opening the car door for her, Eloise jumped in the booster seat as he set her backpack down beside her. She buckled herself in as he got into the driver's seat.

Before starting the engine, Jay eyed her from the rearview mirror. "So, what's this bone you've got to pick with me?"

"It's about movies," she began.

"Should've guessed," Jay returned.

"Uncle Patrick was over."

He put the car in reverse. "I'm aware."

"Well, he told me that if you didn't teach me how to make movies, he would because he's my godfather, and that's a big, big deal."

Jay huffed out a laugh. "So, the moral of this story is that you're now going behind my back to get intel on filmmaking? Cool, got it. Betrayals hurt, Eloise."

He smiled at her through the rearview mirror. She scrunched her nose.

"Then *you* should teach me, father."

A hearty laugh flew out of him. "So, I'm 'father' now? What is this 1812?"

"Yes, because I'm mad!"

His lips curved into a pout. "Will you still be mad if I let you have ice cream before dinner?"

"Perchance," she answered.

He let out another laugh. "Who'd you hear that from?"

"Aunt Lexie said it today when Uncle Patrick invited her to something. And then she told me it means *maybe*."

"I mean, if the whole directing thing doesn't work in your favor, you could be an English lit professor. Specialize in Shake-speare or something?"

"Perchance not."

He shook his head. *This kid.*

They drove in silence for a moment until she spoke again.

"Does your pretty friend also make movies?"

He knew she was talking about Sahar, and his heart expanded three sizes.

"She's on Broadway like Aunt Lexie."

Eloise's eyes went wide. "Was she in the same show?"

"No, she's in a different one."

She swung her feet back and forth. "Can I see that one?"

"It's for adults. You'd be bored."

"Is it like Shake-sphere?" she asked.

"Shake*speare*," he gently corrected. "And yeah, something like that," he answered.

"Perchance, she will be in a fun one someday."

Jay smiled at her. "Perchance she will," he repeated.

Midnights at Pemberley was far more exciting than Shake-speare, but Eloise didn't need to know that.

"I'm not mad at you anymore. Can we go to the beach again soon? But on a day when Aunt Lexie is also home and maybe Uncle Patrick, too? I want to show them the horseshoe crabs."

"Happy to be back in your good graces. Um..." he thought about his upcoming schedule. Maybe Monday? He was off next week. "I'll figure something out with Aunt Lexie." If he was back on her good side, Jay figured now would be the time to rip the Band-Aid off of what he and Sahar actually were to each other.

Eyeing her from the rearview mirror, he said, "Remember when you mentioned that you wanted me to find my own Gavin?"

She excitedly tilted her head. "*OH MY GOD! Did* you?"

"You're calling her my pretty friend, but I'd like her to be more than that, if you're okay with it."

Eloise gave him a big smile. "Yeah! She can come to the beach, too, if she wants."

"I'll pass the message along," he replied finally.

Alex called him as soon as he'd parked in his designated spot. He answered and handed Eloise the apartment keys. She ran ahead in the corridors as he followed.

"Yeah, hey," he said.

"Pat told me about the dinner Sunday night. Is Sahar coming?" Alex asked.

"I'd told her about it, but I'm not sure yet. Why?"

"Just curious. If she does, we can leave the city together since our shows end at the same time."

He helped Eloise with the door when he noticed her twisting in the wrong direction. "That sounds like a plan. I'll let you know," he said over the phone.

Eloise beelined straight toward the kitchen. "Wash your hands," he called out.

As he was kicking off his shoes by the door, a *yelp* chirped out of Alex on the other end of the line. "You good over there?" he asked.

"Almost tripped on a flat tennis ball. Anyway, that's why I called. Let me know what she says. I'm walking into work now. Adios."

"Have fun," Jay said. "Bye."

He *really* wanted Sahar with him at Patrick's. He wanted Sahar with him everywhere.

Walking into his kitchen, Jay opened the freezer and pulled out the ice cream he'd promised Eloise as she picked out bowls.

34

SAHAR

Sahar had seen Jay for a few short minutes earlier in the day as he came by the theatre to kiss her before he went home. She'd come in before her usual time for physical therapy, so he'd caught her right as she was about to go in. It'd been blissful, but short. Too short.

And work had been good. Especially when she'd had a moment where she thought about the flashback episode again, and it gave her another idea that she couldn't wait to run by him. Now, in her bathroom, and about to hop into the shower, she remembered to text him about it.

SAHAR

I have an idea…

As she waited for him to respond, she set her phone down and washed off her makeup. His text came through as she was drying her face.

JAY

I'm listening.

She applied toner with a cotton pad, then opened the

rubbish bin with its foot pedal to discard it inside, and picked up her phone.

SAHAR

What if you snuck in an undercover lovers scene in the flashback episode? Maybe during the moment at the club? Where K and H are watching the handoff? The majority is all there, you've just got to spice it up a bit. 😉

JAY

I thought about something like that during the initial outlining process because it'd be another hint that the Logan brothers had been aware of Katherine's importance all along. What'd you have in mind specifically?

A few weeks ago, she wouldn't have dared to tell him exactly what she'd been thinking. But now, it was...effortless. *Right.*

SAHAR

I don't know how closely you were paying attention during Midnights (or even if you remember) because the scene I'm thinking of usually happens when Darcy and Elizabeth are arguing?

But there's a moment where Jane and Bingley are off on the side and doing their own thing.

JAY

No offense to Ethan and Naomi, but I only had eyes for you, so yeah. I know exactly what scene you're talking about.

SAHAR

Okay, so you know how Jane sits on Bingley's lap?

JAY

Sure, but a demonstration would also work.

SAHAR

Pay attention! I'm trying to help you.

JAY

I can't because now I'm thinking about you on
my lap.

To be fair, so was she.

SAHAR

Fine, pretend it's me.

JAY

You home yet?

SAHAR

Yeah, just got in like twenty minutes ago.

JAY

Can you talk?

She let out a laugh and rang him, putting the phone on speaker. He answered immediately.

"How do you expect me to pay attention to you talking about fictional characters when I'm picturing you on my lap?" he drawled.

"Because *this* is important."

"Okay, okay. I'm listening," he said.

"I think Katherine being on Henry's lap, the two of them very briefly battling their real feelings while simultaneously staying in character, could really show the audience a bit more of that longing that's already present. The flashback does a brilliant job, and you know I love it, but this can be a small addition that shows it as well."

"I like that. I'll start tweaking that scene tomorrow. God, your fucking brain," he uttered, his voice deep and raspy. She wanted to melt into it. Did he know how hot his voice was? Had anyone ever told him that?

"Yes! I'm glad you approve. I thought about it during the show and couldn't wait to tell you."

His laugh echoed through the speaker. "Is there space in that imagination for us or just the characters?"

Sahar smiled to herself, leaning against the sink, worming her foot over the textured purple rug. "I mean, now I'm definitely thinking about sliding onto your lap," she admitted. "Among other things."

A delicious groan tumbled out of him in lieu of words.

She exhaled a laugh. "Would you be able to have lunch with me tomorrow? Post-matinee or before, if that would be better?" she asked.

"I can do it before if it works for you. I'm off at twelve. But Ellie's got art class, so after would be tricky."

"Before works for me," she returned. "We've got to be near the theatre, though. Is the same Japanese restaurant we went to that first time okay with you?"

"On one condition. This time, we sit on the same side of the booth, so I can soak up every second I have with you."

Contentedly, she sighed. "I wouldn't have it any other way."

"Have you given any more thought about Patrick's invite for this Sunday?"

Moving her foot left and right onto the rug again, she pondered it once more. "You said Alex will be there?"

"She will, yeah," Jay answered.

Sahar hated that she was still hesitant to go somewhere with his close friends, even though he'd *already* proven to her how attentive he was during the premiere. She'd met his mum, for crying out loud. She was comfortable around his little sister. Still, this was a little different. It was Patrick's house. They were a couple now. It'd be significantly more intimate.

"There's no pressure, sunshine. Pat just really wants to meet you, and I want you there," he added.

"He does dinners like this a few times a year, you said?"

"Yeah, his dad would always host dinners and game nights with his fellow firefighters, and he used to encourage Pat and Hayden to do the same with their people. After he passed, it's something they stuck to."

Sahar had Googled Patrick's father and learned that he'd died in an apartment fire six years ago. She'd watched *Cuts*; she'd seen how it had destroyed the character Patrick likely wrote in as himself. She also knew how much he'd meant to Jay, how Mr. Sharp had been there for him when his own father wasn't.

"So it'll be us, Alex, and you said three other writers and Eddie? Who's in *Grunge* with Patrick?"

"Yeah, and Eddie's fiancée. Tanya?"

"Tina," she corrected. "Tanya's in *Midnights* with me."

"See, you know better than I do."

Sahar *did* like Eddie. She'd known him since they'd been in a run of *Les Mis* together, and she knew Tina by association from social media.

She should do it, rip the plaster off. She *had* to trust in Jay's promises.

"Okay, I'll be there. Maybe I can talk to Alex, so we can head over together," she suggested.

"She had the same thought."

Oh.

"That's comforting," she let herself say aloud.

THE FIRST TIME they'd had lunch at Summer Nori, the space hadn't felt as significant. Sure, Jay's wink had ignited a steadfast spark in her, but now, it all felt lovelier. Sweeter. She noticed every detail about the restaurant, from the oak panels to the small chips along the sides of this very table. The interior's color palette of browns and beiges contributed to the warmth swelling inside of her.

They'd eaten and had about thirty-ish minutes to spare before she had to go into work for the matinee performance.

Side by side in the ensconced booth, Jay's arm entwined around her shoulder, bringing her closer to him.

Sahar pressed a quick kiss to his mouth. "Did you write the additional scene yet?"

He hummed his response against her temple.

"And when do I get it?"

"It's already in your inbox."

"Yeah?" she whispered.

"Yeah," he whispered back, running his fingers over her shoulder.

"What do I get after this? You did say something about a bonus episode. What if I want the most achingly romantic scene ever?"

Pressing his mouth to her cheekbone, he lingered. "I'll work on that, too."

"Are you ever going to say no to me?"

"Unlikely."

Sahar threaded her fingers with his. "Careful, it'll go to my head."

"Let it," he replied, dipping his head and kissing her shoulder blade.

Oh, she was happy. Wildly so, every part of her entranced. Sahar's gaze held his, locked in a silent conversation.

I love you. I love you. I love you.

"Has anyone ever told you that your jaw looks like it was sculpted by Michelangelo? Maybe God, himself?"

Red flared across his face. A low, closed-mouth laugh bubbled out of him. It sounded fucking delectable. Now that she allowed herself to really *look* at him—to outright check him out, she couldn't believe that he was hers. Jay had the type of face that belonged *in front* of the camera, not behind it. *He* should've been an actor.

But a small, possessive part of her reveled in the fact that she didn't have to share him with the world.

Mine, her heart squealed. *All mine.*

Jay pressed a kiss to her forehead, another on her nose, one across both her cheeks. *Mine* his actions said in return.

After a few short moments, he spoke again. "Hey, so Ellie's been asking to go to the beach on Monday. Lex and Patrick will be there, too. If you feel comfortable, bring extra stuff with you on Sunday and stay the night."

The idea sounded nice. *Really* nice.

Grabbing the remaining iced water she had, Sahar took a sip. "It wouldn't confuse Eloise?"

Jay's fingers still danced along her shoulder. "She keeps calling you my pretty friend, so I think we're passed that. And I've also told her that you're more than a friend."

Something in her heart squeezed as the corners of her mouth twitched upward. "Do you not have pretty friends?"

"You're the prettiest," he declared, kissing the tip of her nose again.

Affectionately shaking her head, she felt her smile growing bigger. "I'm in."

35

SAHAR

Sahar and Alex stood at the train station in Smithtown, waiting for Jay to pick them up. Since he wasn't with him, they'd spent the entire ride over, talking about their love lives, learning that they were both hopeless romantics who kept giving the wrong people chances in hopes of finding someone who could be the right partner.

Only in the last few years, Alex was understandably more reserved with her time. And given the trauma her family had endured, she'd seldom let things go beyond a third date if she sensed that it wouldn't last. There were occasional one-night stands here and there, and only one serious but short-lived relationship while she was in her last year of drama school.

Sahar looked over at the girl as she glanced down at her phone, grimacing. "My car chose the worst time to require servicing, and Jay's usually never late. He has my location, so he should've been here by now. I wonder what happened."

Lowering her tote from her shoulders and holding it out in front of her, Sahar leaned against a pole. "Let's give him five minutes, then maybe we can call?" she suggested.

Alex crossed her legs and carefully lowered herself down on

the pavement. "Sounds like a plan." She looked up at Sahar then. "You nervous?"

"Not so much now," she answered candidly.

Alex smiled. It was reassuring. "Pat's really good about making sure the people he associates with are solid. I think you'll get along with them all."

It was sweet to know that Alex was not only close to her brother but his friends, too. It made her heart ache for a moment as she missed the days when she and Amina weren't living in different countries.

"That makes me feel even better," Sahar added. "Have you always been close to Jay's friends?"

Shaking her head from side to side, Alex said, "No. I mean, I always knew Pat because he was our neighbor, but I started hanging out with them about two-ish years ago now. Are you and your sister close in age?"

"She's three years older than me," Sahar answered. She was about to ask when her contract with *Hatchard's Academy* was set to end when Jay's white Honda CR-V pulled over to where they'd been waiting.

Alex hopped up and went straight for the backseat as Sahar went to the passenger's.

"Did you lose track of time?" Alex asked.

He shook his head, and upon glancing over at him, Sahar noticed the furrow in his brows that signaled he was upset about something.

She ran her fingers over his bicep. "You alright?" she asked.

Checking his left side for traffic, he swerved back onto the road. "Yeah, I was headed out the door, but then Ellie started crying." He eyed Alex through the rearview mirror. "Mom accidentally mentioned that I was picking you up, and she wanted to come. I had to convince her that we were going to a boring meeting for work, but she probably thinks I'm lying, and we're going to the beach without her."

"Stop! My little unicorn. Let's go get her!" Alex replied. "She also knows it's August, and that she has to go back to Philly soon, so every time you've left in the last three days, she gets really sad at first and then eventually feels okay," Alex said.

"Fuck, Lex. Don't tell me that shit."

Sahar looked at him. She couldn't imagine what it was like to have two good parents and live away from one of them.

"I didn't say it so you'd get upset. I'm saying it, so you know she'll be okay in a bit," Alex countered.

"It doesn't help."

He turned to Sahar then, his eyes sadder. "I told her that you might come with us tomorrow, and you're much better at *Zelda* than I am, so you can show her all the ropes."

"See, she just needs a good bribe," Alex commented.

Sahar smiled, squeezing his shoulder in a reassuring gesture. "You know Zelda's my girl, and I'm more than happy to, but isn't she a bit young? Some of it might be scary or overwhelming."

"Her cousin, Maya's sister's daughter, has gotten into it recently, and she's ten. Since their city trip, Ellie's been feeling left out and wants to try. She should be fine during the day, I think."

The tension in his body eased a bit as he slowed the car at a red light.

"That makes sense. Everything I did when I was younger was because my sister did it first. Which version do you have?"

"*Breath of the Wild* and *Tears of the Kingdom.*"

Nodding, Sahar said, "*Breath of the Wild* will definitely be more suitable as a way to ease her into it."

"You're the expert," Jay acknowledged, taking his foot off the brake as the traffic light turned green.

Sahar grinned widely. "This is so exciting. I've been wanting to replay it for a while."

Having a few days to prepare for the fact that she'd be meeting Eloise more formally, Sahar was less nervous now. It wasn't like they'd be announcing marriage tonight. She would just actively be spending time with her, and given how kids generally liked her—Ravi being her little dinosaur-loving bestie —she felt more calm about the whole ordeal.

It was another significant step. A leap she wanted to take *for* Jay and *with* him. It was further proof of how real this was, unexpected and right in ways she'd never thought possible.

As they parked in front of Patrick's house, Alex was actively typing something on her phone when she said, "You two go ahead. I'll come inside in a few."

Jay eyed her quizzically, then passed her his keys.

Once they were outside, he fanned his fingers along Sahar's back as they walked on.

They moved through a cobblestone driveway, hedged with two large maple trees, toward a backyard, where she could hear chatter growing louder.

Abruptly, nerves congregated inside of her again, but she shoved them aside. *Not now. Not today.*

Jay opened the fence gate and guided Sahar inward.

They hadn't even fully entered when a tall man with brown hair, blue eyes, and a killer smile bellowed their names. *Patrick.* She recognized him instantly from photos.

Patrick drew Sahar into a bear hug. "It's so nice to finally meet you! The rewrites are all insanely better because of you." He eyed Jay, adding, "And so is this guy."

Sahar blushed. She wasn't sure what to say, and Jay's eyes proudly boring into hers deepened the flush, making her knees a little wobbly. "It's nice to meet you, too. I've heard lovely things about you."

"Aw, buddy, you say nice things about me?" Patrick aimed at Jay.

Jay reacted with a closed-mouth smile and an eye roll.

Then, at once, Patrick's smile shifted into an uneasy frown. "Where's Alex?" he asked.

"In the car. Said she'll be in soon," Jay replied.

He nodded, gesturing for them to come further inside, and Sahar wondered if she'd just caught him sighing in relief at the confirmation that Alex would be here. *Did he—*

Eddie and Tina were already seated at the rectangular glass table, alongside one other blond man, whom Sahar didn't recognize. There was a wooden pergola above them, covered in twinkling lights, and she could already imagine how dreamy it'd be when the sun went down.

Tina stood up and skipped over, giving Sahar a hug. "Ah! I'm so glad you're here. How long has it been?"

"Two years now, I think?" she answered into their embrace. "And congratulations again, you two," she added, referencing her and Eddie's engagement, which she'd also initially said something about on social media a few weeks ago.

"Small freaking world," Eddie commented, giving Jay a pat on the back before he went in on a quick hug with Sahar.

"Good to see you, mate," Sahar returned.

"Dec's still walking around shirtless, I imagine?" Eddie added.

Sahar laughed. "Wouldn't be Declan if he wasn't." She turned to Jay. "Dec was also in *Les Mis* with us."

Jay's brows curved in an understanding *ah*.

Then, the door behind them creaked open, and Alex stepped in. "Hi hi," she said aloud to everyone. Patrick, who'd been next to Jay, sprinted over to her, arms wide open. With a mischievous smirk twisting along her lips, she shook her head and hugged him. *Did they—*

Jay nudged Sahar forward and pulled up a chair for her. He introduced her to the other guy, Tim, and later, when one of his writing mates, Geoffrey, showed up, he introduced her to him, too. Sahar was generally an extrovert, but it was nice not to do all the work herself—to have someone who was happy to stay beside her.

Throughout dinner—taco night—he kept his hand at the back of her chair or on her knee. It'd been lovely. Warm. As it should be.

After dinner, they'd all migrated from the backyard to Patrick's living room, where there were conversations about the industry, what a horror AI was continuing to be, and how they were all genuinely nervous for the future of creative endeavors.

Seated at the end of a comfortable, suede sofa next to Jay, Sahar looked toward where Alex and Patrick were standing by the screen door. He was leaning against the handle, and whatever she said must've been hilarious because Patrick's guffaw echoed through the chatter surrounding them. As Alex turned sideways, Sahar caught her rolling her eyes before she affectionately shoved Patrick aside and walked out.

Where was she going? And why had Patrick's entire face dropped when she left the room? It was the same frown that had materialized on his face when he realized she hadn't been with Sahar and Jay when they first arrived. She looked at Jay to see if he noticed what was happening in front of them, but he was on his phone, texting his mom.

"Everything okay?" she whispered, leaning into him.

He snaked his arm around the curve of her hip and pulled her close to him. "Yeah, my mom says Ellie's okay now."

"That's good to hear," Sahar returned.

Inching forward, he hovered his mouth along the side of her temple. "What about you? Is any of this too much for you?"

He isn't afraid of showing everyone that you're his.

Sahar shook her head, dropping her hand to his knee. "I'm good," she promised.

And she was. She really, truly, *wholeheartedly* was.

Pressing a featherlight kiss to her forehead, Jay then darted his attention to where Patrick stood, his eyes fixed on the wooden floors.

"Pat," he called out, hurling two fingers toward him and gesturing for him to come by.

Patrick pulled up a chair from the dining table, flipped it backwards, and sat.

"Wanna tell her the news?" Jay asked.

His whole face lit up, and Jay beamed, too.

Sahar flipped her gaze between them. *What on earth was going on?*

Patrick cleared his throat. "So, I'm not sure if you know this, but our director for *Grunge* is Roman Dane's brother—the producer."

"I know your director, but haven't heard about his brother."

She looked at Jay again, trying to figure out where this was going. Unfortunately, his expression gave away very little.

"Roman is currently contracted with Wild Card Pictures, and he's been hunting for a limited series. He'd been by the theatre, and we got to talking when he told me he was reading scripts." Sahar didn't think it was humanly possible for someone's amusement to be as vast as Patrick's, but it kept growing. "I told him about what had happened to *Every Speck of Dust,* and how we'd basically rewritten the entire thing, so he asked for the episodes."

All at once, it clicked. Sahar pieced the puzzle together as her heart pounded with inimitable elation.

"Jay sent it to him on Tuesday night. He stayed up reading and accepted the pitch right away. The network is in, we just need to get everything settled before selling..."

Jay's gaze tipped toward hers, and he reached for her hand. "I didn't want to agree to anything without talking to you first."

She looked back at him, trying not to scream out her joy. Still, she said, "Talk to me about what? This project belongs to you two."

Jay squeezed her hips, pulling her even closer to him. "It belongs to *you*, too," he asserted. "Though nothing is settled. They can still decide they don't want it, but—"

"But in the hands of Roman, we have a significantly better chance of it seeing the light of day," Patrick finished. "He thinks the romantic arc will draw in more viewers because of how the shows that feature it are currently performing."

"And he's right about that," Sahar added giddily.

"So, you're in? I also need to get you in charge of the music somehow," Jay said. *God, he's so fucking perfect like this—happy.*

She leaned further into him, gripping the hand that was still fixed at her waist. "Whatever we need to get Henry and Katherine on my screen, I'm in."

Patrick tipped closer, squeezing both their shoulders. "Fuck yeah! This is a long time coming. It just needed the *right* touch," he emphasized. Hers, he meant, and it felt so...gratifying. Apart from selfishly begging for a happy ending, she hadn't really done anything, but if she could be responsible for even a fraction of Jay's happiness, she'd do *anything*. Christ, how she hoped again—with every fiber of her being—that this would be *it* for Jay.

Everything he'd tirelessly worked for.

Everything he'd ever wanted.

Everything he'd fought to achieve.

Sahar faced Jay when Patrick left and clapped her hand over her mouth, beaming at him. "Jay, I think I might actually burst. I'm so bloody proud of you."

He stood up, holding his hands out to her. She took them, letting him guide her wherever he wanted.

Now, tomorrow, forever.

They stepped out into the yard where cicadas screamed and a light breeze had finally made its way over to combat the sticky heat. He pulled her in for a tight hug, rocking her back and forth.

"I really fucking thought I was done. I had nothing left in me, and your refusal to give up on me is the only reason there's hope today." His voice cracked a bit, and she squeezed him tighter in return.

Parting from her, his fingers lifted to cup her cheek. "God, I'm so in love with you," he divulged, his voice rumbling with transcendent happiness. His confession wrapped around her, carefully mending every scar left by someone else. "I don't want any of this without you. No man has ever had a better muse."

She looked up at him, his brown eyes glinting behind his glasses from the twinkle lights hung over the pergola. "I love your words, Jay. I love your brain. I love your vision. I love *you*," she paused, thinking of his tender heart and all his jagged edges, too. "Wanting more of *you* and in every way has been as easy as breathing."

Jay's mouth landed on hers in a sweeping kiss that was unlike any of the others they'd shared. Sweeter somehow. Softer. *Special.*

Mine, her heart squealed again. *All mine.*

An idyllic exhale left his lips as he enclosed his arms around her again.

Her heart sang louder than the cicadas. He'd told her he was hers, and he meant it. No one admitting their feelings aloud to her felt this overwhelming. Immaculate. *Right.*

Lifting her head to look up at him, Sahar held his face in her hands, and a breathy, freeing laugh leapt from somewhere deep inside of her. "Is it silly to wholeheartedly believe that we were made for each other? Because I do. Now more than ever, I *really* do."

His lips landed back on hers like a hearty agreement, and they stayed like that in each other's arms, away from everyone else. A minute or two, maybe five.

Ten.

"Lovebirds," they heard from Alex then. "If you don't get back inside to start game night, Pat might actually start throwing things."

They laughed, parting.

Then, they walked back in, spending the rest of the night as sworn enemies because there would never be room for love when it came to a game of Werewolf.

36

———

JAY

"So, you're sure Eloise is okay with this? Should we just tell her I'm your friend?" Sahar asked from the passenger's seat.

"My *pretty* friend," he specified, his whole heart buzzing. "And I'm positive. The kid has apparently wanted me to find love before I even considered it."

Switching the car engine off, Jay leaned forward and pressed a kiss to her forehead before walking out to his mom's house.

After saying bye to the two of them, Alex bolted inside, promising Sahar that she'd be filling her in on something Jay wasn't privy to.

"Say hi to your mum," Sahar added.

It was good to know that Sahar and Alex were already getting along so well, and she fit in so effortlessly with his friends, too. Each new milestone now would continue to matter, and he was eager for Sahar to spend time with Eloise.

Jay walked into the house from the front door, where Eloise was putting on her shoes.

"Was she really okay?" he whispered to his mom.

She gave him a genuine grin. "There's nothing a trip to Barnes and Noble can't fix."

Smiling, he thanked her, passed Sahar's message along, then bent down and lifted his daughter off the ground with a bear hug.

Eloise leaned forward in Jay's arms and hugged his mom. "Bye, Grandma. Love you."

"Love you more, sweetheart."

As they stepped out the door, Eloise wrapped her arms tightly around his neck, making him stop in his tracks.

"What's up, baby? You okay?" Jay asked, gently squeezing her back.

"Is your pretty friend nice?"

"Would I ever introduce you to someone who was mean?"

"No," she confirmed.

He kissed the side of her head. "She's the nicest, and she always shares her ice cream."

"And tomorrow we're going to the beach, right? With Aunt Lexie, too?" she asked again.

He stepped down the porch stairs. "We are."

"Promise?"

"A thousand times," he assured.

When they drew closer to his car, she sprang out of his arms, and Jay opened the door to let her in. He watched as Sahar tilted her head, a bright smile shining on her face. "Hi, Eloise," she said.

"Hi," Eloise repeated, a little less shy than before. Progress. Good. She buckled herself in as he got in the driver's seat.

"Dad, can you put on the 'Elephant Love Medley?'"

Sahar's jaw dropped open, and she spun back to face Eloise. "That is some *amazing* taste in music you've got there," she commented.

Jay put on the playlist Maya had curated for Eloise, with the movie version, featuring Ewan McGregor and Nicole Kidman.

"I'm not allowed to watch the movie, but my mom was listening to this song, and I love it a lot."

Jay put the car in reverse, everything in him at ease.

"The movie's really sad. You're better off not knowing that kind of pain for a while," Sahar added.

"Yeah, that's what she said, too," Eloise replied.

The song blared through the speakers, as low hums from both Sahar and Eloise echoed in the small space.

ELOISE AND SAHAR both stared at him from the other side of the island. "You two look like lost puppies right now."

"I consider myself more of an orange cat when I'm promised ice cream, and it isn't delivered quickly enough," Sahar noted.

Eloise squared her shoulders. "Me too," she said.

"Do you even know why she specified an orange cat?" Jay asked.

Eloise shook her head and angled closer to Sahar. "Why an orange cat?" she whispered.

"Because they look like they're harmless and super cute on the outside, but they can get a little spicy when things don't go their way."

Jay laughed, taking a scoop of strawberry cheesecake ice cream for Eloise. "Spicy. That was certainly an adjective choice."

"You met Tulip on a good day," she reminded him. "She's a real piece of work when she's not chuffed. The cutest and spiciest cat in all of New York City."

"Tulip, like the flower?" Eloise asked Sahar.

"Tulip, like the flower," she confirmed. "She's my friend's cat, and she actually looks like an orange tulip." Pulling out her phone, Sahar searched for a photo and showed it to Eloise, as he continued prepping their desserts.

"She's so cute!" Eloise exclaimed, then aimed the next words out of her mouth at Jay. "Dad, can I have a cat?"

He slid the two bowls in their direction, coffee for Sahar and strawberry cheesecake for Eloise. The sight of the two of them sitting beside each other made his damn heart soar. "You can have ice cream. We can talk cats later."

Smiling, Sahar added. "You've got to start buying coffee in bulk now that you'll be sharing with me."

"I don't have to share mine with anybody because he doesn't like strawberry," Eloise singsonged.

"Lucky you. I'd share mine with you, though," Sahar said.

Eloise gave her a big smile. "I don't like coffee that much, but thank you."

Jay leaned forward and gently poked Eloise's hand. "You're not going to offer to share yours?"

"Oh, right. I could share with *you*," she specified to Sahar.

Sahar's lips curved upward in an adorable grin. "Thanks, cutie. But I'm good with the coffee right now."

"Dad, is Sahar coming with us tomorrow?"

Jay looked at Sahar, hoping she'd answer the question herself.

"If you'd like me to, I will," she responded.

Eloise nodded enthusiastically. "Yeah! And in the morning, can you teach me how to play *Zelda*? Daddy says you're better than him."

"I sure can! I've played both games all the way through twice."

"Twice?" Eloise asked.

Sahar nodded, taking another spoonful of ice cream into her mouth. "Twice," she confirmed.

"Whoa."

"Told you she was the one to help," Jay repeated.

Eloise slid her empty ice cream bowl in front of him. "All done!"

"Put it in the dishwasher, please. Then go get ready for bed, and I'll come give you my phone, so you can talk to your mom."

Eloise hopped off the stool and took the bowl with her.

"Goodnight, Sahar," she said.

Sahar gave her a big smile. "Sweet dreams. See you tomorrow."

"I'm so excited I don't know how I'm going to sleep," she muttered on her way out of the kitchen.

"I'm going to die. I can't handle how cute she is," Sahar added.

Moving across the island, Jay stood next to her and leaned against the marble countertop. She took a spoonful of ice cream and brought it to his mouth. He licked.

"Would you mind getting me a towel, so I can quickly shower while you tuck her in?"

"The only thing I'd mind is if you said you wanted to leave."

"Nope," she confirmed, kissing the tip of his nose, her lips cool from the dessert.

Sahar gave her last bite of ice cream to him, pressed her lips to his mouth, then got off the stool. She placed her bowl right next to Eloise's in the dishwasher, and his heart fucking levitated again.

It was the little things—two bowls next to each other, Sahar's sneakers right next to his by the front door, his zip-up black hoodie draped over her shoulders—that was what his world would look like from now on. Pieces of her fusing with parts of him.

Jay walked over to Eloise's room, where she was sitting up in her bed, FaceTiming Maya, and then stepped out to give Sahar a clean towel. He lingered in the bathroom for a bit and kissed her, trying to grasp that this was indeed his new reality and not a perfect dream he refused to wake up from.

When he went back into Eloise's room, she was already underneath the covers. "Mommy says she's happy I like your pretty friend."

"Is that so?"

"Yeah," she confirmed enthusiastically.

Smiling at her, Jay kneeled beside her bed. "Wanna talk to me about why you got upset earlier today as I was leaving grandma's?"

"It's okay, Daddy. I feel better now."

He brushed the back of his fingers along her cheek. "I'm glad you're feeling better, but I don't like knowing that something was bothering you. Did you really think I'd go to the beach without you?"

She released a somber little sigh. "Yeah, and um, I heard Aunt Lexie say that it was August, and I got sad because I'm leaving soon."

"Sweetheart, I need you to first know that I would never break my promises to you."

Nodding, she whispered, "The summer's almost over."

Jay sighed, everything in him twisted and coiled. "I know."

"I wish you and Mommy lived in the same place."

Fuck. That one hurt. It would always hurt.

"I'm going to visit more, Ellie. I promise you."

A barely there smile rose across her lips. "I know. And I know that you have to live in New York because it's better for your job. It just makes me sad sometimes."

"It makes me sad all the time," he admitted. "Being away from you is the worst kind of sadness I know, baby girl. But if you ever need me, I told you I'd move mountains to get to you. I want you to remember that, okay?"

Her little hand landed on top of his, and he held it, his heart shattering.

"I love you times infinity," he said.

"I love *you* times infinity," she repeated. "Can you tell me one story?"

"I can tell you two."

Eloise's eyes lit up. "Okay, for the first one, what's your next movie about?"

Jay let out a low laugh and got up to sit at the edge of her bed. "Sneaky girl. You know what, I can actually tell you this one. You've gotta keep it a secret, though, okay?"

She brought her pinky up to lock it with his.

"This one's a TV show. And it's a love story," he started. "What do you want for the second?"

"Promise you'll teach me something about directing a movie?"

The excitement in her gaze momentarily healed every wound that'd ever ached inside of him. "Yeah, baby. I will. We'll start with all the basics."

He started by telling her the PG, fairytale version of *Every Speck of Dust*, giving credit to Sahar for the happy ending of it all. He even gave her his word that by the time it was out, she'd be old enough to maybe watch the *happier* parts of it.

The ending, maybe. The *beginning*.

JAY WENT over to his bedroom first, but Sahar wasn't there. He trekked to his living room, finding her on his couch, with her headphones in. He was about to approach her from behind when he remembered how easily she spooked. So, he walked over to her carefully from the front. As though sensing his footsteps, she peered up at him, pausing whatever was playing on her phone.

"Is she asleep?" she asked.

He nodded and plopped himself down beside her.

"You alright?"

He inhaled and released a forceful exhale. Placing his head on her shoulder, he said nothing. His eyes darted to Eloise's glittering mermaid backpack on the other side of the couch next to Sahar's floral tote, taking in the small pops of color filling his gray space with more vibrancy. *Life.*

Her arm vined around him, carding her fingers through his hair.

"It's going to be so fucking hard to be away from her again. I hate it," he let himself say.

"Jay," she began, her voice melodic and soothing against the pounding inside of his chest. "You can visit her more often, can't you?"

He nodded. "Yeah, I can. It just sucks."

"I know. But you're going to leave the coffee shop soon, and it'll be easier when your hours aren't all over the place."

"How do you know I'm leaving soon?" he asked, looking up at her.

She tilted her head in a musing gaze. "Because I *do.* You're still holding on to the fear that they'll shelve *Every Speck of Dust* again, but your life is about to change. I'm sure of it."

"*Our* lives," he corrected her.

A kiss on his lips told him she agreed. *Their lives.*

He drew his mouth to her neck, lingering there as his fingers hiked up her thigh. She was wearing the same style of drawstring shorts and a matching tank top like the one she'd worn when her ankle was injured, only this pair was a bright shade of orange. He pressed a kiss to her collarbone, another along her jaw, one more to the column of her throat. Wrapping his arms around her middle, he lifted her onto his lap.

"What were you listening to?" Jay asked, inhaling the

fragrance of her body wash. The citrusy smell he was growing to associate with *home*.

"'All I've Ever Known' from *Hadestown*."

"Oof. How hard did that one make you sob?"

"Wait, wait. Have I never mentioned my love for Orpheus and Eurydice to you?"

Peering up at her, he shook his head. "You have not."

She looked like she wanted to cry. The enormity of her heart made him want to cry, too. "It's haunted me since I was a little girl. It took me over a year to finally watch *Hadestown* because I knew it'd destroy me."

"Did it?"

"I had to bite down on my fist so I wouldn't sob hysterically. Willa basically had claw marks on her skin from my nails digging into her arm. And I mean like ugly snot-filled tears."

He wrapped his arms tighter around her waist.

"Would you turn back? If it were me," she asked, her peachy pink nails tracing his face.

"Yeah," he answered without a second thought. "But I think that's why the story hits the way that it does. When you love someone, *really, really* love them—how could you not double-check? I'd trust you, but I wouldn't trust Hades. I'd want to make sure you're okay. I'd *need* to hear your voice. I'd *need* to make sure no part of you was harmed. That's what would kill me. Not knowing whether you're okay."

Her breath hitched. "I'd follow you—all the way through."

His grin grew a little lopsided. "Yeah?"

Dipping her chin, she pressed her mouth to his and sealed her promise with a kiss. "Yeah. I love you," she whispered.

He'd never get tired of hearing those words from her.

"I love you more," he said. "And I'd walk through any purgatory to bring you back home to me."

A different kind of smile dawned on her face, light sparkling in her beautiful brown eyes. "Fuck, Jay. That's it. That's why Katherine and Henry got me so hard. It's that feeling that's almost always there with fiction. How I've always wanted them to *just once* walk out together."

She trailed the pad of her thumb over his lips. "Thank you for giving me a version of that."

"And I'll keep giving you whatever you ask for."

37

SAHAR

Sahar proudly watched Eloise nail every instruction she'd given her about starting *Breath of the Wild*. The game was mirrored onto Jay's TV as the two of them sat side by side while he made waffles behind them in the kitchen. Between Eloise's adorably audible reactions to her actions within the game and the sounds of Jay shuffling around in the kitchen, so much of the quiet morning was already idyllic.

It was strange how the things people were often afraid of chasing ended up being the loveliest. She had on Jay's zip-up hoodie over her tank top again, and she twirled a drawstring in her hand as Eloise made another giddy hit in the game. "Oh, that was a brilliant move. One day, and you're already a pro, Eloise," she said, encouragingly.

The little girl beamed at her, and Sahar's heart sang a new favorite song.

At the same time, Jay announced, "Waffles are ready, you two."

"One...more...second," Eloise mumbled as she animatedly twisted her body and expression while she figured out her next task.

At the kitchen room table, Jay had set down four plates with a chocolate chip waffle on each. The fourth, for Alex when she'd eventually come over after picking up her car from the dealership.

Eloise patted a chair beside her, saying, "Can you sit next to me, Sahar?"

"Best seat in the house? I'd be honored," Sahar answered, lowering herself onto the chair. She heard Jay's laugh as he closed the refrigerator door, the sound comforting. *Home.*

Stepping behind her, he placed a forest green mug in front of her. "Lavender syrup is the same one we use at work, but the coffee's from Door County, and it's better," he added, before taking his own seat.

"Ooh, where's Door County?" she asked.

"In Wisconsin. My aunt—mom's side—moved to Green Bay when she got married, and when we'd visit her, she'd drive us up there. All other ground coffee pales in comparison."

Sahar smiled, curling her fingers around the warm ceramic. She took a sip, chuffed to confirm that Jay was right about the rich Colombian flavor mixing with the lavender she loved.

"Have I been there, Dad?" Eloise asked.

"Once when you were four."

"We should go again now that I'm older."

Jay nodded, taking a sip of his own drink. "Agreed."

Taking a bite of her waffle, Sahar let herself get used to this new normal. For most people, Mondays were the eighth circle of hell, but the unconventional day off for a Broadway performer often made it feel like a Sunday, brewing with the blues and apprehension. One day of rest.

Except today, it felt different—nothing would be the same after this moment, and it made an arbitrary Monday during one of the hottest days at the beginning of August feel like the best day of the year.

For someone who often fell in love quickly, this had been the slowest and deepest descent yet. It was the one that mattered most. Jay was the only man whose intentions she would never doubt. He had split his heart wide open, so she could see inside every secret treasure trove. She'd give him all of her in return.

"You good over there?" he asked.

"Hmm?"

"You zoned out."

Smiling, she bobbed her head up and down before taking another bite.

And then, out of the blue, Eloise said, "Dad, it's very boring that your name is just Jay."

Sahar choked a little on her breakfast, and Jay exhaled a low huff. "Very humbling, El. But you have a point. I'm not even sure I can make an argument for it."

"I like your name," Sahar said to him.

"*Your* name is the coolest," Eloise pointed out.

Dropping her mouth with an awe-struck expression, Sahar didn't withhold her amusement. "I don't think any compliment I get will be more brilliant than that, so thank you, Eloise. But you win here—you get all sorts of adorable nicknames that go along with yours."

The little girl gave her a big, toothy grin, then turned back to look at her dad. "So, Father..."

"Oh, God," Jay blurted, and a snort toppled out of Sahar. *Father?*

"If we sneakily bring a horseshoe crab home, who's going to find out about it?"

"We're not having this discussion again, *Daughter*. First, your mother will single-handedly murder me if I send you home with anything that crawls. Second, you can't have a horseshoe crab as a pet. Third, stop calling me father."

Sahar watched the exchange with her lips curled inward.

Eloise snickered, pure satisfaction making its way into her mischievous little eyes. "Actually, Uncle Patrick looked it up, and you *can* keep them as pets."

Some sort of a low grunt tumbled from Jay's throat. "Uncle Patrick needs to be banned from the internet."

"That's not very nice," the little girl added.

Jay rolled his eyes, affectionately. "Stop calling me father when you want to get your way, and I'll let you *stare* at the crabs for as long as you want."

"Will you take me back to the beach again before I go home? If I can't keep one, then I need to see them more than two times."

Resting her chin on her hand, Sahar added. "She has a point. You can't expect her to get her horseshoe crab fix if she isn't seeing them multiple times."

Eloise's eyes gleamed as she looked at Sahar, then back at Jay.

"Deal," he accepted.

With sheer, wondrous excitement, Eloise squealed, putting her hand out in front of her dad for him to shake. Jay dipped his head and dropped a kiss to her knuckles instead.

The cracks in Sahar's heart slowly pieced together, moments of shared joy wrapping themselves around her like threads of sparkling gold. Enveloping her hands around the mug again, she took another sip of the coffee, warm liquid and even warmer company. A perfect world indeed.

Eventually, Alex showed up, and the conversation about horseshoe crabs continued. Everything grew a little loud and a lot happier.

~

JAY'S FINGERS snaked around Sahar's hips as Eloise and Alex ran ahead of them toward the still, smooth water.

The beach was crowded, but not as bad as it would've been on a weekend. Salt air filled her nose, mingling with the intoxicating scent of Jay's cologne.

"Now that she's out of earshot, what's with the horseshoe crabs?" she asked him.

She felt him shaking his head. "I have no idea, but it's slightly concerning. The last time we saw them, she said they're cuter than dogs, and with this newfound desire to keep one as a pet, I've been trying to figure out exactly where Maya and I went wrong in our parenting."

"How is she not creeped out by them? Where are their eyes?" Sahar added, squinting through her sunglasses.

Jay shrugged, tightening his grip on her.

"By the way, you could've warned me that you were going to wear that dress," he rasped in her ear.

Tilting her head to the side, she moved her sunglasses to her head and looked up at him. "It's not out of your system yet?"

"Never."

His lips hovered over her temple before he kissed her there. Soft and sweet, like all of Jay's kisses.

She fixed her eyes on the sight of Eloise and Alex giggling before them. Something comforting rose inside her again and squeezed—something permanent.

She took out her phone and snapped a photograph of the scene ahead. Turning the camera then, she took one of her and Jay, too, his face buried in the slope of her shoulder.

Love had never been a solid fortress for Sahar. Instead, like castles in the sand, it had always been unsteady, temporary—built only for the moment until the tides came and washed them away. But the love she had for Jay was made of stone, impenetrable and timeless.

Walking a few steps after Jay as he settled on a spot to set up the beach towels, everything hit Sahar at once. How lucky she was to find love that was made *just for her*.

Sahar had read stories of grand gestures as proof of love's existence, but she never thought she'd find its immensity in the small, simple moments. She never imagined uncovering magic in the ordinary.

Alex and Eloise were beside them now as they discarded the clothes worn over their bathing suits. Jay was trying to convince Eloise to drink a few more sips of water when a loud voice bellowed, "Callahans!"

"Uncle Patrick," Eloise screamed and ran toward him, wobbling over the grainy sand.

"Asshole," Alex mumbled, setting her folded T-shirt dress onto the beach towel.

Jay and Sahar turned to her in unison, questioning the insult.

She rolled her eyes, half-amusement, half-something Sahar couldn't place forming in her expression. "He told me he wasn't coming because I'd be here, and he didn't want to see me after yesterday's game."

Sahar glanced at Patrick as he came closer with Eloise in his arms, his eyes fixed on Alex, and a lopsided grin plastered on his face. *That expression.* She'd noticed it last night, too, but Jay seemed so clueless that it was almost hilarious. Did he really not see it?

Was there something? Or was Sahar so happy and in love now that she was romanticizing every little interaction?

Eloise hopped out of Patrick's arms and dragged him to the horseshoe crabs. He waved off Jay and Sahar as Alex followed behind them, standing by the water, eyes set on the horizon.

When they were alone, Sahar turned to Jay again. "So, after Henry and Katherine reunite at the beach. What happens right afterward?"

His eyes sparkled as he plopped himself down on the beach towel and pulled her down with him.

She didn't suppress the giggle bubbling in her throat.

He wrapped his arm around her, nestling his face in the crook of her neck. Delicious notes of cedar and sunscreen filled her nose. Her heart galloped in her chest. Over and over and over again.

Gently pinching the side of his rib, where the crow rested, she whispered, "Tell me."

A kiss on her cheek. "They go back to his place." A kiss on her forehead. "He makes her breakfast." A kiss on her nose. "He tells her he loves her." A kiss on her other cheek. "He repeats it a hundred more times." A kiss on her lips. "He never lets her go."

"Forever?" Sahar asked, pressing her forehead to his.

One more kiss. "Forever," he promised.

At some point, Patrick and Alex disappeared, leaving Jay and Sahar with Eloise and a million questions about the show they were going to make together. The verbal promise from Jay that he'd let her come to set to see how an episode was filmed, and the vow that he'd teach her everything he knew if she did end up choosing filmmaking as a career. The PG version was still a thing of beauty—an example of endurance and evidence that love was real and worth every risk. Sahar would be lying if she said that horseshoe crabs didn't eventually grow on her after Eloise's strange little obsession forced her to see them in a new light. "Their legs are so small and cute!" the little girl exclaimed as she showed them to Sahar up close. *Yeah, yeah, they are.*

On any other day, 3 p.m. in August would be the point where she'd complain about humidity, the heat, and all things summer, but not today. Today was all about bear hugs on a beach towel and salt air lingering with the breeze, sticking to their skin, and immortalizing as a sacred scent in the healed coves of her heart where she'd permanently store the memories of this perfect day.

Sahar took photographs throughout their time there, added them to her Polaroid filter, and sent them to the people who were in them.

Eloise had even taken one of Sahar and Jay, a little crooked in its aim but immaculate in capturing the essence of them in the middle of a hug. A showcase of how this little love story started from glass shards on the floor and ended in a framed mosaic. Proof of the fact that his arms were home and love would last this time.

They'd last.

"I love you so much," she'd breathed into his arms at the end of the night.

"I love you more, sunshine, and I'll spend the rest of my life making sure I deserve you."

EPILOGUE

3 YEARS LATER - SEPTEMBER

INTERVIEW: *Jay Callahan and Ethan Everett Breakdown Key Moments in 'Woodlawn' and The Importance of a Hopeful Ending*
By: Louisa Quinn

It's always a source of admiration when a dark and heavy series subverts expectations of the audience by delivering a happy ending. Or, in the case of Jay Callahan's Woodlawn, a quietly poignant reminder of how love endures in the face of all tragedies. There's plenty to process with the ten-episode limited series, yet the romantic arc is where it shines as we explore second chances and a love that examines what it truly means to be someone's person. Daring, gritty, and at times, heavy, every beat of the final episode— and the entire show, really— is one that will stay with us for a long, long time.

In an interview with Geeky Declarations' Louisa Quinn, director Jay Callahan and actor Ethan Everett, who plays Henry Palmer, break down the final scene, the character journeys, and discuss a potential second season

The following contains spoilers for all ten episodes of Woodlawn.

LOUISA QUINN: Hi, I'm Louisa Quinn from *Geeky Declarations.*

JAY CALLAHAN: Hi. Nice to officially meet you. I've read some of your reviews.

ETHAN EVERETT: Hi. Reading reviews scares me, but I'm sure yours are amazing. [Laughs]

Really? That's such an honor. *Beneath the Sun* is one of my favorite movies of all time. I promise, I've only ever said nice things about your projects, Ethan. [Laughs]

CALLAHAN: Wow, thank you so much for saying that. It means a lot.

EVERETT: I trust you. [To CALLAHAN] *Beneath the Sun* is also my favorite. Did I ever tell you that?

CALLAHAN: You did not. But thanks, man.

Naturally, I jumped at the chance to cover *Woodlawn* because it has all my favorite narrative archetypes wrapped up in one. I wanted to preface by saying that I've seen the entire thing and would love to talk spoilers, but keep publication until after release, if that's okay with you both?

CALLAHAN: Yeah, yeah. I'm good with that.

My first question is for you, Jay. Having watched both *Beneath the Sun* and *Cuts* as well as some of your earlier shorts, I fully expected this to break my heart into a million pieces. So imagine my surprise at *that* ending. What made you want to give viewers a happy ending with this series?

CALLAHAN: [Smiles] I can't take credit for that. It was all my partner—fiancée. She took one look at the original script, which was completely different in every way, and said *no*. Just straight up. So, a lot of what you see in the final product is a direct result of her nudging me to write something happier. And honestly, it's a better story this way, so I'm really excited to shock people who know my work by delivering something hopeful.

This certainly isn't to say that your other projects aren't hopeful, because it's sort of what I've always appreciated about them, but the melancholy is louder. Here, it feels incredibly earned to go through this journey where we have characters fighting for survival and finally reaching that point.

CALLAHAN: Thank you again for saying that. That's very much what we wanted to get across, so I'm glad that's the effect it had on you.

The cast is also incredible, truly. Ethan, you and Rae Mullins as Katherine really elevate so many of the underlying emotions. Do you both have a favorite moment throughout the series where you sort of realized the story was coming together as you wanted it to?

EVERETT: I'm going to let the captain take this one because I want to know his answer first.

CALLAHAN: Oh, yeah, they're both unreal. Fun fact is that I'd seen Ethan perform in *Midnights at Pemberley,* and I thought he'd be great as Henry, but all we had at that time were parts of the script's rewrites and no guarantee of anything else, so I didn't think anything of it. But it's really rewarding to have him on because they've both made it hard for me to really choose a moment. The whole cast has been so phenomenal. Did you have a moment in mind?

I do, actually. And I have a feeling *a lot* of people are going to adore this moment.

CALLAHAN: Which is it?

The flashback in episode four. The whole episode *I* feel is one of the best things of the year, and I'm more than happy to run the FYC campaign for it, but there's a line where Henry says, *In my perfect world, you and I would be together,* and I haven't watched something that poignant in a long time, especially when we're made to believe they'll never see each other again in the present.

CALLAHAN: [Nods] That's one of the first lines I wrote, so it's gratifying that it sticks out. But all credit goes to Ethan for it. The first time he said it out loud during the table read, a few people literally gasped. We got really lucky with him. [Affectionately pats Everett's shoulder] He's stuck with me now.

EVERETT: You know what's hilarious? And I'm not trying to downplay this moment and the gravitas of that line, but like when I heard those gasps, I think one of them came from Sahar [Peck] because she was at the table read? I immediately thought, oh shit, I fucked up. I'd just gotten out of *Midnights,* and I was so used to Regency British that I'd forgotten how to act with my own accent—without a dialect coach. So, I thought I'd done something wrong.

CALLAHAN: Did you not hear the part where I said you're stuck with me? And we got really lucky. They were good gasps.

EVERETT: [Laughs] I do really love that line, though. My wife cried when she saw the final cut, so I guess I did something right there. And Rae really nails the quiet response, too. She was a fantastic scene partner to work with.

Can we have this be the next Christopher Nolan and Cillian Murphy duo?

CALLAHAN: [Laughs] That's a big compliment, and Ethan's definitely up to par. I've got a ways to go, but let's do it. I'll cast him in everything I make.

EVERETT: We're the worst people to pair up. Neither of us can actually take a compliment. But yeah, no. You're right. Jay's the best director I've had, so I'm going to have a hard time with others. Never work without me, man. Wait, okay, also he gave a fun fact, here's mine. I had no idea I was auditioning for his show when I went in. My agent sent me the script, and then I got super sick with a bad cold, so I forgot to look at it until the day before the audition. I breezed through it and really loved it, then I walked into the audition, and Jay's sitting there. I straight up thought I went to the wrong place.

CALLAHAN: We gave him the job on the spot.

EVERETT: [Laughs] Is it nepotism if we connected through our wives—girlfriends at the time? Is that a thing?

Nepotism is only bad if there's no real talent, but we've got a real winner with both of you. This might not be a sheer coincidence, but I have to ask, Jay. Is this Henry the same one briefly mentioned in *Beneath the Sun?* The line about "calling the detective, H. Palmer?"

CALLAHAN: You know, Patrick didn't even pick up on that?

EVERETT: There's a Henry in *Beneath the Sun?*

Wait, so he *is* the same guy?

CALLAHAN: Yeah, yeah. He is. He sort of just stayed with me, and it never really made sense until I started writing this show *why,* but that's an excellent catch.

EVERETT: I, for one, am stunned by this. Now I need to go rewatch.

I watch it often. I wasn't exaggerating when I said it's one of my favorites. But going off of that, is there hope of seeing any of these characters again? In another project, or a second season, possibly?

CALLAHAN: Honestly, I'm not sure. We marketed it as a limited series, and I haven't really thought of where it could go beyond that point. The story would have to work in order for me to agree to more of it. So, it's a matter of 'we'll see.' As far as the possibility of hearing mentions of these characters again, there's a bigger chance of that. I apparently have a hard time letting go of them. They feel like my kids.

EVERETT: If I could play Henry for another ten years, I would. Make it happen, *Dad*.

CALLAHAN: [Laughs] Sure, buddy. If that's what you want.

I think viewers would appreciate that sentiment, even if it's just a mention of them elsewhere. Like your own little multiverse. Also, there's a directorial choice in the finale that really floored me. The last scene and how it all comes together: Jay, can you talk a bit about that? It *feels* like a montage, even though it isn't one, and we're in a public place like the beach, but it still feels so achingly intimate, and I don't necessarily think that's because they're in a secluded area. What was the thought process behind that?

CALLAHAN: Thank you again. The intimacy of that scene is something I wanted to come across in the screenplay, and once more, credit where it's due, the writing in that final scene is all my fiancée, Sahar [Peck]. She's the one who said it should be a hug, and I wholeheartedly agreed. But what I really wanted was for the scene to feel like something that was theirs and theirs alone. But, at the same time, we wanted the audience to be locked in on the frame, even while the characters move through that space before they come together. Shooting it was tricky, but the end result was also largely due to Ethan and Rae and the blocking they worked through themselves. Ethan's background in theatre certainly helps with that. But I really wanted to emphasize that they'd never stopped moving these puzzle pieces to find each other.

Yeah. That's what it felt like, and with Mark Ingram's cine-matography and Rhonda Blake's editing, it's such a stunning moment. Plus, the song choice? Sam and Priya Butler's "Home" was perfect.

CALLAHAN: Oh, yeah, they're out of this world. And all credit to Sahar [Peck] for the song. She had the idea very early on in the pre-production that it should be an original number, so we got Sam [Butler] and Priya [Sharma] the entire script and they started writing it immediately. It's hard to imagine anything else but that song.

And then for you, Ethan. What was it like tapping into that place of Henry finally getting a modicum of hope back? You've played a lot of angsty characters, but there's something about Henry's journey that's so dark that his exhaustion weighed on us, too. Essentially, what was it like embodying all these facets of him from the beginning to that final scene?

EVERETT: That's such a great question. I say this with a lot of love, but Henry is the hardest character I've played. And he wasn't all that different from Tim in *Detective Vice,* but there was something bigger in his pain. It almost felt more personal to me, even though I have very little in common with him outside of the fact that I'd do the exact same things if anything happened to my wife. But there were days when I'd go to my hotel room after shooting, and I couldn't talk to anyone because his heartache was so visceral that it really struck something in me, too.

So, when we got to shooting that final episode, there was a bit of ease in me, too. Like this guy can finally breathe, and I can breathe with him. In general, I'm somebody who loves the come-down from the third act. Whatever it is, I love the way that a final shot makes me feel. My favorite part of anything is usually the end because you always give so much to get there that when you do, it feels extra rewarding. So, to have a scene *this* poignant and profound come at the very end made it feel almost tailor-made for me. It also always helps to have a great scene partner, and while Rae [Mullins] and I naturally didn't get to spend too much time in the same frame because of the characters' separation, we both understood them and their relationship so well that it helped.

Two questions before we wrap up: One, of all your characters, who do you think you'd get along with most? And two, what are you currently watching?

CALLAHAN: Oh, that's an interesting question. I mean, it feels like cheating a little if I don't say Henry. Maybe that's just because Ethan and I get along so well, but who knows? [Laughs] We've been rewatching *Shrinking* from the beginning. It's such a good one.

EVERETT: Too bad you'd never get in front of the camera; otherwise, I'd choose you. But I think for me, my characters are all so broody, I feel like we'd all just sit in silence and stare at each other. But maybe Henry, too. We're also watching *Shrinking*. And *The Pitt.*

Yes! Both of those are such great shows. Thank you both again for talking to me. I really can't wait to see how people react to this series. You should all be so proud of yourselves.

CALLAHAN: Thank you so much. Your support is greatly appreciated. And thank you for such incredible questions.

EVERETT: Thank you! And yeah, your questions were spot-on.

JAY

Kyle stopped the recording in front of them.

"She was delightful," Ethan noted.

"Yeah," Jay confirmed, a small smile curling at the edge of his lips. "She's a solid writer, too."

They stood up from the gray chairs they were sitting in as Teyona, the PR representative, said, "Ethan, you've got three more with Rae in room 34 and then you're done for the day, too." Nodding, Ethan clapped Jay on the shoulder and hurried out of the room.

Jay took off the microphone from his shirt and thanked Kyle and Teyona before turning away. Sahar had been sitting on a couch in the hotel room, too, wordlessly shining her irreplaceable light on him.

She stood up as she saw him walking toward her. "First round of press done! You feeling okay, baby?"

Inching closer, he dropped his head to her shoulder. "Yeah, my brain feels a bit like spaghetti, but I'm good."

She reached for his hand, and then her bright, beaming smile played on her face like *his* all-time favorite movie scene. "I can't believe she mentioned *that* line. You know she wrote my favorite review of *Midnights?*"

"Yeah?" he asked.

Sahar nodded. "Yeah."

He traced his thumb over the bracelet she had on her wrist, one made by Eloise with navy blue beads to match his. But instead of *Eloise*, Sahar's said, *crow,* like her favorite animal—

their tattoos, their perfect little world. "Thank you for taking the day off to be here with me."

"I mean, hello, I've got a producer's credit. Where else would I be? Plus, I gave the notice in advance, so the people coming in to see *Parchment Paper* today know I'll be out." She paused, smiling. "But in all seriousness, anytime, anywhere—always, my love."

Jay glided his fingers along the diamond ring on her finger. He remembered how he'd proposed to her: in England, at a Man City game, a quiet moment in the stands between the two of them, and a small gathering with her immediate family afterward. He remembered her gorgeous smile and the tears streaming down her face as she said *yes.*

Always wasn't just a word anymore.

It was a truth and a promise with them. A *truth* from the moment she brought him back to life. A *promise* from when she told him she loved him, and every time she repeated it afterward. *A truth* from the moment he vowed to love all of her. *A promise* from when he realized that he was only capable of falling harder and harder with each passing day.

She let out a low laugh then added, "Oh, I texted Maya and Alex a photo from the junket earlier, and Eloise took the phone to say, 'Is he going to let me watch now that I'm 11, or am I still too young? Also, is he wearing the bracelet?'"

Eleven. God, how had that happened? Where had the time gone? After finally quitting his job at the coffee shop shortly before filming for *Woodlawn* began, Jay made sure to visit Eloise every other weekend during the school year. He'd also flown her and Maya to the filming location for a relatively tame shooting day. Eloise had been so giddy. So excited. And she still wanted to follow in his footsteps, which was slightly less terrifying these days.

He smiled and said, "I hope your response was 'Only the

office scene you watched during filming, but the rest? Not until you're forty.'"

"You know very well I did *not* say that. Maya and I agree she gets a full PG cut, and we're watching it when we go to Philly next weekend. You're outnumbered here."

Affectionately shaking his head, he draped his arm over her shoulder as he guided her out of the room and walked out of The Bill Hotel. Little did he know, when they had been at this very spot for an after-party three years ago, he would get the chance to see his series come to life. Sahar would go on to do two shows after her contract at *Midnights at Pemberley* ended, including her current role in *Parchment Paper*, where she was reunited with Miles and Innila.

They had made long-distance work and came back together again.

Little did *they* know...

Sunlight cascaded down upon them as they stepped outside to birds chirping and competing with New York City's bustling soundtrack. Sahar squeezed his waist, looking up at him as they waited for the valet employee to return his car. Her pretty eyes held his gaze and kept him steady. Happy. Content. *Perfect.* "We have wedding plans to finalize now."

Jay nestled her close, pressing a kiss to her forehead. "That's right, sunshine. We do."

ACKNOWLEDGMENTS

There was a point as I was writing the performances and technical aspects of *A Certain Step* where I thought, well, at least this is the hardest thing I'll ever write. God probably let out an affectionate guffaw then. Because, really, nothing could have prepared me for the roller coaster of emotions that *Absolute Certainty* turned out to be. The ways I cracked my heart wide open and am *still* utterly terrified that this story is now out in the world for people to read.

Jay and Sahar challenged me, broke me, stitched me back together, and changed me for the better. There are parts of me in all my books, but I don't know if a story will ever have such a huge chunk of my heart the way this does. In more ways than one, so much is tethered to the state of the world and the industry. Romance novels are a beautiful place to momentarily believe that happy endings are possible, but I'd be lying if I said I have that same faith outside. As I type this, working as an entertainment journalist who's constantly terrified of how AI will take over, I genuinely have no clue what the future holds. In filmmaking, in the literature world, in journalism—any of it. It's a scary, horrific thought to consider that the people who believe in authentic creativity might get to a point where they'll be forced into different careers. I hope I'm wrong in fearing this. I hope that one day, AI can be behind us and people can feel the security in a job they love again. But for now, I'm going to keep writing. And I won't beat myself up over the typo that we missed with multiple rounds of edits because human brains are tired and strange little things.

Once more, with feeling, if this were an acceptance speech or anything, God would be my first thank you. Always. Every prayer I sent up. Every sign I got. Every blessing. It's all because of Christ.

My family and my friends—the people who got an absolute wreck at times because of this release. Thank you for still loving me and supporting me.

When I was a little girl, I wanted to be just like my dad. So, writing a story about fathers and daughters was always inevitable for me. I only wish I could share it with my own. Thank you for all those Friday night trips to the video rental stores, so I can pick up the next new movie and Taco Bell. I'll never stop giving you credit for how I appreciate beautiful words and sentences. Thank you for making me the writer I am.

Jenna, I know I say it with every cover, but you're an absolute dream to work with. Plus, the print!? The PRINT. You already know that this one has my whole heart. But also, the shit you put up with behind the scenes. The constant reassurance. The never-ending support. My books cannot exist without your part in them and your friendship. I love you as much as Eloise loves making Jay rewatch *Barbie*.

Kate, there aren't enough words for how much I put you through with this one. Every text and every Marco Polo and every gentle pat on the back have meant the world to me. Thank you for loving Jay and Sahar the way that you do. And thank you for continuously taking on this journey with me. I love you to the damn moon.

Sarah, I'm sorry that I made Jay and Sahar Man City fans. You can blame Jamie Tartt. I promise I'll someday write Liverpool fans. Thank you for your eyes on this and for continuing to take on my books with your busy schedule. Your input always means so much to me, and I love you to pieces.

Arezou Amin, thank you for always being a text away when I need someone to tell me I'm not losing it. Thank you for your constant support and friendship. As a friend, a journalist, and a fellow author, all of this is brighter because of you. I love you and cannot wait until the world reads your stories. I can't wait to see *you* shine*!*

Amy, I know I keep saying it, but I'm so grateful that you'll read the roughest draft and still cheer me on. I'm so beyond thankful for you and your friendship. I love you and can't imagine this writing journey without your support.

Snigdha at Beyond the Books, your infectious energy and support have been an incomparable light. Thank you for all that you've done. I'm so wholeheartedly and *beyond* grateful.

Ada at Archetype, thank you for squeezing me into your busy schedule. I can't imagine my books without your gorgeous graphics, and I'm so glad we get to continue working together.

Finally, best for last as always, every reader who's picked up *A Certain Step* and asked for Sahar's story. I hope I've done our girl proud. They're yours now, too. Every kind word, every sweet graphic, every page turn has meant more to me than I can ever say.

ABOUT THE AUTHOR

Born and raised in California, Gissane Sophia (pronounced Geese-Enny) is a hopeless romantic who ceaselessly champions that vulnerability is a strength. She's a fan of complex characters, found families, her bright, brilliant family and friends, coffee, forests, and all things autumn. When she isn't dabbling in writing romance novels, she's reading them. And when she's doing neither, she's devouring fiction through TV and film, working full-time as an entertainment editor and writer.

ALSO BY GISSANE SOPHIA

MIDNIGHTS AT PEMBERLEY BOOK I: Ethan and Willa's Story

A CERTAIN STEP

www.ingramcontent.com/pod-product-compliance
Lightning Source LLC
Chambersburg PA
CBHW031513010826
48973CB00013B/1258